"THE NORTHWESTERNERS is the fifth volume in a series of Western fiction anthologies. This one celebrates frontier life in Idaho, Washington, and Oregon.

"We hope you enjoy this imaginative journey through the Great Pacific Northwest and that this volume and the others that preceded it—*The Texans, The Californians, The Arizonans,* and *The Northerners*—prove worthy of a permanent place in your library of Western fiction."

Bill Pronzini and
Martin H. Greenberg
From the Introduction

Other Western Anthologies
Edited by Bill Pronzini and Martin H. Greenberg:

TREASURY OF CIVIL WAR STORIES

THE WESTERN HALL OF FAME: *An Anthology of Classic Western Stories Selected by the Western Writers of America*

THE BEST WESTERN STORIES OF STEVE FRAZEE

THE LAWMEN*

SECOND REEL WEST

THE COWBOYS*

THE WARRIORS*

THE THIRD REEL WEST

THE RAILROADERS*

THE STEAMBOATERS*

THE CATTLEMEN*

THE HORSE SOLDIERS*

THE GUNFIGHTERS*

THE TEXANS*

THE CALIFORNIANS*

THE ARIZONANS*

THE NORTHERNERS*

*Published by Fawcett Books

THE NORTHWESTERNERS

Edited by
Bill Pronzini and
Martin H. Greenberg

FAWCETT GOLD MEDAL • NEW YORK

Contents

Acknowledgments

"Border Incident," by Bill Gulick. Copyright © 1962 by Western Writers of America, Inc. First published in *Legends and Tales of the Old West*. Reprinted by permission of the author.

"The Patriarch of Gunsight Flat," by Wayne D. Overholser. Copyright © 1950 by McCall Corp. First published in *Blue Book*. Reprinted by permission of the author.

"The Pilgrim," by Loren D. Estleman. Copyright © 1981, 1989 by Loren D. Estleman. First published in *The Best Western Stories of Loren D. Estleman*. Reprinted by permission of the author.

"Where the Wind Blows Free," by Bill Gulick. Copyright © 1961 by Grover C. Gulick. First published in *The Saturday Evening Post*. Reprinted by permission of the author.

"Chain of Command," by D. B. Newton. Copyright © 1970 by Western Writers of America, Inc. First published in *With Guidons Flying*. Reprinted by permission of the author.

Introduction

The Northwesterners is the fifth volume in a series of Western fiction anthologies celebrating frontier life in various Western states, in this case the three states—Idaho, Washington, and Oregon—that make up the Great Pacific Northwest. It contains stories that not only are set in these states but fictionally re-create the many aspects of their colorful and exciting history—stories written primarily by authors past and present who have lived within their boundaries.

The thirteen tales in these pages are told through the eyes of soldiers, traders, settlers, ranchers, cowhands, newspaper reporters, loggers, stevedores, steamboat captains, and frontier politicians. In them you'll visit the Snake River country, Boise City, Portland, the waterfront of old Seattle, the Willamette valley, and the logging camps of southern Oregon; you'll travel on a wagon train on the Oregon Trail, on a steamboat on the Willimette River, and by horseback and oxcart across the high plateau and desert country of eastern Oregon; and you'll meet such fascinating characters as the patriarch of Gunsight Flat and the legendary Jedidiah Kelly.

We hope that you enjoy this imaginative journey through the Pacific Northwest and that this volume and the others that preceded it—*The Texans, The Californians, The Arizonans,* and *The Northerners*—prove worthy of a permanent place in your library of Western fiction.

—Bill Pronzini and
Martin H. Greenberg

A writer of quality traditional and historical Western fiction for nearly fifty years, Washingtonian Bill Gulick has twice won the Best Short Story Spur Award from the Western Writers of America—in 1958 for "Thief in Camp" and in 1960 for "The Shaming of Broken Horn." His novels of the Pacific Northwest include Bend of the Snake *(1950),* A Drum Calls West *(1952), and the recent outstanding three-volume saga of the Nez Percé Indians,* Distant Trails, Gathering Storm, *and* Lost Wallowa *(all 1988). His short fiction can be found in the collections* White Men, Red Men, and Mountain Men *(1955) and* The Shaming of Broken Horn *(1961). He is also the author of two fine nonfiction books,* Snake River Country *(1971) and* Chief Joseph Country *(1981). Gulick's sense of humor is evident in much of his fiction; in "Border Incident" he is at his tongue-in-cheek best.*

Border Incident

★★★★★★★★★★★★

Bill Gulick

To the average American emigrant of that day the simple fact that a Britisher should wish him not to settle in any certain part of the undivided territory was of itself sufficient incentive for him to select that spot, provided it was not much worse than any other.

—Bancroft's *History of Washington*

YES, it's ours now. Has been for just a shade over a hundred years. We call it Washington. The state of Washington, understand, not that Washington, D.C., place where the chief products are laws and hot air. We raise timber and fish and apples and wheat and mountains—and sometimes a bit of hell when the loggers come to town. Which is sort of beside the point—the point being that it should be made clear in the beginning that we're talking about a state-sized piece of property and how come it turned out to join the U.S.A. instead of Canada, which is exactly what would have happened if it hadn't been for Jedidiah Kelly.

I know. You Swedes are going to rare back and say, "Look here,

1

son. It was the Swedes and their axes and calked boots made Washington, not no fool of a shanty Irishman."

Just hold onto your snoose cans a minute. This happened long before there were shanty Irish or Swedes with calked boots. Far as that goes, I'd argue that nobody made Washington—not the Swedes or the Irish or even Paul Bunyan, though I'm willing to admit they all maybe altered it some. But when you come right down to it, you've got to agree it was God that made it, and a right fine job He did of it too. He made it and it laid there for a few million years and nobody much paid it any mind till the Britishers came. You know how Britishers are. They looked it over, saw it was a good thing, and then kept their mouths shut, figuring as long as they didn't come right out and tell anybody it was a good thing, nobody would ever guess—least of all those fool Americans.

Well, they might have got away with it if it hadn't been for Jedidiah Kelly, who, being Irish and from Kentucky to boot, had a bad habit of not believing a single damn thing he was told.

Jed came West with an emigrant train in '44. Condition he was in, he shouldn't have come West at all, shouldn't even have got out of bed. But he did. And the way it happened was this.

He'd come down with a fever and a bad cough and had lain abed two, three weeks, when his wife Deborah decided maybe he was really sick, not just lazing it off. She sent one of the kids to town for the doctor. Old Doc Berringer rode out on his mule, thumped Jed's chest, peered at his tongue, poked him, prodded him, rolled back his eyelids and took a squint at the pupils, then shook his shaggy head.

"You got it, all right."

Jed coughed for a spell. "Got what?"

"Lung fever."

"You mean," Jed said, "I'm goin' to die?"

"Afeard so."

Jed lay there, thinking it over. It was coming on autumn and the trees on the hills outside the cabin were all golden and red and a faint blue haze hung in the distance. More Jed thought about dying the less he liked the idea. So he decided he wouldn't.

"Doc," he said, raising his gaunt, skinny body up on his elbows, "you're a damned old meddlin' fool comin' in here an' tellin' me I'm goin' to die. Because I ain't."

Well, Doc Berringer took that as a personal insult to his medical integrity, and he laid into Jed right proper. Said he'd seen hundreds of cases of lung fever and they all died. Said if Jed had a lick of sense he'd just give in to the inevitable, make his will, and take it like a man. Jed jawed right back, saying who did Doc think he was to tell a man whether he could live or die? Maybe Doc did know lung fever, Jed said, but he damn sure didn't know *him*, because if he made up his mind not to die, well, he just wouldn't die—and that was that.

"Won't do any good to argy, Doc," Deborah said. "Jed's some stubborn, he sets his mind to a thing."

Doc Berringer snorted and went prancing off down the trail on his mule, allowing as how anybody as pigheaded as Jed Kelly could just go ahead and live if he didn't have any more respect for sound medical advice than that; he was washing his hands of it.

So Jed put his mind to living, and come Christmas he was tottering around the cabin some, still weak, still coughing—but still breathing. Neighbors came to call frequent, and they acted so kind and sympathetic it made him want to cuss and spit. So he cussed and spat.

"Mind ye," he'd say after getting rid of a mouthful of spittle and profanity, "they ain't a thing wrong with me that a mite of fresh air an' sunshine won't cure, come spring. Outside of feelin' a shade puny, I feel fine. Why, if it wa'n't that I'm forty past an' got this farm an' a family an' all, I'd . . ." He thought for a minute on what he would do. Naturally he came up with just the thing most contrary to what a sick man had ought to do. "I'd pull up stakes here an' go West!"

"Shore," a neighbor said, nodding indulgently as one will to an invalid. "Fine idea, goin' West, but like you say, a man past forty's too old—"

"Me?" Jed said, getting a look in his eye. "Too old?"

"Well, I meant—"

Well, the upshot of it was that just because somebody said Jed was too old to pull up stakes and go West, Jed decided nothing would do, come spring, but that he pull up stakes and go West. Soon as the hill folk heard he was really going, they started giving him all sorts of advice. Some said why didn't he try Arkansas, which they'd heard had hills just as pretty as these in eastern Kentucky; some said Missouri would be fine, account of the trade 'tween St. Looie and Santa Fe; some claimed he'd like Iowa better, where the corn land just couldn't be beat.

Then some fool young fellow who'd been to school and learned how to read and was all the time showing off his knowledge by bragging about what he'd read in the city newspapers that now and then found their way back into the hills said self-importantly,

"If it was me, I'd go to Oregon. 'Course a man in poor health couldn't hardly tote his family way out there."

"Oregon," Jed said, and the word tasted strange on his tongue. "Oregon," he repeated, and this time the word had a roll to it, a lift to it, a power to it. "How fur'd that be?"

"From where?" said the youngster, stalling for time—for the truth was he couldn't rightly say.

"From hyar. Right hyar. How fur'd it be?"

"Well, couldn't tell you in miles. But they do claim it takes all spring and summer to git there should you start from Westport. That's on the Missouri, a piece west of St. Looie."

What happened was, as you might suspect, that Jed did some inquiring around, and the more he inquired, the more people he heard say that a man with a hill farm as good as his and a family as big as his and him as sick as he was would be plumb crazy to even consider selling out and starting to Oregon. So he didn't consider it hardly at all. He just sold out and started.

There's no need to say much about the trip. Say it was worse than some, not quite as bad as some, and that covers it pretty well. Out of Westport and along the Little Blue there was April rain and mud and mud and rain and rain and mud, and Jed coughing and cussing and spitting and laying the whip into the oxen. There was dust and hunger and June heat along the Platte, cholera and new graves dug on the wide plain. There was sagebrush and space and wagon tires dropping off when the dry air shrunk the wheels. Fourth of July on a high wind-swept ridge beyond which all waters flowed to the Pacific. A soda-water spring that seemed to help Jed's cough, and August dust that made it worse along the blistering Snake River Plain. A fool Hudson's Bay Company man at Fort Boise that tried to tell Jed it'd be impossible to cross the Blue Mountains with wagons.

"Better leave them here," he said. "Trade them and your oxen in on horses—that's the only way you'll get through."

Jed coughed and squinted off to the northwest, where mountains shimmered in the heat haze. "Can't take wagons through, you say? Why not, young'un? Why the hell not?"

"Well . . ."

Well, the more the young Britisher talked, the less Jed believed him. Jed was captain of the train by then. Forty wagons, forty families Oregon-bound, forty tough, trail-hardened men arguing around a campfire that night whether they'd ought to try it or not. Jed let them argue just so long. Then he coughed and said, "Come mornin', I aim to start. Who's comin' with me?"

There was the Snake to raft across and beyond it the tangle of Burnt River Canyon to chop a trail through and the rocks and steep grades and finally the descent from the Blues to the Columbia desert. At last there was the Dalles, gateway to the last mountain barrier.

It was October by then and the rains had begun. Rain at the river level, snow up yonder in the mountains. And no more trail. No trail at all, they told Jed. Only thing he could do was sell the wagons and hire Injuns to take his party the rest of the way downriver by boat. How much for the wagons? They made him an offer, which was six cents less than nothing. How much to boat the party through? A million dollars, take or give a few pennies.

Jed coughed and cussed and spat and said to hell with 'em all; he was going downriver and he was taking his wagons—fly 'em or float 'em, he'd find a way. They laughed and said, "You're crazy! It can't be done!"

Well, as I pointed out in the beginning, he was Irish and from Kentucky and not in the habit of believing one damn thing he was told. Not being a riverman, not knowing what kind of a river the Columbia becomes once it pours itself into that crack in the Cascades they call the Gorge, he didn't have any better sense than to rip those wagons apart and make rafts of them, lashing the wheels aboard so they could be turned back into wagons again as soon as they'd floated through. Then families and dogs and belongings were piled aboard, and away they went.

Most got through, though it took a month. A month, with the cold rain never stopping, rafts awash, clothes wet, camp at night on a rocky ledge with wood too wet for a fire. Food running short, hands blistered from the ropes you had to use lining the clumsy rafts down the rapids, shoes ripped off by the rocky bottom, children sick, someone swept away every now and then, never to be seen again—and Jed, coughing and cussing and coughing and outworking three men day in and day out just because somebody had been fool enough to tell him it couldn't be done.

And then, one gray, rainy November day, there was Oregon.

At least it was what Jed called Oregon. They'd tried to tell him he'd reached Oregon way back yonder in the Snake River country, but he hadn't believed them, wouldn't believe them. Because he'd got it in his mind that Oregon lay at the end of somewhere, that it'd be a place you'd know the minute you saw it and wouldn't want to go a mile farther. The country back yonder was just space that lay between him and Oregon, he figured, and who cared what the maps said?

But this, now, this looked right. The river quiet and wide between soft green foothills. The Hudson's Bay Company post of Fort Vancouver there on the north bank. A valley yonder stretching off into the mists from the south bank. The rain like a fine spray that a body hardly recognized as wet at all. Yes, this was Oregon. Yonder, south of the river, and he was still alive and he'd proved something to somebody, though he wasn't quite sure who or what.

All right, you Washington Swedes, I'll get to the point if you'll just be patient and hang on to your snoose cans like I told you. Sure, you set down to read a story about how come an Irishman from Kentucky saved Washington for the U.S.A. and all you've read so far has been about Oregon and what a great place it was. But history is a pretty complicated subject and takes a bit of unraveling.

As I explained, nobody in those days knew anything about Washington except the British, and they were keeping mighty mum. You see, they were in a delicate spot. Seems Tom Jefferson had made a cash deal with a Frenchie name of Napoleon for a hunk of land somewhere west of the Mississippi. Napoleon had been kind of hazy as to where the boundary fences were, so Jeff sent out a couple of boys to look the real estate over. They had so much territory to cover and were so impressed with finding such a big river included in the deal that it didn't occur to them there was anything worth seeing north of the Columbia. So the Britishers just quietly moved in one dark night and took over.

Well, it wasn't quite as simple as that. There was a war in there somewhere, and the fur business was on the upgrade, and even though Daniel Webster did say when he was Secretary of State that he'd gladly trade all the Pacific Northwest country for one good Newfoundland codfish bank, the United States wasn't about to agree to anything the Britishers proposed as regards territorial settlements, going on the sound theory that no matter what kind of a trade you made with a Britisher, you were bound to lose. But we did agree to the damnedest temporary treaty you ever heard of. The British thought it up.

"What we'll do," says John Bull to Uncle Sam, "we'll neither one of us claim anything out thataway for a while. We'll have joint occupancy for say ten years, then if that works out we'll try it another ten years, et cetera."

Likely they figured to hook us on the "et cetera" sooner or later, but anyhow, that was the way it was set up. Then in come the British very quietly and set up a whole string of Hudson's Bay Company forts and start trading for furs with the Indians. Those traders go out in all directions—south to California, east to the

Rockies, west to the ocean, everywhere. They're just sitting there waiting, these Britishers, till the proper time, at which they're going to ask for everything and then settle for a couple of acres less. At the very least the Columbia River would be their southern boundary, understand?

See where that leaves Washington? Yeah. You Swedes would be singing "God Save the King," and how do you think you'd like a steady diet of cricket instead of baseball?

Well, you can thank Jed Kelly it didn't turn out that way.

With all his faults, no one could ever claim Jed was a man to forget a favor, and for the rest of his life all you had to do to get him fighting mad was say a bad word about Dr. McLoughlin, chief factor at Fort Vancouver. Because British or not, McLoughlin was a human being. He took just one look at those drowned-rat people in Jed's party and started snapping out orders. Warm clothes, shoes, food, medicine, dry quarters. Quick as that Jed's people were taken care of, and if it bothered McLoughlin at all that he was giving away company supplies for which he'd likely never get paid and would catch hell from Sir George Simpson when Sir George found out, he never let on.

His advice was free, too, and it was good advice. Settle south of the river, he said. Lots of fine, fertile land there. Help yourself. You need supplies, you can draw on the company and we'll put it on the cuff till you're in shape to pick up the tab. No, I can't sell you any cows because I'm trying to build up the company herds, but I'll loan 'em to you and you can keep the milk and butcher the male calves for meat should the fish and wild-game supply run low. You want lumber, come to my sawmill and I'll sell it to you and put that on the cuff for a while too.

Yes, Dr. McLoughlin was a kind, human sort of a man, and Jed took to him right off. After the party had stayed at Fort Vancouver a week or two and everybody got to feeling better, Jed and the rest took their rafts across the river to the south side, put the wheels back on the wagons, and went up the Willamette Valley looking for homesites. In a month or two they'd all settled down, had built cabins, and were in out of the weather with nothing to do but sit by the fire for the rest of the winter, listening to the rain fall.

Jed set for maybe a week, resting up, then one day long about New Year's he decided he'd go to Fort Vancouver and pay Dr. McLoughlin a social call and maybe say thank you. He had to wait a spell on the south bank of the river till he could hook a ride across with a Frenchie in a rowboat. As men will, they got to talking.

"How come," Jed said, eyeing the twin flags hanging soddenly on the flagpole within the fort stockade, "they's two flags yonder?"

"Wan is ze flag of ze companee," says the Frenchie, shocked at such ignorance, "an' wan is ze flag of ze King."

"King? What's a King?"

Now this Frenchie was a fat, jolly, grizzled little fellow who had spent a lifetime in the service of the company and the King, receiving at last as his well-earned reward a parcel of land in the Willamette Valley, credit at the company stores, and the privilege of sending his seven half-breed children to the company school. In his travels he had met many Americans, all of them crazy or ignorant or both (in his opinion), but never—no, never—had he met one so crazy-ignorant as this lank, coughing man in the boat with him now. Not to know what a king was—*sacre du nom!*

"Ze King is ze—how you say?—ze beeg boss of ze people. Lak ze President of your countree. He say do somezing, ze people do eet."

"That so?" Jed said, and thought on it a moment. "How come you stand for it?"

"Je ne comprends pas."

"I said, why do you take that guff? How come you jump when this king fella says 'frog'?"

"Mon Dieu, he rules ze countree. He tal' everbodee what to do."

"Doc McLoughlin, he work for this hyar king?"

"Everbodee work for ze King."

Well, that was a totally new idea to Jed. More he thought about it the less he liked it. It came to him that if Dr. McLoughlin was working for the King, like the Frenchie said, then when McLoughlin advised people to do something it must be because the King had told him to advise them to do it, and the way that ended up the King was actually bossing Jed himself because Jed, for once in his life, had taken a piece of advice from somebody without throwing up his head and balking.

Jed thought some more. Cross the river, McLoughlin had advised, and settle in the country to the south. Jed squinted off to the north. Far as he could see the country wasn't any different up that way. Same wide green valley and foothills veiled with rain. Only difference was it was on the north side of the river and the other country was on the south side of the river. But he got to wondering.

When the boat touched the dock, he hopped out and walked right up the slope to the stockade, walked right in through the open gates, past the big brass cannon, up the curving steps that led into the chief factor's house, past three clerks that tried to stop him, right on into where Dr. McLoughlin himself sat at his desk in his private office. This McLoughlin was a big fellow, six feet six or seven, with long white hair, eyes sharp as an eagle's, and a voice that could be as gentle as a woman's one breath and as loud as thunder the next. You could go a thousand miles north or east or south and not find a single Indian that wouldn't tremble at the mere mention of his name, for it was known all over that wide reach of land that the Great White Tyee's arm was long, his justice swift, his word immutable as iron.

The slight frown on his face as he rose to greet Jed would have frozen any one of the hundreds of men in company employ, but Jed stood there squinting up at him, coughing, as calm as he would have been if he were addressing his own brother.

"Well, Mr. Kelly," said McLoughlin, "to what do I owe the pleasure of your visit?"

"Doc," Jed said, "you've behaved right well to us. I'm purely obliged. But I got to thinking. How come you told us to settle south of the river?"

"Because that's where the best land is. That's where all the Americans are settling."

"Ain't none of 'em goin' north?"

"No."

"How come?"

Well, McLoughlin was a patient man, so he explained it to Jed as best he knew how. The country north of the Columbia was rougher. There were no trails. There were several nasty rivers which were difficult to cross; the Indians were unfriendly; the timber was too thick in most places for farming, and so on and so on. When he had finished he spread his hands and smiled.

"In view of all this, I'm sure you'll agree it would be extremely foolish for any of you people to settle north of the river."

Jed stood there a minute, thinking it over. Then he thanked McLoughlin and left. Then he found a trail that led back into the timber to the north for a way and started walking, and when the trail petered out after a while he kept on walking, making his own. . . .

That's about all there is to the story. All worth telling, that is. Because the truth is I've never been able to find a thing in the history books that says Jed Kelly ever found anything better north of the river than what the other settlers had already found south of the river. But the point is he kept on looking, and pretty soon other Americans came along and started looking around too—just because they heard Jed Kelly was up there and they figured he must have come onto a good thing or he wouldn't have stayed.

First thing you know the country was aswarm with Americans, all of them looking around. Wasn't much the Hudson's Bay Company could do to keep them out or throw them out once they got there. Oh, the company did have a charter from the King that gave it authority to use force if necessary in keeping "uncivilized, unchristianized people" in line. These fool Americans were civilized—well, supposed to be, anyhow. Christianized, too, after a fashion. So the company's hands were tied, and pretty soon it was put up to those Britishers: either make a permanent boundary settlement or risk a war with the U.S.A.

You know how that came out. The Britishers put in a claim for everything as far south as California, and the U.S. topped that by claiming everything clear up to the North Pole, and after a President got himself elected on that "Fifty-four Forty" slogan it all simmered down and they hung the boundary fence right where it is now.

But only because Jed Kelly had let the cat out of the bag about what a good thing Washington was, get it?

I know. They called it all Oregon at first. But a river as wide as the Columbia makes a good boundary between states, and presently the people north of it were saying damned if they'd be tied to the webfoots, and the webfoots said damned if they'd put up with the sawdust eaters—so Oregon and Washington split up with no tears shed on either side.

Far as I know, none have been shed since.

The first great novel of the Old West and one of the most influential ever penned was Owen Wister's The Virginian *(1902), a best-seller for more than ten years. Wister also wrote other memorable tales of the Wyoming range, among them the novel* Lin McLean *(1897) and many of the stories in such collections as* Red Men and White *(1896),* The Jimmyjohn Boss and Other Stories *(1900),* Members of the Family *(1911), and* When West Was West *(1928). Wyoming, however, was not the only setting utilized by Wister for his fiction; he traveled widely throughout the West and wrote equally fine stories set in Arizona, Texas, California, and the Pacific Northwest. Idaho's Boise City and Snake River Valley are the settings for "The General's Bluff," featuring General Crook and Specimen Jones.*

The General's Bluff

★★★★★★★★★★★★

Owen Wister

THE troops this day had gone into winter quarters, and sat down to kill the idle time with pleasure until spring. After two hundred and forty days it is a good thing to sit down. The season had been spent in trailing, and sometimes catching, small bands of Indians. These had taken the habit of relieving settlers of their cattle and the tops of their heads. The weatherbeaten troops had scouted over some two thousand aimless, veering miles, for the savages were fleet and mostly invisible and knew the desert well. So, while the year turned, and the heat came, held sway, and went, the ragged troopers on the frontier were led an endless chase by the hostiles, who took them back and forth over flats of lime and ridges of slate, occasionally picking off a packer or a couple of privates, until now the sun was setting at 4:28 and it froze at any time of day. Therefore the rest of the packers and privates were glad to march into Boisé Barracks this morning by eleven and see a stove.

They rolled for a moment on their bunks to get the feel of a bunk again after two hundred and forty days; they ate their dinner at a table; those who owned any further baggage than that which partially covered their nakedness unpacked it, perhaps nailed up a photograph or two, and found it grateful to sit and do nothing under a roof and listen to the grated snow whip the windows of the gray sandstone quarters. Such comfort, and the prospect of more ahead, of weeks of nothing but post duty and staying in the same place, obliterated Dry Camp, Cow Creek Lake, the blizzard on Meacham's Hill, the horse-killing in the John Day Valley, Saw-Tooth stampede, and all the recent evils of the past; the quarters hummed with cheerfulness. The nearest railroad was some four hundred miles to the southeast, slowly constructing to meet the next nearest, which was some nine hundred to the southeast; but Boisé City was only three-quarters of a mile away, the largest town in the Territory, the capital, not a temperance town, a winter resort; and several hundred people lived in it, men and women, few of whom ever died in their beds. The coming days and nights were a luxury to think of.

"Blamed if there ain't a real tree!" exclaimed Private Jones.

"Thet eer ain't no tree, ye plum; thet's the flagpole 'n' th' Merrickin flag," observed a civilian. His name was Jack Long, and he was pack-master.

Sergeant Keyser, listening, smiled. During the winter of '64–65 he had been in command of the first battalion of his regiment, but, on a theory of education, had enlisted after the war. This being known, held the men more shy of him than was his desire.

Jones continued to pick his banjo, while a boyish trooper with tough black hair sat near him and kept time with his heels. "It's a cottonwood tree I was speakin' of," observed Jones. There was one—a little, shivering white stalk. It stood above the flat where the barracks were, on a bench twenty or thirty feet higher, on which were built the officers' quarters. The air was getting dim with the fine, hard snow that slanted through it. The thermometer was ten above out there. At the mere sight and thought Mr. Long produced a flat bottle, warm from proximity to his flesh. Jones swallowed some drink, and looked at the little tree. "Snakes, but it feels good," said he, "to get something inside y'u and be inside yerself. What's the tax at Mike's dance-house now?"

"Dance 'n' drinks fer two fer one dollar," responded Mr. Long, accurately. He was sixty, but that made no difference.

"You and me'll take that in, Jock," said Jones to his friend, the black-haired boy. " 'Sigh no more, ladies,' " he continued, singing. "The blamed banjo won't accompany that," he remarked, and looked out again at the tree. "There's a chap riding into the post now. Shabby-lookin'. Mebbe he's got stuff to sell."

Jack Long looked up on the bench at a rusty figure moving slowly through the storm. "Th' ole man!" he said.

"He ain't specially old," Jones answered. "They're apt to be older, them peddlers."

"Peddlers! Oh, ye-es." A seizure of very remarkable coughing took Jack Long by the throat; but he really had a cough, and, on the fit's leaving him, swallowed a drink, and offered his bottle in a manner so cold and usual that Jones forgot to note anything but the excellence of the whiskey. Mr. Long winked at Sergeant Keyser; he thought it a good plan not to inform his young friends, not just yet at any rate, that their peddler was General Crook. It would be pleasant to hear what else they might have to say.

The General had reached Boisé City that morning by the stage, quietly and unknown, as was his way. He had come to hunt Indians in the district of the Owyhee. Jack Long had discovered this, but only a few had been told the news, for the General wished to ask questions and receive answers, and to find out about all things; and he had noticed that this is not easy when too many people know who you are. He had called upon a friend or two in Boisé, walked about unnoticed, learned a number of facts, and now, true to his habit, entered the post wearing no uniform, none being necessary under the circumstances, and unattended by a single orderly. Jones and the black-haired Cumnor hoped he was a peddler, and innocently sat looking out of the window at him riding along the bench in front of the quarters and occasionally slouching his wide, dark hat brim against the stinging of the hard flakes. Jack Long, old and much experienced with the army, had scouted with Crook before and knew him and his ways well. He also looked out of the window, standing behind Jones and Cumnor, with a huge hairy hand on a shoulder of each, and a huge wink again at Keyser.

"Blamed if he ain't stopped in front of the commanding officer's," said Jones.

"Lor'!" said Mr. Long, "there's jest nothin' them peddlers won't do."

"They ain't likely to buy anything off him in there," said Cumnor.

"Mwell, ef he's purvided with any *kind* o' Injun cur'os'tees, the missis she'll fly right on to 'em. Sh' 'ain't been married out yere only haff'n year, 'n' when she spies feathers 'n' bead truck 'n' buckskin fer sale sh' hollers like a son of a gun. Enthoosiastic, ye know."

"He 'ain't got much of a pack," Jones commented, and at that moment "stables" sounded, and the men ran out to form and march to their grooming. Jack Long stood at the door and watched them file through the snow.

Very few enlisted men of the small command that had come in this morning from its campaign had ever seen General Crook. Jones, though not new to the frontier, had not been long in the army. He and Cumnor had enlisted in a happy-go-lucky manner together at Grant, in Arizona, when the General was elsewhere. Discipline was galling to his vagrant spirit, and after each payday he had generally slept off the effects in the guardhouse, going there for other offenses between-whiles; but he was not of the stuff that deserts; also, he was excellent tempered, and his captain liked him for the way in which he could shoot Indians. Jack Long liked him too; and getting always a harmless pleasure from the mistakes of his friends, sincerely trusted there might be more about the peddler. He was startled at hearing his name spoken in his ear.

"*Nah!* Johnny, how you get on?"

"Hello, Sarah! Kla-how-ya, six?" said Long, greeting in Chinook the squaw interpreter who had approached him so noiselessly. "Hy-as kloshe o-coke sun" (It is a beautiful day).

The interpreter laughed—she had a broad, sweet, coarse face and laughed easily—and said in English, "You hear about E-gante?"

Long had heard nothing recently of this Pah-Ute chieftain.

"He heap bad," continued Sarah, laughing broadly. "Come round ranch up here—"

"Anybody killed?" Long interrupted.

"No. All run away quick. Meester Dailey, he old man, he run all same young one. His old woman she run all same man. Get horse. Run away quick. Hu-hu!" and Sarah's rich mockery sounded again. No tragedy had happened this time, and the squaw narrated her story greatly to the relish of Mr. Long. This veteran of trails and mines had seen too much of life's bleakness not to cherish whatever of mirth his days might bring.

"Didn't burn the house?" he said.

"Not burn. Just make heap mess. Cut up feather-bed hy-as tenas [very small] and eat big dinner, hu-hu! Sugar, onions, meat, eat all. Then they find litt' cats walkin' round there."

"Lor'!" said Mr. Long, deeply interested, "they didn't eat *them*?"

"No. Not eat litt' cats. Put 'em two—man-cat and woman-cat—in molasses; put 'em in feather-bed; all same bird. Then they hunt for whiskey, break everything, hunt all over, ha-lo whiskey!" Sarah shook her head. "Meester Daily he good man. Hy-iu temperance. Drink water. They find his medicine; drink all up; make awful sick."

"I guess 'twar th' ole man's liniment," muttered Jack Long.

"Yas, milinut. They can't walk. Stay there long time, then Meester Daily come back with friends. They think Injuns all gone; make noise, and E-egante he hear him come, and he not very sick. Run away. Some more run. But two Injuns heap sick; can't run. Meester Dailey he come round the corner; see awful mess everywhere; see two litt' cats sittin' in door all same bird, sing very loud. Then he see two Injuns on ground. They dead now."

"Mwell," said Long, "none of eer'll do. We'll hev to ketch E-egante."

"A—h!" drawled Sarah the squaw, in musical derision. "Maybe no catch him. All same jack-rabbit."

"Jest ye wait, Sarah; Gray Fox hez come."

"Gen'l Crook!" said the squaw. "He come! Ho! He heap savvy." She stopped, and laughed again, like a pleased child. "Maybe no catch E-egante," she added, rolling her pretty brown eyes at Jack Long.

"You know E-egante?" he demanded.

"Yas, one time. Long time now. I litt' girl then." But Sarah remembered that long time, when she slept in a tent and had not been captured and put to school. And she remembered the tall young boys whom she used to watch shoot arrows, and the tallest, who shot most truly—at least, he certainly did now in her imagination. He had never spoken to her or looked at her. He was a boy of fourteen and she a girl of eight. Now she was twenty-five. Also she was tame and domesticated, with a white husband who was not bad to her, and children for each year of wedlock, who would grow up to speak English better than she could, and her own tongue not at all. And E-egante was not tame and still lived in a tent. Sarah regarded white people as her friends, but she was proud of being an Indian, and she liked to think that her race could outwit the soldier now and then. She laughed again when she thought of old Mrs. Dailey running from E-egante.

"What's up with ye, Sarah?" said Jack Long, for the squaw's laughter had come suddenly on a spell of silence.

"Hé!" said she. "All same jack-rabbit. No catch him." She stood shaking her head at Long, and showing her white, regular teeth. Then abruptly she went away to her tent without any word, not because she was in ill-humor or had thought of something, but because she was an Indian and had thought of nothing, and had no more to say. She met the men returning from the stables; admired Jones and smiled at him, upon which he murmured "Oh fie!" as he passed her. The troop broke ranks and dispersed, to lounge and gossip until mess call. Cumnor and Jones were putting a little snow down each other's necks with friendly profanity, when Jones saw the peddler standing close and watching them. A high collar of some ragged fur was turned up round his neck, disguising the character of the ancient army overcoat to which it was attached, and spots and long stains extended down the legs of his corduroys to the charred holes at the bottom, where the owner had scorched them warming his heels and calves at many campfires.

"Hello, uncle," said Jones. "What y'u got in your pack?" He and Cumnor left their gambols and eagerly approached, while Mr. Jack Long, seeing the interview, came up also to hear it. "Ain't y'u got something to sell?" continued Jones. "Y'u haven't gone and dumped yer whole outfit at the commanding officer's, have y'u now?"

"I'm afraid I have." The low voice shook ever so little, and if Jones had looked, he would have seen a twinkle come and go in the gray-blue eyes.

"We've been out eight months, yu' know, fairly steady," pursued Jones, "and haven't seen nothing; and we'd buy most anything that ain't too damn bad," he concluded plaintively.

Mr. Long, in the background, was whining to himself with joy, and he now urgently beckoned Keyser to come and hear this.

"If you've got some cheap poker chips," suggested Cumnor.

"And say, uncle," said Jones, raising his voice, for the peddler was moving away, "decks, and tobacco better than what they keep at the commissary. Me and my friend'll take some off your hands. And if you're comin' with new stock tomorrow, uncle" (Jones was now shouting after him), "why, we're single men, and y'u might fetch along a couple of squaws!"

"Holy smoke!" screeched Mr. Long, dancing on one leg.

"What's up with you, y'u ape?" inquired Specimen Jones. He looked at the departing peddler and saw Sergeant Keyser meet him and salute with stern, soldierly aspect. Then the peddler shook hands with the sergeant, seemed to speak pleasantly, and again Keyser saluted as he passed on. "What's that for?" Jones asked, uneasily. "Who is that hobo?"

But Mr. Long was talking to himself in a highly moralizing strain. "It ain't every young enlisted man," he was saying, "ez hez th' privilege of explainin' his wants at headquarters."

"Jones," said Sergeant Keyser, arriving, "I've a compliment for you. General Crook said you were a fine-looking man."

"General?— What's that?— Where did y'u see— What? *Him?*"

The disgusting truth flashed clear on Jones. Uttering a single disconcerted syllable of rage, he wheeled and went by himself into the barracks, and lay down solitary on his bunk and read a newspaper until mess call without taking in a word of it. "If they go to put me in the mill fer that," he said sulkily to many friends who brought him their congratulations, "I'm going to give 'em what I think about wearin' disguises."

"What do you think, Specimen?" said one.

"Give it to us now, Specimen," said another.

"Against the law, ain't it, Specimen?"

"Begosh!" said Jack Long, "ef thet's so, don't lose no time warnin' the General, Specimen. Th' ole man'd hate to be arrested."

And Specimen Jones told them all to shut their heads.

But no thought was more distant from General Crook's busy mind than putting poor Jones in the guard-house. The trooper's willingness, after eight months hunting Indians, to buy almost anything brought a smile to his lips and a certain sympathy in his heart. He knew what those eight months had been like; how monotonous, how well endured, how often dangerous, how invariably plucky, how scant of even the necessities of life, how barren of glory, and unrewarded by public recognition. The American "statesman" does not care about our army until it becomes necessary for his immediate personal protection. General Crook knew all this well; and realizing that these soldiers, who had come into winter quarters this morning at eleven, had earned a holiday, he was sorry to feel obliged to start them out again to-morrow morning at two; for this was what he had decided upon.

He had received orders to drive on the reservation the various small bands of Indians that were roving through the country of the Snake and its tributaries, a danger to the miners in the Bannock Basin and to the various ranches in west Idaho and east Oregon. As usual, he had been given an insufficient force to accomplish this, and, as always, he had been instructed by the "statesmen" to do it without violence—that is to say, he must never shoot the poor Indian until after the poor Indian had shot him; he must make him do something he did not want to, pleasantly, by the fascination of argument, in the way a "statesman" would achieve it. The force at the General's disposal was the garrison at Boisé Barracks—one troop of cavalry and one company of infantry. The latter was not adapted to the matter in hand—rapid marching and surprises; all it could be used for was as a reinforcement, and, moreover, somebody must be left at Boisé Barracks. The cavalry had had its full dose of scouting and skirmishing and long exposed marches, the horses were poor, and nobody had any trousers to speak of. Also, the troop was greatly depleted; it numbered forty men. Forty had deserted, and three—a sergeant and three privates—had cooked and eaten a vegetable they had been glad to dig up one day, and had spent the ensuing forty-five minutes in attempting to make their ankles beat the backs of their heads; after that the captain had read over them a sentence beginning, "Man that is born of a woman hath but a short time to live, and is full of misery"; and after that the camp was referred to as Wild Carrot Camp, because the sergeant had said the vegetable was wild carrot, whereas it had really been wild parsnip, which is quite another thing.

General Crook shook his head over what he saw. The men were ill-provided, the commissary and the quartermaster department were ill-provided; but it would have to do; the "statesmen" said our army was an extravagance. The Indians must be impressed and intimidated by the unlimited resources which the General had—not. Having come to this conclusion, he went up to the post commander's, and at supper astonished that officer by casual remarks which revealed a knowledge of the surrounding country, the small streams, the best camps for pasture, spots to avoid on account of bad water, what mules had sore backs, and many other things that the post commander would have liked dearly to ask the General where and when he had learned, only he did not dare. He did not even venture to ask him what he was going to do. Neither did Captain Glynn, who had been asked to meet the General. The General soon told them, however. "It may be a little cold," he concluded.

"Tomorrow, sir?" This from Captain Glynn. He had come in with the forty that morning. He had been enjoying his supper very much.

"I think so," said the General. "This E-egante is likely to make trouble if he is not checked." Then, understanding the thoughts of Captain Glynn, he added, with an invisible smile. "*You* need no preparations. You're in marching order. It's not as if your men had been here a long time and had to get ready for a start."

"Oh no," said Glynn, "it isn't like that." He was silent. "I think, if you'll excuse me, General," he said next, "I'll see my sergeant and give some orders."

"Certainly. And, Captain Glynn, I took the liberty of giving a few directions myself. We'll take an A tent, you know, for you and me. I see Keyser is sergeant in F troop. Glad we have a noncommissioned officer so competent. Haven't seen him since '64, at Winchester. Why, it's cleared off, I declare!"

It had, and the General looked out of the open door as Captain Glynn, departing, was pulling at his cigar. "How beautiful the planets are!" exclaimed Crook. "Look at Jupiter—there, just to the left of that little cottonwood tree. Haven't you often noticed how much finer the stars shine in this atmosphere than in the East? Oh, Captain! I forgot to speak of extra horseshoes. I want some brought along."

"I'll attend to it, General."

"They shouldn't be too large. These California fourteen-and-a-half horses have smallish hoofs."

"I'll see the blacksmith myself, General."

"Thank you. Good night. And just order fresh stuffing put into the aparejos. I noticed three that had got lumpy." And the General shut the door and went to wipe out the immaculate barrels of his shot-gun; for besides Indians there were grouse among the hills where he expected to go.

Captain Glynn, arriving at his own door, stuck his glowing cigar against the thermometer hanging outside: twenty-three below zero. "Oh, Lord!" said the captain, briefly. He went in and told his striker to get Sergeant Keyser. Then he sat down and waited. " 'Look at Jupiter'!" he muttered, angrily. "What an awful old man!"

It was rather awful. The captain had not supposed generals in the first two hours of their arrival at a post to be in the habit of finding out more about your aparejos than you knew yourself. But old the General was not. At the present day many captains are older than Crook was then.

Down at the barracks there was the same curiosity about what the "Old Man" was going to do as existed at the post commander's during the early part of supper. It pleased the cavalry to tell the infantry that the Old Man proposed to take the infantry to the Columbia River next week; and the infantry replied to the cavalry that they were quite right as to the river and the week, and it was hard luck the General needed only mounted troops on this trip. Others had heard he had come to superintend the building of a line of telegraph to Klamath, which would be a good winter's job for somebody; but nobody supposed that anything would happen yet awhile.

And then a man came in and told them the General had sent his boots to the saddler to have nails hammered in the soles.

"That eer means business," said Jack Long, " 'n' I guess I'll nail up me own cowhides."

"Jock," said Specimen Jones to Cumnor, "you and me ain't got any soles to ourn because they're contract boots, y'u see. I'll nail up yer feet if y'u say so. It's liable to be slippery."

Cumnor did not take in the situation at once. "What's your hurry?" he inquired of Jack Long. Therefore it was explained to him that when General Crook ordered his boots fixed, you might expect to be on the road shortly. Cumnor swore some resigned, unemphatic oaths, fondly supposing that "shortly" meant some time or other; but hearing in the next five minutes the definite fact that F troop would get up at two, he made use of profound and thorough language and compared the soldier with the slave.

"Why, y'u talk almost like a man, Jock," said Specimen Jones. "Blamed if y'u don't sound pretty near growed up."

Cumnor invited Jones to mind his business.

"Yer muss-tache has come since Arizona," continued Jones, admiringly, "and yer blue eye is bad-lookin'—worse than when we shot at yer heels and y'u danced fer us."

"I thought they were going to give us a rest," mumbled the youth, flushing. "I thought we'd be let stay here a spell."

"I thought so too, Jock. A little monotony would be fine variety. But a man must take his medicine, y'u know, and not squeal." Jones had lowered his voice and now spoke without satire to the boy whom he had in a curious manner taken under his protection.

"Look at what they give us for a blanket to sleep in," said Cumnor. "A fellow can see to read the newspaper through it."

"Look at my coat, Cumnor." It was Sergeant Keyser showing the article furnished the soldier by the government. "You can spit through that." He had overheard their talk, and stepped up to show that all were in the same box. At his presence reticence fell upon the privates, and Cumnor hauled his black felt hat down tight in embarrassment, which strain split it open halfway round his head. It was another sample of regulation clothing, and they laughed at it.

"We all know the way it is," said Keyser, "and I've seen it a big sight worse. Cumnor, I've a cap I guess will keep your scalp warm till we get back."

And so at two in the morning F troop left the bunks it had expected to sleep in for some undisturbed weeks, and by four o'clock had eaten its well-known breakfast of bacon and bad coffee, and was following the "awful old man" down the north bank of the Boisé, leaving the silent, dead, wooden town of shanties on the other side half a mile behind in the darkness. The mountains south stood distant, ignoble, plain-featured heights, looming a clean-cut black beneath the piercing stars and the slice of hard, sharp-edged moon, and the surrounding plains of sage and dry-cracking weed slanted up and down to nowhere and nothing with desolate perpetuity. The snowfall was light and dry as sand, and the bare ground jutted through it at every sudden lump or knoll. The column moved through the dead polar silence, scarcely breaking it. Now and then a hoof rang on a stone, here and there a bridle or a sabre clinked lightly; but it was too cold and early for talking, and the only steady sound was the flat, canlike tankle of the square bell that hung on the neck of the long-eared leader of the pack-train. They passed the Dailey ranch, and saw the kittens and the liniment-bottle, but could get no information as to what way E-egante had gone. The General did not care for that, however; he had devised his own route for the present, after a talk with the Indian guides. At the second dismounting during march he had word sent back to the pack-train not to fall behind, and the bell was to be taken off if the rest of the mules would follow without the sound of its shallow music. No wind moved the weeds or shook the stiff grass, and the rising sun glittered pink on the patched and motley-shirted men as they blew on their red hands or beat them against their legs. Some were lucky enough to have woolen or fur gloves, but many had only the white cotton affairs furnished by the government. Sarah the squaw laughed at them: the interpreter was warm as she rode in her bright green shawl. While the dismounted troopers stretched their limbs during the halt, she remained on her pony talking to one and another.

"Gray Fox heap savvy," said she to Mr. Long. "He heap get up in the mornin'."

"Thet's what he does, Sarah."

"Yas. No give soldier hy-as Sunday" (a holiday).

"No, no," assented Mr. Long. "Gray Fox go téh-téh" (trot).

"Maybe he catch E-egante, maybe put him in skoo-kum-house [prison]?" suggested Sarah.

"Oh no! Lor'! E-egante good Injun. White Father he feed him. Give him heap clothes," said Mr. Long.

"A—h!" drawled Sarah dubiously, and rode by herself.

"You'll need watchin'," muttered Jack Long.

The trumpet sounded, the troopers swung into their saddles, and the line of march was taken up as before, Crook at the head of the column, his ragged fur collar turned up, his corduroys stuffed inside a wrinkled pair of boots, the shotgun balanced across his saddle, and nothing to reveal that he was anyone in particular, unless you saw his face. As the morning grew bright and empty, silent Idaho glistened under the clear blue, the General talked a little to Captain Glynn.

"E-egante will have crossed Snake River, I think," said he. "I shall try to do that today; but we must be easy on those horses of yours. We ought to be able to find these Indians in three days."

"If I were a lusty young chief," said Glynn, "I should think it pretty tough to be put on a reservation for dipping a couple of kittens in the molasses."

"So should I, Captain. But next time he might dip Mrs. Dailey. And I'm not sure he didn't have a hand in more serious work. Didn't you run across his tracks anywhere this summer?"

"No, sir. He was over on the Des Chutes."

"Did you hear what he was doing?"

"Having rows about fish and game with those Warm Spring Indians on the west side of the Des Chutes."

"They're always poaching on each other. There's bad blood between E-egante and Uma-Pine."

"Uma-Pine's friendly, sir, isn't he?"

"Well, that's a question," said Crook. "But there's no question about this E-egante and his Pah-Utes. We've got to catch him. I'm sorry for him. He doesn't see why he shouldn't hunt anywhere as his fathers did. I shouldn't see that either."

"How strong is this band reported, sir?"

"I've heard nothing I can set reliance upon," said Crook, instinctively levelling his shotgun at a big bird that rose; then he replaced the piece across his saddle and was silent. Now Captain Glynn had heard there were three hundred Indians with E-egante, which was a larger number than he had been in the habit of attacking with forty men. But he felt discreet about volunteering any information to the General after last night's exhibition of what the General knew. Crook partly answered what was in Glynn's mind. "This is the only available force I have," said he. "We must do what we can with it. You've found out by this time, Captain, that rapidity in following Indians up often works well. They have made up their minds—that is, if I know them—that we're going to loaf inside Boisé Barracks until the hard weather lets up."

Captain Glynn had thought so too, but he did not mention this, and the General continued. "I find that most people entertained this notion," he said, "and I'm glad they did, for it will help my first operations very materially."

The captain agreed that there was nothing like a false impression for assisting the efficacy of military movements, and presently the General asked him to command a halt. It was high noon, and the sun gleamed on the brass trumpet as the long note blew. Again the musical strain sounded on the cold, bright stillness, and the double line of twenty legs swung in a simultaneous arc over the horses' backs as the men dismounted.

"We'll noon here," said the General; and while the cook broke the ice on Boisé River to fill his kettles, Crook went back to the mules to see how the sore backs were standing the march. "How d'ye do, Jack Long?" said he. "Your stock is travelling pretty well, I see. They're loaded with thirty days' rations, but I trust we're not going to need it all."

"Mwell, General, I don't specially kyeer meself 'bout eatin' the hull outfit." Mr. Long showed his respect for the General by never swearing in his presence.

"I see you haven't forgotten how to pack," Crook said to him. "Can we make Snake River today, Jack?"

"That'll be forty miles, General. The days are pretty short."

"What are you feeding to the animals?" Crook inquired.

"Why, General, *you* know jest's well's me," said Jack, grinning.

"I suppose I do if you say so, Jack. Ten pounds first ten days, five pounds next ten, and you're out of grain for the next ten. Is that the way still?"

"Thet's the way, General, on these yere thirty-day affairs."

Through all this small talk Crook had been inspecting the mules and the horses on picket-line and silently forming his conclusion. He now returned to Captain Glynn and shared his mess-box.

They made Snake River. Crook knew better than Long what the animals could do. And next day they crossed, again by starlight, turned for a little way up the Owyhee, decided that E-egante had not gone that road, trailed up the bluffs and ledges from the Snake Valley on to the barren height of land, and made for the Malheur River, finding the eight hoofs of two deer lying in a melted place where a fire had been. Mr. Dailey had insisted that at least fifty Indians had drunk his liniment and trifled with his cats. Indeed, at times during his talk with General Crook the old gentleman had been sure there were a hundred. If this were their trail which the command had now struck, there may possibly have been eight. It was quite evident that the chief had not taken any three hundred warriors upon that visit, if he had that number anywhere. So the column went up the Malheur main stream through the sagebrush and the gray weather (it was still cold, but no sun anymore these last two days), and, coming to the North Fork, turned up toward a spur of the mountains and Castle Rock. The water ran smooth black between its edging of ice, thick, white, and crusted like slabs of coconut candy, and there in the hollow of a bend they came suddenly upon what they sought.

Stems of smoke, faint and blue, spindled up from a blurred acre of willow thicket, dense, tall as two men, a netted brown and yellow mesh of twigs and stiff wintry rods. Out from the level of their close, nature-woven tops rose at distances the straight, slight blue smoke-lines, marking each the position of some invisible lodge. The whole acre was a bottom ploughed at some former time by a washout, and the troops looked down on it from the edge of the higher ground, silent in the quiet, gray afternoon, the empty sage-brush territory stretching a short way to fluted hills that were white below and blackened with pines above.

The General, taking a rough chance as he often did, sent ground scouts forward and ordered a charge instantly, to catch the savages unready; and the stiff rods snapped and tangled between the beating hoofs. The horses plunged at the elastic edges of this excellent fortress, sometimes half lifted as a bent willow levered up against their bellies, and the forward-tilting men fended their faces from the whipping twigs. They could not wedge a man's length into that pliant labyrinth, and the General called them out. They rallied among the sagebrush above, Crook's cheeks and many others painted with purple lines of blood, hardened already and cracking like enamel. The baffled troopers glared at the thicket. Not a sign or a sound came from in there. The willows, with the gentle tints of winter veiling their misty twigs, looked serene and even innocent, fitted to harbor birds—not birds of prey—and the quiet smoke threaded upward through the air. Of course the liniment-drinkers must have heard the noise.

"What do you suppose they're doing?" inquired Glynn.

"Looking at us," said Crook.

"I wish we could return the compliment," said the captain.

Crook pointed. Had any wind been blowing, what the General saw would have been less worth watching. Two willow branches shook, making a vanishing ripple on the smooth surface of the treetops. The pack-train was just coming in sight over the rise, and Crook immediately sent an orderly with some message. More willow branches shivered an instant and were still; then, while the General and the captain sat on their horses and watched, the thicket gave up its secret to them; for, as little light gusts coming abreast over a lake travel and touch the water, so in different spots the level maze of twigs was stirred; and if the eye fastened upon any one of these it could have been seen to come out from the center toward the edge, successive twigs moving, as the tops of long grass tremble and mark the progress of a snake. During a short while this increased greatly, the whole thicket moving with innumerable tracks. Then everything ceased, with the blue wands of smoke rising always into the quiet afternoon.

"Can you see 'em?" said Glynn.

"Not a bit. Did you happen to hear any one give an estimate of this band?"

Glynn mentioned his tale of the three hundred.

It was not new to the General, but he remarked now that it must be pretty nearly correct; and his eye turned a moment upon his forty troopers waiting there, grim and humorous; for they knew that the thicket was looking at them, and it amused their American minds to wonder what the Old Man was going to do about it.

"It's his bet, and he holds poor cards," murmured Specimen Jones; and the neighbors grinned.

And here the Old Man continued the play that he had begun when he sent the orderly to the pack-train. That part of the command had halted in consequence, disposed itself in an easygoing way, half in, half out of sight on the ridge, and men and mules looked entirely careless. Glynn wondered; but no one ever asked the General questions in spite of his amiable voice and countenance. He now sent for Sarah the squaw.

"You tell E-egante," he said, "that I am not going to fight with his people unless his people make me. I am not going to do them any harm, and I wish to be their friend. The White Father has sent me. Ask E-egante if he has heard of Gray Fox. Tell him Gray Fox wishes E-egante and all his people to be ready to go with him tomorrow at nine o'clock."

And Sarah, standing on the frozen bank, pulled her green shawl closer, and shouted her message faithfully to the willows. Nothing moved or showed, and Crook, riding up to the squaw, held his hand up as a further sign to the flag of peace that had been raised already. "Say that I am Gray Fox," said he.

On that there was a moving in the bushes farther along, and, going opposite that place with the squaw, Crook and Glynn saw a narrow entrance across which some few branches reached that were now spread aside for three figures to stand there.

"E-egante!" said Sarah, eagerly. "See him big man!" she added to Crook, pointing. A tall and splendid buck, gleaming with colors and rich with fringe and buckskin, watched them. He seemed to look at Sarah, too. She, being ordered, repeated what she had said; but the chief did not answer.

"He is counting our strength," said Glynn.

"He's done that some time ago," said Crook. "Tell E-egante," he continued to the squaw, "that I will not send for more soldiers than he sees here. I do not wish anything but peace unless he wishes otherwise."

Sarah's musical voice sounded again from the bank, and E-egante watched her intently till she was finished. This time he replied at some length. He and his people had not done any harm. He had heard of Gray Fox often. All his people knew Gray Fox was a good man and would not make trouble. There were some flies that stung a man sitting in his house, when he had not hurt them. Gray Fox would not hurt anyone till their hand was raised against him first. E-egante and his people had wondered why the horses made so much noise just now. He and his people would come tomorrow with Gray Fox.

And then he went inside the thicket again, and the willows looked as innocent as ever. Crook and the captain rode away.

"My speech was just a little weak coming on top of a charge of cavalry," the General admitted. "And that fellow put his finger right on the place. I'll give you my notion, Captain. If I had said we had more soldiers behind the hill, like as not this squaw of ours would have told him I lied; she's an uncertain quantity, I find. But I told him the exact truth—that I had no more—and he won't believe it, and that's what I want."

So Glynn understood. The pack-train had been halted in a purposely exposed position, which would look to the Indians as if another force was certainly behind it, and every move was now made to give an impression that the forty were only the advance of a large command. Crook pitched his A tent close to the red men's village, and the troops went into camp regardlessly near. The horses were turned out to graze ostentatiously unprotected, so that the people in the thicket should have every chance to notice how secure the white men felt. The mules pastured comfortably over the shallow snow that crushed as they wandered among the sagebrush, and the square bell hung once more from the neck of the leader and tinkled upon the hill. The shelter-tents littered the flat above the washout, and besides the cookfire others were built irregularly far down the Malheur North Fork, shedding an extended glimmer of deceit. It might have been the camp of many hundred. A little blaze shone comfortably on the canvas of Crook's tent, and Sergeant Keyser, being in charge of camp, had adopted the troop cookfire for his camp guard after the cooks had finished their work. The willow thicket below grew black and mysterious, and quiet fell on the white camp. By eight the troopers had gone to bed. Night had come pretty cold, and a little occasional breeze that passed like a chill hand laid a moment on the face and went down into the willows. Now and again the water running through the ice would lap and gurgle at some airhole. Sergeant Keyser sat by his fire and listened to the lonely bell sounding from the dark. He wished the men would feel more at home with him. With Jack Long, satirical, old, and experienced, they were perfectly familiar, because he was a civilian; but to Keyser, because he had been in command of a battalion, they held the attitude of schoolboys to a master—the instinctive feeling of all privates toward all officers. Jones and Cumnor were members of his camp guard. Being just now off post, they stood at the fire, but away from him.

"How do you like this compared with barracks?" the sergeant asked conversationally.

"It's all right," said Jones.

"Did you think it was all right that first morning? I didn't enjoy it much myself. Sit down and get warm, won't you?"

The men came and stood awkwardly. "I 'ain't never found any excitement in getting up early," said Jones, and was silent. A burning log shifted, and the bell sounded in a new place as the leader pastured along. Jones kicked the log into better position. "But this affair's gettin' inter-esting," he added.

"Don't you smoke?" Keyser inquired of Cumnor, and tossed him his tobacco-pouch. Presently they were seated, and the conversation going better. Arizona was compared with Idaho. Everybody had gone to bed.

"Arizona's the most outrageous outrage in the United States," declared Jones.

"Why did you stay there six years, then?" said Cumnor.

"Guess I'd been there yet but for you comin' along and us both enlistin' that crazy way. Idaho's better. Only," said Jones, thoughtfully, "coming to an ice-box from a hundred thousand in the shade, it's a wonder a man don't just split like a glass chimbly."

The willows crackled, and all laid hands on their pistols.

"How! How!" said a strange, propitiating voice.

It was a man on a horse, and directly they recognized E-egante himself. They would have raised an alarm, but he was alone and plainly not running away. Nor had he weapons. He rode into the firelight, and "How! How!" he repeated, anxiously. He looked and nodded at the three, who remained seated.

"Good evening," said the sergeant.

"Christmas is coming," said Jones, amicably.

"How! How!" said E-egante. It was all the English he had. He sat on his horse, looking at the men, the camp, the cookfire, the A tent, and beyond into the surrounding silence. He started when the bell suddenly jangled near by. The wandering mule had only shifted in toward the camp and shaken his head; but the Indian's nerves were evidently on the sharpest strain.

"Sit down!" said Keyser, making signs, and at these E-egante started suspiciously.

"Warm here!" Jones called to him, and Cumnor showed his pipe.

The chief edged a thought closer. His intent, brilliant eyes seemed almost to listen as well as look, and though he sat his horse with heedless grace and security, there was never a figure more ready for vanishing upon the instant. He came a little nearer still, alert and pretty as an inquisitive buck antelope, watching not the three soldiers only but everything else at once. He eyed their signs to dismount, looked at their faces, considered, and with the greatest slowness got off and came stalking to the fire. He was a fine tall man, and they smiled and nodded at him, admiring his clean blankets and the magnificence of his buckskin shirt and leggings.

"He's a jim-dandy," said Cumnor.

"You bet the girls think so," said Jones. "He gets his pick. For you're a fighter too, ain't y'u?" he added, to E-egante.

"How! How!" said that personage, looking at them with grave affability from the other side of the fire. Reassured presently, he accepted the sergeant's pipe; but even while he smoked and responded to the gestures, the alertness never left his eye, and his tall body gave no sense of being relaxed. And so they all looked at each other across the waning embers, while the old pack-mule moved about at the edge of camp, crushing the crusted snow and pasturing along. After a time E-egante gave a nod, handed the pipe back, and went into his thicket as he had come. His visit had told him nothing; perhaps he had never supposed it would, and came from curiosity. One person had watched this interview. Sarah the squaw sat out in the night, afraid for her ancient hero; but she was content to look upon his beauty and go to sleep after he had taken himself from her sight. The soldiers went to bed, and Keyser lay wondering for a while before he took his nap between his surveillances. The little breeze still passed at times, the running water and the ice made sounds together, and he could hear the wandering bell, now distant on the hill, irregularly punctuating the flight of the dark hours.

By nine next day there was the thicket sure enough, and the forty waiting for the three hundred to come out of it. Then it became ten o'clock, but that was the only difference, unless perhaps Sarah the squaw grew more restless. The troopers stood ready to be told what to do, joking together in low voices now and then; Crook sat watching Glynn smoke; and through these stationary people walked Sarah, looking wistfully at the thicket and then at the faces of the adopted race she served. She hardly knew what was in her own mind. Then it became eleven, and Crook was tired of it, and made the capping move in his bluff. He gave the orders himself.

"Sergeant."

Keyser saluted.

"You will detail eight men to go with you into the Indian camp. The men are to carry pistols under their overcoats, and no other arms. You will tell the Indians to come out. Repeat what I said to them last night. Make it short. I'll give them ten minutes. If they don't come by then, a shot will be fired out here. At that signal you will remain in there and blaze away at the Indians."

So Keyser picked his men.

The thirty-one remaining troopers stopped joking and watched the squad of nine and the interpreter file down the bank to visit the three hundred. The dingy overcoats and the bright green shawl passed into the thicket, and the General looked at his watch. Along the bend of the stream clear noises tinkled from the water and the ice.

"What are they up to?" whispered a teamster to Jack Long. Long's face was stern, but the teamster's was chalky and tight drawn. "Say," he repeated, insistently, "what are we going to do?"

"We're to wait," Long whispered back, "till nothin' happens, and then th' Ole Man'll fire a gun and signal them boys to shoot in there."

"Oh, it's to be waitin'?" said the teamster. He fastened his eyes on the thicket, and his lips grew bloodless. The running river sounded more plainly. "—— —— it!" cried the man desperately, "let's start the fun, then." He whipped out his pistol, and Jack Long had just time to seize him and stop a false signal.

"Why, you must be skeered," said Long. "I've a mind to beat yer skull in."

"Waitin's so awful," whimpered the man. "I wisht I was along with them in there."

Jack gave him back his revolver. "There," said he; "ye're not skeered, I see. Waitin' ain't nice."

The eight troopers with Keyser were not having anything like so distasteful a time. "Jock," said Specimen Jones to Cumnor as they followed the sergeant into the willows and began to come among the lodges and striped savages, "you and me has saw Injuns before, Jock."

"And we'll do it again," said Cumnor.

Keyser looked at his watch: four minutes gone. "Jones," said he, "you patrol this path to the right so you can cover that gang there. There must be four or five lodges down that way. Cumnor, see that dugout with side-thatch and roofing of tule? You attend to that family. It's a big one—all brothers." Thus the sergeant disposed his men quietly and quick through the labyrinth till they became invisible to each other; and all the while flights of Indians passed, half seen, among the tangle, fleeting visions of yellow and red through the quiet-colored twigs. Others squatted stoically, doing nothing. A few had guns, but most used arrows and had these stacked beside them where they squatted. Keyser singled out a somewhat central figure—Fur Cap was his name—as his starting-point if the signal should sound. It must sound now in a second or two. He would not look at his watch lest it should hamper him. Fur Cap sat by a pile of arrows, with a gun across his knees besides. Keyser calculated that by standing close to him as he was, his boot would catch the Indian under the chin just right and save one cartridge. Not a red man spoke, but Sarah the squaw dutifully speechified in a central place where paths met near Keyser and Fur Cap. Her voice was persuasive and warning. Some of the savages moved up and felt Keyser's overcoat. They fingered the hard bulge of the pistol underneath and passed on, laughing, to the next soldier's coat, while Sarah did not cease to harangue. The tall, stately man of last night appeared. His full dark eyes met Sarah's, and the woman's voice faltered and her breathing grew troubled as she gazed at him. Once more Keyser looked at his watch: seven minutes. E-egante noticed Sarah's emotion, and his face showed that her face pleased him. He spoke in a deep voice to Fur Cap, stretching a fringed arm out toward the hill with a royal gesture, at which Fur Cap rose.

"He will come, he will come!" said the squaw, running to Keyser. "They all come now. Do not shoot."

"Let them show outside, then," thundered Keyser, "or it's too late. If that gun goes before I can tell my men—"

He broke off and rushed to the entrance. There were skirmishers deploying from three points, and Crook was raising his hand slowly. There was a pistol in it. "General! General!" Keyser shouted, waving both hands, "No!" Behind him came E-egante, with Sarah, talking in low tones, and Fur Cap came too.

The General saw and did not give the signal. The sight of the skirmishers hastened E-egante's mind. He spoke in a loud voice, and at once his warriors began to emerge from the willows obediently. Crook's bluff was succeeding. The Indians, in waiting after nine, were attempting a little bluff of their own; but the unprecedented visit of nine men appeared to them so dauntless that all notion of resistance left them. They were sure Gray Fox had a large army. And they came, and kept coming, and the place became full of them. The troopers had all they could do to form an escort and keep up the delusion, but by degrees order began, and the column was forming. Riding along the edge of the willows came E-egante, gay in his blankets, and saying, "How! How!" to Keyser, the only man at all near him. The pony ambled, and sidled, paused, trotted a little, and Keyser was beginning to wonder, when all at once a woman in a green shawl sprang from the thicket, leaped behind the chief, and the pony flashed by and away, round the curve. Keyser had lifted his carbine but forbore, for he hesitated to kill the woman. Once more the two appeared, diminutive and scurrying, the green shawl bright against the hillside they climbed. Sarah had been willing to take her chances of death with her hero, and now she vanished with him among his mountains, returning to her kind and leaving her wedded white man and half-breeds forever.

"I don't feel so mad as I ought," said Specimen Jones.

Crook laughed to Glynn about it. "We've got a big balance of 'em," he said, "if we can get 'em all to Boisé. They'll probably roast me in the East." And they did. Hearing how forty took three hundred but let one escape (and a few more on the march home), the superannuated cattle of the War Department sat sipping their drinks at the club in Washington, and explained to each other how they would have done it.

And so the General's bluff partly failed. E-egante kept his freedom, "all along o' thet yere pizen squaw," as Mr. Long judiciously remarked. It was not until many years after that the chief's destiny overtook him; and concerning that, things both curious and sad could be told.

*This brief, amusing account of "A Trip to Oregon" is one of many such satirical letters to the editor of various newspapers written by John Phoenix (Captain George Horatio Derby, 1823–1861) in the years prior to the Civil War. Flour and pork merchant Amos Butterfield, a wry observer of the rough-and-tumble society of the Far West, was just one of the author's fanciful creations. Two volumes of these letters were collected and published in 1861—*The Squibob Papers *and* Phoenixiana—*shortly before Captain Derby died of sunstroke while supervising the building of a lighthouse in the South.*

A Trip to Oregon

★★★★★★★★★★★★

John Phoenix

O N the sixteenth day of September I received a letter from my correspondent in Australia which convinced me that flour was about to make an unprecedented and unheard of rise. I have been nipped slightly heretofore in flour speculations; green and inviting appeared the floury paths before my mental vision, and I regret to say that I returned from their pursuit with just a shade of the greenness adhering to me, in a figurative point of view; but this time I determined to make a sure thing of it.

The last quotation from Oregon (which I never hear mentioned without associating it with the idea of Bartlett pears at one dollar apiece and particularly rotten inside) showed that flour might be purchased there at five dollars per barrel. "If, then," said I to Mrs. Butterfield, "I repair to Oregon, my dear, and purchase two thousand barrels of flour at five dollars per barrel and returning to San Francisco incontinently sell the same at eleven dollars per ditto, our circumstances will be slightly improved."

Mrs. Butterfield had seen at Guerin's a perfect love of a velvet mantle: a brown velvet mantle profusely embroidered, for which they asked but one hundred and twenty-five dollars, and she said she thought "it would be a good thing." And so I went down to the steamship *Columbia,* and purchased "A" stateroom, and had my trunk "dragged into camp" in stateroom "A." I detest and despise going to sea; it makes me sick at my stomach and I cannot agree with that young man who, on being reminded that "a rolling stone gathers no moss," replied, "Never mind the moss—*let us roll!*" I do not like to roll at all, and I sincerely believe that the man who first invented going to sea was some most abandoned rascal, who could not under any circumstances be permitted to live on shore, and I wish from my heart he had been drowned, and the invention lost with him. So that when I had paid sixty dollars to Purser Meade, who, like the beverage that bears his name, is of a mild, though sparkling disposition, and is moreover constantly effervescing with good humor, I went below, and gazing with a discontented air at stateroom "A," thought to myself I had given a very high price for an emetic. However, when one has made up his mind to be slain, it is certainly the best plan to employ a regular physician and have it done *secundum artem,* and it was a great relief to my mind to find the *Columbia* a clean and comfortable steamship, where if one had to die, he could at least die with decency. The Captain, too, had such a cheery good-natured smile on his handsome face, such a roguish twinkle in his eye, such a strong expression of wishing to make every one happy about him that it was difficult to conceive that anything very disagreeable could happen where he commanded.

The *Columbia* went to sea, and I went to bed in the second berth in stateroom "A." As Lever's hero, Charles O'Malley, invariably remarks after getting a lick on the back of the head, "I knew nothing more" until the arrival at Mendocino Mills. Confused visions of Mrs. Butterfield nursing a fifty pound sack of flour, which changed occasionally into a bowl of gruel, and then into a large wash basin, prevailed in my mind, I remember, during this period; but at Mendocino Mills I arose, girded up my loins, and the *Columbia* being very quiet, came forth like a young giant refreshed with new wine. In fact, as the Captain pleasantly remarked, I "opened like a psalm book."

Even as a tortoise draweth suddenly in his head when smote from the rear by some evil-disposed urchin with a stick, so suddenly did I disappear within the shell of stateroom "A," when the *Columbia* left Mendocino Mills. Then an interval elapsed, and we arrived at Trinidad. This place derives its name from the Latin words *Trinis,* three, and *Dad,* father, having been originally discovered by three Catholic priests. The town consists of about thirty mules, being packed with whiskey for the mines on Trinity River. Another interval of wash basin and gruel and we anchored at Crescent City. This little place has quite an active and bustling appearance. It is the depot of the Klamath mines and appears to be very much of a business place. At the door of the principal public house sat a forlorn, lost looking girl, who had once been beautiful; she was neatly and handsomely dressed, but there was a look of suffering about her pale and care-worn face that I shall not soon forget. I was told she was the proprietor of the establishment. Poor thing.

There is some surf at Crescent City, and unless you embark cautiously you are very liable to get your trousers wet. I never do anything cautiously. We arrived at Port Oxford one night, and disembarked Lieut. Kautz and eight mules belonging to the 4th U. S. Infantry. Lieut. Kautz commands the military post at Port Oxford, I was told, but what the military post is, I am not informed; probably they use it to tie the mules to. I heard that the *Columbia* once got up steam and left here, without casting off one of her stern lines, and accidentally towed the whole city up the coast about forty miles before the line parted, very much to the confusion of one Tichnor, who, having been elected a member of the Oregon Legislature, sailed off in a small schooner to find that body, but being unsuccessful, attempted to return to Port Oxford but did not get in for some time owing to that accident.

Imagine the feelings that animated my mind as we arrived—I sprang hastily from the steamer; I saw my friend Mr. Leonard G. Green, the great Portland jobber and importer, on the dock. I seized him by the arm and led him one side—"Butterfield," said he, "how do you do?" "Never mind," replied I in a faltering voice; "I want to buy two thousand barrels of Oregon flour!"

Leonard G. Green smiled; he was not at all excited, and he answered, "Probably!"—I gasped for breath. "Tell me," said I, "how is flour selling?" Leonard G. Green looked me calmly in the eye and answered slowly, "Eleven dollars and a half a barrel!" I am not a profane man; I attend the Rev. Dr. Scott's church regularly, have family prayers in my household, and say grace over my frugal repasts, but dog-gorn—never mind, as the man said, "I couldn't begin to do justice to the subject."

I wrote a letter, a doleful letter, to Mrs. Butterfield that night, and the brown velvet embroidered mantle still hangs in Guerin's window.

I walked up the streets of Portland and heard a man scream out, "J. Neely Johnson is governor of California, ha! ha! ha!" Confound Portland and Oregon Territory; I wish from the very bottom of my heart that Pierce would appoint John Bigler governor of it.

Yours in deep disgust,

AMOS BUTTERFIELD
Flour and Pork.
Near the corner of Battery and Front
Orders from the country promptly filled.

The son of pioneer parents, Wayne D. Overholser grew up in Washington and Oregon and was a high school history teacher before turning to full-time fiction writing in 1945, ten years after his first professional sale. During his long career he has published one hundred Western novels and hundreds of short stories, none better than the affecting tale of an Oregon homesteading family that follows. He is the recipient of two WWA Best Novel Spurs—for Lawman *(1953, as Lee Leighton) and* The Violent Land *(1954)—and was recently presented with WWA's highest honor, the Golden Saddleman Award, in recognition of his outstanding achievements in traditional Western fiction.*

The Patriarch of Gunsight Flat

★★★★★★★★★★★★

Wayne D. Overholser

THE sins of man are many. He will kill. He will take that which belongs to others—money and cattle and all that can be turned into money. Aye, and other things: a good name—a woman's virtue—a man's home—a friend. And who can say with certainty that murder is a greater crime than thievery?

Dave Cray was hitching up when Gramp hobbled out of the cabin and came across the trodden earth of the yard. Sometimes Dave wondered if he hated the old man. The years had made his hair white, had scarred his gaunt face with deep lines. They had brought rheumatism to his gnarled and twisted muscles until there were days when he could not walk. But Gramp didn't hate or speak ill of anybody.

No, it wasn't that Gramp had ever done anything wrong. It was just that he'd brought Dave out here to Gunsight Flat to dry up with the wind. There'd come a day when Dave's bones would whiten under a hammering sun set in a brassy sky. A million years from now somebody would dig them up like the Gable kids had dug those queer-looking bones out of the sand dunes to the north, bones that must have gone through uncharted eons since some misty day when creatures that were no longer here walked the earth.

"Don't lose your head with Solly," Gramp said in the same even tone he used whether it was a good day or a bad day, whether the rheumatism was giving him its special brand of hell or had for the moment forgotten him.

"I ain't making no promises," Dave replied, climbing into the buckboard.

"You got Luke's list?"

"I've got it."

Dave spoke to the team and wheeled out of the yard, keeping his gaze ahead on the twin tracks that cut straight north through the sagebrush. He didn't hate the old man. He knew that. You couldn't hate a man who had waited for death with the uncomplaining fortitude Gramp had. It was just that Dave Cray's life would have been different if Gramp hadn't settled here. . . .

There were the early treasured years in the Willamette Valley with its people and cities. There was Dave's gem box of memories: the valley in spring and the smell of its rich life-swelling earth; the first lamb tongue; Indian summer days when the Cascades were blurred by smoky distance; the cries of other children as they played tag through a July twilight, the thrill of the game itself, and his first kiss when he had caught Ruthie Norton back of the big oak.

Dave had been twelve when the news of Lee's surrender came to Oregon. That was when Gramp sold the place. "Ain't much sense in going west—just fall into the Pacific. We'll go the other way, and I aim to keep on believing what I believe."

So they had gone east—over the Cascades, through the Douglas firs and then the pines on the east slope, around the lava flows that an enraged nature had spewed out upon the earth like the fiery vomit of an animated prehistoric gargoyle.

Across the Deschutes—the Crooked River—the John Day: searching, always searching, while the empty miles twisted behind in trackless solitude. Rimrock and sage and pine forest—or pine forest and sage and rimrock. No reception committee, unless it might be a marauding handful of Snake Indians. No band to blare out a brassy welcome. . . . Only the lonely miles.

Then Gramp found it: Gunsight Flat, an emerald in a gray sage setting—pines in the near-by mountains—a crystal-clear creek—fish—antelope—deer—bear—and hay land in the flat that would never want water, for water was always there.

Dave, watching Gramp, knew this was the end of the search. The twisting, seeking tracks would go no farther. But the empty miles were there, all around them, running away in any direction as far as Dave could see and on beyond into the unmeasured distance.

"We won't starve," Gramp had said. "Fish and game a plenty. A fine land to become a man in." He pulled at his beard that had been black then, and a glint was in his eyes that comes only to a man when he feels the ultimate in satisfaction. "A land where a man can think what seems fitting to think."

They had gone back the next summer for more horses and stock, for seed and tools. It was the last time they had seen the Willamette Valley. Others had come: Luke Petty, Fred Gable and his cabinful of kids, Jared Frisbie, loud-talking Abe Mack, and more and more, until the whole flat was taken.

Then came Smiling Jim Solly with his wagons and cattle and his fine riding buckaroos; and there was pigtailed Ann Solly, riding a bay mare up at the head of the column alongside Smiling Jim. Seeing her that first time, Dave thought her corn-yellow hair was as fine as real silk, as beautiful as gold in the sun.

Aye, the sins of man are many. . . . Standing with the thief and the murderer is the one who says his daughter shall not see the man she loves. If they run away together, he will follow them and hang the man and black-snake his girl and bring her back. Smiling Jim Solly would have done exactly that—and kept his smile through all of it.

"Don't lose your head with Solly," Gramp had said.

Well, maybe Dave wouldn't lose his head, but he'd kill Smiling Jim Solly. Ann wouldn't hate him for it. . . .

The buckboard left the sage flat and climbed the bald face of the rimrock by a twisting route, dropped over, and came down to Solly's store. There was no money in Gunsight Flat except what Solly had brought, but there was a deal of swapping. Solly had cattle and winter shelter, but he had no hay land. The Flatters, as they were called, had hay. Every autumn, wagons rumbled into Solly's canyon with the hay and built credit for the Flatters at the store.

Only this winter it would be different, for Solly had steadily built a carry-over of hay until now he wouldn't need any for another year. Dave, his eyes sweeping the long row of round weather-browned stacks, choked with the fury of his anger. Smiling Jim Solly would look at you and say you could buy his sugar and salt and coffee and dried peaches if you had money. That was the way it had been with Jared Frisbie and loud-talking Abe Mack—the week before, when they had come.

As Dave tied his team in front of the store, he saw Ann working in her yard. He grinned; he wanted to yell; he wanted to get up on the buckboard seat and holler like a rooster when a hen comes off the nest with fifteen chicks. Smiling Jim Solly could laugh in your face and say he'd starve you to death if you didn't sell to him, but he couldn't keep his girl from loving one of the Flatters he despised.

Dave picked up a rock and weighted down the letter he'd written the night before to Ann. Smiling Jim Solly was slick, but he wasn't as slick as his daughter and one Dave Cray. Solly would raise Cain if he ever found out. Dave's jaw set stubbornly. Let him find out. It had to come to a showdown sometime.

Smiling Jim Solly was in the back of the store, one of his long cigars tilted at a cocky angle between his teeth. Half a dozen buckaroos squatted on the floor or sat on a counter, listening and laughing to the big tale Solly was telling. He was a bragger, Smiling Jim was. He liked to talk, and he liked to hear his audience laugh.

There were some Flatters over there, too. Jared Frisbie and Abe Mack were helping themselves out of the cracker barrel, only Abe wasn't as loud as usual. The only racket he made was when Solly finished his story. Then Abe laughed louder than any other two men in the store.

Dave stood there in the door, half turned so he could watch Ann run across to his buckboard and get his note. It was the way they always worked it. If Dave stepped out of the doorway, Ann knew her father was watching.

As soon as Ann had the letter and had slipped it inside the bosom of her dress, Dave stalked into the store. Smiling Jim saw him, all right, but he didn't pay any attention. He tilted his cigar a little higher and started on another windy.

There were several things crowding Dave, but mostly it was Abe Mack and Jared Frisbie coming back after the way they'd been turned down cold last week. It was worse standing there filling their bellies with Solly's crackers. But it was a hell of a lot worse for Abe to laugh like that at Solly's sorry jokes.

"Here's some things Gramp wants." Dave shoved a ragged corner of paper under Solly's nose. "Likewise there's Luke Petty's list."

Solly looked mad because Dave had butted into his yarn. He chewed on his cigar a minute. His mouth was still smiling, but his eyes weren't. He said, "Got any money?"

"No, but we've got hay."

"You know damned well I ain't taking no hay."

"How do you expect us to eat?"

"Eat your hay, if you've got so much."

They laughed—especially Abe Mack. Funny about that laugh: it sounded like a mule's bray. The Flatters eating hay might be funny to Solly's buckaroos; but it wasn't funny to a Flatter, and Abe was a Flatter.

"Maybe you're horse enough to eat hay, Solly," Dave said evenly, "but we ain't. You don't need to get so smart about not taking any hay, neither. There's gonna be another year."

"By that time you Flatters will be starved out, and you'll sell your places to me like I've been asking you to for the last five years."

"Then you're nothing but a thief."

When a man was rich like Smiling Jim Solly and had the power and dignity that money gave him, and when he liked to have other folks bow and scrape around, you didn't call him a thief—not more than once. Solly wasn't smiling. Nobody was laughing. It was the first time Dave had seen Solly when he wasn't smiling.

"You're a brave man or a fool," Solly said slowly. "Either way I'm telling you something you'd better listen to. Get out of this country and don't never come back."

Dave laughed. So Smiling Jim was going to run him out of the country! Suddenly everybody was still. Nobody else had laughed. Dave took a long breath. He said, "Solly, what would you do if your hay burned up?"

He shocked them. Seems it's all right for a man like Jim Solly to make threats and talk tough, but the little fellows like Dave Cray weren't supposed to do that.

They had forgotten to breathe. Everybody but Abe Mack, who took an extra-deep breath—the way a man does when an idea has crawled up his spinal cord into his brain.

"You threatening me?" Solly asked.

"No. I'm just giving you something to chew on along with that cigar. I reckon big talk can blow both ways."

Solly laughed. "Only I wasn't making big talk, kid. I'm just telling you that if you stay in these parts you're likely to meet up with an accident."

They all laughed then, all but Dave. The laughs were a little shaky, as if it wasn't real funny but they knew Solly expected them to laugh. Abe Mack's was the biggest and loudest.

Dave said: "I'm sure gonna run, Solly. I'm gonna run like hell." He picked Abe Mack up, turned him over, and dropped him head-first into the cracker barrel. Then he walked out.

Anne wasn't in sight when Dave stepped into the buckboard.

That was the way it should be. She'd come. He turned the team and wheeled up the grade to the top of the rim. He was a little uneasy about what Gramp would say when he heard the way things had gone.

A dozen times since Smiling Jim Solly had come to the canyon, Gramp had said: "He's a bad one. You can't trust a man who smiles all the time. There'll come a day when we'll have to have it out; and if we don't handle it right there'll be some shooting."

Dave hadn't handled it right. Uneasiness deepened in him. He felt he shouldn't have called Solly a thief. It was up to Dave now to fight or run, and he didn't want to do either. Not till Gramp said it was time.

He turned off the road when he reached the plateau above the rim and followed it until he came to a cluster of junipers. There he waited—and presently Anne came, as he knew she would.

Looking at Ann was like seeing a million stars flash across a sky that was gloomy black a moment before. When he kissed her, he forgot his uneasiness, he forgot about the empty miles and the lonely years, forgot the childhood memories that had been his treasury. He even forgot that Smiling Jim Solly was her father.

Then she was motionless in his arms, head on his chest, and his heart was pounding with great hammering thuds. He was remembering things now, the things that he had forgotten a moment before.

"It can't be this way," he said. "Turn your horse loose. He'll go back."

"I can't."

What he saw in her brown eyes frightened him. He had seen something like that in a doe's eyes when she was badly hurt. He said more roughly than he intended to: "You don't owe him anything. You owe it to yourself—and to me!"

She drew his arms away from her and walked to the rim. The wheel ruts of the road were like tiny threads laid through the sage. The flat lay below her, the dots that were houses, the brown haystacks squatting in the grass stubble.

"No, I don't owe him anything," she said, "but I have seen him kill men. I know the pride that is in him, and I know what it will do. I couldn't stand it if he killed you."

She mounted and rode away. That was the end of it. The stars were gone. It was a black sky again, gloomy black, and the years lay ahead like the twin tracks through the sage. Only they didn't end here in the flat. Somewhere out there, beyond the horizon, lay Dave Cray's destiny. It wasn't here.

Ann Solly was gone. Dave would never look back again; there

was nothing to hold him now. Gramp would be dead soon. There was a world to see, a distant world that waited out there beyond where the twin tracks disappeared in a sea of sage.

But he didn't go that day. Gramp listened to what had happened in the store. He packed his pipe and lighted it, eyes narrowed with feeling, face lines as deep as irregular furrows plowed across a brown and aged field. But there was no reproof.

"It's been a good place to live," Gramp said at last, "but I knowed, the day Jim Solly drove his herd across the flat, that we'd have to fight. I've been hoping we'd get it settled afore you had to plant me. Saddle up, Dave. Tell the folks to meet here tomorrow night."

Dave rode that day, uneasiness biting at him again. He couldn't leave today—nor tomorrow. He'd have to wait until he'd buried Gramp up there on the rim, a spot he'd picked out years before. It was a gossamer bond, but it held him as no clanking chain or jail bars could have held him.

He told them all, and they said they'd come. Smiling Jim Solly would have to get up in the morning if he wanted their places. It'd take more than a year to starve them out. They'd got along before he'd started his store. They'd sent their own freight wagons to the Dalles, and they'd do it again. Dave didn't have the heart to tell them that they had had money in those days and didn't now. They had hay, but they couldn't haul hay across those unmarked miles, and nobody would buy it if they did.

Even loud-talking Abe Mack listened, a grin on his lips that was meant to be friendly; but his eyes had a way of touching Dave's face and sliding off like the slimy trail that marks a snail's passing.

"I'll be there," Mack promised. "Solly ain't gonna push us off this flat."

They were there, with the sun still showing a red arc above the western horizon, the promise of tomorrow a shining brightness above the edge of the earth.

They hadn't brought their women, for this was men's business. Nor had they brought their guns. First there would be the talk. Then the fighting if it had to come. But there was no talking yet. They respectfully waited for Gramp to start it. All but Abe Mack, who had much to say whether anybody listened or not.

Then Gramp got up from where he'd been sitting under a poplar, a poplar he'd planted the second year he'd come to the flat. He knocked the dottle from his pipe into the palm of his hand.

They stopped their chatter. Even Abe Mack braked his tongue to silence.

"We all came here for our own reasons," Gramp said in his even-toned voice. "That ain't of no importance. What is important is that we put a part of our hearts, aye, our souls, into what we've made home. When folks do that, they don't move off 'cause Smiling Jim Solly gets it into his head to have what is ours."

"Trouble is, Solly's smart. He knows it's too late in the year to get wagons to the Dalles and back. Besides, we ain't got money. Now I've been thinking about this ever since Dave came back from the store yesterday, and I can't see no way out. Come spring, most of us will be riding over to the store with our tails dragging. We'll be begging Solly to give us anything he feels like for our places."

It was true. What would life be without coffee, or tobacco, or salt? They had always stocked those things in the fall when Solly's wagons got in from the Dalles. It was late summer now, and they were out. There was no hope except from the shelves of Jim Solly's store.

"We can steal from him," Fred Gable said. "He's fixing to steal from us."

"You reckon a winter's supply of coffee is enough to pay your kids for the loss of their pappy?" Gramp asked. "That ain't the way, Fred."

They were silent then. They knew that Gramp was right. They looked at one another, a hopelessness spreading among them like a psychic plague. The sun was almost gone now, just a red slash along the horizon. The glitter of the sunset had spread to be echoed by clouds low in the east. The deep purple and dusk began building below the rimrock. It seemed to move in now, as it always did when the day had spun its allotted thread.

They were still silent when they heard the thunder of hoofs on the road between them and Solly's store. They fell back, edging toward their horses, thinking of their women at home, of the guns they did not have.

"Don't nobody go," Gramp said. "Solly's a patient man. He won't be pushing—not yet."

It was Ann. Dave recognized her before the others, bent low on her horse's neck, riding as only a girl raised in the saddle can ride.

She came thundering into the yard and pulled up, dust rolling around her. She coughed and stepped down into Dave's arms. She coughed again, and he led her out of the dust.

There was no telling what they thought. Even Gramp stared at her with cold eyes. They didn't know, and Dave didn't tell them—not then. He waited, like the others—not knowing and, like them, a little scared.

"Somebody burned our stacks," she said. "Dad's coming with his men."

They stood like chiseled granite, thinking of this and what it meant, but mostly they thought about what Smiling Jim Solly would do and what this gave him a right to do. But to Dave Cray it meant something else. It meant that Ann had at last cut loose. She was giving to him what a woman owed to the man she loved. Suddenly the golden childhood memories were gone. This was his life. This was his home. Here was his destiny. His arm tightened around her to hold this thing that was his.

"Thank you, Ann," Gramp said. "Does he know you're here?"

"No."

Dave had never told Gramp about him and Ann, but Gramp saw it now. He had a way of knowing things like that.

"Go inside, girl," Gramp said. "I think the way has been shown us."

She went without question. They waited while that last trace of the sun was lost to sight and the scarlet began to fade in the west, while purple slid out across the flat from the rimrock. They heard the horses. "A dozen," Luke Petty said. "We ain't got a weapon amongst us, Gramp. What have you got inside?"

"The weapons I've got inside will stay there," Gramp said, more sternly than he usually spoke. "This ain't the night for fighting."

They shuffled uneasily, and Mack muttered; but they stayed until Smiling Jim Solly came out of the dusk, a dozen buckaroos fanning out on both sides, guns cased on their hips.

"My stacks were burned today," Smiling Jim Solly said coldly. "Nobody was home but Ann. She was in the store, so she didn't see who done it. Rest of us was north on Cold Creek, but I don't have to have anybody tell me. Cray, you asked me yesterday what I'd do if my stacks burned. You denying you fired 'em?"

"*I* didn't do it!" Dave shouted. "It'd be like you to fire 'em yourself—just to blame it onto me."

Solly's cold smile broke now into a raking laugh. "No, I wouldn't do that, Cray. I told you yesterday to get out of the country. I reckon you're fixing to, but first you had to fire my stacks so I'd buy your crop this year."

Dave, staring at the man, knew that was the way it would look to anyone. He said: "I didn't do it, Solly. Gramp knows I was here all day."

Solly lashed them with his raking laugh again. "So you think

I'd believe the old coot? Not me, Cray. I knew about this meeting you was having, and I'm guessing you figgered you'd boost the price on me. All right. I'll make a deal, but I'll make it my way: I'll buy your places, and I'll pay you a fair price—but you're turning in this year's crop for nothing, to pay for what Cray burned."

"Hell, Solly, you can't do that!" Abe Mack yelled. "We've got to have stuff out of your store this winter."

It was plain enough to Dave. Jared Frisbie, who had been in the store with Mack the day before, must have had the same thought, for he said in cold fury: "Abe heard Dave ask Solly what he'd do if his hay burned. . . . You knew Solly would jump Dave, didn't you, Abe?"

"How would I know?" Mack cried, and backed away.

"How did you hear about this meeting, Solly?" Gramp asked.

"Mack told me," Solly said. "He told me he saw Cray riding over the rim early this morning."

"You got a limb that'll hold Mack's carcass?" Fred Gable bellowed. "We don't want the likes of him around."

"There will be no act of that kind," Gramp said sternly. "Mack, be out of the country by morning. You've got no family to hold you. What you did was bad enough, but putting it off on Dave was worse. Git, now!"

Mack left in haste and without dignity. Solly said darkly: "Don't make no difference who done it. Mack was a Flatter. You'll make that hay good."

"You can have Mack's hay," Gramp said quietly, "but you'll pay the rest of us. I wouldn't be surprised if you put Mack up to burning your hay just to give you an excuse for shoving us off the flat. I know what you are, Solly. You came after the rest of us were here. You came after we'd made it safe for your money and your cattle, all the time thinking you'd work it around to own the land that's ours. We'll never go, Solly. If you murder us, our blood will be on your shoulders. It will be in your dreams and in your soul."

"I ain't worried about my dreams," Solly said contemptuously.

"We've had our dreams, Solly, dreams about our homes. You had money to hire your work done. We had our two hands. Maybe we won't live to see the day, but it will come when a million people live in this country. A million people with hands and faith. Your kind can live with us if they want to. If they don't, they'll have to go like Abe Mack went."

"You're a fool, old man," Solly raged. "I ain't worrying about the million people. I'm worrying about the hay I've got to have to get me through the winter."

"You'll have it for a fair price. You'll be fair with us, Solly, because you've got to live with us the same as we've got to live with you. You think your money gives you the power to ride us down. That makes you a fool. Your money can't even buy you the thing you want more than anything else in the world."

There was silence with only the breathing of thirty men rasping into the stillness. Then Smiling Jim Solly, who had lost his smile a moment before, asked: "What do you mean?"

"Ann!" Gramp called.

She came out of the cabin and across the yard until she stood beside Dave. Her hand sought his. She held her head high, proud and defiant.

"Tell him why you're here, girl," Gramp said.

"Go home," Solly said through gritted teeth.

"It's not my home now. I'm staying here."

"You see how it is, Solly," Gramp said. "All the money and power and pride in hell can't buy your girl's love, and it can't keep her away from the man she loves. We understand that, Solly, but you don't. You'll have to work for her love if you ever have it."

Aye, the sins of man are many, and there must be compensation for them. There must be life, as there is death; there must be love, as there is hate. Smiling Jim Solly shriveled in the eyes of those who looked at him. Dignity garbed Gramp like a cloak, but there was no dignity about Solly. He turned his horse and rode away, his men lining out behind him.

"You can go home and sleep well tonight," Gramp said. "That was the only way anybody could touch Jim Solly."

Then it was just Dave and Ann and Gramp, and the sound of horses' hoofs dying across the flat. There would come a day when the empty miles would not be empty, when train whistles and the shrill scream of whirring saws slicing pine into lumber would cut the high thin air. There would be people and cities; there would be the echo of children's laughter. There must be compensation, the companionship of tomorrow to replace the loneliness of yesterday, the goodness of the Gramps to balance the sins of the Jim Sollys. It takes time to understand these things: time and human dignity and a willingness to understand.

And Dave Cray did understand. It was a fine land to become a man in—a land where a man could think what it seemed fitting to think.

Loren D. Estleman has won numerous awards for his Western and detective fiction, both of which he writes with originality and facility. In the Western field he has won the WWA Spur for Best Novel of 1981 (Aces and Eights) and Best Short Story of 1986 ("The Bandit"). He has also been nominated for the National Book Award and the Pulitzer Prize. "The Pilgrim" was originally intended as the first chapter of his novel The Wolfer (1981) but was excised as a result of a difference of opinion with his then editor. It stands alone quite nicely in its brief but vivid portrait of an eastern newspaperman on a visit to the Snake River Valley, "the wolfing capital of the Northwest."

The Pilgrim

★★★★★★★★★★★★

Loren D. Estleman

IT has been my great good fortune during my sunset years to have made the acquaintance of former President Theodore Roosevelt and to consider myself, in spite of our rather savage differences (for no other adjective will suffice) over his attempt to split the Republican Party in 1912, his friend. He it was who suggested I set down the facts attending the brief period I spent with that great frontiersman and forgotten American, Asa North; and should I succumb in my present extremity to the damnable cough which my physicians predicted would claim me thirty years ago before I have had time to prepare a proper dedication, let it be known henceforth that he alone is responsible for the narrative which follows.

Before I proceed, some background is necessary. Having been born in 1846 to a family of scriveners and schoolteachers in Portsmouth, New Hampshire, and graduated from Harvard at a tender age, I was disappointed though not much surprised upon joining the Army of the Potomac in 1865 to find myself a company clerk in Rhode Island. The only action I saw there had to do with a heated correspondence between myself and a quartermaster sergeant at Fort Leavenworth involving a shipment of flannel underwear issued in response to a requisition for twelve cases of new

47

Springfield rifles. Following Lee's surrender, and contrary to the wishes of my parents, who had envisioned for me a career in law, I emigrated to New York City and there applied for and was given a position as reporter on James Gordon Bennett's New York *Herald*. In that assignment I distinguished myself so far as to persuade Bennett's son, James Gordon, Jr., not to give me the sack when he assumed control of the journal following his father's death in 1872.

I toiled for eleven more years without rising above my original station and had given up all hope of so doing when I received a telegram from Joseph Pulitzer, founder of the fledgling New York *World*, offering me fresh status as city government reporter with editorial responsibilities at a monthly salary fully twice what I was receiving at the *Herald*. Naturally I accepted, and it was as a Pulitzer employee that I embarked upon the adventure which has inspired this volume.

Lest the reader think my life impossibly barren prior to that winter of 1885, I should add that during my residency in Babylon-upon-the-Hudson I had married and become separated from a young widow from Albany who proved to have the morals but not the discretion of the common alley cat, immersed myself deeply in municipal politics, served two terms as city alderman, and been a delegate to the Republican national convention which nominated Garfield for the Presidency in 1880—continuing all the while to discharge my journalistic duties at first one paper and then the other. Along the way I had also contracted a most serious case of emphysema which, threatening to turn into consumption, influenced my decision to seek a healthier climate out West.

The official excuse was a proposed series centered around a number of those colorful characters with which the frontier was said to be filled, but in truth the general interest in things western was not what it had been, and to this day I am convinced that the assignment was little more than a working exile designed to relieve the newsroom of my constant hacking and the fear of exposure to the miasma which was said to surround sufferers of my type of malady. I flatter myself that my ability to transform the Machiavellian concepts of party politics into the most puerile terms for the benefit of our readers was what prevented my editors from discharging me.

I do not know what it was exactly that made me settle upon Rebellion, other than a determination to avoid such picked-over territory as Dodge City and Tombstone. I am fairly certain that I had never heard the name before I booked passage on the Great Northern Pacific bound to the Northwest, along whose right-of-way lay the last vestiges of the frontier, but by the time I found myself trading the luxury of a Pullman for a seat in a rickety day coach on the Oregon Short Line I had heard enough from those of my fellow passengers who were returning to be convinced that I had stumbled upon an untapped vein of pure gold for the journalist.

My first glimpse of the bonanza was not promising. Huddled between the Caribou and the Big Hole mountains on the twisting thread of water that gives Idaho Territory's Snake River Valley its name, it was a cluster of dark log buildings that looked as if they had started out weary and had long since sunk past despair into tragic resignation. Directly overhead, a sky the color of mildew hung so low, it seemed to cast its shadow over the dull snow upon which the shelters lay scattered as if cast by a gambler's hand. A terrible dread settled over me as I stepped off the platform, bags in hand, into the muddy street—not of death or danger, which would merely have stimulated the creative impulse that had brought me, but rather that I should have to spend the rest of my days amid such cruel boredom.

"Is it always like this?" I asked my traveling companion of the past four hundred miles, a lean old ranch foreman by the name of Dale Crippen, whose great grizzled moustaches appeared by their sheer weight to be dragging his sun-browned flesh away from the bone beneath. A handful of bearded men in patched logging jackets were gathered near the platform but made no move to greet any of the trio of road-weary passengers, all male, that had alighted with us. I suspected that this was the highlight of their day.

"Why, hell, no," said the cowhand, around a plug of tobacco the size of a baby's fist (which I had been waiting all day for him to expectorate, in vain). "It will be like this here for a couple of days at the most, and then things will settle down and get downright dismal for a while."

His reply took me aback until I glanced at him, saw a faded blue eye watching me slyly from the forest of cracks at the corners of his lids, and realized that I had just been treated to an example of that famous frontier humor about which I had heard so much. I countered with the Manhattan equivalent.

"Good. I am in need of rest."

To my surprise, for I had expected the subtlety to escape him, Crippen winked broadly and served me a nudge in the ribs with a bony elbow that gave me an uncomfortable moment lest I subside into a coughing fit. Thus far in my journey, no one west of Park Row knew of my real reason for leaving New York, and that was the way I would have it. By the time I had mastered myself sufficiently to renew our conversation, we had reached the hotel.

This was a square, three-story frame building, one of only two in town, whose sign running the length of the front porch identified it as the Assiniboin Inn. Though it was of fairly recent construction, the paint on one of the porch pillars came off in a grayish dust onto my sleeve when I brushed against it and the iron sconces in which a lantern rested on either side of the door were brown with rust. In general the building was a twin of the structure upon the opposite corner, which sported no sign but which I was to come to know as "Aurora's place," whose frilly curtains concealed the sort of activity one might expect of an establishment popularly referred to, from the nickname of the hotel that faced it, as "the other side of Sin." I remember experiencing a recurrence of the nameless dread as I stepped up onto the booming hotel porch behind Crippen and glimpsed a pair of mannish-looking matrons watching us idly from the balcony of the other building. In the harsh light of day their shimmering dressing gowns and faces splotched with rouge and mascara made me think of corpses shrouded and painted by an inexperienced mortician.

I asked Crippen about the stench that seemed to be coming from the alley which wound behind the Assiniboin. Borne upon the crisp winter air, it was overpowering.

"Skins," he replied. "That's where they tally them before paying out the bounties. This here is the wolfing capital of the Northwest."

The front of the building was something of a town bulletin board, plastered over with posters describing various rustlers and horse thieves and offering inducements to cattlemen to ship stock on the Union Pacific, all but buried beneath scribbled advertisements enumerating various items for sale by local citizens. It was indication enough that the town had no newspaper. One poster in particular caught my eye for the black boldness of the block capitals that made up its top line, reading as follows:

$600 REWARD $600

For the Whole Hide, or other Proof of Death or Capture, of a Black-Mantled Wolf weighing in excess of 100 Pounds, and known as Black Jack, Leader of a Large Pack in the Caribou Foothills whose Depredations among local Herds of Cattle and Wild Game have been the Source of much Concern among the Good Citizens of Rebellion.

$5 BOUNTY $5

For each Wolf Scalp taken in the vicinity of the Snake River Valley, or more than Twice what the Territory of Idaho is offering for the same Item.

Redeemable from any Member of the Idaho Stockmen's Association.

(signed) Nelson Meredith,
President.

Meredith's signature was a daring indigo slash above the printed name.

"Six hundred dollars seems rather a stiff bounty to pay for a wolf," I commented, indicating the circular.

"Not for this wolf."

Though far from elegant, the lobby of the Assiniboin carried a simple dignity in its sturdy construction and utilitarian furnishings to which no amount of gilt fixtures or burgundy carpeting could add. A broad staircase of hand-rubbed oak led to the upper floors on the other side of a large desk fashioned of the same dark wood, behind which a middle-aged clerk with a round, florid face and blond hair brushed back carefully from a scanty widow's peak stood beaming at us as we entered. He was wearing a black beaver coat in need of brushing and a high starched collar whose exposed seams revealed that it had been freshly turned. When Crippen greeted him I learned that the gentleman's Christian name, unfortunately, was Thanatopsis.

"Is he in?" asked the foreman after answering a number of questions about his trip to Chicago. He jerked his head in the direction of the stairs.

The clerk nodded. "With the others. He said to send you right up when you arrived."

Crippen started in that direction, leaving behind the worn carpetbag that was his only luggage. "Keep an eye on that. And take good care of my friend here from back East. He knows a joke when he hears one."

" 'R. G. Fulwider,' " read the clerk in his off-key tenor when I had signed the register. "Is that your full name, sir?"

I assured him that it was and accepted the key to a room on the second floor. There being no bellboy, and the man behind the desk pleading gout, I was carrying my own bags up the complaining staircase when a number of men passed me on their way down. There were eight of them strung out in a line, middle-aged and older, dressed in suits of varying quality under overcoats which seemed a bit heavy for the rather mild temperature outside. Their headgear ranged from derbies not unlike my own, perched at jaunty angles, to the storied "ten-gallon" Stetson, which had proved rarer among the wide open spaces than I had been led to believe. Their faces were either very dark or very pale, with no gradations in between, and there was not a clean-shaven lip among them. To a man they moved with that air of being late for an important appointment elsewhere which I had so often noted in financiers on their way to and from the stock exchange.

Dale Crippen was on my floor speaking with a man who stood in an open doorway with his back to a room full of chairs upholstered in black leather. The stranger was stocky and solid-looking, with a square face admirably suited for his sidewhiskers and a head of thick, wavy auburn hair going silver at the temples. His complexion was hickory brown, fading out as it climbed the planes and hollows of his face and ending in a creamy swath across his forehead where the broad gray brim of the hat he held in one hand would have prevented the sun from reaching. His suit was cut western style, his high boots tilted forward upon two-inch heels and hand-tooled in the Mexican manner, but I suspected that nothing like them was available in town, or anywhere else west of New Bond Street.

Seeing my approach, the foreman broke off the conversation to introduce us. Nelson Meredith regarded me with eyes the shade of blue one sees at the very edge of a tempered blade after a professional sharpener has finished with it, and which flees almost in the time it takes to put it away. It hurt to look at them.

"I hope you will enjoy your stay in my Idaho," he said, offering his hand. I set down a bag to accept it. His grip was like his speech, controlled strength in a guise of softness. He had an English accent. Had I not been told his name, I think I would still have connected him with that bold signature I had seen on the bounty notice downstairs. I guessed our ages to be about the same.

I responded to his welcome with an inanity which escapes me now and explained the official reason for my trip. He laughed softly, a low, silken rumble that barely stirred the lines of his face.

"I fear that you will be disappointed," he said. "The sort of creature you are hunting no longer exists out here, if indeed he ever did. There is but one Wild Bill Hickok to a century."

"But I am not searching for a Hickok, necessarily. I am certain that our readers back East would be just as eager to learn about big ranchers such as yourself."

"Perhaps, but I am hardly a typical example. My father came to this territory when it was populated only by red Indians and herds of buffalo to whom his title of Knight of the Realm meant nothing. He carved out an empire larger than some European kingdoms with his bare hands and a little help from Mr. Colt. He would have been worth writing about. I was educated at Cambridge and only came out here ten years ago upon my father's death." He smiled without showing his teeth. "I am something of a carpetbagger, you see."

"And the others?"

"You passed some of them on the stairs just now. What is your impression?"

I told him of the comparison I had made with financiers back home. He nodded.

"An apt analogy. They are speculators, mainly, from Europe and elsewhere, who purchased their holdings from men like my father and expanded them by homesteading the sources of water. Which is an illegal practice, though hardly heroic. If it is stories of adventure you want, Dale Crippen is your man. He has brought more cattle up from Texas than the city of Chicago could consume in a decade, and has fought red Indians and outlaws to do it. Unfortunately, his experiences do not greatly differ from those of hundreds of others whose stories have already been repeated for print. I fear that you could merely be covering old ground."

"You paint a bleak picture," said I.

He shrugged, a minimal movement involving but one shoulder. "I am using what colors are available."

"I should like to visit your ranch sometime."

"Dale and I will be returning in the morning. If you would care to accompany us, you will be most welcome."

My lungs were beginning to close up. I replied hastily that I would very much like to accompany them, agreed to meet them in Meredith's suite at dawn, and took my leave. I barely got to my room with my luggage when the awful racking began.

When it was done, I sat down weakly on the edge of the bed and inspected my handkerchief closely. There was no blood yet. Unstrapping my portmanteau, I excavated a quart bottle of gin from among my shirts, uncorked it, and without bothering to search for a glass tipped it up to dissolve the phlegm which had accumulated in my throat. It worked admirably well. My problem was that I did not stop once it had accomplished its purpose.

Although a California native (his grandfather sailed around the Horn in 1850 and jumped ship in San Francisco Bay), Steve Hail had an abiding interest in Oregon logging history and wrote several authentic yarns about that state's lumber camps for the pulp magazines of the forties and early fifties. "Timberland Troublemaker," which is set in the Coos Bay region, demonstrates his sure hand with the "Big Woods" story. Hail was also adept at the action-packed traditional Western tale, contributing many of this type to such publications as Zane Grey Western Magazine *and* Street & Smith's Western Story.

Timberland Troublemaker

★★★★★★★★★★★★

Steve Hail

I

THE stranger didn't call out, as was the custom, when he stepped into the clearing on the far side of the slash. Nor had he come striding carelessly up the skidroad that led to the Coos and thence to the trail that followed the river twelve miles downstream to the coastal town of Baypoint.

It was these two facts that awoke the first suspicions in the mind of Pop Hardigan. Hardigan was down on the time sheets as foreman of the Hammerhead claim, though he was acting as bull o' the woods now while the Old Man was in town arranging the milling rights for the season's cut.

Favoring his gimpy leg, he had gone over to the bunkhouse doorway for a breath of air and a routine look-around. He rammed a chaw of rough cut into one seamed cheek, meanwhile shaking his graying head at his lack of judgment in failing to back up a pair of kings with nothing better than a four-spot hole card in the game of stud that had been going on in the room behind him for two days past.

His faded eyes went to the turn of logs chained to skidways on the bank above the camp, ready to cut loose for the next morning's drive. He nodded in satisfaction and turned his head. That was when he caught the movement in the shadow of the crown cover, though a moment before he would have sworn only emptiness had been there. Except, that is, for the patient and eternal stomping of the corraled oxen, and the flies buzzing lazily in the shimmering heat of the late afternoon. Though the sun was already down behind the humped ridges of the Coast Range, the dead air still made dancing mirages of the jagged stumps crowding the slash, so Hardigan shaded his eyes, watching the stranger come toward him.

The man's red shirt was an open wound against the backdrop of fir and underbrush bordering the claim. His steps were no longer hesitant, Hardigan saw, now that he was in the open. His calks twisted tiny flecks of dirt from the hard-packed earth, like a man who has made a decision and is determined to see it through. Better light outlined him then, and it hit the Hammerhead foreman what he was.

He saw a young man, big, but with the supple leanness of a first-growth sapling showing in the chest muscles that stood out behind the wool shirt open to his navel. The wool was sweat-stained beneath the arms, yet his forehead, burned to the color of heartwood, was dry. He had been a while, Hardigan thought, sizing up the camp. And he looked as tense as a cornered cougar and as dangerous.

The bedroll slung over one shoulder was thin, as was his mouth when he said, "I'm hunting me a job—for a day or two. You pushing this show?"

"I am." Hardigan spat amber to the slash and swiped his stained mustaches. "The Hammerhead doesn't hire one-blanket boomers."

The stranger frowned, and there was a sudden brittleness to his pale eyes, but he said evenly enough, "Most claims I've worked pay a jack for what he can do with an ax and peavey, not for the way he parts his hair. I can buck a Svenska fiddle with the best."

Hardigan looked at the other's hands. They were hard, callused, with lean thumbs hooked into his belt as if it were a means of keeping them still. The foreman's jaws stopped working. He would have been willing to give odds that the stranger could, at that. He noticed for the first time, too, the pitted marks of steel calks, logger's smallpox, showing white against the tan of that sober face.

With more respect, yet still wanting no part of a man on the dodge, Hardigan said, "Work's done here for a week or more. We haven't turned a wheel in two days. We're taking the drive down in the morning at the top of the flood tide. I've plenty of men to handle it."

He hesitated, and not knowing why, said, "You might try the Broken L, five miles up river. They'll be driving too, but they've been short-handed right along. Maybe they could use an extra jack—if you can keep your feet under you on a floating log."

The stranger's voice was level, matter-of-fact. "I can, but I'm heading the other way." He glanced once over his shoulder, then let his soogans slide to the ground, carefully. "I've been on the trail a spell. I'd thank you for beans and tea before I move along."

Hardigan nodded, knowing that it was the least he could do. In Oregon Territory no one turned a man away or refused him a meal, no matter who he was or what he was running from.

"You can wash up behind the shack," he said. "Chow won't be long." He turned and went into the bunkhouse.

II

The stranger followed a moment later, dropping his bindle carefully to a bench beside the door. But he didn't drop it quite carefully enough. In the sudden silence of his entrance there was a muffled thud as something within the blanket struck the wood. It sounded to Hardigan like steel. Heavy steel. Probably .44 caliber.

No one said anything for a moment, then Whitey Bjorlund, the side push bossing the falling crew, eased his bulk casually along the bench before the table, making room. His calk-slashed hands riffled the cards absently as he watched the stranger's face.

"Dealer's choice, friend," he said, "if you'd like to sit in. Two-bit ante, dollar limit. We cold use a little foreign money."

The stranger's eyes were blank, but one corner of his mouth lifted in a twisted grin. "Thanks." His eyes hit Hardigan and went back to Bjorlund. "But the ante's a little steep for me."

Bjorlund's heavy lip curled, his little eyes squinting and bright. "For a jack who carries a gun, it'd be my guess you're playing for bigger stakes than are on the table."

In the sudden silence that settled like a flung blanket across the room, Hardigan heard his own breath sucking in, in great, lung-filling breaths. He shook his head. That was Whitey Bjorlund, all right—cocky, swaggering, minding everybody's business but his own. He was thick as a fir butt, sullen, conscious of his own power—and a troublemaker since the day he'd hit the Coos.

Outside of Hardigan and the Old Man himself, the side push was top man in camp—and he knew it. He had proved it often enough, Hardigan recalled, with his clubbing fists and slashing calks. Always spoiling for a fight, Whitey's temper for the most part was taken out in work, driving the crew. But now, with two days of idleness to hone his appetite for trouble, he seemed to be looking to the stranger to satisfy it. And judging from the look in the stranger's eyes, Whitey Bjorlund didn't have too long to wait.

Hardigan sat down hastily in the vacant space. "Deal me in, Whitey," he said gruffly. "You'll have trouble enough on the drive." He hoped that would ease the tension piling up like a thunderhead in the stale air of the room. After all, it was none of Bjorlund's concern, or his, Hardigan's, or anybody's, whether the stranger carried a gun or not. There were cougar and bear on the timber trails to the north, and a man was entitled to protection. Nor did it really matter what his business was, whether it be within the law or without. The stranger had been invited to accept the hospitality of the Hammerhead, and he wasn't expected to pay—either in money or information.

The foreman started to reach for cards, but the stranger, speaking slowly, stopped him. His lips were as pale as his eyes, a slow flush crawling up his cheeks above the lumped line of his jaw. The thumbs unhooked from his belt, the fingers twitching as they hung by his side. He spoke directly to Bjorlund, measuring his words.

"If it's dealer's choice, I think I can meet the ante."

His hand went into his pocket and he flipped a quarter dollar to the polished pine of the table. The coin hit spinning, coming to rest finally in front of Bjorlund's suddenly clenched fists. "I call for a civil tongue from any boxhead who hasn't got savvy enough to keep it behind his teeth until he's invited to do otherwise."

Beside him, Hardigan felt Bjorlund's legs bunching under him, saw the side push's big hands bracing against the table's edge. There was an expectant smile of battle on his full mouth. Hardigan reached for the faller's arm and was late by a split second. The rough table went over with a crash, and Bjorlund rushed. His head was down, logger fashion, huge arms flailing. Stopping that rush, Hardigan knew, was like snubbing a free log coming off a skidway. He'd seen it tried before and never successfully.

There was an answering grin, tight-jawed but with an expectancy matching Bjorlund's, on the stranger's face. He shifted his weight, hardly seeming to move, and lashed out with a left hand as Bjorlund rushed. It landed flush on the faller's ear, sounding in the low-ceilinged room like the flat slap of a Winchester carbine.

Then, instead of waiting, setting himself for another rush, the stranger was after Bjorlund like a river pig riding a renegade log on white water. His feet shifted, feather-light in his calked boots, following the bigger man in and out and around. And his fists were keeping time, slashing, hacking, driving, finding a mark on every swing, never missing.

Bjorlund raised his head, spitting blood. He said, "Come in and fight, you dancing master. I—" and the stranger laid his knuckles across that bleeding mouth before the other could finish. He crossed a right hand and laid Bjorlund's cheek open to raw bleeding meat, and when the other's head rocked sideways on rubber-neck muscles, the big man hit him again, his calks biting into the floor to give him added weight. Bjorlund staggered, spun along the wall, and went crashing to the earthen floor like an undercut pine. He didn't move.

The stranger stood over him for a moment, boots poised, ready to rake the fallen man's skull with the half a hundred lethal calks that studded his boot soles. Then abruptly the pale fire was gone from his eyes, the blood draining from his cheeks, and he was staring at Bjorlund as if he had really seen him for the first time. His big shoulders shook uncontrollably for a moment, then sagged, and he turned away. His eyes looked like those of a man who has been staring into the past.

From his place by the wall Hardigan saw that look and wondered, but then his eyes fell to the limp, snoring heap by the table, and he shook his head. His eyes raised and met the stranger's.

"You could handle a crew, mister," he said. "Any crew. If you can do as well with an ax, you've got a job. Permanent."

The big man rubbed bleeding knuckles across his shirt. He smiled faintly, then shook his head. "I'm heading south. How far is it to the California line?"

"A hundred miles or so," answered Hardigan. "Mostly up and down. I'd think . . ."

The gut hammer cut him off and the cookie's voice shouted: ". . . or I'll throw it away!"

III

Nobody said much during the meal. Loggers have a way of eating as if each bite of food might be their last. It seemed especially that way with the stranger. He wolfed down his beans and salt pork, yet seemed to enjoy each mouthful as if it had been a long time since the last and might be even longer until the next.

Maybe he figured right, at that, Hardigan thought, for when they came back to the bunkhouse, the stranger untied his pack and began cleaning and reloading his gun. The way he went at it, it looked as if he had made it a daily chore for some time past. The food seemed to have thawed him, though, or maybe it was the fight with Bjorlund, for when Hardigan spoke to him, he seemed to warm up a little.

The foreman started it off by saying, "You'd better figure on bunking here tonight. You won't get far trying to keep to the trail in the dark." He paused. "I don't mean to be prying, but we ought to have a handle to call you by."

The other looked up sharply through narrowed eyes, but after a moment he smiled faintly. "I worked a spell east of the Cascades," he said. "How would Idaho do?"

"That's as good as anything. Idaho it is."

It was growing dark outside and the rest of the crew began wandering in. Someone lit a lamp, and the poker game began where it had left off, though Bjorlund didn't take a hand. He was lying face down on one of the muzzle-loading bunks, breathing in long noisy gasps through a broken nose. He made no attempt to speak, nor did anyone go near him.

Idaho took a place at the table near the door, almost facing it, where he could see anything or anyone that approached across the slash. Everyone talked in monosyllables, just enough to keep the betting going.

That appeared to suit Idaho. He won his share of the pots, though it didn't look to Hardigan as if he was listening to much of what was going on. His mind seemed to be somewhere else, beyond the camp, not even hearing the slither of the greasy cards or the restless movements of the cattle over near the edge of the slash. He was listening for something far beyond the river, past the ridge even, where the trees were beginning to rustle gently in the night breeze, to where . . . But that was impossible, Hardigan knew. And yet Idaho appeared to be trying.

And then it came, far down the skidroad where it joined into the trail from town. A hail, barely heard at first, then louder. "Hello, the Hammerhead!" and Idaho was on his feet, the cards forgotten and spilling out on the table in front of him. His eyes went around the room as if he were looking for a back door or window that he knew wasn't there. Then his eyes went to his bedroll on the spare bunk where he had stowed his gun.

He was halfway to it, everybody quiet, staring at him and at the same time backing away from in front of the door, when Hardigan got to him. The foreman hooked his fingers into the big man's arm.

"There'll be no killing on this show," he said quietly. "But that goes for the law, too—if it is the law. I'll guarantee it. You were invited to bunk down for the night. Any argument you two have can wait till tomorrow."

Idaho hesitated, and Hardigan felt the other's arm muscles tightening in his grip like a coiled spring. Then the pale eyes flicked over to where Bjorlund was lying, still face down on his bunk, and the tension in him relaxed. He nodded almost imperceptibly and went back to the table and sat down.

Hardigan sighed his relief, but somehow he had the feeling that it hadn't been his own words that had stopped Idaho. It had been . . . But he had no time to think it through, for Idaho was shuffling the cards and looking at the men. He said, "Ante up," but no one sat down with him. They just stood where they were, waiting, and a moment later the doorway filled with the figure of a tall, rawboned man, lantern-jawed, blinking at the lamplight with blue eyes.

The night was still warm, and the newcomer's mackinaw was drawn back across his shoulders. There was a gunbelt buckled around his middle, and the silver star pinned to his galluses was polished and bright, reflecting back the lamplight and the quiet tenseness of the unmoving men. He shoved his rain-test hat back over gray hair that was darkened with sweat.

A look at Hardigan seemed to satisfy him that he was addressing the man in charge, and he said casually:

"I've had quite a walk. Wasn't sure I was going to make it by dark." His eyes were raking the room, not missing a thing. They hit Idaho then, and they didn't change, but his hand fell slowly to the gun hanging at his side and poised there, waiting.

Idaho kept his hands in plain sight on the table, shuffling the cards. His eyes went to the sheriff, then back to the cards. He said nothing.

The sheriff nodded to himself and said to no one in particular, "Looks like the trail is done." He sat down near the door, fished a corncob from his pocket, and began loading it.

Idaho dealt himself a hand of solitaire, slow and studied. "You're looking for somebody?" he asked softly.

The sheriff tamped down the tobacco. "Yep. Man named Riley. Wanted for murder in Pocotah County, Idaho. Or manslaughter maybe, if he's lucky. Depends on how a jury looks at it." He struck a match. "You've lost some weight, Riley."

Idaho cut three cards and turned the fourth. "I thought I was a couple of days ahead of you, Sheriff Cobb. Maybe three." He put a black queen on a red king. "It was a saloon fight, but fair. No guns or knives. I should have stopped it before I did, but it could as well have been me. I don't figure on paying for that."

Sheriff Cobb sucked noisily at the pipe, drawing it to life. His eyes looked through the flame at Idaho. "I've worked timber most of my life, and I've had my share of fights—before I learned that temper can lead to trouble." He blew out the match and flicked it toward the dark rectangle of the doorway. "But I'm not the judge or jury. I was sent to bring you back. We can make Baypoint by daylight if we start now. Right?"

Idaho made himself a cigarette and licked the paper flat. "Wrong. I'm not going back to the county seat to face a city jury. I don't feel that lucky. The least I'd get would be ten years. There are easier ways to die than rotting in a cell."

The sheriff got up and opened his mouth to speak. Hardigan stopped him. "The man's a guest of the Hammerhead for the night," he said. "Tomorrow'll be soon enough." He yawned elaborately. "I'm going to get some shut-eye."

The sheriff's eyes went to the blackness outside hemming in the camp, and Hardigan knew he was thinking of what could happen on the pitch-black river trail alone with a wanted man. He looked his relief, sighed, and sat down again. "Tomorrow, then."

On the far side of the room, Bjorlund sat up. He spoke thickly to the sheriff through pulped lips. "He's got a gun in his bindle on that lower bunk."

Hardigan said, "I'm sleeping on the lower bunk."

The sheriff looked sharply at Bjorlund, studying his beaten face, then back at Idaho. Idaho shrugged and his mouth corners moved faintly, but he nodded at Cobb.

The sheriff didn't say anything, but he began peeling off his mackinaw and boots. He hung his gunbelt on a peg and lay down on the bunk nearest the door, and Hardigan knew the unspoken truce had been accepted.

Someone blew out the lamp, and within a few minutes everybody had turned in. The poker game had been forgotten. In that thing at least, Hardigan thought, Bjorlund had been right. There were higher stakes on the table now.

Hardigan lay on his back, feeling the bulk of Idaho's gun between himself and the wall, listening to silence settle over the room. The only sound was the soft gurgle of the sheriff's pipe and the occasional and uneasy rustle of a straw mattress. Across the room Idaho's cigarette was a pinpoint glow, dimming and brightening. Like a pulse, Hardigan thought, the difference between life and death. It was still burning when he dropped off to sleep.

IV

Hardigan awoke to a raucous clamor as the bull cook made music on the gun hammer outside the cook-shack. He swung his feet out of the bunk and into his boots. In the faint light of dawn washing through the doorway from across the slash he saw that Idaho was already up, fully dressed, sitting on the edge of the bunk. He didn't look as if he had slept much or well. And standing in the doorway, Sheriff Cobb waited, his gunbelt hanging loosely around his middle. His eyes were red-rimmed as if he hadn't slept too well, either.

"Grubpile," Hardigan called to the rest of the crew. "We'll eat and move out. High water's at ten." He led the way out the door.

The sheriff and Idaho ate with the others. Neither one of them had anything to say. Hardigan made conversation, explaining the forthcoming drive to the sheriff.

"A little different here along the coast than the water you get up north. No current to speak of, except tide." He grimaced. "But that's enough sometimes. We dump the cut at the month's highest tide, and the ebb carries it down. No white water, as you know it, but the channel shoals out on the bends pretty bad. Two, three hours after slack the river is really running. That's where our trouble comes—if we have trouble. A jam on a bend with the tide behind it can be bad."

The sheriff nodded absently, but didn't seem to be listening. He kept glancing at Idaho from under his bushy eyebrows. Idaho ate in silence, chewing his food mechanically. When he finished, he got up from the table, let out a notch in his belt.

"I didn't sleep much," he remarked. "Too long, I guess, since I had a mattress under me. Gave me some time to think."

His eyes went to Bjorlund, eating silently at the end of the table, then away. He went on quietly:

"Sometimes it takes a lot of years for a man to learn things about himself that he had never thought much about. Again you learn them in a day, or an hour. Like for instance, how your temper can get you into things you'd never thought could happen. Yesterday I nearly killed a man. Another one. A thing like that can pile up. Like a snowball on a downgrade." He looked at the lawman. "I think I could kill *you*, Sheriff Cobb. At least it wouldn't be a bad gamble for my freedom." He shrugged. "But, shucks, a man can't run forever, especially from himself. I reckon I'll head back north and sit in with that city jury. I won't give you any trouble, Sheriff." He started for the door.

The sheriff sighed and looked his relief. Hardigan, staring after

Idaho, wasn't sure whether Cobb should feel relieved or not. Maybe Idaho was merely playing along, waiting things out, counting on events of this day or another day on the long trail north to give him a chance for a break. He shrugged then and put it from his mind. After all, it was a thing that lay between Idaho and the sheriff. He called Whitey Bjorlund to him.

The side push wasn't pretty. His battered face was drawn in a sullen scowl as he listened to his orders. There was a sneer curling his lips as his eyes followed Idaho. Hardigan didn't have to be told that he wasn't alone in his judgment of the big man from Idaho.

But when Hardigan finished with his instructions, Bjorlund nodded shortly and picked out his men, assigning them to stations at strategic points on the down-river trail. The faller shouldered a peavey and moved out ahead with the first group. Hardigan saw the sheriff and Idaho following a little while later. Then he forgot them. It was time to go to work.

It was nearly midmorning when, after a final inspection, Hardigan was ready to dump the logs down the rollway. Bjorlund's crew, he knew, had had time to reach their tending-out stations well downstream. The water was high on the banks, the tide almost at the stand. Chips floating idly upstream a moment before had been sucked into back eddies near the bank and were swirling, hesitating, beginning to reverse their course. Hardigan nodded in satisfaction and raised his hand in a signal to dump the load.

The logs thundered down the skids like a ten strike in a valley of the giants. Exploding spray misted over the river, painting a hundred rainbows in the sunlight as they struck the surface of the water. The drive settled, leveled off, and moved downstream, grudgingly at first, then faster as it felt the force of the growing ebb behind it.

Hardigan started down river along the trail, keeping pace with the brown carpet, his eyes on the leaders. Small jams, a few logs caught crosswise, started even before the first bend had been cleared, but waiting rivermen tore them apart with pike poles and peaveys before they had a chance to lock.

The foreman legged it along the bank, alert to the ever-present danger of the drive hanging up on hidden snags. He spread the crew as the need arose, gathering them when trouble threatened. Gradually the head of the drive forged on, the leaders out of sight past Seven Mile Creek, halfway to Baypoint.

Hardigan was beginning to breathe more easily as he climbed a rise where the trail cut inland across a projecting point. That was when he heard the dull booming, sounding at first like distant artillery, then louder, sifting through the timber between himself and the river. He felt his heart pounding against his ribs in the same irregular rhythm as he broke into a shambling run, cross-country toward the point.

A riverman met Hardigan halfway there, sweat streaming down his face, words tumbling from his gasping throat. "She jammed on Seven Mile Bend. Hung up on a snag and piling fast. She's a bad one! Whitey—"

Hardigan didn't wait to listen to the rest. He'd heard enough. He yelled over his shoulder, "Head back up the river. Get every mother's son you can find. Quick! Highball 'em down here! Send a man upstream to the Broken L and tell 'em to hold their drive." He left the other standing there and made tracks for the river.

He was a quarter hour making the rise above the bend where he could expect his first glimpse of the jam. The river pig had been right. It wasn't good. The first logs had fouled the hidden snag almost in midstream, and the rest were pressing in behind them, piling up slantwise, completely blocking the river. Already, he saw wings were building to both ends, crowding up on the banks, higher by the moment, as the current swept the writhing, twisting carpet of timber down on it. The river itself was rising along the banks, backing the water upstream.

Hardigan saw then that Bjorlund already had a dozen of the crew out on the dam working feverishly with peaveys, levering at the logs on the downstream side, trying to pry them loose. Hardigan cursed the man for a bull-headed fool. This wasn't the Penob-scot or the Saginaw or any place else where the current was forever behind them. This was tidewater and bad enough, but at worst it could only be a matter of hours until the current would change, lessening the weight bearing in behind them. Then would be the time to attempt to break the jam, letting the force of the incoming tide help them in their effort.

True, with every minute lost, there was more timber coming down, thudding into the solid mass, some of it splintering and certain to make for a grading down at the mill. But it was better to accept the damage and the loss rather than gamble the lives of rivermen in an attempt to save the whole.

V

He saw Bjorlund, feet planted wide on a fir butt, his checkered sleeves rolled back over brawny forearms. The side push was straining on his peavey handle with both hands, prying at a big blue canted at a sharp angle close beside the butt. By the looks of him he had found the key log already, but it was rooted as solidly as if it had been planted.

Hardigan started forward, climbing and leaping as best he could, shouting at the other, trying to make himself heard above the grinding thunder of the jam. He had taken only a half-dozen steps when he saw the butt on which Bjorlund stood begin to tremble.

Hardigan's cry became a wordless growl in his throat as the butt twisted, half-rolled, and sent the faller flying. There was a grinding jar for a moment, and the whole mass slid a few feet like a gathering avalanche. It hesitated, moved on, and stopped. Bark dust and Bjorlund's scream hung for a moment in the still air and were gone. The scream was enough to halt the headlong rush of the crew, leaping frantically for the safety of the bank. They stopped and turned. Behind them Whitey Bjorlund had disappeared.

The foreman's eyes went instinctively to the open stretch below the dam, waiting. Nothing broke the surface of the water, and he knew then where Bjorlund was—somewhere down in the tangled mass of logs piled up like huge jackstraws and rising now a dozen feet above the river's surface.

Hardigan fought his way across the pile, feeling for the first time the aching weariness in his crippled leg. He looked down. Bjorlund was there, all right, buried under three or four of the logs, but miraculously thrown into an angle that the big fir butt made with the other timbers. Hardigan felt rather than heard the crew gathering at his back, peering down between the gap in the logs. All that any of them could see was the side push's checkered shirt and his blond hair spilling across his face. It was impossible to tell whether he was alive or dead. Then as he straightened, Hardigan saw the face below him move and the flicker of an eyelid as Bjorlund came back to consciousness. A thin trickle of blood welled from the corner of his mouth.

The foreman dropped to his hands and knees and put his mouth to the gap. "You hurt bad, Whitey?"

Bjorlund's eyes rolled wildly for a moment, then steadied. His broken mouth widened in what started out to be a smile. It didn't quite make it.

"My leg," he gasped. "Must be broke. I can't see it . . . but I can't feel it, either."

Hardigan got to his feet, looking around him, thinking. If they were very lucky and given time enough, they could break the jam. Black powder would do it, of course, but now that possibility was out. It was a matter of breaking the key log free and . . .

He shook his head. That wouldn't do, either. With Bjorlund down there, injured and unable to help himself, it meant certain death when the jam let go. The only thing to do was what should have been done in the first place. That was to wait for the turn of the tide—another couple of hours at most. It would ease the pressure behind the dam and give them a chance to pry Bjorlund free. He grimaced. Providing, of course, the side push didn't bleed to death before then. There was no way of telling how bad his leg might be.

His shoulders lifted helplessly. It was a chance they'd have to take. He stooped again to tell Bjorlund of his decision, and at that moment he heard the muted thunder from up river, rolling over and above the lessening drumming of their own jam, and he knew without turning that his messenger hadn't been in time. The Broken L had dumped their cut, and it was on its way down river, hell-bent for destruction, with the full force of tide and current behind it.

A voice, forgotten these past hours, spoke from behind Hardigan, and he turned and saw Sheriff Cobb standing spraddle-legged on one of the top logs. A step or two behind him, waiting silently, was Idaho. The sheriff, thumbs hooked into his gunbelt, angled his lantern jaw upstream.

"That solves one of your problems, mister," he said grimly. "Once that drive hits, your jam'll break soon enough. You'll have logs flying from here to Baypoint, crown high."

"I thought you were hitting the trail to Pocotah." Hardigan spoke mechanically.

The sheriff shrugged. "I was. But I'm a timberman, and it looks like you could use some help. What can I do?"

The foreman felt his jaw muscles tightening. "Nothing—unless you want to die. And that wouldn't help much either. A man with strength enough and guts enough and"—he smiled wryly—"and two good arms and legs might have a chance to finish what Bjorlund started—lever out that big butt yonder and get this mess on its way. But he wouldn't live a hundred yards in the hell the lower river's going to be once this tears loose."

His shoulders lifted wearily. "And what's the use? Whitey would go with it. He wouldn't have a prayer." His eyes turned up river, where every minute he expected to see the Broken L drive rounding into the reach above the bend. "Well, there's always a chance," he told the other, knowing it was only wishful thinking, "that the Broken L will foul and jam."

"After your cut has swept the channel clean?" the sheriff scoffed grimly. "About the same chance as a windfall in hell, I'd

say." He shook his head. "Your only gamble is to break it now
and try to reach Bjorlund before he's crushed or drowned."

Hardigan nodded, admitting reluctantly to himself that the
other was right. The job—the first part of it, anyway—was not
impossible for a . . . He thought of his own words: "A man with
strength and guts and two good arms and legs." He looked at the
crew standing by listening to his argument with the sheriff. Nobody said anything. They shuffled their feet and looked at their
boots. Then there was movement in the group and Sheriff Cobb
was peeling off his coat.

Hardigan looked at him in wonder. He started to speak, then
stopped, really noticing Idaho for the first time. There was the
same tight smile on Idaho's face as he stood there watching the
sheriff. And Hardigan thought of what it would mean to him with
the lawman dead in the river.

It would mean freedom, without the necessity of a fight or a
killing to gain it. He could merely turn and walk away. No one,
Hardigan knew, would try to stop him. Idaho knew it too, and
it looked as though he was enjoying the prospect and was aware
that he didn't have long to wait. For upstream now, the first advance logs of the Broken L drive were rounding the turn above
the straight reach heading into Seven Mile Bend.

It would be ten minutes, a quarter of an hour at the most, before
the drive reached the Hammerhead jam. Unless, of course, Sheriff
Cobb could wrench the big blue loose before. But either way it
was certain that the sheriff was a dead man. He was halfway out
of his coat already, shrugging out of the sleeves. Then Idaho
moved, stepping forward quickly, grabbing the gun from the sheriff's holster, palming back the hammer.

VI

Hardigan stared at him, unbelieving, wondering if Idaho didn't
think drowning good enough for the lawman; if he had to add another personal killing to his record. But then Idaho was stepping
backward toward the center of the jam instead of toward the
shore. He backstepped carefully, his calks chewing bark, with the
gun leveled in one steady hand, covering all of them.

"Get out of here, the lot of you," he said. His voice was hard,
flat, yet soft somehow like a man whose thoughts are in the past.

They must have been at that, Hardigan realized, for he heard
Idaho say almost to himself, "I killed a man a few weeks back.

yesterday I nearly killed another. I guess it's time I started working the other way."

The foreman started forward. He heard himself saying, "You fool! I'm pushing this show. One man dead down there in the jam is bad enough. Nobody is—"

Idaho didn't let him finish. "Get back! My killing days are over, one way or another, but I've carried a gun this far and so help me I'll cut the legs out from under the first jack who tries to stop me."

He looked at the sheriff, then at Hardigan, and his smile widened. "I've worked a little timber myself and run my share of white water. And I'm a younger man by twenty years than either of you." His shoulders lifted. "As for dying, do you know of a better way?" His eyes flicked upstream then, at the swift death rushing down on them. The grin died, and he said sharply, "Move!"

Hardigan led the way, knowing there was little that he or anyone could do to help. It was a one-man chore from here on in. The others were on his heels, none of them hesitant now, leaping from log to log, scrambling for the safety of the bank.

As his calks found dirt beneath him, the foreman looked back and he saw Idaho throw the gun in a long-looping arc out into the river as if it were a symbol of something he wanted to forget. In almost the same movement Idaho snatched up a peavey and slammed the point into the big blue at his feet.

Hardigan watched him work and knew immediatley that it wasn't the first jam that the man from east of the Cascades had broken—even though it was going to be his last. Idaho's feet were planted wide, calks set deep. His big body bent slightly, getting a purchase on the hickory handle. Then he straightened slowly, putting steady pressure on the log.

Nothing happened. It was as solid as a piling driven into sand. Idaho tried again, twisting this time, alternating the movements with short vicious tugs. Hardigan could see moisture glistening on his face, body sweat staining his shirt across the small of his back. Still the log didn't budge, and Hardigan found himself half hoping that it wouldn't. Bjorlund was as good as dead no matter what happened. Even if Idaho did dislodge the key log, it would pop out of the breast of the jam like a bung from a barrel, with all the pressure of the drive and the dammed river behind it. And suddenly Pop Hardigan wanted Idaho to live.

He looked upstream to where the Broken L drive was boiling down river, lifting and thrashing and now only a few short minutes away. He was aware of his heart hammering against his ribs, and he started forward again, drawing in breath to call out a last warning. Idaho had tried and failed and that should be satisfaction enough. It was time for him to go, while he still had a chance.

Idaho looked up then, but not at Hardigan. He measured the onrushing drive coolly, almost scornfully, and turned his back on it. He studied the key log. It was still upended, sticking out of the pile at an angle for nearly half its length. Idaho nodded to himself in seeming satisfaction, then dropped down to a level with the water and planted his calks again, ankle deep in the river. He shouted something to Bjorlund that Hardigan couldn't hear above the thudding and booming of the drive, then he spat on his hands deliberately and drove home the point of his peavey and set himself for another try. Hardigan knew it would be his last.

He saw the big man bend his knees almost double, keeping his back straight, letting his bunched thigh muscles do the work. Slowly he increased the pressure, the wooden handle bending in his effort. Then with a last savage lunge he threw the whole weight of his body into a twisting tug.

The big blue trembled, rolled slowly, then faster and outward like a flywheel feeling the impulse of steam. The peavey straightened in Idaho's hands, then shot suddenly into the air, its polished handle looking like a hurled javelin in the midday sunlight. Beneath him the mass of timbers grumbled, grew louder, grinding and crunching. And suddenly the log squirted loose, arrowing into the air. The whole jam tore free behind it.

Idaho leaped, clawing air, as the log he stood on went out from under him. He landed on his feet, almost falling, but dipping to one knee in the same movement, groping for something beneath Hardigan's line of vision.

Then the river was a wild maelstrom of tossing timbers before him, all brown with the bark of a thousand logs charging downstream and white where they lashed the water to foam. Only one spot of color was in it all, crimson where Idaho's shirt made a flame in the midstream current. He was crouching, calks digging bark, riding a pine log like the wild thing that it was. It was something to see.

But there was something else there then, and Hardigan sucked in his breath, forgetting to let it out again and breathe. It was checkered cloth gripped in Idaho's hand, and a head with blond hair, wet and tumbling wildly. Idaho, fingers hooked into the shirt, clung to it as though it was life itself. Then, even as Hardigan watched, the big man hauled Bjorlund up onto the log, holding him there somehow while his feet moved, swiftly as a ballerina's, keeping balance.

At last the brown flood leveled off and men were shouting, streaking along the bank, paralleling the two figures on the log. Hardigan remembered to breathe again and followed, yelling crazily like the rest. Idaho, he saw, had managed to lift Bjorlund free of the water, had slung him across one shoulder as carelessly as his one-blanket bindle, and was gradually working himself in toward the bank across the flooring of logs. He made the shore on the next bend, jumping into hip-deep water, wading up the bank. He laid Bjorlund on dry ground, the side push whimpering in the agony of his crushed leg. Idaho sat down beside the man he had rescued, almost falling in his exhaustion.

Hardigan bent over Bjorlund. After a moment he straightened. He said to no one in particular, "He's got to have a doctor quick. And he can't walk to one. It's still five, six miles to Baypoint. Somebody'll have to go for help."

Sheriff Cobb fumbled for his pipe. "That'll be me. I was on my way north anyhow."

Idaho got up and stood, waiting.

The sheriff looked at him and through him as if he'd never seen him before. He struck a match to his pipe, staring thoughtfully at the flame, but beyond it, too.

"A man has a right to change his opinion, I think," he said finally. "I've changed mine. About being judge and jury, I mean."

He puffed slowly, then went on, "I heard a sermon once when I was down on my luck in Tacoma." He smiled. "It was the price of a flop and a free meal, as I remember, but I guess it didn't do me any harm. it was something about an eye for an eye, a tooth for a tooth." He broke the match absently and tossed it away. "That's the way the law looks at it, too. But it seems to me there's more than one way of interpreting a thing like that. A man's life saved, we'll say, when by all odds, he should be dead, ought to go a long way toward squaring a debt."

He had his pipe going good then, and he turned and walked away, taking the trail north toward town and Pocotah County, Idaho.

Hardigan watched him go, and when he disappeared into the timber, the foreman turned and looked down at Whitey Bjorlund lying there on the ground.

Slowly his eyes raised to Idaho and he said, "I'll be needing a man to help finish the drive. After that, a boss for the falling crew. A man who could control his temper. Maybe you'd do."

A slow grin broke through the mask of weariness on the big

man's face. "Maybe I would, at that," he said. "That is, if you're paying a jack for what he can do with an ax and peavey, not for the way he parts his hair. If that's the way it is, you've hired yourself a hand."

"That's the way it is," Hardigan told him. "I've seen worse with a peavey. Now, let's see what you can do with a crew." He turned his back and limped away, hiding his grin.

Verne Athanas (1917–1962) was a native of the Pacific Northwest and, in the words of one critic, "sang songs of prose about his home region." One such "song of prose" is "The Pioneers," a grimly evocative and suspenseful tale of an Oregon farmer on the trail of a band of marauding Rogue Indians who have abducted his wife. During Athanas's all too brief career, he published more than fifty short stories and novelettes in magazines as wide-ranging as Country Gentleman, Frontier Stories, Railroad Magazine, Adventure, *and* The Saturday Evening Post *and three full-length Western novels—* The Proud Ones *(1952),* Rogue Valley *(1953), and* Maverick *(1956).*

The Pioneers

★★★★★★★★★★★

Verne Athanas

THERE was this steady, hurting, hammering thud inside his skull every time his heart beat. It hurt worse than anything he could remember, and deep down in the secret places of his mind, he wanted to get away from it, to slide back into the soothing, unhurting dark. But his heartbeat smashed at the splintering bones of his skull until he opened his eyes to see the brown faces hovering over him.

He came up at them, fighting with an animallike clawing and roaring, but the strong brown hands caught and pinned him before he could do any damage. Then slowly the man inside came through the fear and hurt, and he knew who he was and where. He was Byron Martin, and the brown faces weren't the Indians, they were Mexican muleteers.

The *Caporal,* in his dandy's outfit of black all trimmed in red and gold, knelt down and wiped Byron's face with a cloth and murmured something in Spanish. Byron pushed him aside and sat up, suddenly remembering.

The stench of smoke was in his lungs; deep, where he couldn't get it out; the smell of things that were never meant for burning— cloth and flour and scorched meat. The horses lay where they had

72

crashed down in the harness, one stiff and still, the other still bubbling and groaning from the Rogues' clumsy gut-shooting.

Byron got his hands and knees under him. He crawled the four feet or so to the rear wagon wheel and pulled himself up by the spokes. He started to fall and clutched desperately at the iron rim. It was hot under his hand. He heard the *Caporal*'s inquiring voice, and his own words were a mushy paste he had to force through his teeth.

"Carrying the woman down to Clayburne's," he said. "Heard the Rogues was raising up, and Clayburne's got a stout house and four growed boys. Me and the woman and the boy. I loaded up the wagon to carry them down—" Then the thought hit him like a bullet, and he almost screamed in the man's face, "They got Ruth! They got my boy! My God, man, where are they? What have they done with them?" He turned loose of the wheel to reach despairingly at the man as if to shake the answer out of him. He lost his balance and fell to his hands and knees.

The Mexican stooped and helped him up. His skin was smooth and darkly tan, and his liquid eyes were sympathetic. *"Compadre,"* he said, "you come now."

Byron moved under the gentle support of the *Caporal*'s arm, seeing the little brown *arrieros* hustling to shift packs on some of the string of mules patiently standing to the side.

He'd seen them many times before. The mule trains were about the only transport to and from the valley, for the only wheel-trace in the Rogue River Valley was the Applegate trail in from the east on the Bear Creek end and on out north to the Willamette; anything south over the Siskiyous or west to the coast went mule-back or not at all.

The *Caporal* had a canteen and a cloth, and he reached up to the back of Byron's head and nearly tore it off with his first gentle swabbing touch. Byron groaned. The *Caporal* clucked and said, "Vair close, *compadre, Los Indios bala* come one hair more—poof! you are dead."

Byron endured while the *Caporal* swabbed and bandaged and put on his hat cocked well forward so it did not touch the thick pad at the back of his head. "Now," said the *Caporal,* "if you weel moun' thees mules, *compadre*—"

Byron understood then. He made a lurching turn. "The woman," he said. "My boy."

The *Caporal* shrugged uneasily. He gestured flamboyantly at the crowding timber which threatened to push the narrow track off into the near-dry creek bed. *"Los Indios,"* he said. "Where are they? Coyotes. *Diablos.* Like wolves—poof! They are gone! You come, now. *Mañana,* with friends—*los soldados,* perhaps—"

"No," Byron said. The fear had him by the throat. He knew if they left him here he could not bear it; but he could not go—not without knowing.

The *Caporal* studied him with his soft sympathetic eyes. "*La mujer,*" he said. "The woman." He sighed and hunched his shoulders resignedly. "And no weapon, no nothing." He turned away and went to his mount, a sleek black mare, and came back with a long-barreled pistol. "You comprehend the revolver *pistola, señor?* To load, bite the *cartucho*—cartridge—so. Into the *cámara*—chamber—so; and then the rammer; and again and again, to five. Caps on the neeples, so. One *cámara* vacant, so the hammer has a home place. So."

Byron accepted the pistol and the box of cartridges and percussion caps numbly. He could not even say thanks. They were going to leave him. He began to tremble, and the thin silent shrieking of fear began again inside. The *Caporal,* looking away suddenly, said softly, "*Vaya con Dios, compadre.*" Then they were gone, with just the faint smell of their dust left, the rear rider touching his hat in solemn final salute from the far turn.

The silent dismal secretiveness of the forest closed in on him, surrounded him, and no matter where he turned, he felt the silent pitiless waiting eyes of the Rogues, out there. He backed up against the wagon, between the wheels so that his back was flat against the sideboards. The pistol butt was slick and awkward in his sweating fist.

In these sickening moments he knew he was a coward. He couldn't do it. He wasn't a woodsman; the little brown devils were. They were watching him now, torturing him with silence and waiting; they had him either way. If he broke and ran for it, they'd kill him from behind. If he went into the brush after them, they'd come up through the leaves and open him up with a knife or gutshoot him with his own rifle. The half-dry creek behind him made little sucking noises of sardonic mirth. Then a bird cried, back in the timber, and his outraged mind translated it into a woman's distant scream. He moved suddenly—without willing it, without thinking—up the slope and into the timber in a heedless rush that trampled brush and twigs underfoot.

The inner desperation drove him into a frenzy of desire to get it over with, and he cursed in a strangling voice and rushed into a thicket of brush, lashing the limber-leaved branches aside with the pistol barrel. There was nothing in the brush clump. He crashed through and wheeled around, crying in a choked voice for them to come out and get it over with. He backed into a tree, and the jar against the back of his head sent him to his knees.

He was helpless as he knelt there, he knew that. He was almost blind with hurt, and he'd dropped the pistol. But the Rogues didn't come—they weren't coming. That certainty finally got through the frozen layers of his brain. They had been scared off by the mule train coming up the trail.

Slowly now the blindness went away, and his reinjured hurt faded to a steady thumping ache. He picked up the pistol, and with absentmindedly careful motions he brushed it off, really looked at it for the first time. He wasn't a hand-gunner. Armand Clayburne and most of the rest of the valley men carried pistols as a matter of course, and he tried to remember what he'd heard.

"They've got a helluva kick," Clayburne had said once. "Get close to your man and hold low," he said. "Put your sights right on his crotch and cut 'er loose. Let 'er r'ar back into a stiff wrist and you got your man. Hell with picking your spot. A .44 slug hits him anyplace atween the crotch and the eyebrows he ain't goin' to bother you no more."

Byron held the pistol out now, looked down the sights. The weapon was clumsy in his hand, and the sights wavered. He got up and started to walk.

He was no woodsman. He'd come this way because the *Caporal* had waved this way, vaguely. He walked, almost aimlessly, among bare trunked pines like bronze pillars rising from their own litter of shed needles and the straggling little brush that was all that grew in their shade. He found something finally, a long scuffed spot where the needles were turned and stirred—nothing more. It wasn't much, but a questing eagerness came on him suddenly, and he moved along in the direction of the scuffed place.

He found a little manzanita with one twig doubled back under the one above; the oval leaves showing their pale grayish underside. Something had pushed by here forcibly, and the slow inevitable reaction of the bush hadn't gotten around to rearranging it yet.

He cursed his stupid lack of skill at this. He was a farmer. He knew pasture land and corn land and potato land, and he could squeeze a lump of soil in his callused hands and predict almost to the hour when it would be ready for the plow. He could rub seed corn between his palms and bite a kernel or two and tell pretty close how many would sprout to the hill; but the brush was not his world. They called it the brush, but it wasn't. It was virgin timber, uncounted miles of it, pine and fir and cedar and others he didn't know. His own holdings made a single flea-bite in this vast shaggy rug that covered this wild, raw, new Rogue River Valley and its hills. And he'd spent a year of his life hewing out that flea-bite patch.

He'd been a fool in the first place, he could see that now. But land-hunger made a fool of a man. He'd been a tenant farmer in Kentucky and Ohio; free land, they'd said, out in Oregon, for the taking. Well, it wasn't free—it is never free. The cleared bottoms were all staked, and the miners rooting in the creeks bid the prices of everything out of a poor man's reach; he and the wagon and the team all beat down so thin by two thousand miles of shoe-stringing it that the canyon passage to the Willamette was impossible . . .

The story of my life, he thought bleakly. *Biting off more than I could chew. Bulling ahead with my eyes shut and figuring a strong back made up for a weak mind.*

He'd gotten along with the Indians all right. Hunted with them, sometimes. Ruth was afraid of them. Inscrutable little brown men with an animal's wiry strength and an animal's unthinking cruelty; they'd bird-dogged the brush and chased deer out in front of his rifle; grunted without expression and taken their share and disappeared back into the shadowy creeks where their brush huts were. He didn't understand them—he conceded a certain respect for their wild woodsman's skills, but he didn't fear them, as Ruth did, until Tyee John's bucks rose up and burned every cabin along the creek.

For some reason they'd bypassed his shack. He'd had a hard time believing the hurried little knot of miners that came by on their way to Jacksonville to warn him.

It had scared Ruth. Scared her worse than she was already. And finally, reluctantly, he'd packed up the wagon to carry her down to the Clayburnes'. They'd passed two burnings; the Wiggins and Macafee places; Ruth wouldn't look when they passed the smoldering piles. . . .

He crossed the ridge now and started down the far side, mostly on hunch. Marks were so few and scattered, he couldn't be sure of anything. But he kept moving. It was dark almost, as soon as he dropped off the ridge, and by the time he reached the next creek bottom, he was wandering like a lost and blinded spirit in a tangle of ghostly formless shapes. He drank from the creek until he was almost sick; his lips were cracked and dry. He could go no farther, and he pulled back instinctively from the creek and lay on his left side with his back against a half-rotten windfall. He crumpled his hat to soften the stub limb under his dully aching head, thrust the pistol under his shirt against the skin, his right hand still hooked around the butt.

He came awake, fully awake, with alarm shouting, shrieking, shaking at him. It brought him sharply and alertly awake, without a muscle moving but his eyelids, and he saw the Indian. Fear ran screaming down all the fine burning nerves of his body.

The Rogue stood on the creek bank, across from Byron. He stood like a hunched statue, harking alertly as the mountain grouse do, turning his head in tiny flirting motions to sound the wind. Then, quite suddenly, the Rogue dropped flat and started sucking water from the creek. Byron moved then, instinctively doing what he had to do without thought, picking the instant he had his man in a bind.

He slid the pistol out of his shirt and cocked it, holding the trigger back so the sear would not click. He thought he did it without sound, but as the hammer came back to full cock, the Rogue raised his head in a sudden jerk and stared straight at him. Over the sights, the Rogue's chin sat on the blade of the front sight, and his frozen features were those of a gargoyle carved in walnut, water drooling from the slack, surprised lower lip, black obsidian-chip eyes without depth or life, the only movement the tiny flare and sag of nostrils under slow labored breath.

Byron didn't know how long they posed thus. The black eyes over the pistol's sights were almost hypnotic in their steady un-winking stare. This one wasn't a full-grown buck. Maybe 14, maybe 16—who can tell the age of a Rogue Indian? But he had him, and they both knew it. And without thinking about it, he was dredging his mind for the few words of jargon he knew, for he knew without conscious cerebration that he was going to use this Rogue cub if he could.

"*Tillicum,*" he said. That meant friend. The Rogue stared at him with unblinking eyes. He seined his brain again. Boston. That was the universal word for white man. Klooch—kloochman—that was woman.

"*Boston kloochman?*" he said, putting the question in the tone. He pointed across the creek. Nothing.

"God damn you," he said through his teeth. "*Kloochman. Boston kloochman.* You see her?" Eyelids suddenly blinked across those black bottomless eyes. What was the word for *you*? *Kipa? Kima?* No—*mika*. "*Mika—boston kloochman?*" He went toward the Rogue with the pistol thrust ahead, and the Indian pulled back before him as he splashed through the ankle-deep water. He came to his knees, still blinking rapidly, and Byron laid the gun on the bigger target of his belly. "Damn you," he said, "I'll kill you. You understand? *Mamook mamaloose!* Speak up, damn you!"

The Rogue was afraid. He could almost smell it. And suddenly the Rogue's mouth opened and he said in a breathless gobble, *"Klatawa yah'wa boston kloochman."* He pointed *'Tyee Zhon man is'kum kloochman ko'pa skookum chuck."*

Byron cursed himself for not knowing more jargon. But it sounded as if this one knew where she was. Then the chilling thought came. *"Kloochman mamaloose?"* he demanded fiercely. "Woman dead?"

The Rogue said, *"Wake,"* and shook his head no.

"All right," said Byron. "You take me. *Mika klatawa yah'wa. Boston kloochman. Hyak!"*

The Rogue stood up. He wore a ragged cotton shirt and, unless there was a breech clout under the flapping tails, nothing else except his moccasins. A twisted rawhide cord was belted twice around his waist and tied, and a sheathed butcher knife was pushed under it. Byron took the knife, tied one end of the belt around the Rogue's wrist, and held the other.

"All right," he said, and motioned with the barrel of the pistol. *"Klatawa. Hyak!"* The Rogue backed away to the length of the tether, then finally turned and led off into the timber.

The Rogue's shuffling, almost shambling pace was deceptively fast. Byron couldn't see the trail the Rogue seemed to be following so easily, and twice he was sure they had left it. But eventually some sign always turned up that even he could see. Once it was a tag of cloth, no bigger than a fingernail, which the Rogue plucked off a dry spur of manzanita. The Indian looked at it, raised it to his nostrils and sniffed inquiringly as an animal might, shrugged, and tossed it aside.

They crossed two more ridges and two creeks. On one soft bank, the Rogue pointed out a flat curved depression, the mark of a hard shoe-sole, said *"Kloochman,"* contemptuously, as if any fool should know more than to leave as clear a marker as that. Byron prodded him on with the pistol.

The pace was tiring him, though the Indian lad seemed as fresh as ever. Byron wondered how the boy had stood it if his captors had traveled this fast. Shortly after the sun passed overhead in its nooning, he got his answer. The Rogue harked alertly at something, swinging his eyes off the trail. He paused, just the slightest hesitation, and Byron sent a quick sweeping glance around and brought up the pistol. The Indian started on, and Byron stopped him with a twitch of the leash. "What is it?" he demanded low voiced.

The Indian grunted something and started on, and Byron saw something wrong in the stiffness of his shoulders. He stopped him again and searched the surrounding area carefully with his eyes. He saw the scuffed mark off in the needles to the side and knew he had something when the Indian reluctantly went toward it under his prodding. He found his son's body not twenty feet off the trail, carelessly hidden in the scrub brush.

Somehow it didn't make sense. The little face was so pale and expressionless that it might have been a wax doll's face. He lay in a sprawling sleeping pose, his cheek against the shed leaves, and only the fact that his head was turned too far from the angle of his shoulders showed where a strong hand had broken the tender bones of his neck with one savage twist.

Byron didn't touch him. He squatted there a long time while his tired mind rejected it, refused to consider it, even.

It was an ant that broke the spell. A common little black ant that skittered up over the boy's pale cheek. Byron waited for him to reach up and brush it off, and he didn't. It was as if a red bomb had exploded in his brain. He made a screaming sound of pain and came to his feet and in one wheeling motion clubbed with the pistol at his tethered Indian.

In that instant he knew he'd waited too long. The Rogue had picked up a club, a ragged-ended limb three feet long, and he swung it in a countering blow that drove the pistol out of Byron's fingers and spinning aside.

He was scared, the Rogue. His eyes were round and his mouth was slack, and he jerked back hard on the rawhide that tethered his wrist to Byron and yanked it free. Still on the defensive, he backed away, holding the stick poised, but Byron ignored it completely as he flung himself after him. The lad cried out something in a scared voice, threw the club at him, and then wheeled and broke for it. Byron plunged heedlessly through a stand of brush, dodged through a spindly fence of pine reproduction, before the red mist cleared and he knew he couldn't match the Rogue at this game. He thought of the pistol, then, and he ran back. It was still there. So was the pitiful doll-body of his son.

He was trembling now from reaction, but he moved almost calmly. He picked up the weapon and brushed it off. He thrust it into the waistband of his trousers and pulled out the tails of his shirt. With infinite but almost impersonal care, he wrapped the body in his shirt. He tore up scrub brush and little saplings until he had a bed of them. He laid his burden on them and covered it with more; it was the best he could do for now. He carefully didn't think about it. About anything.

*   *   *

He became aware that there were two of him somewhere along in the afternoon. The feeling came on him so sharply that he suddenly lifted his right hand and stared at it as if he had never seen it before. It was his hand, and it wasn't.

He was tired, and he had to have a drink, and he was scared—with a deep, cringing, weeping scaredness. But he was also an eager hunting wolf who sneered and raged against the rebellion of a body that wanted to quit. His head started to ache again, and he impatiently slapped it on the side as if to teach it better. He trotted, and when those numb impersonal legs that wouldn't obey started to stumble, he dropped back to a walk. Then, impatiently, he drove them back to jogging again.

He crossed the last ridge at dusk. He knew it was the last one, somehow; maybe it was his ingrained husbandman's knowledge of drainage slopes. He'd never been here before, but he somehow knew that this slope led to the river. His feet fell upon a deer trail that wended easily through the timber, and he followed it.

He smelled smoke and collapsed in his tracks. It was that instinctive. He fell on his belly, and he had the pistol in his hand. He left the trail and wormed through the brush as silent as a snake, while the scared tired part of him marveled admiringly. With the sure attraction of a magnet to filings, he slid toward the one clump of trees that called him, though it was no different than half a hundred others on this slope.

He smelled smoke again, and his heart set up a steady drumming against his ribs. A down-curving spike of dry brush raked him from shoulder to flank, and he did not move an inch to relieve himself of the pain.

The brush thinned and dwarfed off into scrub, as it would where it was so shaded, and he caught the first warm color of the fire. Something stirred almost within arm's reach, and he froze instantly. A rabbit peered at him from a shallow burrow in the brush roots and then suddenly broke into a skittering silent run away at right angles. He moved up again.

He was curiously matter-of-fact about it. He held the cocked pistol ahead and slid up to it, using the elbow as a lever, the other hand back level with his chest to raise his weight and slide it ahead.

Five of them. And Ruth. He counted them as he might count hogs in a pen, with no particular feeling one way or the other. With a queer dispassion, he knew that Ruth looked pretty bad. One braid had come loose, and she looked odd, lopsided, sort of, with one side of her hair hanging free and loose and the other still rather neatly braided.

Her dress and petticoat were ripped and torn; only one shoulder held up her petticoat, and her dress was little but a ripped rag of skirt; he wondered impersonally whether the Rogues or the brush had done that; her hands were behind her, and as she shifted in her cramped seated position, he could see they were tied. One of the Rogues had what looked like a couple of rabbits spitted on a stick over the fire. Another was rubbing at a heavy flintlock rifle with a rag—part of Ruth's dress, maybe. One moved away and out into the brush and then came back. Byron could hear the river talking over there, a few hundred feet beyond the fire.

The one with the spitted rabbits pulled back the stick now and tested them with a pinching thumb and finger. He burned himself apparently, for he shook his hand disgustedly. A thought came to him, almost visibly, and he lurched up and went around the fire and thrust the stick at Ruth, close to her face. He was grinning a humorless animal grin.

She flinched back from the sizzling carcasses, and he gave a grunt and grabbed her braid and snatched her head forward while he wiped the scorching meat on her face. Byron took a deep breath, steadied his right wrist with his left hand, and shot him through the belly.

The thunderous shocking roar of the pistol jarred him, and the double flash of cylinder and muzzle blinded him for an instant. The recoil was so rough, he wondered fleetingly if the weapon had blown up on him. The Rogue he'd shot took two limber-legged steps back and sat down abruptly.

The one with the flintlock started up, and Byron's second shot took him in the right shoulder blade and spun him aside, and the flintlock went off with a bellow and a shower of fire that followed the ball six feet in the air.

Byron surged to his knees to get above the scrub brush and got his third man low in the back as he dove into the brush on the far side. He made a clean miss with his fourth bullet, and the fifth sent bark spinning off a tree, chest high, where one of them dodged.

He started running with the third shot, in a charging crouch with the pistol thrust ahead. The last Rogue, slower-witted perhaps than his fellows, cowered across the fire and scarcely moved until Byron burst out of the brush. He turned then and made a clawing scramble of it, not running or crawling, and Byron hurled the heavy handful of steel and walnut with the full sweep of his arm and hit him across the small of the back.

The red roaring rage was on him again, and he moved with the jerky precision of a killing machine. There was a light hand axe by the fire. He scooped it up without breaking stride and whirled it over and down against the back of the scrambling buck's head. He caught a flash of movement as the one behind the tree made a break for it, and he hurled the axe at the movement. He heard it hit, and a scream of wordless hurt, but the brush crashed as his man kept on going.

Byron snatched up the pistol and dug into his pocket for the flat cartridge box the *Caporal* had given him. He pulled the slide cover and tumbled waxed paper cartridges into his hand and methodically loaded and capped the cylinders.

The first one he'd shot through the belly was still alive. He was crawling and squirming like a crippled snake when Byron stepped over to him.

"This is for the boy," he said in a flat, even voice. "You didn't have to do that." He shot the Rogue through the head at three feet.

He stalked to Ruth without looking back. She stared up at him silently. Her face was white with shock, but there was no readable expression on it. Her head turned to follow him like a fascinated bird's as he knelt beside her and cut the cruelly taut twisted rawhide that bound her wrists. Her hands fell free, and she put them in her lap and rubbed them clumsily together. Her body shook as if she were weeping, and her face was a mask of sorrow, but no tears came, and no sound.

"Ruth," he said, a ragged frightened sound. She looked at him again with that queer, twisted, weeping face, and he helped her up. She was shaking as if with the swamp-ague, and he steadied her, and then she said in a choked crying voice, "Oh, Byron!" She pushed her face against his dirty bare chest and rocked her forehead to and fro. "They killed him. They killed little Jimmy."

"I know," he said. "I know." Then she collapsed against him, completely limp.

They met the mounted patrol a mile before they reached Clayburne's. Byron trudged ahead with his son's body in his arms and the pistol in his belt. Ruth came behind, carrying his rifle, with one of the Rogues' ragged shirts over her torn petticoat. And something in the way they walked and looked at the mounted men kept their questions to a minimum and their voices low.

At Clayburne's, Ruth's eyes scarcely left Byron. Even when Mrs. Clayburne came running and put her arms around her and tried to lead her into the house, she kept watching Byron over Mrs. Clayburne's plump shoulder. And not until he said quietly, "Go along, Ruth," did she let the woman lead her inside.

The mounted men and the Clayburnes, father and sons, stood in a rough semicircle about Byron, staring at him as at one risen from the dead. He looked more like a savage than any Rogue.

Two days' beard blurred his jaw, and his bandage made a dirty, bloody headband. His body, bare to the waist, was streaked with dirt and blood, and his eyes had low, smoldering coals of fire behind them.

But he said, in a voice completely dispassionate and matter-of-fact, "Armand, would you favor me with the loan of a team and wagon, or even a horse?"

"Why—why, sure," said Armand Clayburne. "But—"

"I'm obliged," said Byron carefully. "I'd like to get along back to my place. I'd like to lay the boy away on—on his own land. And I'll have to look to my crops."

"You're daft, man," said Clayburne. "The Rogues—"

The little coals of fire blazed up brighter behind Byron's steady eyes. "They'll never do me any more hurt than they have," he said. "If they come, I'll be there. On my own land. Behind my own walls. I'm past fearing them. If you'll hitch up the team for me. I don't want to put the boy down again."

They stared at him as at some strange monster, but they got out a light wagon and hitched in a team. Byron mounted over the wheel without aid and carefully laid the bundle on the seat beside him.

"I'll be obliged," he said, still with that careful passionless precision, "if you'll look after the woman a bit. I'll be back, when she's up to it, and find some way to get her back to her folks."

Then Mrs. Clayburne's voice came, with a frightened note in it. "Wait. Ruth, wait!"

And Ruth came, almost running, pushing her way through the men. She still had on the ragged shirt and carried the long caplock rifle, and she said steadily, "Byron, wait. I'm going with you."

He looked down at her from the seat. "I'm going back to the house, Ruth."

"Not alone," she said. "I'm going with you."

He stared down at her, boring at her with those strange eyes that were fiery and dead all in one; and then the stiff strictness of his face broke and softened. "Yes, Ruth," he said softly. He leaned down to give her a hand up, and she leaned the rifle between them and picked up her son's body and held it in her lap.

Byron Martin shook the reins out over the team, and the wagon creaked into motion. The mounted patrol fell in silently, respectfully, making a queer formality of this escort.

As the wagon turned out of the yard and onto the narrow track, the eldest Clayburne son said to his father, "By God, Pap, that's guts!"

And Armand Clayburne said softly, "It's more than guts, son. There goes a man. And a woman. Take a good look, son, for you'll not see many like them in a lifetime."

The wagon creaked, a homely, comforting sound as the Martins drove down the long road home.

A longtime resident of Oregon, Dwight Newton has been a prolific writer of Western fiction for nearly half a century. Under his own name and such pseudonyms as Dwight Bennett, Clement Hardin, Ford Logan, and Dan Temple, he has produced numerous short stories and more than sixty novels. Standouts among his books are Shotgun Guard *(1950),* Fire in the Desert *(1956),* Cherokee Outlet *(1961),* The Big Land *(1972), and* Disaster Creek *(1981). He also contributed dozens of teleplays to such early TV Western series as* Wagon Train *and* Death Valley Days. *He is at his fictive best in "Chain of Command," a vivid tale of E Company of the First Oregon Volunteers during the Civil War.*

Chain of Command

★★★★★★★★★★★★

D. B. Newton

TWENTY horse soldiers belonging to E Company of the First Oregon Volunteers had been all the commanding officer of the undergarrisoned post on Burnt Creek could spare for this assignment. Under a captain and the usual complement of noncoms, they swung at an easy pace through the ripe September sunlight, following the normal cavalry routine of canter, walk, rest, down, and lead the horses. It was those horses that would have marked it anywhere as no regular unit but a lowly detachment of Volunteers.

No cavalry remount officer would have accepted any one of them. Instead of the solid colors demanded by the regular mounted army, they came in all markings and sizes, a good many so gaunted by three years of wearing service in the field that it was hard to see how they kept up; and the men who rode them—men clothed and armed with what might have been the cast-off equipment of a better organization—looked nearly as hard-worn and used.

The talk that drifted along the column was the familiar enlisted man's banter, unchanging the world over—the talk of men who knowingly faced loneliness, discomfort, and a constant possibility of death and treated him in the only sensible way—as a bad joke.

85

Still, their griping held a note of particular seriousness, and with reason.

Like every other outfit in the Volunteers, this fall of 1864, E Company was understrength and overworked. Recruits just weren't coming in, and meanwhile the first batch of three-year enlistments would be up in a matter of weeks. Amid speculation about the future, someone called up to a big yellow-bearded trooper in the middle of the column: "O'Mara! What's this I hear about you signing for another hitch?"

"What lyin' bastard told you a thing like that?" O'Mara demanded bitterly. "Send him to me, and I'll kill him. I don't even want to hear jokes about it!"

"Why, ain't you been happy in the Volunteers?" his questioner asked in mock surprise. "You know *somebody's* got to make it safe so them fellers over on Wilson Creek can take out all that there gold dust. It's a real privilege."

"Where we off to this time?" another man wanted to know. "Some brave pioneer see his own shadow on the outhouse wall and put out a yell for the cavalry?"

Trooper Tom Swenson, newest to the outfit and nervous because this was his first patrol, spoke up. "Reckon maybe it's actual. I heard Colbrook talkin' to the guy that come larruping into the post asking for help." He nodded forward toward the civilian—one of the Wilson Creek miners—who rode at the head of the column now with Captain Ash. "I guess the Snakes must of jumped 'em good!"

"In that case," O'Mara said sourly, "it's a lucky thing we got five days' saddle rations with us. We'll be eatin' sage roots before *we* see camp again! But I'll tell you now—the day my enlistment's up, I take off. And that means, wherever I happen to be. . . ."

The scarred banks of Wilson Creek were littered with brush shelters, with sluice boxes and prospect holes, and with the stumpage of timber that had been carelessly chopped out: men on a quest for quick wealth never seemed to care what squalid wreckage they left behind. Jingling up the shallow canyon, where yellow leaves of alder and cottonwood streamed on the slight wind, E Company found that most of the workings had been temporarily abandoned; but a number of hardy and reckless souls were still hanging on to their claims in the face of Indian danger instead of seeking the protection of numbers in Canyon City or the other eastern Oregon camps. When Captain Ash signaled a halt, a couple of dozen men came hurrying, looking a little wild-eyed and most of them clutching weapons of some description.

Sergeant Mead Colbrook automatically shouted the orders that dismounted the troop and sent scouts up onto the canyon rim; then he joined the captain, who was sifting through some excitedly garbled accounts of the dawn raid. It seemed the Snakes had made a heavy fire attack from the rim just at daybreak. Then—in the midst of the shooting, while the whites were being kept occupied— one daring bunch of bucks had swooped down onto the grassy upward end of the canyon where the miners' livestock was loose held. They'd made off with better than thirty head of horses and mules, leaving a couple of Indians behind, dead. The defenders had lost one man to a lance thrust, and three more had taken injuries of varying seriousness.

Ash listened to all this; afterward, probably to escape some of the confusion, he took Colbrook and two of the miners inside a tent, where they could sit down to check over one of E Company's inadequate field maps.

Out on the creekbank a strained silence settled, with troopers and civilian gold-seekers exchanging stares in two sullen and vaguely hostile groups. Trooper Swenson's bay horse had been worrying the reins, trying to free its head as it caught the scent of nearby water. Now, as Swenson gave in and led his animal to the creek through muddy litter, he was instantly aware of suspicious eyes following him; it was as though these men thought he meant to take something that didn't belong to him. Wiping sweaty cheeks on his neck cloth, the young fellow muttered, "The hell with them! Water's free, I guess!" and refused to hurry the bay while it drank.

One of the troopers indicated a sluice box and a long-handled shovel thrust into the muck beside it. "You take much out of that?" he asked the owner—an unintelligent-looking redhead in stag pants and muddy boots and sweaty underwear rolled to the elbows.

The man looked him over coldly, switched a chew of quid from one cheek to the other. "Could do worse," he admitted with a shrug.

"I'll swap with you," the disgruntled veteran named O'Mara offered; another trooper said sourly, "Sure! You rather be making sixteen bucks a month wearing a uniform? Just speak to the captain: he'll fix you up. You can eat beans and sowbelly and spend your time chasing Indians all over this backend of Oregon. Think you'd like some of that?"

The man sneered openly. "Not this year! I'll leave it for suckers like you boys!"

That brought a snicker from some of the miners, causing an

angry stir in the ranks that ended only as a corporal yelled sharply, "All right! You men are at ease!"

The conference in the tent was over now. Captain Ash emerged, ducking the flap and buttoning a folded map into a pocket of his tunic. Colbrook, inspecting his troops, saw Tom Swenson leading his horse back from the creek, and he let out a roar. "Swenson, who gave you permission to break ranks?"

"Nobody, Sergeant. I was only—"

"At ease, trooper!" Colbrook turned his back and strode away. Swenson caught the grins on the faces of the lounging miners and felt the flood of heat moving up from his throat into his cheeks, even to the hairline.

The redhead who had done most of the talking switched his chew into the other cheek and looked him over knowingly, not missing the new and ill-fitting uniform. "Reckon you ain't been in long, have you, sojer boy? You better watch it. Don't you forget, you ain't a civilian anymore. You button your pants by the numbers—and when the sergeant tells you." Young Swenson's jaw muscles bunched, but he stood with eyes straight ahead, the reins clamped tight in one hand.

One of the scouts was back down from the rim, reporting to the captain; apparently he'd found sign, for Ash crisply returned his salute and issued an order. His horse was brought up, and he swung astride, saber glittering in sunlight. An edgy excitement ran through the column.

"You just better see you git our livestock back—hear?" someone yelled at them. "That's what for we pay you dogfaces your wages."

O'Mara swore under his breath. The order came back then: "Prepare to mount—*mount!*" Leather creaked and accouterments rattled; tight blue britches slapped saddle leather.

"Can't even git on or off a horse without being told!" the redheaded miner said. "Be damned if I'd ever put myself under anybody's thumb that way. It ain't fitting to a man's dignity—like he had no will or mind of his own. Me, anytime I take a hankering to spit, I'm gonna spit!" And looking straight at Trooper Swenson, he slanted his head and loosed a juicy brown gobbet, hitting the rock beside Swenson.

At once a second bait of chaw hit, precisely atop the miner's own mark—but at such an angle that it bounced. The man yelled and leaped back as his boots were splattered; he looked up glaring and subsided as he saw Sergeant Colbrook staring at him icily.

The sergeant spurred on to the head of the column then; but as he pulled away, his eyes found Tom Swenson's and held there for a brief and wordless moment. After that, to another shouted order, the column struck out at a canter, southward along the creek.

Where the canyon shallowed, they found a break in the east rim and climbed out onto high, rolling plateau land; here Captain Ash sent out his flank scouts, and striking sign of the Indians and their stolen horses, the column pushed on—a slender probe of men and horses and guns testing the silent vastness of this wide and empty land. Trooper Swenson watched the hills, dark with timber, and felt a gnawing in his solar plexus. Once he cried out, startled, and pointed as a distant bunch of antelope swirled away, drifting a pall of dust above the yellow-blooming sea of rabbit brush. His cheeks turned crimson under their sheen of sweat when the men riding about him laughed scornfully.

"Sure, kid," one of them told him. "You can figure on it: until you get the hang of this country, you'll be seeing Injuns behind every clump of sagebrush."

"Hell! That bunch has got six hours' lead on us. We ain't likely to see them *or* the stock they run off."

"So why are we killing our own horses for nothing?" he demanded, and this time raised an answering mutter of agreement.

This was only the newest in a long list of grievances. Just before the troop left the rock and log buildings of the encampment on Burnt Creek, word had passed among the men of E Company that someone high up had gone back on the promise, made them at the time of enlistment, of forty cents a day allowance for supplying their own mounts. Some of those horses had been in the field with their owners now for three years and were worn to nearly worthless piles of bone and hide. Trooper Swenson knew he voiced a rankling sense of injustice and betrayal shared by all these other men as he said, "It ain't fair and it ain't sense! Let that crowd back on the crick worry about their own damned livestock. They can afford losing it a sight more than—"

"Swenson!"

It was Colbrook again; he had ridden along the column, and his expression, as he put his mount alongside the recruit's, was dangerous. Swenson looked into the red face with its cheeks raddled by drink and weather, its pale, cold eyes, and the hard set of the mouth under the drooping and grizzled mustache; and he thought for the hundredth time how much he hated this man. "You criticizing orders?" the sergeant demanded harshly.

The boy flushed. "All I said—"

"I heard what you said! Just why are you in this outfit anyway?"

"Because," he snapped, forgetting his fear of Colbrook in the spill of anger, "I ran into one of your damn recruiting officers over in Portland!"

The pale eyes narrowed. "That's no answer."

"You think it ain't? I could have been East right now, with General Grant—doing my part to win this damn war. It's all I've wanted, all the time I been waiting for my kid brother to get old enough he could take care of the folks and the farm without me." His mouth twisted bitterly. "So then I meet this feller who says I'm needed worse at home, helping the Volunteers that was formed to hold Oregon together after the regulars pulled out. And like a fool I believed him!"

"So you figure you was sold a bill of goods. . . . You still think you'd like it better with Grant?"

Trooper Swenson shrugged. "I ain't *that* green, not anymore! A fellow learns fast, whether he's in the regulars or a scratch outfit like this one. Either way, it's still the Army! All this damn saluting and drilling and standing at attention! Like the fellow said back there at the crick, seems like you could make a soldier out of a man without trying to beat his brains out and turn him into some kind of machine, or something. . . ."

He broke off, resolutely meeting the fierce light in the sergeant's stare. Around him, the other troopers rode in a waiting silence that was broken only by the sound of hoofs and creak of leather and jingle of accouterments. Trooper Swenson firmed his jaw, determined to brave out whatever the sergeant would do to him.

Colbrook's voice, when he spoke, was like iron. "Just how old are you, kid?"

"Old enough."

The sergeant didn't like that answer. He turned his head and spat across the crupper of his mount, scrubbed a fist across his mouth and heavy mustache. "I'll talk to you later," he said finally, and lifting the reins, he spoke past Trooper Swenson to the man who rode beyond him. "Might not be a bad idea, Gilliam, if somebody was to tell the kid just what happens to deserters in this outfit."

He was gone then, with a kick of the spurs and a lifting wrench of the reins in his strong fist. He rode on along the column to take his place beside Captain Ash at its head; after a moment of slogging silence Tom Swenson sneaked a look at Gilliam. "Well?" he demanded harshly.

"About deserters, you mean?" The trooper shrugged. "Why, what I hear is, if they catch you, they burn you. They take down your pants and brand a nice fat D—right on your butt."

Trooper Swenson swallowed. "You're funnin'!"

"No he ain't," Trooper O'Mara said over a shoulder. "Kid, I seen it done to a guy once. You should of heard him yell!"

He felt his gut crawl a little. A brute like Colbrook would really enjoy that, he thought; but why pick on *him*?

Everybody in this outfit griped. Yet, let him once open his mouth and the sergeant had him pegged as ready to go over the hill. Well, by God! Treat a man so and you could drive him to it. . . .

Timbered ridges crowded about them now; pine spires scraped the bellies of clouds that thickened as the long day wore on. Those clouds shut out the sunlight presently, and it grew shadowy and a little awesome. A small rain began and was quickly ended, leaving a stink of sodden wool to hang about the column. The flank scouts—the ones who really rode with the smell of death in their nostrils—continued to have nothing to report.

O'Mara, the complainer, said once, "I ain't sure them dogfaces know Injun sign even when they see it. If the legislature would only let loose enough dough to let us hire a few friendlies to do our scouting . . ."

This was another long-standing grievance with the Volunteers, who claimed their hands were tied because the elusive Snakes could always manage to shake them off. Just a few grudging dollars a month for the hire of trail-wise scouts would have given them a fighting chance to close in pursuit—perhaps even accomplish the jobs they were sent to do.

Sometimes it looked as if nobody at all gave a damn. . . .

After a rest, the order to remount came back. Leather creaked and bit chains rattled, and the column swung out again. They were running east and north again, into timber; someone said the Snakes must be planning to bypass the settlements along the John Day and cross north into the safety of the Blue Mountain fastnesses. Trooper O'Mara commented drily, "One thing you can bet on: they know by now we're after them. Maybe they don't care. On the other hand, maybe they figure to do something about it. . . ."

"How do you mean?" Trooper Swenson demanded a little anxiously, but the veteran wouldn't elaborate, leaving him to stew on it.

The troop rode silently now, for the most part; talk had been worn out of them by the attrition of the long hours. By this time they were going on dogged soldiers' will, munching cold saddle rations and looking no further than to enduring the balance of the day's march and waiting for the order to make camp.

A horse went lame, its rider wearily cursing as he saw it had played out at last. On Colbrook's order he swung up behind another trooper, who resentfully emptied a stirrup. "Just great!" O'Mara grumbled. "Now the animals are starting to go!" The sergeant gave him a look but said nothing. There was no letup in the pace.

Sometime toward three o'clock, although no word had been given, excitement began to stir in the column; the men knew somehow that their captain had ridden ahead to confer with a scout, that something had been sighted. There was a brief halt for consultation. Then they moved out again, under the tall pine heads.

Sergeant Colbrook was back with terse orders: "First squad follow the captain. Second squad, peel off and come with me. And take it easy!" Moments later the detachment had split and Trooper Swenson found himself working his way down the tilted spine of a long slope, keeping to the cover of heavy pine growth. It was his guess that Ash had ordered a pincer movement, which, if it worked, might catch the Indians between the two prongs of his column. Every man sensed now that action could be very close. They dropped into a steep ravine choked with tough *manzanita*, then angled across an intervening ridge and, in the draw beyond, pulled rein as the sergeant raised a hand.

On their front, straight-standing ranks of yellow-barked pine marched up a steep rise.

Sergeant Colbrook faced his men, scowling. "All right," he told them. "What we're looking for is in a clearing just beyond that ridge. The red devils know that we know it. It's a trap, of course, and maybe they figure we're stupid enough or just damned wore out enough to ride into it.

"Instead, we're gonna try to spring it for them. The captain and his squad will ride in through the draw just like they're expecting. The rest of us are to jump the varmints from the flank. You all got that?"

He waited, challenging an answer. Trooper Swenson clamped his lips tight and stared straight ahead, holding himself stiffly at attention, but his stomach was beginning to act strangely.

"All right—check your weapons."

His hands feeling stiff and clumsy now that it was the real thing and not arms practice, Tom Swenson went through the motions, drawing the pistol and looking to the seating of the caps on their nipples. Afterward he unshipped the Sharps carbine on its sling, worked the lever, and dropped a linen cartridge into the breech. As he finished, Colbrook gave the order to move out. Carbine gripped tensely, Trooper Swenson spurred his mount forward.

The hill was steep and slick beneath the pines with a spongy brown matting of old needles. Halfway up, the angle increased, and Colbrook ordered his men out of saddle to lead their mounts.

Trooper Swenson set his face toward the comb of the ridge, which was almost lost in the rising pillars of yellow-barked pines. The bay horse turned balky, and Swenson cursed and dragged at the reins with main strength. "Come on!" he gritted. "You trying to hold me back? You're coming up this hill if I have to carry you!"

Sweating and panting, he fought the stubborn animal and the slope and the slickness underfoot. For every yard of gain he seemed to slide back two. Once his boot slipped and brought him down heavily, wrenching his knee; but he was up again in an instant.

By this time he'd lost all sight of his fellow troopers through the wide-spaced tree trunks; he wasted no time searching, taking it for granted the rest would already have reached the top. He was using the butt of the carbine now to aid him, digging in with it and thus pulling himself up the last difficult yards, with blue sky and clouds showing now just ahead through the trees.

"Swenson!"

Colbrook's deep roar came from behind and below him, so startling that he nearly dropped the reins as he whirled. The sergeant was climbing toward him, lifting thick legs high, his head thrust forward with the effort of climbing. "Now what?" the boy asked himself. He set himself to stand up to the bully; but when Colbrook was close enough for him to see the congestion of blood darkening his face, the young fellow's courage forsook him, and he quailed.

"Goddamn it!" Colbrook's heavy hand dropped onto his shoulder with a crushing weight and tightened until nerves screamed in protest. The sergeant's eyes blazed, and the mustache seemed to bristle with a rage so great that for a moment the man appeared unable to form words. He let his hand fall away, and it was absolutely trembling.

"What the hell you planning to do?" the sergeant managed to get out finally. "Capture 'em single-handed? Now, you follow orders! Stand hitched and wait for the rest to catch up—you hear?"

Turning, bewildered, Trooper Swenson looked back and saw the others still toiling up the slope, a good dozen yards below. It occurred to him he must not have heard a command to hold up for a moment and rest both horses and men. He felt so suddenly and completely a fool that he reddened to the ears and was stung to retort: "I just didn't want to give you any excuse for calling me a coward!"

Eyes narrowed, Colbrook regarded him for a long moment. Finally he said, in a quieter voice, "I never called you a coward, Swenson. In as short a time as this, I got no way of knowing *what* you are. I just know you're pretty damn young—and this is your first action. And when we get down that hill, I want you where I can keep an eye on you. Understand?"

"I don't need any nursemaid!"

"You've got an order!" Colbrook snapped, and didn't wait for argument. Instead he turned and yelled for one of the nearing troopers to bring up his horse, which he had left to catch up with Swenson. The man grabbed the animal's reins and dragged it forward with his own.

Seething, Trooper Swenson busied himself with checking the cinch on his saddle. He found himself straining to hear some sound from beyond the ridge, but he supposed it was still too far. Everything was covered by the stir of pine tops in the golden September afternoon, the sounds of men and mounts assembling along the ridge top. The trees were too thick to see more than a few yards.

When the first rattle of gunfire broke the stillness, Colbrook's squad was mounted and lined out, waiting. That was the signal. Without any command, the men of Colbrook's squad went pouring down through the timber—a breakneck, murderous spill.

Trooper Swenson found himself so busy managing his horse, he nearly forgot what would be waiting for him at the foot of the ridge. His heart slogged in his throat as he wrenched at the reins and tried to avoid the trees that came pelting at him with crazy speed. Following orders, he attempted dutifully to keep a close distance to the big sergeant; it wasn't easy. Intervening trees and brush kept getting in the way.

Of only one thing he was certain: He'd be damned if the heavy-handed bastard was going to get down off this hill a single step ahead of him!

The trees were thinning a little, giving an occasional glimpse of green meadow and a glitter of water. There was a steady popping of gunfire now. Suddenly Trooper Swenson felt his mount break stride in a tricky patch of pine needles and loosed a yell of warning that brought Colbrook's head whipping around. His homely face showed alarm as he saw the boy, out of control, barreling down toward him. Just as Swenson, with a jerk at the reins, managed to help his mount regain its footing, the two horses met in a sideswiping collision.

Colbrook was not so lucky. His horse slewed wildly under him. Swenson saw the tense look on the sergeant's face. In the last split second, with a true cavalryman's instinct, Colbrook remembered to toss away the saber he held; he was scarcely rid of it when man and mount crashed full against a thick-boled tree, the horse neighing its terror as they went thrashing down.

Trooper Swenson frantically hauled rein; the bay slid a dozen feet with him, on braced haunches, before it could come to an uneasy halt. Shakily the boy leaped down, remembering to keep hold of the leathers, and got to Colbrook as the fallen man's horse was struggling and pawing to its feet. Ducking a lashing hoof, he reached and caught the bridle, got both mounts settled.

Dropping the reins, Tom Swenson turned to look at Colbrook then—half afraid too, not wanting to see a man with his brains dashed out or with broken bones probing torn flesh.

But the sergeant's number must not have come up yet. Swenson saw he'd been thrown clear in the fall; already he was climbing to his feet. As the boy stared at him, the sergeant groaned and shook his head. His hat lay on the ground. He shoved thick fingers through his grizzled hair and looked around him; his eye settled on Trooper Swenson, and it became terrible. The young fellow saw his chest swell.

"Damn it, trooper! Can't you even manage that animal?"

It was suddenly too much. Tom Swenson didn't even know he was going to hit until something seemed to explode behind his eyes and his arm started its brief, chopping swing. The aching smash of knuckles against the man's hard head astonished him and felt infinitely satisfying in the same moment. Colbrook's head jerked back on his shoulders, and his boots slid apart, breaking stance. But then he had his balance, and the blow didn't seem to have done more than surprise him.

Slowly his chin lowered against his chest, his pale eyes turned to flint. The breath seemed congested in his throat. He lifted a stubby finger to the sleeve of his sweated tunic and gently tapped the chevrons. "I wasn't wearing these when you did that, you understand?" he said hoarsely. The muscles of his solid jaw bunched. "And I ain't wearing 'em now," he added as his own fist swung.

Trooper Swenson was sent flying before a blow of stunning, staggering power. A pine's rough bark struck his shoulders; the back of his head slammed against it hard. His vision clouded, cleared again, and he saw the sergeant closing the distance. He found the voice and the courage to hurl his defiance, a trifle hysterically: "Go right ahead, you bastard! Now's your chance! You been trying to break me ever since I joined this stinking outfit!"

Sergeant Colbrook came to a stand, so close that Swenson could feel the man's breath hot against his face. He pressed his back hard against the rough tree bark and made himself meet the pale eyes. Colbrook's voice held quiet, but it shook with emotion.

"Now, you listen careful—because I just got time to say this once! I've only been trying to make a soldier out of you. I been trying harder than I ever done with anyone before because I know you're young and you're green; and the way you use up your strength hating me and the Army, I got a notion you may not last long!"

Trembling, Trooper Swenson tongued a small thread of blood from a cut lip, "What's the difference?" he retorted. "You can get more replacements where you got me from!"

The big man drew back a trifle. Slowly he shook his head. "I don't guess," he said, in a strangely altered tone, "you'd understand I could be tough on you because I happen to *like* you! I was a kid about as young and about as green and full of notions when I set out to help Phil Kearny lick the Mexicans. It was a long time ago, kid; nobody took any trouble with me, and I survived in spite of it. But a man remembers how it was. . . .

"You don't believe a word I'm saying, do you?" he added, the harshness returning as he looked into the other's unyielding, sweaty face. the growing racket of gunfire called Colbrook back to the present then. He stepped back. "The hell with this!" he barked. "It's a fight we got down there—and we ain't in it!" He gave the other a staggering blow on the shoulder, shoving him toward his horse. "Now get in that saddle!"

Trooper Swenson stumbled to obey. Colbrook had picked up his hat and was dragging it on as he ran for his own mount: the saber scabbard banged empty against his leg, but he wasted no time looking for the weapon. He leaped to the saddle, got his mount straightened around, and headed him downhill at the gallop; and Tom Swenson spurred hard after.

They broke through the last of the trees, and, enclosed by a neighboring ridge, a sheltered pocket of grass stretched before them. It was brown with autumn, and beyond was the yellow slash of cottonwood and alder that marked the flashing course of a stream. Yonder, too, Trooper Swenson glimpsed a dark mass he knew must be the livestock they'd been sent to recover—though it looked to him like considerably more than thirty head. At the moment that wasn't important, for immediately below them and to their left, where the timbered ridges pinched together, he looked upon the confusion and dust and drifting smoke of a gunfight.

Towed blindly after Sergeant Colbrook's mount, as though at the end of a line, he stared appalled at the first thing of this kind he had ever actually seen.

Plainly it was no mere handful of Indians they had been chasing but a good-sized, stock-raiding sweep through these hills along the John Day; and now the bunch who attacked the prospectors at Wilson Creek had led them straight into the main body. They had laid their trap at the point where the ridges narrowed in, digging their fire pits and screening them with brush. But the captain, having guessed their intention, had made the daring decision to spring the ambush with half his force while the rest came in to take it by surprise.

The second squad, veterans that they were, didn't seem to need orders to tell them what had to be done. Even now they were bursting out of the trees and driving straight in without slackening pace. They ran right over the fire pits, killing some of the Snake warriors where they lay and flushing the rest like quail into the open. After that it was a melee of milling horses, half-naked Indians, and men in Army blue. Men yelled and horses screamed; pistol and rifle fire rattled echoes off the near ridges. Somewhere E Company's trumpet was squalling. And Trooper Swenson's throat locked tight as he followed his sergeant into that.

Too much was happening at once for him to grasp. He glimpsed Colbrook maneuvering his horse with the skill of an expert, throwing his pistol over to fire at any target that came his way. A riderless cavalry mount collided with Swenson's, made it squeal with terror as it scrambled for footing. He felt something cushion his mount's hoofs briefly, wouldn't let himself look down to see what it was.

Suddenly a bronzed shape flung itself at him, clawing for the reins. Trooper Swenson found his carbine in his hand without knowing how it got there, and frantically he drove its stock twice, with all his strength, into the upturned face. The buttplate smashed home; he felt the crunch of bone and a pulpy yielding. He had a glimpse of spurting blood, and his stomach churned as the hands slid away and the man dropped back.

Dust and smoke were blinding, and noise split his ears. He plunged blindly on, hunting a target. Out of the streaking pall of dust he saw a ghostlike shape resolve itself into Colbrook, still mounted but with hat gone and a smear of powdersmoke across one cheek. As Trooper Swenson spurred toward him, a second horseman loomed blackly—a nearly naked figure in buckskin leggings, clinging to a saddleless horse; the dark face was smeared with paint and sweat, the braided hair as black and straight as a horse's mane.

A rifle spoke into the uproar—it sounded like a repeater, a newer and better weapon than any of the carbines carried by the

Volunteers. Swenson saw the blast of muzzle flame, and suddenly Sergeant Colbrook's horse was crashing under him, so solidly that it must have been dead before it left its feet.

Colbrook lit rolling, thrown free of the animal's dead weight but obviously stunned. Perhaps the Indian had seen the stripes on the sergeant's tunic; he held his wild-eyed pony on a tight rawhide rein so that it danced in a complete circle and brought him back again to the white man sprawled helpless in the dirt. The rifle, held like a lance, tilted down, and the muzzle probed at Colbrook's chest for a shot to finish him.

Then Trooper Swenson, who was yet to fire the carbine in his hand, broke out of his lethargy. Scarcely thinking, he dropped the carbine's barrel across the arm that held the reins and, steadying it there, sought a point on the Indian's naked chest and triggered. He wasn't braced for the shot, and the shock of it all but unseated him and nearly tore the weapon from his grasp. The film of muzzle smoke swept into his face and choked him. But when it cleared, the painted face and naked body of the warrior had vanished. Swenson saw the Indian pony galloping away, already swallowed up in the drifting fog of battle.

Still dazed, Swenson looked for the sergeant.

Colbrook couldn't have been badly hurt, for already he was trying to pull himself to his feet. Reining over, Trooper Swenson reached him the barrel of the carbine; the sergeant groped for it, and Swenson hauled him easily off the ground. The noncom had an odd look on his face as, leaning nearer, the boy heard him say gruffly, "I guess I have to thank you. Another second and he'd of done for me. . . ."

Tom Swenson managed an angry retort. "Don't get any wrong ideas! Far as I'm concerned you weren't wearing your stripes that time either."

Yet he knew he would never forget the look the other gave him.

There was a strange stillness, now the fighting was done. The Indians who hadn't died when their position was overrun had been beaten and scattered, leaving upward of a hundred head of raided stock behind; but it had been done at a cost. Now E Company was licking its hurts—tallying the dead, caring for the wounded. One of the dead was Trooper O'Mara, who would never get his discharge from the Volunteers after all.

Forgotten for the moment, Trooper Swenson was standing off by himself, trying to absorb all he had seen and been through, when he heard a step and a voice that tightened his nerves and quickly put him on the defensive. He whirled as Sergeant Colbrook came to a glowering stand, arms akimbo. "*Now* what are you doing?"

"Nothin'," the young man blurted, and then defiance made him add, "Not a damn thing. Just waiting for orders—and enjoying the scenery."

Colbrook's stare moved past him to the little valley that was a bowl of golden light in this hour before the settling of the sun. His next words were a surprise. "Kind of nice, ain't it?"

Trooper Swenson completely forgot what he might have said—about the bodies of men and horses that fouled the grass, the blood that soaked it. He could only nod slowly. "Never seen a better piece of farmland. Matter of fact, I was just thinking it looked almost as though somebody had tried to work it one time or another."

The sergeant put a searching look on him. He said suddenly, "Come here. I want to show you something I found."

He turned and walked away toward the tree-lined creek. A little puzzled, the boy followed. He pushed through new growth of alder bushes, halted on the creekbank, and looked around him. Trees had been taken out here; there were the stumps of them, and there were the signs of cultivation, partly reclaimed by rank growth.

A step farther, he cleared the brush and there joined the sergeant in staring at the charred logs and litter that once had been a cabin but now was only a scar of ugliness, not yet grassed over. Wordlessly, Colbrook pointed with one boot toe. Trooper Swenson looked, saw the sunken mound of earth and the wooden plank that was starting to sag sideward. He moved closer and made out the letters crudely carved with a knifepoint: "My dear wife JENNY, kilt this day by Indians March 9, 1862."

Slowly he straightened, sickened and shaken more than he would have believed. He turned on the sergeant; his hands were clenched as he cried tightly, "Damn you! Why'd you have to go and show me this?"

The pale eyes skewered him. "Why? Because I thought it might give you something else to think about besides how much you hate the Army. . . . Just lemme ask you, trooper: Do you expect anything *else* in this world to be perfect?"

Swenson stammered a little. The sergeant didn't wait for his answer.

"Well, neither is the Army! The job we done here today was a real good piece of work: The captain, he used his head, and he outthought them devils, and we outfought 'em even if we did lose six good men. We got back the stock we was sent after, and a sight more besides. But do you think anything will come of it, except maybe a couple paragraphs in a field report?"

He snorted. "Look what's happening back there in Virginia! The privates and the noncoms and the field officers licked Bob Lee at Antietam, and McClellan threw it all away. They done it again at Gettysburg—whipped Lee clean to the socks—and then Meade let him escape with his whole damned army, and the war goes on. Right now Grant says he's headed for Richmond. Maybe he'll even get there. But like as not, after all the sacrifices his men are making, he'll take and let the victory slide right through his hands again!

"The chain of command, they call it. At the top are the generals, and the lousy politicians who should never have let this war build up in the first place. Yeah—and the damn civilians that only care about their own easy lives and their profits! And down here at the bottom, you and me and the captain do the fighting, and if we die, maybe our dying will even buy something. Like maybe some general gets him an extra star on his shoulder straps. . . ."

Trooper Swenson could contain himself no longer. "That being how you feel, why the hell have you stayed with it for twenty years?"

"Damn it, that's what I'm trying to tell you! Aside from the fact I happen to like this Army—which I'd never expect *you* to understand!—there's a lot of jobs only the Army can do." Colbrook indicated the heap of ashes and the grave. "If this Oregon's to be tamed so a fellow like that can plow his fields and raise his family, he'll never do it alone; it's up to us. And guys just like us, spilling out their guts on Virginia soil, will finally win *that* war, too, and then we'll have a country again—until the ones up top blunder us into another mess and we have to pull it out for them. It's bound to happen. It always has!

"And what of it? *Somebody* has to pay the price because the world ain't perfect. This happens to be our turn. . . ." The sergeant broke off talking. "Oh hell!" he muttered. "I'd never in a million years make you see what I'm getting at. I dunno why I try!"

He swung away and pointed toward the creek and the timber ridge beyond. "Another ravine, yonder, leads to the river. From there you should be able to find your way to the gold camps—even make it back to the Columbia and Portland if you're lucky. Don't worry—I ain't gonna stop you. I won't turn in the alarm before you've had a chance at a start. But remember, this outfit ain't easy on deserters if it catches them!" He hesitated, nodded curtly. "Good luck!" he added, and turned and walked away.

Trooper Swenson stared after him. He looked at the timber beyond the chuckling run of the creek. His horse stood handy; there were rations on his saddle. He could probably make it.

He took a long breath. He lifted his voice.

"Hey, Sarge! Wait up!"

Colbrook, halting, watched the young fellow coming after him. Slowly something that was almost like a parody of a grin began to split the homely face. Sergeant Colbrook turned his head aside to loose a mahogany stream of tobacco juice between strong, yellow teeth.

"All right—trooper!" he said in a voice that would never lose any shade of its gruffness. "Damned outfit won't wait all day for us. Let's go!"

This lusty, good-humored tale of the Seattle waterfront in the summer of 1896 is typical of the work of James Stevens (1892–1971), who knew intimately and from firsthand experience the history, people, and locales of the Pacific Northwest. For many years he was head of public relations for the old West Coast Lumberman's Association, a trade organization once among the most powerful in the world, but still found time to write both fiction and nonfiction as well as a newspaper column called "Out of the Woods." He was the author of the first and most famous book-length version of that "Big Woods" legend, Paul Bunyan (1925); two northwestern novels, Brawnyman (1926) and Big Jim Turner (1948); and many short stories set in Oregon and Washington, some of the best of which can be found in his 1928 collection, Homer in the Sagebrush.

Ike the Diver's Friend

★★★★★★★★★★★★

James Stevens

I

THE plank sidewalks were jammed with people who were out to enjoy the illuminated bicycle parade, the climax of Seattle's mammoth celebration of the Fourth of July. The bicyclists, men and women, boys and girls, some three thousand in number, pedaled in wide ranks down the city's main avenue, the wheel spokes flashing from the colored lights that shone in the fir bough arches fastened to the seats and curving over the riders' heads. The crowds on the sidewalks shrieked and cheered.

Edward Matthews, Esquire, still salty and rope-scarred from an enforced voyage from Liverpool and around the Horn, watched the parade with a severely critical eye. At last his throat swelled unbearably with censorious words. Utterance became a necessity. He turned to his left-hand neighbor, a tall, lean, stooped, broad-backed man who gazed down at him with mild, pale-blue eyes as he spoke. Said Edward Matthews, Esquire:

"It's perty enough, I'll s'y that. But you 'aven't the genooine science of cyclin' over 'ere at all. 'Oo in the paryde 'as the correct' poscher, I arsk you now? They 'ump theirselves like they was blinkin' rycers. It's the fault of their trynin'. They've never learnt the correc' cyclin' form, y'see. Scorchin', scorchin' is all yer blasted Yank cyclists think of. Now, you arsk me, I'll tell you wot's wot about the science of cyclin'. It's this w'y."

So Edward Matthews, Esquire, gabbled on about the science of cycling until the parade was over. The other man looked mildly down at him and never said a word. Then Edward Matthews, Esquire, remembered he was hungry. This big man who had listened to him with such attention must be liberal and kind. He'd try him out.

"I s'y, ol' cull, I'm a bit dry. 'Ungry, too. 'Ad a blinkin' lot of 'ard luck. Shanghaied out of Liverpool and 'ere just three d'ys. A strynger 'ere and I can't get work. On my uppers fer fair. Wot s'y you set 'em up? You do and I tell yer wot yer blarsted Fourth of July's all about. The American Rebellion, and all that."

The big man spoke for the first time, in a deep, flat voice.

"You'll have to write 'er, friend. I'm deefer'n hell!"

For a minute Edward Matthews, Esquire, was knocked cold. But only for a minute. His throat was parched, his insides were lank, and the big stranger still looked kind. Edward Matthews, Esquire, made the motion of hoisting a drink to his mouth. The deaf man grinned.

"Throat's itchin', is she? Let's drift into Ole's."

He pushed through the crowd, and the little hungry man followed. There was no more gabbing until three schooners of beer and some fistfuls of rye bread, cheese, and bologna were downed. Then words began to throb in his tongue. He hated to waste them on a deaf man. The born talker was puzzled. A kind, liberal man stood beside him. A good-natured giant kind of a man. A man worth having for a friend. A man who was anxious to have his mind improved by fair and reasonable words. But a man without ears to hear. That was the blinkin' trouble. Then the deaf man solved the problem himself.

"Have another, mate," his flat voice boomed. "Have another and go after the free lunch much as you want. You seem like a pore, starved critter. You go on and talk some more, though. I like to be talked to. Nobody will hardly ever do it, for I'm deefer'n hell. I ruint my ears at deep-sea divin'. I'm longshorin' now. The boys on the beach call me Ike the Diver. I'm deaf, but you go ahead and talk. You're a born talker, I see. I've took a likin' to you. Don't know your name, so I'll call you Mouthy. Have another beer, Mouthy, then you talk."

This seemed to be a mighty long speech for Ike the Diver, as it made him sweat. Edward Matthews, Esquire, didn't need a second invitation; he started right in and he talked and grabbed until a stuffing of beer, free lunch, and hoarseness laid him out. Ike the Diver hadn't said another word but kept his pale-blue eyes smiling on "Mouthy." Now he carried his new friend down to his tideflat shack. In the morning Edward Matthews, Esquire, was awakened by the sweet smell of frying bacon and steaming coffee. He sat up in his blankets, and his tongue started to rattle. Ike the Diver smiled and nodded his head.

"Talk some more, Mouthy," he said. "Mouthy, you just keep on talkin'."

That was how the strange pair got to be friends. Before long their friendship was famous all along the Seattle beach.

II

Edward Matthews, Esquire, would have had a tough time of it in Seattle that summer of 1896 if it hadn't been for Ike the Diver. Seattle then was only a sawmill town and lumber port. There had been a big fire in '89, but the place had grown again from the labor of men driving dock piling; logging the big timber; sawing lumber and stowing it in the holds and stacking it on the decks of ocean freighters; mining coal; and building houses and stores until the town was growing all over the clearings between the timbered hills that circled Elliot Bay. In August '96, George Cormack was finding gold in the dirt of Bonanza Creek up in the Klondike territory, but the news was eleven months away. The people of Seattle were still only doing their work around the town. They never dreamed that in another year the town would be booming into a city, and all because the whole country was in a fever over the news of frozen Northern gold.

It was a lean year for workingmen. The waterfront saloons along Railroad Avenue had more penniless men lounging around them than they had customers. Whenever a ship tied up at one of the docks, the chief stevedore picked his men at the pier shed gate. The saloons were always emptied then, and the longshoremen made a yelling, milling mob at the gate; leg-aprons buckled around their waists and knees, wooden-handled iron hooks swinging from their belts. The boss stevedore picked his favorites. The lucky ones were formed into gangs of hatchmen, slingmen, and truckers. The discharged cargoes were barrels, bales, and cases of dry goods and groceries, crates of machinery and furniture, sacks of vegetables, tubs of butter, casks of wine, and kegs of beer. In the empty holds were stowed cargoes of lumber and coal. Long-shoring was grinding labor in '96. There were twenty-hour shifts.

If there was a rush to get a cargo stowed, the longshoremen were held to the hatches and slings for a straight ten hours. No time off for lunch. No blowing spells. Let a man kick and he was shoved off the dock and a tougher one was picked at the gate. Stowing green lumber would exhaust a man with the back of a mule. Stacks of rough green timbers and boards ten feet high on the dock floor. Heave the lumber off the stack. Pile it on the sling till a load was made. Straighten up for the ten seconds it took the winch-driver to hoist the load head-high. Then bend over and heave lumber till another sling was filled.

That was the work of the men on the sling gangs.

Down in the holds the hatch gangs sweated in half-darkness, dragging the lumber into place, binding each board and timber so that the cargo would not shift in the roughest sea. It was labor for broad-beamed men like Ike the Diver. Edward Matthews, Esquire, might have been a first-rate handler of light cargo on the wharves of Liverpool, as he claimed, but the boss stevedores turned him down on the Seattle docks.

"Avast. You're no good for this lumber cargo. All right, Ike, you deef Siwash. All right for you, Ike."

That was it, nearly every time.

Edward Matthews, Esquire, never allowed himself to grow resentful and bitter over the treatment he had from the boss stevedores. Whenever there were enough ships in port for him to be picked at the gate, he showed there were no hard feelings by telling the walking-boss all the details of the superior style of Liverpool longshoring, telling it on even after he was asked to shut up. When he was turned down he was never bitter and resentful but only philosophical. He would philosophize to the general public in Pat Noonan's saloon, he would philosophize to himself as he tidied up the tideflat shack, and he would philosophize to Ike the Diver when his friend dragged in, half-dead from rassling green lumber. This was how he put it up to Ike one early winter night, after he'd sliced the bacon and had it sizzling on the stove.

"It's perty orful, Ike, ol' man; it's orful and sickenin' for a civilized chap like me to 'ave been lugged orf like a dead cow and berried in a blinkin' 'ole like this 'ere. I feel sometimes like I'd lose all my sperit, I do. 'Ere I am, Edward Matthews, Esquire, of Liverpool, England, and I 'ave to stoop and truckle to the boss stevedores of a mud 'ole of a port like this 'ere one. Berried to my eyes in it, I am. A pearl 'as been cast before swine, if I do s'y it myself. All they can s'y is, 'Cast orf! Avast, you blighter!' And me knowin' more about stowin' cargo than the 'ole blarsted lot of 'em. If it wasn't for you, Ike, ol' man, I'd starve, s'elp me! Much they'd care. Well, I'm wytin' and wytin'. I'm a patient philersophical man, I am. That's Edward Matthews, Esquire, of Liverpool, England. My time'll come, says I. 'Be a philoserpher, Edward,' I always says to me when the boss stevedores turn me down at the gate. And I always am. My time'll come, Ike, ol' man. And when I'm a boss stevedore myself, or a wharfinger, more likely, if I get a bit more of ejucation, I won't be forgettin' yer friendship. You don't know 'ow you've comforted this pore exile, Ike—"

"Hey, Mouthy, the bacon's burnin'!" bawled Ike the Diver, rising on his bunk until he rested on his elbows. "Go on talkin', Mouthy, but turn over the bacon!"

The philosopher had been tapping his left palm with a fork as he talked. Now he turned and jabbed the bacon in such a hurry that he splattered sizzling grease on his bare arm.

" 'Ow!" he yelped. " 'Ell!"

The burns hurt, and he only swore about them to himself while he stirred the frying potatoes, threw a dash of cold water into the pot to settle the coffee, and sliced some bread on the scarred oilcloth of the homemade table.

"Hurry up with them spuds and bacon, Mouthy!" boomed Ike the Diver. "I'm so hungry I could eat the tar off a rope! Get the grub on the table, then talk all you want. Get the grub on first, though, Mouthy!"

"In a jiff, Ike ol' man. In a jiff. Yer ol' woman'll soon have yer supper fixed. A bit of patience, Ike ol' man."

It was a good meal, and Ike the Diver's pale-blue eyes beamed as he scooped down the bacon and potatoes and watched his friend talk. Nothing he enjoyed better than seeing Mouthy talk. He liked to watch the lights change in the wide, solemn gray eyes, the liveliness of the wrinkles above the working jaws, the sober downturning at the corners of the mouth under the thin, drooping mustache. Ike couldn't understand what the talk was about, but then he couldn't remember any talk in the days before he was deaf that had been particularly worth understanding. Mouthy sat and talked and the tideflat shack wasn't so lonesome any more . . . But he was tired. . . . Twenty hours of heaving lumber.

"Got to roll in, Mouthy. Like yer talkin' but I got to roll in."

III

That was it with Edward Matthews, Esquire, and Ike the Diver, nearly every night. Their friendship grew stronger as the winter months passed. For four months the little Englishman failed to be picked at the gate for ships that steamed and sailed through the winter fog of Puget Sound for Seattle docks. But Ike was often picked, and he kept grub in the tideflat shack. Every kind of work was scarce, and Pat Noonan's and the other saloons along Railroad Avenue were packed with idle men. Below Yesler Way loggers and sawmill hands in pitch-stained overalls, mackinaws, and ducking coats loafed in joints like Billy the Mug's or in the lobbies of flophouses and stared through the windows at dray teams plodding through the everlasting rain.

By the middle of December the news of George Cormack's strike on Bonanza Creek had reached Circle City and Forty Mile. But Alaskan news was still ice-bound, and Seattle never heard it. She was still just a working coast town, building up on lumber and coal.

Spring days and work opened up. Loggers and other working stiffs drifted to the woods, the mines, and the mills. Fishermen sailed the sound again. Hatch gangs, sling gangs, and truckers were busy along the beach. Edward Matthews, Esquire, was picked at the gate twice in ten days. He made fifty dollars, and he bought two slabs of bacon and a sack of potatoes for the tideflat shack. And he gave good old Ike a royal night of it. For the first time he was the one who bought all the beer over Pat Noonan's bar, the one who led the way below Yesler, took a whirl at the games in the Standard Gambling Hall, and paid for performances in the Paris House.

All the while they were blowing in Edward Matthews, Esquire, philosophized. And he allowed himself a few dreams. The boss stevedores were learning at last what a man he was. His time was at hand. He'd be a walking boss himself in a short while. Then he'd prove that what he was doing to-night for good old Ike was nothing at all. Nothing at all.

"You're talkin' good, Mouthy," Ike the Diver said again and again. "Mouthy, you just keep on talkin'."

Edward Matthews, Esquire, felt sore and heavy in his head the next morning. His stomach didn't feel exactly right, either. And he seemed to have a poor hold on his philosophy. He was silent at least half the time as he and Ike tramped up to Pat Noonan's and waited with other longshoremen for a boat. There was no

work that day or the next. It was another slack spell on the Seattle
beach. It lasted until the *Portland* steamed down from Alaska with
a load of wild-eyed miners and a ton of gold dust from the Klondike. Then Seattle began to boom and roar. Every man was thrown
into a fever by the marvelous gold stories of the miners. Every man
except Edward Matthews, Esquire. He philosophized louder than
ever; he got so interested in telling everybody about the folly of
mankind in going crazy over gold that he couldn't work a ship.
Nobody would listen to him. The boss stevedores fired him off the
docks because, as he told Ike, he was talking too much common
sense to the longshoremen. But Ike the Diver wasn't watching him
much of evenings now, for he was always reading the newspapers
when he came off shift.

IV

One sunny afternoon Edward Matthews, Esquire, was sitting on
a beer keg in the deserted barroom at Pat Noonan's, philosophizing to himself about the folly of poor, blind humanity. All fair in-
sane about the Klondike. All mad with a fever for the yellow dust
of gold. Folly! Folly! Any thinking man would know that the rich
big bugs would flock up to the Klondike now with their lawyers
and hog everything. The poor should stay where they belonged.
The poor should be made to see. But they wouldn't listen to fair
and reasonable words. It was a mad, foolish world. Edward Matthews, Esquire, kicked the beer keg with his heel and hummed:

"It's the rich gets all the gryvy;
  It's the pore that gets the blyme!"

But the poor helped the poor anyway. Good old Ike. Their
friendship was fair beautiful, it was. The rich big bugs could hog
it all they pleased but they couldn't touch the friendships of the
poor. . . .

His philosophizing was broken up by the roaring voice of Hooks
Bartell, boss stevedore of the Sound Steamship Company.

"What the hell you know about it?" growled Hooks to Pat Noonan. "What you know about it, Pat? These longshoremen's been
starvin' for four years, but now they's plenty of ships and good
cargo they're all achin' to hang up their hooks and hit for the gold
cricks. How many's bought passage on the *Alki* and the *Portland*
I don't know. Hope they all rot with the scurvy. Grief ahead, you

bet! All the good boys pullin' off the beach and the wharf rats that'll take their places'll make it lousy as Liverpool."

Edward Matthews, Esquire, slid off his beer keg and made for Hooks Bartell like a bantam rooster flying at a bulldog.

"S'y, big feller, wot's the matter of Liverpool, I'd like to know? Wot you got to s'y agin Liverpool, you big stiff? Wot the blinkin' 'ell do you know about Liverpool anyw'y, I'm arskin' yer? Well, stand and stare when I arsks you a civil question, you 'ook-eyed blighter!"

"Do you want a drink?" asked Hooks Bartell calmly. "Have one. Anything you like. Only shut up."

"Talkin' about this beach gettin' lousy as Liverpool—w'y, you couldn't even dream about this beach bein' like Liverpool in any w'y, shype, or form! W'y not, you arsks me. And I tell you. Becorse this blinkin' ol' pill of a beach is such a blighted little ol' pill of a beach it couldn't even *smell* like Liverpool! Now, mytey, yer arskin' me something about Liverpool, w'y, I'll tell yer something about Liverpool, in fair and reasonable words. It's this w'y—"

"Oh, shut your jaw!" bawled Hooks Bartell. "Shut up or I *will* amputate that jaw of yourn, as I've threatened time and again! Here, Pat, give him a scoop of suds. No such luck as this dock rat hittin' for the Klondike and freezin' his vokel cords or his jaw-bone—"

"Me? You arsk if I'm goin' in this blinkin' ijiotic gold rush? Me—gorblimeny, you arsk me if me, Edward Matthews, Esquire—"

"Get away from me!" yelled the tormented boss stevedore. "I'll have you shanghaied, damn' if I don't! Cast off! Avast, you mouthy hellion!"

Edward Matthews, Esquire, resigned closed his mouth before a shaking hairy fist. It was always like that, he thought, as he drained the roomy scoop. They would never listen to him, the chief stevedores wouldn't. But he was patient and meek. Waiting for his time to come.

He returned to his beer keg, went to philosophizing to himself again, and shut his ears to the talk of the ignorant boss stevedore until he heard Ike the Diver mentioned by name. . . . "Yeah, he's just another of the good boys that's hangin' up their hooks. Walked off the beach not an hour ago and booked passage on the *Portland*. Hell's bells, Pat, I'll have to stay full of redeye all the time or else take out for the Klondike myself. . . ."

Edward Matthews, Esquire, started to get up and tell the boss stevedore he was a blinkin' liar, that he showed just how much a boss stevedore on this beach knowed when he made a statement like that about Ike the Diver. But he sat down again. He remembered how Ike had been reading the papers since the *Portland* reached Seattle. Never watching him any more while he talked. Ike was only a poor simple soul—and even the mayor of the city had resigned his office and was joining the rush. It was likely true. Ike the Diver was going to the Klondike! The first real friend he'd ever had! It was shocking, that's what it was.

"Gorblimey!" groaned Edward Matthews, Esquire. A black cloud settled over his mind, making life seem foolish and foul. "Gorblimey, it's a rotten ol' lay agin. I feel like I could bawl. Ow! 'Ell!"

The boss stevedore went on talking to Pat Noonan.

"Pour me another snifter, old settler. . . . Hear about 'em drydockin' and paintin' the *Eliza Anderson*? Oldest sidewheeler on the sound. Been laid up for five years with the tides runnin' through her. I was down to the drydock, and I could jab my fingers into her side anywhere below the waterline. She'll prob'ly drown a hundred on her first try for St. Michaels. Well, it's not my funer'l. I'm stowin' cargo."

Edward Matthews, Esquire, wanted to tell the real facts about the outfitting of rotten ships for Alaska but he was too downhearted. His philosophy was all gone. He could only think about Ike the Diver, and sit, and groan:

"Ow! 'E's leavin' me. Only friend I ever 'ad. 'Ell!"

V

The next afternoon it seemed like all of Seattle was on the waterfront. Edward Matthews, Esquire, and Ike the Diver stood on the Schwabacher Dock, a mad crowd milling around them. The *Portland* had steam up. The rattling winches were lowering the last of the Klondike outfits into the hold. A line of men was pushing up the gangplank; the decks were already alive with faces and loud with shouts. Ike the Diver stuck out his paw, his pale-blue eyes got their friendliest shine, and the two friends had a long, solemn handshake. Edward Matthews, Esquire, felt his throat choke up and his mouth turn dry. His eyes were wet. He couldn't say a word, not one blinkin' word; he could only look up into the gaunt, wrinkled, good-natured face of old Ike and think of all the grief that was ahead. But there was nothing he could say or do about it.

Last night, when the two were alone in the tideflat shack, he had tried to write a philosophical warning that would wean old Ike away from folly. But his pencil could never throb out the words like his tongue could. It hadn't been any use. it wasn't now. Here in this drowsy sunlight, with the waters of the sound smooth and shining, with the city so peaceful on her green hills, it was easy for unthinking men to see treasure for the digging at the end of an ocean and river steamboat run. A philosopher like himself could see all the hardships and dangers of cold and starvation, scurvy and fever, and the greed and power of the rich big bugs and their lawyers. But it was too late for philosophy now. Gold! Gold! Gold! The *Portland* had brought down a ton of it. Men were mad to get to the Klondike territory . Poor old Ike no less than the others.

The handshake was ended.

"So long, Mouthy. You stick to the shack and whenever you feel downhearted you just start talkin'. Talk about the times we'll have when I come down with a ton of dust. So long, Mouthy."

Ike the Diver was gone, tramping up the gangplank.

Edward Matthews, Esquire, hadn't been able to say a word of farewell, though many words were throbbing in his head. It was no use to try to say them. Ike the Diver was mad with the blasted gold fever. He was going. For how long? Forever, most likely. . . . The *Portland*'s whistle boomed, and the steamship moved away from the dock piling. The crowd whooped and cheered. An answering cheer thundered from the decks. The smoke from the steamship's stacks rolled blackly against the blue of the sky. Her wake boiled and foamed. Rowboats and small sailing craft rocked over her waves as she swung out into Elliott Bay. The faces on her decks became splotches of white. The cheers sounded faint and far. The crowd on the waterfront was silent as the *Portland* turned into a fading black smudge at Three Mile Point. She was gone. Husbands, brothers, and sons were gone—and friends, thought Edward Matthews, Esquire. . . .

"Yeah, you'll do for a hatch gang this ship," growled Hooks Bartell from the gate of the Sound Steamship Company. "But keep your trap shut or you'll cast off. Well, step along! Avast, Swanson, you're oary-eyed. All right for you when you sober up. Step along. . . ."

Edward Matthews, Esquire, was longshoring alone on the Seattle beach.

VI

There were plenty of ships at the Seattle docks in the summer days. The *Excelsior, Capilano, Alki, Mexico, Queen, Hueneme, City of Topeka, George W. Elder, Roanoake, Islander, Cleveland, Rosalie, Ohio, Willamette, Humboldt*, steamships and schooners, all that would float, were loaded with passengers and freight for Alaska, the Yukon, the Klondike. River steamers and monster scows were towed behind the ships. So Edward Matthews, Esquire, made the hatch gangs all summer long. The Klondike cargoes were like the light stuff he'd handled in Liverpool. Longshoring now wasn't the back-breaking, strong-arm labor of stowing rough green lumber. Down to the docks the drays carted crates of bacon, barrels of flour, boxes of evaporated fruit and vegetables, sacks of corn meal, rice, coffee, and beans, bales and cases of corduroys, rubber boots, hobnail shoes, wool socks, mittens and gloves, suits of heavy underclothes and mackinaws, hats and caps, blankets and fur coats, bundles of picks and shovels, axes and saws, stacks of gold pans, rolls of tarpaulins, kegs of whiskey, wine, beer, and nails.

He knew the stowing of such cargo, did Edward Matthews, Esquire. His philosophy bloomed again. His faith in himself got big once more. Until the winter days were on again he saw a boss stevedore's job always within his reach. If he had kept his hope to himself and only dreamed about it as he did when he was in the tideflat shack, the hope might have been realized that year. There at his lonely meals he saw Ike the Diver coming off an Alaskan ship next year; ragged, hungry, half-dead; greeted by a boss stevedore, greeted by Edward Matthews, Esquire, risen in the world but still loyal and true, offering his old friend a soft checker's job— oh, it was fair wonderful, that dream!

But Edward Matthews, Esquire, was bound to tell his hopes and dreams all along the beach, in the holds, and at Pat Noonan's. No one would listen, and some, especially the boss stevedores, would threaten to amputate his jaw and slit his tongue. That was how much sympathy and understanding there was in this blinking pill of a port.

"If you know so much about stowin' cargo, try to show us with something else besides your jaw!" Hooks Bartell, that ignoramus, would yell. "All I've ever seen your mouth do is to hold up a ship. Fall to or cast off!"

Thus unappreciated, Edward Matthews, Esquire, was still being picked at the gate, a plain longshoreman, when the winter rain

and fog came to Puget Sound. Alaska shipping was stopped by
the Northern ice. Now it was lumber and coal cargoes again.
Never mind! The gold fever was still raging. By spring tens of
thousands would be flocking to Seattle from all over America to
go North on the first ships to sail. There would be more green
longshoremen on the beach. The old-timers who had not been
caught by the gold fever were stirred up now by the promise of
fifteen-dollar-a-day wages in the Klondike. Edward Matthews, Esquire, warned them. A meal up there cost a dollar and a half. A
pair of brogans cost a fortune. Whiskey was fifty cents a glass. Tobacco was out of sight. There was the scurvy and the Yukon fever.
He felt it was his duty to warn the old-time longshoremen who
were left. But if they did go in the spring, well, so much the better
for him.

Many of them did go on the first ships, and it was better for
him. Seattle boomed and roared more than ever when the passage
to Alaska was open again. Thousands swarmed First Avenue
night and day. Below Yesler Way the gamblers, pimps, and dance
hall girls coined gold. What's the use of carting money to Alaska?
That was everybody's cry. The city threw off her working clothes.
Seattle became a dance hall queen of a town; that was what she
was, a queen in a dancing skirt, with a red sash shining rakishly
over her white shoulder, a glass of wine sparkling in her jeweled
hand. The gold rush boomed and glittered its highest in the summer of '98 and Seattle got to be a regular dance hall queen of a
town. She was never to lose that beautiful and devilish young spirit
of hers.

Ships from the Alaska coast brought down more Klondike stories and more Klondike gold. In hotel lobbies, saloons, dance
halls, parlor houses, and gambling halls hot-eyed men chanted the
mighty story of the Yukon River, White Horse Rapids, Lake
Lindeman, Circle City, Forty Mile, Dawson, the Chilkoot Pass,
Skagway, and the gold-bottomed creeks—Indian, Dominion, Bonanza, Eldorado—trickles from the laboring old glaciers of the
North. They chanted and sang. Dirt piled up in the long, dark
hours of winter! Gold washed out in the light of the midnight sun!
Gold! Gold! Gold! Tons of yellow dust on every ship! Set us out
another snifter, bartender! All promenade to the bar! Yea, Bill,
we're on our way to the Klondike and her gold-bottomed creeks!
Gold! Gold! Gold. . . !

"It's no use talkin', I know," Edward Matthews, Esquire,
would declare in Pat Noonan's. "No use. But I feel it's my
bounden duty to call yer attention to the fac' that for every blighter
wot packs a full chammy skin poke down a gangplank they's

twenty be'ind 'im wot's ragged and 'arf-starved, scurvy-eaten and fever-blarsted, 'avin nothin' but their gladness to be 'ome. 'Ow about the Copper River district, I arsk you now? 'Ow about the pore devils starvin' up there? And 'ow about the big rich bugs in the Klondike? You 'ear 'ow they're 'oggin' it all, don't you, mytes? 'Oo can buck a feller like this McDonald—king of the Klondike, they calls 'im. The rich bugs 'ave their lawyers and their gangs. I prophesied 'ow it would be. I warned 'em. But it's no use of talkin'. I only 'opes I'll 'ave my boss stevedore's job afore good ol' Ike comes back. A wreck 'ee's sure to be. But I, Edward Matthews, Esquire, 'll tyke care of my friend and myke 'im 'earty and 'ole, a man in 'is right mind agin. 'Ee's all I'm wytin' for, is Ike the Diver. To 'ell with yer blinkin' gold!''

VII

On a day in July Edward Matthews, Esquire, was living the richest and fairest hour of his life. He was living it in Pat Noonan's saloon. In dignity and silence. Yes, sir, he was taking it blinkin' well, he thought, in exactly the proper spirit. His hopes had been realized, but he was still the philosopher and thus dignified and silent. To talk now would mean that he must boast and brag. He would not do it. He only nodded and smiled when Hooks Bartell shook his hand, ordered two mugs of beer, and lifted his own as boss stevedore to boss stevedore. For Edward Matthews, Esquire, was a boss stevedore at last. Thirty minutes ago the manager of the newly organized Far North Steamship Company, an Englishman who could appreciate a longshoreman from the Liverpool beach, had made his hopes come true. He was to begin his new duties to-morrow, he told Hooks Bartell with just the proper dignity.

To-morrow—now let Ike the Diver, good old Ike, come back. He would soon learn what a true and loyal friend he had. He should be cared for as he had cared for Edward Matthews, Esquire, the unfortunate exile. He should be shown that philosophy also had its rewards. He should be shown the folly of going mad over gold. But gently, calmly, with tact. Edward Matthews, Esquire, would never lord it over his good old friend. Ike the Diver should have a decent, easy job. One that would do for him as long as he lived. . . .

The pleasant dream was broken up by an excited bawl that sounded through the saloon door.

"The *Roanoake*'s dockin' at the Pacific Steamship wharf! Loaded with gold! Come on, mates!"

Edward Matthews, Esquire, followed the rushing mob with a dignified step. Seattle was emptying her uptown streets. People were running in droves down the hills and across Railroad Avenue. But Edward Matthews, Esquire, boss stevedore for the Far North Steamship Company, never hurried. Calmly and philosophically he watched the docking of the ship and heard the mad yells of the crowd. He watched the haggard, bearded miners coming down the gangplank with only sober pity in his eyes—until he saw shoulders that had a familiar stoop—a grizzled beard covered the miner's face—but there was no mistaking those pale-blue eyes. . . . "Ike, ol' man, Ike, ol' man! . . ."

"Hello, Mouthy. What's the matter? Ain't you still a-talkin'? How you been makin' it, Mouthy?"

Poor old Ike, all gaunted up and worn down, dressed in ragged coat and pants, rough-shod, not a total wreck as he'd feared, but in a bad shape, as anybody could see with half an eye. Edward Matthews, Esquire, felt his heart swell with pride. This was indeed his golden hour. Good old Ike—but he must let his friend know there was a good time ahead before he started talking. He had started a search for pencil and paper when he saw Ike opening the pockets of his mackinaw. They were crammed with greasy sacks.

"Thousands, Mouthy," said Ike. "I stagger when I carry 'em. We start out right now to paintin' the town, Mouthy—why, Mouthy, what's hurtin' you? Got a bellyache, Mouthy?"

For Edward Matthews, Esquire, had sat down suddenly on a pile of rope; and now he was bending over, holding his face in his hands and groaning.

" 'Ow! It's ever the w'y! 'Ell!"

Gold. Ruinous gold. It was ever a curse in the hands of a man like poor old Ike. It was shocking, horribly shocking, to find Ike a blinkin' Croesus. Staggering under a load of gold. Talking of painting the town first thing, of course. The beautiful plans were in ruins. Ike needed to be guided. He should not paint the town. Edward Matthews, Esquire, his true and loyal friend, would see to that. Ike should be guided and watched, made to keep enough of his gold for a fair living in his old age. He would be hard to manage. But it must be tried. No use to think of the chief stevedore's job now. That would have to be sacrificed. His duty was with Ike. How would he start to guiding, watching, and managing him? He couldn't think just now. Not after such a shocking blow. Poor old Ike a blinkin' Croesus! The plans were in ruins—ow, but his mind was in *such* a blasted stew—

"Come on to the Rainier Grand Hotel, Mouthy," said Ike the

Diver. "We're goin' to get us some swallertails and plug hats, and then we're goin' to start paintin' the town, Mouthy."

"Ow!" groaned Edward Matthews, Esquire, as he got to his feet. "I must think and think. Wot to do? Wot is a philosopher to do with sacks of gold? 'Ell! To 'ave all my 'opes end this w'y! Ain't it a blinkin' shyme?"

The philosophy of Edward Matthews, Esquire, never had a chance against Ike the Diver's gold. It was shaken as soon as the pair entered the gilded lobby of the hotel. The plush and draperies in their magnificent bedroom brought philosophy down. The plug hats and swallowtails smothered it. Its lifeless form was washed away as the champagne flowed.

"We'll start at the Horseshoe, Mouthy," announced Ike the Diver when the two were in their plug hats and swallowtails. "I've always wanted to make a splash in the Horseshoe, Mouthy."

VIII

The Horseshoe was a beautiful uptown saloon with solid mahogany fixtures. Its mirrors were French plate glass. The fixtures had taken the grand prize at the Philadelphia world's fair back in '76. A solid silver horseshoe, with nails, toe, and heel calks of solid gold, shone in the middle of the bar. The great mirror was fenced by little mirrors in horseshoe frames. Bottles with rainbow labels were stacked between polished mahogany columns. Mountains of crystal glasses sparkled and flashed from snowy beds of linen. The floor was the finest colored tile. The brass footrail was polished every hour. There was a great safe built like a vault, with deposit boxes where the Klondikers could safely store their dust.

Ike the Diver tramped to the bar of the Horseshoe, deposited his gold, and ordered champagne for the house. And the story told by Edward Matthews, Esquire, about his friend's great strike in the Klondike was listened to by men whose white fingers sparkled with diamonds.

Philosophy was all forgotten. The Standard Gambling Hall, with its twenty-five games of faro, roulette, chuckluck, fantan, blackjack, and poker, knew the pair on their first night of painting the town, and on many other nights. Ike the Diver bucked the wheel, and when he lost, Edward Matthews, Esquire, told the rubberers how his friend could lose a thousand times as much and never miss it. He was listened to with respect now, for he wore a swallowtail and a plug hat and he was the partner of a Klondike man. He read his name in the newspapers, saw a description of

himself in print. The painted ladies of the dance halls and parlor
houses were enchanted by his society conversation and listened
humbly when he moralized about their life.

Aye, it was fair glorious, it was. How was a man to think, how
was he to keep his philosophy, how was he to remember that it
was his duty to guide his friend and watch over him, when he was
enjoying such glory, wearing a plug hat and swallowtail, drinking
champagne, being admired by the ladies and by sports who wore
diamonds, and, best of all, being listened to whenever he talked?
How was he now? Remember the bitter life he'd always had. And
now it was fair heaven, it was. He'd philosophize with Ike the
Diver soon enough. Show him he should have something for his
old age. There were pounds and pounds of gold dust left. Thousands of dollars. A few would be enough.

The best of all was down at Pat Noonan's. The famous pair
nearly wrecked the waterfront when they got all the longshoremen
of the beach jammed into Pat's place. Ike the Diver bought so lib-
erally that Pat had to hire three extra bartenders. And at last he
had to send to the wholesale house for a load of champagne.

"We'll buy our old mates nothin' but champagne, hey,
Mouthy?" said Ike the Diver.

Edward Matthews, Esquire, solemnly nodded agreement. It
was nothing but right. Give the poor some of the rich big bugs'
fine fun when there was a chance, he said. He talked without a
break for a full two hours; for every time Ike the Diver ordered
another round of champagne, he would say:

"It's good to see you talkin' again, Mouthy. You just keep on
talkin'."

And the longshoremen harkened—they who had scorned him
so before! Aye, it was fair glorious, it was!

The two friends painted the town for a week—two weeks—a
month—two months—and at the end of October the owner of the
Horseshoe showed Ike the Diver an empty deposit box. Ike
blinked his pale-blue eyes for a moment, then he grinned down
at his friend.

"Looks like we'll have to take the old hooks down again,
Mouthy. Guess we'll have to trade our plug hats and swallertails
for mackinaws and overalls, Mouthy!"

Edward Matthews, Esquire, had nothing to say. He was
knocked cold. He'd thought there were thousands there yet. It was
shocking, simply horribly shocking. Broke! Ike the Diver was a
poor man again! Not a blinkin' cent left to protect him in his old
age. And it was all the fault of Edward Matthews, Esquire. Just
when he had needed it most, he had let his philosophy go. Ow!

"Well, Mouthy, we've had a high and hellin' old time of 'er any-way," said Ike, still grinning. "We sure painted the town, Mouthy. Guess it's us for the old tideflat shack now, though. Let's rustle some bacon and spuds and you can cook us a good supper, Mouthy."

The next morning Hooks Bartell was picking them from the crowd of longshoremen that was milling around in the rain before the Sound Steamship Company's gate.

"Hell, here's our millionaires back again! All right for you, Ike. Step along. Cast off, Mouthy. You're no damn good for this lumber cargo. Step along. All right, Swanson. Packin' anything on your hip? Got to stay sober, mind. Step along. . . ."

Swinging his hook, Ike the Diver tramped on through the gate. Edward Matthews, Esquire, turned back toward Pat Noonan's. It would be the same old story all winter, most likely. Loafing at Pat's, waiting for a chance at a ship. Frying the bacon and spuds, boiling the coffee, slicing the bread for good old Ike. No chance to be a boss stevedore next summer. Opportunity only knocked once, all the philosophers agreed. Well, he'd got his own philosophy back anyway; he'd proved it right, and that was a consolation. His time had come. But he'd been ruined by gold. Hereafter he could only hold himself up as a warning.

"Look at me standin' 'ere," he would say. "Once I was full of pride. Onct I was a blinkin' millyunaire, a bloated Croeesus, I was. Look on me, young man, and tyke warnin'. Alw'ys be true to yer-self, as the poet says. . . ."

*Gifford Cheshire was born in 1905 on an Oregon ranch home-
steaded by his grandfather in the 1850s after he had crossed the
plains by wagon train from Tennessee. He published his first short
story in 1934 and followed it with hundreds more over the next two
decades in a wide variety of Western and adventure pulp magazines.
Among his more than twenty-five novels, which appeared under his
own name and the pseudonym Chad Merriman, are several with
Pacific Northwest settings, including* Starlight Basin *(1954),* Thunder on the Mountain *(1960), and* Wenatchee Bend *(1966). Some
of his best fiction deals with riverboating and rivermen in Oregon,
Washington, and Idaho. "Six-Guns Round the Bend" captures the
robust flavor of early passenger and freight traffic on the Willamette
River of south-central Oregon.*

Six-Guns Round the Bend

★★★★★★★★★★★★

Giff Cheshire

I

EASY North hesitated, then turned back down the gangplank,
and as he crossed the splintered wharf, he exhaled sharply,
his breath making floating fog in the air. He cuffed his blue cap
back and stepped into the office. The faint scent of perfume
touched his cold-keened nostrils, and he frowned slightly. It
hadn't been like this in Jim Hammond's day. Then Juliet had
shown little interest in the business. It used to be you caught the
reek of old Jim's pipe, wafting out of his private office after he had
quit the river. And now perfume.

Crossing to his battered, infrequently used desk in the outer office, Easy took a small key from his pocket and locked the center
drawer carefully. Old Alec was half nodding at the other desk in
this outer room, yet Easy saw that one eye had popped open. The
freight clerk cleared his throat and came alert, and, pretending
he had only been sunk in thought, he began to write on a waybill.

Juliet Hammond was working on the books that she did neatly
and well. She had a litter of ledgers and papers on her desk, and

for a moment after he stepped into her room Easy watched her track a transaction. At length she said, "I wondered if you'd come in to the office before you left."

Easy frowned. "I thought I'd better tell you I might lay over in Eugene City a day or so. I'm not letting Walt Undset go this time till I've signed a new contract with him."

Juliet turned over a ledger page and studied it. "We can hardly compel a man to do business with us, Easy."

He held back a quick answer, saying instead, "Undset was glad to tie up with us till lately. Somebody's been working on him, right when our contract's running out. We haven't got enough way business yet to keep our heads above water. We've got to hold on to him. Bromley's paper is also running out, you know." He let irony creep into his voice with this last.

He heard old Alec clear his throat again, beyond the door. Impatience sharpened Easy, with the desire to be on the river where spaces were wide, the air clean, and the way ahead discernible. Yet he experienced a twinge of remorse that he had poured out his worry in the form of sarcasm. But Juliet had asked for it. Ever since Easy had become manager she had been asking for it, with coolness, indifference, and quiet contrariness.

In milder moments, Easy could admit that he had slapped Juliet down pretty hard at the start. She had tried to take her father's place, to pull her weight ever since a bursting cylinder head on the *Antelope* had killed the engineer and mortally scalded Jim Hammond. The old man had lived only long enough to settle the weight of a great responsibility onto Easy North's shoulders.

"I know you two don't cotton to each other, Easy," Jim had said, "but you gotta run the boats till Juliet's learned enough to run them herself. She won't like it, but I'm making you manager till you're ready to turn the outfit over to her. She'll respect my dying wish. I'll tell her."

Juliet Hammond had wanted no such restrictions placed upon her, and she had made that clear, though she had consented to her father's last wish. She had learned to handle the office end quickly, and she began immediately thereafter to assume responsibilities beyond her abilities. At last Easy had been obliged to drop tact and oppose her openly. As now. It had been Juliet's idea to let Walt Undset tie up with anybody he wanted to, if he preferred not to re-sign with the Hammond line.

Easy turned toward the door, then swung back, a thing he had not wanted to mention prompting him suddenly. "I promised to run this business till you're capable of running it. Your playing grain to that peacock Peyton doesn't strike me as showing competence. Rough as it is on your pride, Juliet, I still have an idea he sees a couple of steamboats as plain as he sees their pretty owner. He's the one setting you against me. I've known it for a long time. He'd like to boot me out and marry you and have the works."

Juliet jerked her head then, the creamy skin across her high cheek bones coloring. Easy could see a hot answer forming on her lips, then she shook her head.

"To that I'm not even listening," she said quietly.

Easy stood the shallow-draft *Shoaler* up the Willamette, quartering against a cold morning sun. A responsibility that he had deeply felt at first had clabbered completely. It had been three years since he had signed as captain aboard the new *Shoaler,* by which Jim Hammond hoped to establish his own steamboat service as far south as Eugene City, a rough hundred miles away. Prior to that, the old man had had only the *Antelope,* on the Portland—Oregon City run, bucking the bigger boats.

There were falls above Oregon City, but the venturesome emigrant gentry filling Oregon from across the plains had not been long in establishing service beyond. There was a portage now between Oregon City and the equally thriving town of Canemah, where the Hammond office was located. In those days old Alec York had handled the office end.

And Easy North, who had earned his nickname through a deceptively quiet manner, had bored up the channel above Harrisburg and established Hammond service to the upper Willamette Valley town of Eugene City in competition to a bigger line. Though the growing southern metropolis had contributed considerable snagging and brush clearing, it was still a ticklish reach for a steamboat except in high-water stages.

There was more than a clash of personalities between Juliet Hammond and Easy North. Something was afoot, and Easy had a growing suspicion to that effect. Walt Undset's strange caginess was a sign.

Western Oregon was long and comparatively narrow, with only a rough territorial road running its length. The Willamette River spanned less than half the distance yet was a better transportation artery than the road. Packers from the southern Oregon settlements connected with the steamboats at various landings, such as Eugene City, as did less numerous wagon freight outfits. Steadily rising water rates had been the natural result of this dependence on the river.

Walt Undset packed from Eugene City to the merchants of Winchester, which distributed for a large area in central southern

Oregon. For two years Undset had been glad to deal with the
Hammond line, which was trying to hold its tariffs to reason.
Now, with the contract coming up for renewal, Undset was showing a strange evasiveness. He had not even met the boat the last
two times Easy had put in at the Eugene City landing, though between times he had picked up the freight.

Somebody was working on Undset. Why or how, Easy had no
idea, but one thing was clear to him. Outside the Hammond office,
only Undset was supposed to know the contract was expiring.
Easy was beginning to suspect a leak, and for this reason he had
made an elaborate show of locking the middle drawer of his desk.
The night before he had fastened a silk thread in such a way that
it would be broken if the drawer were opened in his absence. There
was nothing of importance in the desk; he just wanted to deter-
mine if anyone in the office would take the bait and spy into that
drawer. He had to get a lead on who was doing the quiet dirty
work.

Old Alec York had been discontented since Juliet Hammond
had usurped his place in the office. Easy knew very little about
the man, and it was not inconceivable that York was working for
other interests on the sly.

Easy almost hoped that it would be old York, rather than what
he was forced to think and feared more cogently—that Juliet herself was up to something, trying to shake him loose from the man-
agership she found so unacceptable.

Oregon City was presently the transportation hub of western
Oregon, and its saloons and hotels were filled with river men. In
any such aggregation there was bound to be an element of riffraff.
Men like Bing Peyton, handsome and ambitious. Peyton was captain of the *Shoaler*'s sister packet, the *Antelope,* on the lower reach.
Easy had himself hired Peyton, needing a man and lacking the
time to investigate Peyton thoroughly, misjudging him, he told
himself now, from a deceptively friendly manner. Since, he had
been unable to fire him, for the man had at once begun to pay at-
tentions to Juliet Hammond, who responded favorably. Easy was
convinced that Peyton had set Juliet stubbornly on her present
antagonistic course.

Easy could attach no other meaning to what was happening,
and he felt a gnawing uneasiness. There was another factor that
did not seem to fit but which kept crowding into his mind. Shortly
after Jim Hammond's death, one Bromley Graham had filed
against the estate two personal notes for five thousand each, signed
by Jim Hammond. Easy had known little of Hammond's business
affairs, but this development had shocked him.

Graham was a gambler who divided his time between Portland and Oregon City. He had recently returned from an extended trip to the Fraser River mines, and why he had left more profitable pickings to return to Oregon City, Easy could not understand. Maurice Jaffe, the lawyer settling Hammond's affairs, told Easy about the notes. "Graham claims that Jim Hammond ran on borrowed money the last couple of years. Graham let him have it. If the company can't pay them notes off when they're due, he can tie things up plenty."

To this worry, also, Juliet Hammond had seemed oddly indifferent. "If we owe the man, we'll pay him," was her comment. And to Easy's sharp inquiry as to how this might be done easily, she had replied, "I'm getting tired of these alarms. They don't discourage me, if that's what you're after." Yet later, when Easy warned her that Graham's due date was fast approaching, she had said, "I'll see Bromley Graham. I think he'll be reasonable."

It added up to the fact that in every way she could, Juliet Hammond was telling Easy North that she was ready to run the business herself, that she was more than a little tired of his interference. Easy was well aware that Bing Peyton would like to see her succeed in chasing him out, and it could be that Bromley Graham would feel likewise. But it was more than this opposition that set the line of Easy North's jaw a little sharper; it was his memory of Jim Hammond that restrained his impulse to pull out of it. He had made a verbal contract with Jim, and he would keep it.

II

In the first hour the *Shoaler* stepped by the mouth of the Tualatin and threaded the narrow channel past Rock Island. The Willamette was less turgid than the Columbia into which it flowed, Easy knew from experience with both, but full of meanders, thus presenting a greater danger from snags and shoals. It was more like the Mississippi on which he had got his training. They rounded the bend at Peach Cove, thereafter moving westward.

Yawning, Charley Mann, the first mate, stepped into the wheelhouse to relieve Easy for dinner. Though getting on in years and a surly man, Mann was a first-rate river pilot. He took the wheel and, as Easy stepped to the door, put an arresting question.

"Didja know Bing Peyton got Shag Kemble to take his place for a while, Easy?"

Easy heeled around, his stare making it ridiculous to pretend he had known, though it was embarrassing to admit his continual ignorance of company affairs. Kemble usually worked as a relief pilot.

"No, I didn't," Easy said flatly. "Is Peyton on a toot?"

Charley shrugged. "Dunno. I just heard downtown that he was taking time off. Easy, one of these days you'll either have to fire that man or kill him."

"What do you mean?"

The mate expertly targeted the brass spittoon. "What else'll keep a pair of first-rate steamboats out o' his pocket?"

Easy left, frowning thoughtfully. Charlie Mann maintained his home on the Eugene City end of the run and was usually elated when they were upbound. Now the man was morose and preoccupied, but if he had something special on his mind, he was not communicating it.

In early afternoon they made the Champoeg landing, unloading a dab of way freight. The downbound *Dolly* was tied up ahead of the *Shoaler,* and passengers from the Salem stagecoach hurried across the landing to board her to finish their journey by river. Easy North, watching from the pilothouse, squared his shoulders suddenly.

Two men had started leisurely around the corner of the warehouse, heading toward the *Dolly,* then had pulled back quickly. Easy's eyes narrowed as he watched the sharp angle of the building. His special business in Canemah that morning had put him an hour behind schedule. The two men had obviously been surprised to see him here. Then, realizing they had been seen, they came into view again, walking unconcernedly, as if some local distraction there had caused them to duck back for a moment.

They had to pass abreast of the *Shoaler,* and as they came nearer, Easy studied the tall figure of Bing Peyton. The captain of the *Antelope* was dark-complexioned, with a burly handsomeness and a relaxed power showing in his movements. He was a striking figure, Easy admitted; likable, even.

Peyton's companion was Bromley Graham, a blocky man in silk hat and long coat, whose face wore a habitual affability that now looked a little forced.

Both men looked up at the *Shoaler*'s texas as they passed, and Graham called, "Hello there, Easy." Peyton gave no greeting, but he grinned a little.

"Aren't you off the reservation?" asked Easy in a casual voice.

They halted, looking up at him. Graham shrugged his thick shoulders. "A little sporting event in Salem."

It was a plausible enough explanation. Graham had a considerable hand in the sporting affairs of the valley, and his half-mysterious business took him around. Yet ordinarily when he went south he preferred the comfort of the river boats. Salem was on the river, and this staging down to Champoeg rather than taking a through boat had an odd ring to it, unless Graham had had business in one of the inland way towns.

There was no patent reason for Peyton being along. To this point Easy had never suspected a connection between the pair. The man's grin held its continuing masked amusement. He waited for Easy to question him, but Easy refrained. The two walked on and passed calmly aboard the *Dolly*.

Charley Mann had emerged so silently onto the texas that Easy had not heard him. The mate spat over the side, staring southward at the *Dolly*. While knowing his boats and water, there was something intangibly slack about Mann. Some kind of truculence that he rarely let come to the surface seemed to simmer in him, a basic dissatisfaction with life, or at least with his own lot. He drank and gambled and usually had his salary drawn ahead. These things Easy tolerated, because it was hard to keep a competent crew when the bigger boats offered more prestige and better wages and because Mann had a daughter to support.

It was Mann's watch, and he took the wheel and, at Easy's nod, belled for standby. The little *Shoaler* ran steadily up the Willamette, which turned south again above Ash Island. Night caught them passing east of Grand Island, and in its bright, moonlit hours they crept by Salem, Albany, and Marysville, tying up at the Eugene City landing under towering Skinner Butte in the early morning. Each had slept through his off-watches, and now the two men went ashore together.

The ramshackle box house the Manns occupied was on a street north of the butte. Charley carried no key, and at his impatient rap his daughter Nancy came to unlock the door, a wrapper pulled tightly about her slender figure, her russet hair tousled. Her sleepy eyes took in Easy North, and she said without greeting, "Breakfast for two coming up. Though why I should be hauled out of bed when you have a Chinaboy cook aboard is more than I can see."

"You're not looking from where I am," said Easy, with a grin. Mann had tramped on into another room, and Easy tossed his cap onto a table. He turned and watched the slow smile warm Nancy's features. She disappeared, and when she reemerged, she wore a dress and her hair was combed. She went at once to the big range in the kitchen. Easy followed, waiting for her to speak.

At length, when she didn't, he said, "Well, did you see anything of Walt Undset?"

"Yes, but I couldn't get anything out of him. The man's sore about something, Easy. He came in and packed out again while you were downstream, like the other times."

"Then I'll be here when he gets back," Easy said.

Nancy's eyes brightened. "You mean you'll be around a while?"

"Day or so. Till Undset gets back, anyhow. Did you talk to him?"

"Yes, but he wouldn't say much. Claims some sick mules've thrown him off stride, which is why he hasn't been meeting the *Shoaler*. But he spent a lot of time with a couple of men who were at the hotel, Easy."

Easy straightened. "Who were they?"

"Strangers to me. But I saw them pull out in a livery rig."

Charley had come back into the room, and Easy exchanged glances with him. "Well, that explains it," Easy murmured. "Graham and Peyton."

"Why in blazes'd they drive over that hellish road? Why didn't they take the other boat?"

"Too conspicuous," said Easy. "They didn't want us to know they'd been here." He was growing excited, with half-shaped suspicions at last falling into an intelligible pattern. "I'll find out what their business was if I have to choke it out of Walt Undset."

They sat at the table while Nancy served their breakfast. Easy's eyes followed her quick, lithe movements, and with his change of mood they pleased him. Nancy was around twenty, a lighthearted girl who could not remember her mother and whose father was indifferent and mostly on the river. Their glances met by chance, and Easy saw some speculation die in Nancy's gray eyes.

Theirs was an odd relationship. Often Nancy made the round trip on the packet. Easy was always completely at ease, relaxed, yet strangely alive with her. Sometimes he would forget that she was a woman, and again he would be keenly aware of it. For the first time he wondered if this easy acceptance of her bothered her. Yet she had never let on. Once, when he had lightly kissed her for mending his coat, she had stepped away quickly and stared at him with warning eyes. He didn't know how he really felt about her. It was something he had had no impulse to find out.

When Easy got back to the Shoaler, the deckhands, under the third mate, were unloading. When they had finished, he told them that they would stay tied up for a day or two, and he let all but the watchman go ashore. He went to his cabin and napped, and when he awakened it was late afternoon. He passed ashore again and made his way to the main part of the town, idling along the muddy, rutted streets. Cottonwood and balm stood thickly on the flat holding the town. Evening crept down the eastern Cascades foothills, drifting westward toward the vapor-hung Coast Range.

Easy had no idea what impulse halted him before a big general mercantile a little later and turned him in. He went instinctively to the dry goods section, his gaze slowly traveling over the stacks of bolt goods. He saw a yellow printed material and wondered how it would go with russet hair. Turning the problem in his mind, he glanced toward the big front windows. What he saw made him heel about. Pack mules were going along the muddy street toward the river. He headed for the door, waving an approaching clerk away.

Led by a belled pony, a long string of pack mules filed past. Walt Undset was looking straight ahead, and not until Easy called, "Walt!" did he glance around. Letting the animals string on, Undset rode over to the board sidewalk. His eyes were guarded, though he tipped his head in greeting.

"Walt," said Easy, "I've been trying to connect with you."

"Yeah, I know." Undset slowly digested this unexpected meeting. "Hurried back special to talk to you, Easy. I guess we'll be breaking it off, come the twelfth."

"Why, Walt?"

"Easy, I got to tend to my critters. I'll come aboard to see you by and by." Undset wiped the trail mud from his saddle, not looking up, and swung away.

Easy forgot the impulsive gesture he had planned for Nancy Mann, irritation putting a scowl on his face. But he was done with this evasiveness. He hurried after the pack train, following it to the landing. The bell pony turned southward by instinct, halting before Undset's corrals and barn. Undset stepped down with the packer who helped him, and they turned the animals in. Easy North strode up, careless of the deep mud.

"Walt, I'm tired of this beating around the bush," he said bluntly. "Bromley Graham and Bing Peyton've been up to see you. They've been working on you for a long while, looks like. What do they want? What've they been telling you?"

The packer shoved a hand into his pocket, looking at Easy closely. There was a simple honesty in Undset's eyes, a calm courage. "Well, Easy, I guess I misjudged you," he said. "I guess you're a crook."

"I'll have to have more than that, Walt."

Undset weighed his words carefully. "I liked Jim Hammond. When he talked to me a couple years ago about putting the *Shoaler* into competition with the *Starling* up here, I was all for it. Been paying too much freight. I allus liked you, too, Easy, but when I hear about you working to run Jim's girl out o' her pappy's own company, I don't like it. I can't stop you, but I don't have to do business with you."

"So," said Easy softly. "Didn't you wonder why that pair came all the way up from Portland to tell you that, Walt?"

"They were just passing through. I happened to run into 'em, and we got to talking."

"That's what they wanted you to think. But you were acting sore before that."

"Well, Charley Mann'd dropped a couple of hints, and I had time to think it over."

"Charley Mann!"

"Yep. Just gossip. But it all ties together, and I reckon there's something to it. I'd like to help Jim's girl. When you're out o' the company, I'll turn my business her way again." Undset heeled around. "And until you are, I don't want nothin' to do with the Hammond Line."

III

Easy North moved with shocked and angry purpose. There was no use arguing with Undset at this juncture. The man had made up his mind slowly and would stay stubborn until he was presented with something more persuasive than talk. Easy scoured the town's grog shops in search of his crew, boiling to get to Canemah to call for a showdown. He found his fireman and engineer together and sent them hustling for the river, and he rounded up the deckhands.

He swung by the Mann house, fuming and uncertain what he would say to Charley, and found the place dark and locked tight. Wheeling around, he headed for the landing.

At first Easy was more baffled than illuminated by what Undset had told him. If Peyton and Graham were trying to run him out of the company, why were they nipping off its most important piece of business? Walt Undset's through freight to Eugene City furnished a good part of the Hammond Line's revenue. Its loss would be a crippling blow. Particularly when there were those two notes of Bromley Graham's to meet.

It came to Easy then that Graham wanted the business himself and was using Bing Peyton to help him get it. This left Peyton's angle a complete mystery, for the man stood a good chance of marrying the business, thus securing it himself. It became clear for the first time, however, that Juliet Hammond was herself on the skids, whatever they were working for. And she was too inexperienced, or downright foolish, to recognize it.

The engineer had got up steam in the time it took Easy to complete his chores. Standing lights winked on the hog posts through the thickening night. Easy strode up the gangplank, calling to a pair of deckhands to swing it inboard. He turned forward and mounted to the texas and stopped still in the doorway of the wheelhouse.

He thought for a moment that the dark figure inside was Charley Mann, then Nancy's calm voice asked, "Ready to push off, skipper?"

"Where's Charley?"

He heard a sound like a sigh. "In his cabin. I brought him down. He had a little too much to drink, Easy. I'll stand his watches going down."

Anger surged up in Easy, but he remembered that he had told all hands they would probably have a day or so off. The rest of his crew was also probably feeling its oats by now.

"How did you know I wanted to shove off, Nancy?" he asked.

"Guessed it. I saw Undset shag into town. I knew you'd want to shove off right away, no matter what kind of luck you had with him. Did you have any?"

"None."

He did not speak to her of what her father had been doing. That wasn't Nancy's fault. Considering it now, Easy realized that the girl's life had not been pleasant. Her father was a periodic drinker, mean and unpredictable when he was on a jag. Most of his wages went over bars and card tables. It must have been difficult for Nancy at times, maybe most of the time.

Her quick insight into his own desires pleased Easy. She was capable of relieving him at the wheel, for she had cubbed for a long while, to his private amusement. He had been surprised at how quickly and well she had learned to handle a boat. And instead of resenting a woman at the wheel, his crew had liked it.

Easy remembered his interrupted business at the mercantile with a pang of guilt. "You like yellow, Nancy?" he asked suddenly.

Her answer was a little sharp. "In a dress or . . . a man?"

"Why, I mean a dress. And ribbons and the things women like."

"I love it, Easy. But why?"

"I saw some material in a store. I was about to buy it when I sighted Walt."

"For me?" Her voice was incredulous.

"I thought it would look right pretty on you, Nancy."

"Why, Easy!" There was a catch in her voice, and she said no more.

Casually he said, "Your father got it in for me, Nancy?"

Her answer was slow in coming. "I reckon he's got a grudge against the world. Anyhow, the part that has things he's never been able to get. And you don't have to remind me it's his own fault, Easy North. He had a command once and lost it. He's only a good river man when there's somebody else to take most of the responsibility. Why did you ask?"

Once before, this day, Easy had had the feeling that Nancy Mann knew things she was telling no one. He felt the caution in her now. He wondered again if she had come along for some other reason than to substitute for her father. He couldn't bring himself to ask, and it looked as though she wasn't going to tell him. Yet he knew that what he had said about the dress had moved her. If he led her on—he put the thought out of his mind as unseemly.

"Just wondered," he said. "Sometimes Charley sulks."

The *Shoaler* ran steadily through the night, under a good moon, picking through the labyrinthine channels between the McKenzie and Harrisburg Landing. Easy's afternoon nap had drawn the fatigue from him and he kept at the wheel, except to let Nancy take it at times while he relaxed on the chart ledge. They ran faster downstream, and daylight found them on the last short stretch to Canemah.

When they had tied up, Easy had an early breakfast with Nancy in the packet's small galley. Afterward he told her to take his cabin and get some sleep. Excitement, now that he was back in Canemah, put any thought of rest for himself out of his mind. He looked in on Charley Mann and found the mate still sleeping heavily. Returning to the galley, he sat for a long while over coffee, building his plans.

At nine o'clock Easy came out on deck, and instantly those plans left him in a surge of demanding impulse. Bing Peyton came around a far corner and strode along the landing, heading for the Hammond office. By this time the office was open for business, and old Alec York and probably Juliet Hammond would be there. Easy considered these things briefly as he plunged down the gangplank.

Softly he called, "Peyton!"

Bing Peyton swung around, showing no surprise, for he had seen the *Shoaler*. Half in belligerence and half in wonder, he came toward Easy. His eyes held a question that Easy did not answer.

In a tone that was almost bland, Easy said, "Peyton, you're fired."

Disbelief pulled Peyton's shoulders a little higher. "Says who?"

"Say I. From here on you can stay off the works!"

A slight rise in the pitch of Peyton's voice was all that revealed the tension that had come into him. "You got openers, Easy?" he asked softly.

Easy had known that it would be this way, that Peyton would defy him to make his words good. Peyton had got his feet balanced under him, his shoulders set, and he waited for Easy to move. A spasm of fury took Easy. He stepped closer, then Peyton jumped.

Easy met him, and both felt the brain-jolting impact. Peyton let out a breath that had a rising elation in it. He grappled, not punching but trying to get a hold. Easy heaved out of his grip, and Peyton panted, "We'll see who throws who off the works!"

Easy tugged loose and sent in a sizzling punch that grazed Peyton's neck, and then Peyton began to slug. Easy felt knuckles smash his face, leaving only a numbness, but in a minute he felt blood streaming into his mouth. It rocked him, and he drove away the next jabs, sinking a whistling fist to Peyton's belly. Peyton pulled back, disturbed and wary. Then, out of the blue, Easy's toe hooked on his own foot and he went sprawling.

To his astonishment, Peyton kept back while he scrambled to his feet. Easy stared but was no more than balanced when Peyton bore in again. He drove Easy half across the dock, toward its edge, grinning suddenly. That almost good-natured grin didn't fit, and anger at this baffling detail set Easy solidly on his feet again.

Once more he drove a fist into Peyton's belly. Disdaining it, remaining wide open, Peyton launched a withering storm of haymakers that cut and lashed and thudded to Easy's face and head. He stood toe to toe, refusing to retreat, refusing to cover himself. Easy took the punishment and kept hammering at the man's belly. He did not relent when he saw Peyton sag. In the next seconds Peyton collapsed in a heap.

"You fired, Peyton?" panted Easy.

Bing Peyton hoisted himself onto his elbows, stretched bellywise on the splintered wharf, and his head weaved from side to side. Then he went slack.

Easy grew aware then that most of his crew were watching from the main deck of the *Shoaler*. He had no sense of triumph as he stared down at Peyton's limp form. He had accomplished nothing with his upsurging show of authority, hadn't even gained satisfaction.

A voice said, "You'd better fix that face," and Easy turned to see old Alec York standing in the office door. York's mouth wore a sardonic grin. He let his gaze drift to Peyton's still figure, then swung about and disappeared inside, closing the door. Easy saw Juliet Hammond then, watching from the window of her office, and now he realized that the racket couldn't help attracting all this gallery. The look on her face was hard to decipher; he thought that it was almost regret. Shame jabbed at him, and to rid himself of this he brought a scowl onto his face. He turned and went into the office.

He strode past Alec York, who was apparently preoccupied with his work again, and on into Juliet's office. She had left the window and moved to her desk, and now she looked up at him.

"Well, I heard you fired a good man. Have you anybody in mind to take his place?"

"Shag Kemble's been taking it for a week or so, hasn't he?"

Juliet was startled, and she looked at him sharply. "Easy, how did you learn that?"

"Was it that much of a secret?"

"It was something you weren't supposed to know. Who told you? Charley Mann?"

"What difference does it make?" The truculence he had adopted was seeping away from Easy. In a shocked moment of perception he saw himself in an entirely new light. He had fought Bing Peyton in killing fury, and he knew now that it had come from more than any contention over authority in the affairs of the Hammond Line. His feeling of guilt now before Juliet affirmed this. He must have had deeper reasons than he knew for hating, and then suspecting, Bing Peyton. He must be in love with this girl. Which made it quite another matter.

Gruffly he said, "I never had any reason other than what I took to be a verbal contract between your dad and me for meddling in your affairs, Juliet. But I admit you've got a rightful voice in things. If you're ready to sink or swim on your own responsibility, I'll pull out. I know where I can get a job on the middle Columbia."

It was hard to define what showed on Juliet's face then. It wasn't triumph, and it was hardly gratification. It was almost regret again. But she nodded.

"All right, Easy, I expect that would be best." She swept up her coat and hurried out, as if eager to convey the news to someone.

IV

Easy stopped at his desk as he went out, for there were a few personal things in it that he wanted. He didn't remember the locked drawer until it failed to respond to his tug. He fished into his pocket for his key, and old York's voice said, "Nobody's been fiddling with your desk, Easy."

Easy stared at him, but the old man didn't look up from his work. Then York said, "You're barking up the wrong tree, boy."

Easy crossed to him in long strides, sheepish but grinning a little. "All right, I set a trap. Information's been leaking, Alec. I thought it was through the office, but you're right. I was sniffing the wrong tree. It was my own first mate. I've learned enough to see it's been a two-way leak. The man's playing both ends against the middle. What do you know?"

York swiveled around in his chair. "Son, if I really knew what I think is happening, I wouldn't just sit here. Why don't you finish the business?"

"On account of I just quit."

"You're a blasted fool, but can't say I blame you. I get a better picture here than you could on the river. I ain't saying anything I can prove, boy, and I'm only guessing. But was I you, I'd let it stand that I was through, but stick around a while and keep my eyes open."

"Damn it, Alec, can't you come into the open?"

"Not when it'd sure hurt certain people if I'm wrong."

Leaving the office, Easy crossed the wharf and reboarded the *Shoaler*. The packet had brought down no freight, but according to schedule she should be reloading and readying to point her prow upstream again. That was Juliet Hammond's worry now. She could run the line if she could keep it out of Bromley Graham's hands, or she could sell the packets up on Fraser River, where steamboats were in high demand.

Easy had stepped into his cabin before he recalled that he had loaned it to Nancy Mann. He started to withdraw hastily, but she lifted her head from the pillow and looked at him. He grinned and shut the door, turning toward her.

"Nancy, how'd you like to live at Dallas City?" he asked abruptly.

Nancy swung her legs over the edge of the bunk and began to shape her hair with her hand. She digested the question and looked at him. "How come?"

"I could get on up there."

Nancy's eyes were unscrutable. "Are you talking about marriage, Easy?"

Impatiently he said, "Of course. I've never offered you anything else, have I?"

"Precious little at all." Her mouth was bitter suddenly, yet she wiped off the expression and smiled at him. "Last night you asked me how I like yellow, Easy. I told you I like it in a dress. I loathe it in a man."

He was stung and staggered by her words. His gaze slapped her hard. "What do you mean?"

"That I won't help you run from trouble. From the woman who won't have you."

"Is that your answer?"

"That's my answer, Easy North."

He started to speak, reconsidered, and turned and went out.

Charley Mann was still sleeping soggily. He was a cyclic drinker, and a freshly opened bottle of whiskey on the ledge above his bunk showed that he had wakened thirstily, quenched the thirst heartily, and passed out again.

Easy heard Nancy leave his cabin and pass aft. He turned back to the cabin and packed his things. A little later, carrying a cowhide valise and carpetbag, he strode down the gangplank and across the wharf. Maybe it was what she had wanted, but his anger at Nancy's accusation of cowardice had set his mind. He was going to see this through, following Alec York's advice to pretend otherwise.

An hour later Easy took a room in an Oregon City hotel, at the lower end of the portage around Willamette Falls, and half a mile north of Canemah. He slept, and in late afternoon emerged onto the streets, showing himself in the various bars that were social headquarters, for the river breed, advertising his leisure.

At dusk the *Ranger* came in from Portland, tying up in the basin. Watching in apparent idleness, Easy saw Bromley Graham come ashore, accompanied by two hard-faced men he recognized as hangers-on of Portland deadfalls. The trio went at once to Anson's Livery, and a little later a buggy rolled with them over the hill in the direction of Canemah. Easy had been waiting for this with restrained excitement, for idle inquiry had told him that Graham had left downstream suddenly on the *Lurline* at noon.

Action was coming, and Easy felt it in his bones. He struck out on foot toward Canemah, the low rumble of the falls a steady sound, the frozen earth giving his steps a staccato beat.

There was a light in the Hammond office, Easy saw, as he

turned down to the wharf some fifteen minutes later. The fast pace had warmed him, set his blood to coursing, building a hunger for raw action. The *Shoaler* was still tied at dockside. Easy went past the office and warehouse structure with no effort to conceal his presence. He turned up the gangplank and, at the top, halted.

The deck was deserted, except for a dark figure hunched over the rail, obviously staring at the lighted office windows. It was Charley Mann. Easy turned his way, saying harshly, "Well, Charley, I've been waiting for you to recover your speech. You've got some things to explain."

Mann's answer was a low growl. "Like what?"

"You've been trying to spark a fight between me and Peyton. You blackened my character with Walt Undset. You're working for Bromley Graham. What're you up to and what do you hope to get out of it?"

Mann lurched around, pulling his sagging frame erect, his weaving head thrown back. He spat one word, "Lies!" He swung around, back to the rail, supporting himself there.

"You might as well talk," said Easy, in a calm tone. "Or I'll fix it so you'll never get another job on the river. Maybe I will anyhow, much as I hate to have to because of your girl."

"Yeah!" snarled Mann. "Because of my girl!" He moved then, and Easy saw too late that he held a tackle-belaying pin from the rail in his hand. Mann swung it savagely and, though he ducked, Easy felt its terrific impact on the side of his head. Lights danced, and as Easy grappled, Mann swung again. He shoved Easy toward the rail break. Easy fought blackness, fought Mann, fought raw fear, then toppled over the chain toward the water.

V

The water's icy slap went through Easy in a sheet of pain. Dimly he remembered the falls, which made a giant horseshoe across the river, sucking the stream toward them in a vast pucker. He submerged, something internal seeming to drain him, his ears ringing. He fought to the surface, saw lights someplace, but they swirled in his blurred vision. For a moment he seemed to have no will beyond the instinct to keep his head above water. He was swept down past the Hammond landing toward the falls. Reason returned in a rush as he remembered the falls, and he struck out blindly. He pulled himself in to the rocky underpinning someplace along the long river front.

He pulled out of the freezing water and lay for minutes, panting, recovering his wits. Mann's attack had been a total surprise, a sure try at murder. Easy had never believed that the man had motive enough for that. He climbed to his feet presently, stamping them and slapping his arms to get warm. His jaw set, and he made his way to the end of the wharf and came up around it. He tramped back along the north terminus of the strung-out huddle of weathered structures. At the end of the Hammond building, opposite the office, he removed a key from his pocket and unlocked a door which let him into the cavernous freight shed. He moved soundlessly down the cluttered length of the freight room.

There was a small, ledged opening in the partition between the office and freight house for easy communication. He moved up on this cautiously from the side and risked a quick look. The outer office was deserted and dark, except for indirect light from Juliet's private office. Moving cautiously, Easy opened the door and stepped into this space, the room's warmth folding about his chilled body. Keeping close to the wall, he made his way to the inner office door, less worried about a betraying noise now, for spirited talk was flying in there.

Bing Peyton's voice rang out, and there was anger in it. "You're a fool to force it, Graham! You sure had us sidetracked for a long time, but we got on to it finally. That's why I played along with you, to make sure what you were up to!"

"Shut up, Peyton." Bromley Graham's voice was calm, ice-cold. "It's Miss Hammond's say. She admits them two dinky steamboats didn't cost over ten thousand apiece to build. I'm willing to take 'em at that without knocking off a red cent for depreciation."

Juliet's tight voice was a sharp protest. "But the company, the good will. . . !"

Easy heard Graham's quick laugh. "How much good will've you got left? You've lost Walt Undset, and that alone'll probably bust you. I'll take your tubs at what they cost, applying ten thousand on the notes and giving you ten thousand cash. And you're lucky to get a break like that."

At last there was a note of resignation in Juliet's voice. "I guess I am. What do you say, Bing?"

"I say the devil with the man!" It was Easy North's voice. He stepped quickly through the door. Juliet and Bing Peyton stood side by side behind her desk. Across from them stood Bromley Graham. On Graham's right were the two hard-cases he had brought up from Portland. Bodyguards, in case something went wrong with this. Easy saw their hands slide under the skirts of their coats as they stared at him.

Easy fixed his attention on Graham. "I'd bet my life those notes were forged, and I'll sure try to prove it. You've made it plenty smooth, because I couldn't see why you'd try to break the company and take it over, too. It's never been a prosperous enough outfit to be much of a prize. I didn't see it until you made a point just now of how much the *Antelope* and *Shoaler* cost Jim Hammond. It made me think of your trip up to Fraser River a while back. And it popped into my mind how old Turk Adley sold the *Albany* up there. They need steamboats bad to handle the gold rush. I heard Turk got forty thousand for a tub that cost him only eight."

Graham gazed at him. Shock built in his eyes, quickly glazing over with an uneasy malice. "You're just too damned bright, North. That's why we wanted to ease you out of it, and I thought we had." A thoughtful worry worked in the man. "It looks like we've got to make sure of it." There was a deadly venom in Graham's voice.

It was the first proof that Easy's shot at the validity of the notes had hit something. Easy waited in tight wariness, knowing that if Graham was out on a demonstrable criminal limb, he himself was in a tight spot. He saw Graham nod at his two toughs, and the pair stepped forward.

Easy waited no longer. His long body lanced straight at Graham. The man scrambled clear, and then the two bodyguards jumped in, both of them wielding clubbed pocket guns. Easy knew he was playing a slim hand. He fought savagely, grew aware in a moment that Bing Peyton had sailed in to help him. Then a gun exploded and something whistled close to Easy's ear. Graham had pulled a derringer, was resorting to it in desperation. Easy saw Juliet hurl something from the top of her desk, and Graham went down soundlessly.

Bing Peyton had one of the hard-cases down and was mercilessly hammering him. Tipping a shoulder, Easy charged the other fellow, colliding with the man's face. When the man hit the floor, Easy pounced on him, hammering incessantly. In a moment he realized that it was all over. All three were out cold.

It was Bing Peyton that Juliet ran to instinctively. "Oh, Bing, are you all right?"

Peyton placed an arm about her slender shoulders. "Yeah. It was Easy who got it."

"Just tried to part my hair," said Easy with a grin.

Juliet turned a concerned face toward him, and Easy turned the

grin on her. It surprised him that he did not resent seeing the instinctive endearment between these two.

"I don't get it," he said, "but congratulations, Bing. She's a
catch. And maybe you are. I had you figured wrong. I thought
you were trying to drive me out of the company to marry it."

Peyton eyed him in amiable speculation. "Right on both scores,
except I wanted to marry the girl only. At first we really thought
you were trying to euchre her, Easy."

Easy looked at Juliet. "Charley Mann kept dropping you
hints?"

Juliet nodded. "And vague little warnings. Then Bing saw him
and Bromley Graham meet under secretive circumstances for a
talk. It set Bing to wondering. He got friendly with Graham and
confessed he wanted to drive you out of the company. Graham
swallowed the bait, though he wouldn't open up. He suggested
clipping away the company's business to get you discouraged so
you'd pull out voluntarily. They worked on Undset. Graham
claimed to be concerned only about his notes."

"Meanwhile playing all angles by having Charley Mann trying
to set you and me at each other's throats," Easy said. "Charley
even told me I'd have to kill Bing."

Men were coming across the wharf from the *Shoaler,* attracted
by the shot that had been fired. There would be plenty of them
to handle Graham and his toughs when they came to. Easy had
another chore in mind. As the others barged in, he slipped out.

The *Shoaler* was deserted, except for Nancy Mann, who stood at
the rail. She did not speak as Easy came up, staring out over the
darkened river.

"Where's your dad?" Easy asked.

Nancy nodded toward the river. "Down there."

Easy tensed. "The river?"

"Yes, Easy. I saw him. I knew what was coming, what it would
lead to, but it had to be."

"He tried to kill me," Easy told Nancy. "Do you know why?"

"Yes. I talked with him afterward. Graham promised him a lot
of money for his help. Dad was going to take the two boats up
to the Fraser River for Graham. He was going to be able to make
a fresh start. He was drunk, Easy, and when you threatened to
ruin him, he lost his head. He was sorry within a minute after he'd
done it. He was a man for whom happiness was impossible, Easy.
I kind of knew what he would do, and maybe I could have stopped
him, but I didn't try."

The moment was not appropriate, but Easy knew that every-

hing this girl had was gone from her completely. He had to tell
her that he did not want her to help him forget another woman.
He wanted her for herself, and in this hour she needed desperately
to know that.

"Nancy, I want to see you in a yellow dress," he said humbly.
"In a yellow kitchen. I congratulated Bing Peyton a moment ago
and never meant anything more in my life. Won't you believe
that?"

Nancy turned toward him, and there was a catch in her voice.
"I want to, Easy. Maybe it wouldn't be very hard for you to make
me believe you."

Easy pulled her to him, and at last she yielded with a little sigh
of happiness, and her lips met his.

Idaho Territory in the late 1860s is also the scene of Owen Wister's second entry in these pages, and General Crook and Specimen Jones are once again among the cast of characters. Other important components of "The Second Missouri Compromise" are poker, pistols, politicians, the territorial treasurer's strongbox, and an abundance of high good humor.

The Second Missouri Compromise

★★★★★★★★★★★★

Owen Wister

I

THE Legislature had sat up all night, much absorbed, having taken off its coat because of the stove. This was the fortieth and final day of its first session under an order of things not new only, but novel. It sat with the retrospect of forty days' duty done, and the prospect of forty days' consequent pay to come. Sleepy it was not, but wide and wider awake over a progressing crisis. Hungry it had been until after a breakfast fetched to it from the Overland at seven, three hours ago. It had taken no intermission to wash its face, nor was there just now any apparatus for this, as the tin pitcher commonly used stood not in the basin in the corner, but on the floor by the Governor's chair; so the eyes of the Legislature, though earnest, were dilapidated. Last night the pressure of public business had seemed over, and no turning back the hands of the clock likely to be necessary. Besides Governor Ballard, Mr. Hewley, Secretary and Treasurer, was sitting up, too; small, iron-gray, in feature and bearing every inch the capable, dignified official, but his necktie had slipped off during the night. The bearded Councillors had the best of it, seeming after their vigil less stale in the face than the member from Silver City, for instance, whose day-old black growth blurred his dingy chin, or the member from Big Camas, whose scantier red crop bristled on his cheeks in sparse wandering arrangements, like spikes on the barrel

140

of a musical box. For comfort, most of the pistols were on the table
with the Statutes of the United States. Secretary and Treasurer
Hewley's lay on his strongbox immediately behind him. The Governor's was a light one, and always hung in the armhole of his
waistcoat. The graveyard of Boisé City this year had twenty-seven
tenants, two brought there by meningitis and twenty-five by difference of opinion. Many denizens of the Territory were miners and
the unsettling element of gold-dust hung in the air, breeding argument. The early, thin, bright morning steadily mellowed against
the windows distant from the stove; the panes melted clear until
they ran, steamed faintly, and dried, this fresh May day, after the
night's untimely cold; while still the Legislature sat in its shirtsleeves, and several statesmen had removed their boots. Even had
appearances counted, the session was invisible from the street. Unlike a good number of houses in the town, the State-House (as they
called it from old habit) was not all on the ground-floor for outsid-
ers to stare into, but up a flight of wood steps to a wood gallery.
From this, to be sure, the interior could be watched from several
windows on both sides; but the journey up the steps was precisely
enough to disincline the idle, and this was counted a sensible thing
by the lawmakers. They took the ground that shaping any government for a raw wilderness community needed seclusion, and they
set a high value upon unworried privacy.

The sun had set upon a concentrated Council, but it rose upon
faces that looked momentous. Only the Governor's and Treasurer's were impassive, and they concealed something even graver
than the matter in hand.

"I'll take a hun'red mo', Gove'nuh," said the member from Silver City softly, his eyes on space. His name was Powhattan Wingo.

The Governor counted out the blue, white, and red chips to
Wingo, penciled some figures on a thickly ciphered and canceled
paper that bore in print the words "Territory of Idaho, Council
Chamber," and then filled up his glass from the tin pitcher, adding
a little sugar.

"And I'll trouble you fo' the toddy," Wingo added, always
softly and his eyes always on space. "Raise you ten, suh." This
was to the Treasurer. Only the two were playing at present. The
Governor was kindly acting as bank; the others were looking on.

"And ten," said the Treasurer.

"And ten," said Wingo.

"And twenty," said the Treasurer.

"And fifty," said Wingo, gently bestowing his chips in the middle of the table.

The Treasurer called.

The member from Silver City showed down five high hearts, and a light rustle went over the Legislature when the Treasurer displayed three twos and a pair of threes and gathered in his harvest. He had drawn two cards, Wingo one; and losing to the lowest hand that could have beaten you is under such circumstances truly hard luck. Moreover, it was almost the only sort of luck that had attended Wingo since about half after three that morning. Seven hours of cards just a little lower than your neighbor's is searching to the nerves.

"Gove'nuh, I'll take a hun'red mo'," said Wingo; and once again the Legislature rustled lightly, and the new deal began.

Treasurer Hewley's winnings flanked his right, a pillared fortress on the table, built chiefly of Wingo's misfortunes. Hewley had not counted them, and his architecture was for neatness and not ostentation; yet the Legislature watched him arrange his gains with sullen eyes. It would have pleased him now to lose; it would have more than pleased him to be able to go to bed quite a long time ago. But winners cannot easily go to bed. The thoughtful Treasurer bet his money and deplored this luck. It seemed likely to trap himself and the Governor in a predicament they had not foreseen. All had taken a hand at first and played for several hours, until Fortune's wheel ran into a rut deeper than usual. Wingo slowly became the loser to several, then Hewley had forged ahead, winner from everybody. One by one they had dropped out, each meaning to go home, and all lingering to see the luck turn. It was an extraordinary run, a rare specimen, a breaker of records, something to refer to in the future as a standard of measure and an embellishment of reminiscence; quite enough to keep the Idaho Legislature up all night. And then it was their friend who was losing. The only speaking in the room was the brief card talk of the two players.

"Five better," said Hewley, winner again four times in the last five.

"Ten," said Wingo.

"And twenty," said the Secretary and Treasurer.

"Call you."

"Three kings."

"They are good, suh. Gove'nuh, I'll take a hund'red mo'."

Upon this the wealthy and weary Treasurer made a try for liberty and bed. How would it do, he suggested, to have a round of jack-pots, say ten—or twenty, if the member from Silver City preferred——and then stop? It would do excellently, the member said, so softly that the Governor looked at him. But Wingo's large countenance remained inexpressive, his black eyes still impersonally fixed on space. He sat thus till his chips were counted to him, and then the eyes moved to watch the cards fall. The Governor hoped he might win now, under the jack-pot system. At noon he should have a disclosure to make; something that would need the most cheerful and contented feelings in Wingo and the Legislature to be received with any sort of calm. Wingo was behind the game to the tune of—the Governor gave up adding as he ran his eye over the figures of the bank's erased and tormented record, and he shook his head to himself. This was inadvertent.

"May I inquah who yo're shakin' yoh head at, suh?" said Wingo, wheeling upon the surprised Governor.

"Certainly," answered that official. "You." He was never surprised for very long. In 1867 it did not do to remain surprised in Idaho.

"And have I done anything which meets yoh disapprobation?" pursued the member from Silver City, enunciating with care.

"You have met my disapprobation."

Wingo's eye was on the Governor, and now his friends drew a little together and as a unit sent a glance of suspicion at the lone bank.

"You will gratify me by being explicit, suh," said Wingo to the bank.

"Well, you've emptied the toddy."

"Ha-ha, Gove'nuh! I rose, suh, to yoh little fly. We'll awduh some mo'."

"Time enough when he comes for the breakfast things," said Governor Ballard easily.

"As you say, suh. I'll open for five dolluhs." Wingo turned back to his game. He was winning, and as his luck continued his voice ceased to be soft and became a shade truculent. The Governor's ears caught this change, and he also noted the lurking triumph in the faces of Wingo's fellow-statesmen. Cheerfulness and content were scarcely reigning yet in the Council Chamber of Idaho as Ballard sat watching the friendly game. He was beginning to fear that he must leave the Treasurer alone and take some precautions outside. But he would have to be separated for some time from his ally, cut off from giving him any hints. Once the Treasurer looked at him, and he immediately winked reassuringly, but the Treasurer failed to respond. Hewley might be able to wink after everything was over, but he could not find it in his serious heart to do so now. He was wondering what would happen if this game should last till noon with the company in its present mood. Noon was the time fixed for paying the Legislative Assembly the compensation due for its services during this session; and the Governor and the Treasurer had put their heads together and arranged a surprise for the Legislative Assembly. They were not going to pay them.

A knock sounded at the door, and on seeing the waiter from the Overland enter, the Governor was seized with an idea. Perhaps precaution could be taken from the inside. "Take this pitcher," said he, "and have it refilled with the same. Joseph knows my mixture." But Joseph was night bartender, and now long in his happy bed, with a day successor in the saloon, and this one did not know the mixture. Ballard had foreseen this when he spoke, and that his writing a note of directions would seem quite natural.

"The receipt is as long as the drink," said a legislator, watching the Governor's pencil fly.

"He don't know where my private stock is located," explained Ballard. The waiter departed with the breakfast things and the note, and while the jackpots continued the Governor's mind went carefully over the situation.

Until lately the Western citizen has known one everyday experience that no dweller in our thirteen original colonies has had for two hundred years. In Massachusetts they have not seen it since 1641; in Virginia not since 1628. It is that of belonging to a community of which every adult was born somewhere else. When you come to think of this a little it is dislocating to many of your conventions. Let a citizen of Salem, for instance, or a well-established Philadelphia Quaker, try to imagine his chief-justice fresh from Louisiana, his mayor from Arkansas, his tax-collector from South Carolina, and himself recently arrived in a wagon from a thousand-mile drive. To be governor of such a community Ballard had traveled in a wagon from one quarter of the horizon; from another quarter Wingo had arrived on a mule. People reached Boisé in three ways: by rail to a little west of the Missouri, after which it was wagon, saddle, or walk for the remaining fifteen hundred miles; from California it was shorter; and from Portland, Oregon, only about five hundred miles, and some of these more agreeable, by water up the Columbia. Thus it happened that salt often sold for its weight in gold-dust. A miner in the Bannock Basin would meet a freight teamster coming in with the staples of life, having journeyed perhaps sixty consecutive days through the desert, and valuing his salt highly. The two accordingly bartered in scales, white powder against yellow, and both parties content. Some of Boisé today can remember these bargains. After all, they were struck but thirty years ago. Governor Ballard and Treasurer Hewley did not come from the same place, but they constituted a minority of two in Territorial politics because they

hailed from north of Mason and Dixon's line. Powhattan Wingo
and the rest of the Council were from Pike County, Missouri. They
had been Secessionists, some of them Knights of the Golden Circle; they had belonged to Price's Left Wing, and they flocked together. They were seven—two lying unwell at the Overland, five
now present in the State-House with the Governor and Treasurer.
Wingo, Gascon Claiborne, Gratiot des Pères, Pete Cawthon, and
F. Jackson Gilet were their names. Besides this Council of seven
were thirteen members of the Idaho House of Representatives,
mostly of the same political feather with the Council, and they
too would be present at noon to receive their pay. How Ballard
and Hewley came to be a minority of two is a simple matter. Only
twenty-five months had gone since Appomattox Court-House.
That surrender was presently followed by Johnston's to Sherman
at Durhams Station, and following this the various Confederate
armies in Alabama, or across the Mississippi, or wherever they
happened to be, had successively surrendered—but not Price's
Left Wing. There was the wide open West under its nose, and no
Grant or Sherman infesting that void. Why surrender? Wingos,
Claibornes, and all, they melted away. Price's Left Wing sailed
into the prairie and passed below the horizon. To know what it
next did you must, like Ballard or Hewley, pass below the horizon
yourself, clean out of sight of the dome at Washington to remote,
untracked Idaho. There, besides wild red men in quantities, would
you find not very tame white ones, gentlemen of the ripest South-
western persuasion, and a Legislature to fit. And if, like Ballard
or Hewley, you were a Union man, and the President of the United
States had appointed you Governor or Secretary of such a place,
your days would be full of awkwardness, though your difference
in creed might not hinder you from playing draw-poker with the
unreconstructed. These Missourians were whole-souled, ample-
natured males in many ways, but born with a habit of hasty shooting. The Governor, on setting foot in Idaho, had begun to study
pistolship, but acquired thus in middle life it could never be with
him that spontaneous art which it was with Price's Left Wing. Not
that the weapons now lying loose about the State-House were
brought for use there. Everybody always went armed in Boisé, as
the gravestones impliedly testified. Still, the thought of the bad
quarter of an hour which it might come to at noon did cross Ballard's mind, raising the image of a column in the morrow's paper:
"An unfortunate occurrence has ended relations between es-
teemed gentlemen hitherto the warmest personal friends. . . . They
will be laid to rest at 3 P.M. . . . As a last token of respect for our
lamented Governor, the troops from Boisé Barracks. . . ." The

Governor trusted that if his friends at the post were to do him any service it would not be a funeral one.

The new pitcher of toddy came from the Overland, the jackpots continued, were nearing a finish, and Ballard began to wonder if anything had befallen a part of his note to the bartender, an enclosure addressed to another person.

"Ha, suh!" said Wingo to Hewley. "My pot again, I declah." The chips had been crossing the table his way, and he was now loser but six hundred dollars.

"Ye ain't goin' to whip Mizzooruh all night an' all day, ez a rule," observed Pete Cawthon, Councillor from Lost Leg.

" 'Tis a long road that has no turnin', Gove'nuh," said F. Jackson Gilet, more urbanely. He had been in public life in Missouri and was now President of the Council in Idaho. He, too, had arrived on a mule but could at will summon a rhetoric dating from Cicero and preserved by many luxuriant orators until after the middle of the present century.

"True," said the Governor politely. "But here sits the long-suffering bank, whichever way the road turns. I'm sleepy."

"You sacrifice yo'self in the good cause," replied Gilet, pointing to the poker game. "Oneasy lies the head that wahs an office, suh." And Gilet bowed over his compliment.

The Governor thought so indeed. He looked at the Treasurer's strong-box, where lay the appropriation lately made by Congress to pay the Idaho Legislature for its services; and he looked at the Treasurer, in whose pocket lay the key of the strongbox. He was accountable to the Treasury at Washington for all money disbursed for Territorial expenses.

"Eleven twenty," said Wingo, "and only two hands mo' to play."

The Governor slid out his own watch.

"I'll scahsely recoup," said Wingo.

They dealt and played the hand, and the Governor strolled to the window.

"Three aces," Wingo announced, winning again handsomely. "I struck my luck too late," he commented to the onlookers. While losing he had been able to sustain a smooth reticence; now he gave his thoughts freely to the company and continually moved and fingered his increasing chips. The Governor was still looking out of the window, where he could see far up the street, when Wingo won the last hand, which was small. "That ends it, suh, I suppose?" he said to Hewley, letting the pack of cards linger in his grasp.

"I wouldn't let him off yet," said Ballard to Wingo from the window, with sudden joviality, and he came back to the players. "I'd make him throw five cold hands with me."

"Ah, Gove'nuh, that's yoh spo'tin' blood! Will you do it, Mistuh Hewley—a hun'red a hand?"

Mr. Hewley did it; and winning the first, he lost the second, third, and fourth in the space of an eager minute, while the Councillors drew their chairs close.

"Let me see," said Wingo, calculating, "if I lose this—why still—" He lost. "But I'll not have to ask you to accept my papuh, suh. Wingo liquidates. Fo'ty days at six dolluhs a day makes six times fo' is twenty-fo'—two hun'red an' fo'ty dolluhs spot cash in hand at noon, without computation of mileage to and from Silver City at fo' dolluhs every twenty miles, estimated according to the nearest usually travelled route." He was reciting part of the statute providing mileage for Idaho legislators. He had never served the public before, and he knew all the laws concerning compensation by heart. "You'll not have to wait fo' yoh money, suh," he concluded.

"Well, Mr. Wingo," said Governor Ballard, "it depends on yourself whether your pay comes to you or not." He spoke cheerily. "If you don't see things my way, our Treasurer will have to wait for his money." He had not expected to break the news just so, but it made as easy a beginning as any.

"See things yoh way, suh?"

"Yes. As it stands at present I cannot take the responsibility of paying you."

"The United States pays me, suh. My compensation is provided by act of Congress."

"I confess I am unable to discern your responsibility, Gove'nuh," said F. Jackson Gilet. "Mr. Wingo has faithfully attended the session and is, like every gentleman present, legally entitled to his emoluments."

"You can all readily become entitled—"

"All? Am I—are my friends—included in this new depa'tyuh?"

"The difficulty applies generally, Mr. Gilet."

"Do I understand the Gove'nuh to insinuate—nay, gentlemen, do not rise! Be seated, I beg." For the Councillors had leapt to their feet.

"Whar's our money?" said Pete Cawthon. "Our money was put in thet yere box."

Ballard flushed angrily, but a knock at the door stopped him, and he merely said, "Come in."

A trooper, a corporal, stood at the entrance, and the disordered Council endeavored to look usual in a stranger's presence. They resumed their seats, but it was not easy to look usual on such short notice.

"Captain Paisley's compliments," said the soldier mechanically, "and will Governor Ballard take supper with him this evening?"

"Thank Captain Paisley," said the Governor (his tone was quite usual), "and say that official business connected with the end of the session makes it imperative for me to be at the State-House. Imperative."

The trooper withdrew. He was a heavy-built, handsome fellow with black mustache and black eyes that watched through two straight, narrow slits beneath straight black brows. His expression in the Council Chamber had been of the regulation military indifference, and as he went down the steps he irrelevantly sang an old English tune:

" 'Since first I saw your face I resolved
    To honor and re—'

I guess," he interrupted himself as he unhitched his horse, "parrot and monkey hev broke loose."

The Legislature, always in its shirtsleeves, the cards on the table, and the toddy on the floor, sat calm a moment, cooled by this brief pause from the first heat of its surprise, while the clatter of Corporal Jones's galloping shrank quickly into silence.

II

Captain Paisley walked slowly from the adjutant's office at Boisé Barracks to his quarters, and his orderly walked behind him. The captain carried a letter in his hand, and the orderly, though distant a respectful ten paces, could hear him swearing plain as day. When he reached his front door, Mrs. Paisley met him.

"Jim," cried she, "two more chickens froze in the night." And the delighted orderly heard the captain so plainly that he had to blow his nose or burst.

The lady, merely remarking, "My goodness, Jim," retired immediately to the kitchen, where she had a soldier cook baking, and feared he was not quite sober enough to do it alone. The captain had paid eighty dollars for forty hens this year at Boisé, and twenty-nine had now passed away, victims to the climate. His wise wife perceived his extreme language not to have been all on account of hens, however; but he never allowed her to share in his professional worries, so she stayed safe with the baking, and he sat in the front room with a cigar in his mouth.

Boisé was a two-company post without a major, and Paisley, being senior captain, was in command, an office to which he did not object. But his duties so far this month of May had not pleased him in the least. Theoretically, you can have at a two-company post the following responsible people: one major, two captains, four lieutenants, a doctor, and a chaplain. The major has been spoken of; it is almost needless to say that the chaplain was on leave and had never been seen at Boisé by any of the present garrison; two of the lieutenants were also on leave, and two on surveying details—they had influence at Washington; the other captain was on a scout with General Crook somewhere near the Malheur Agency, and the doctor had only arrived this week. There had resulted a period when Captain Paisley was his own adjutant, quartermaster, and post surgeon, with not even an efficient sergeant to rely upon; and during this period his wife had stayed a good deal in the kitchen. Happily the doctor's coming had given relief to the hospital steward and several patients, and to the captain not only an equal, but an old friend, with whom to pour out his disgust; and together every evening they freely expressed their opinion of the War Department and its treatment of the Western army.

There were steps at the door, and Paisley hurried out. "Only you!" he exclaimed, with such frank vexation that the doctor laughed loudly. "Come in, man, come in," Paisley continued, leading him strongly by the arm, sitting him down, and giving him a cigar. "Here's a pretty how de do!"

"More Indians!" inquired Dr. Tuck.

"Bother! they're nothing. It's Senators—Councillors—whatever the Territorial devils call themselves."

"Gone on the warpath?" the doctor said, quite ignorant how nearly he had touched the Council.

"Precisely, man. Warpath. Here's the Governor writing me they'll be scalping him in the State-House at twelve o'clock. It's past 11:30. They'll be whetting knives about now." And the captain roared.

"I know you haven't gone crazy," said the doctor, "but who has?"

"The lot of them. Ballard's a good man, and—what's his name?—the little Secretary. The balance are just mad dogs—mad dogs. Look here: 'Dear Captain'—that's Ballard to me. I just got it—'I find myself unexpectedly hampered this morning. The South shows signs of being too solid. Unless I am supported, my plan for bringing our Legislature to terms will have to be postponed. Hewley and I are more likely to be brought to terms ourselves— a bad precedent to establish in Idaho. Noon is the hour for drawing salaries. Ask me to supper as quick as you can, and act on my reply.' I've asked him," continued Paisley, "but I haven't told Mrs. Paisley to cook anything extra yet." The captain paused to roar again, shaking Tuck's shoulder for sympathy. Then he explained the situation in Idaho to the justly bewildered doctor. Ballard had confided many of his difficulties lately to Paisley.

"He means you're to send troops?" Tuck inquired.

"What else should the poor man mean?"

"Are you sure it's constitutional?"

"Hang constitutional! What do I know about their legal quibbles at Washington?"

"But, Paisley—"

"They're unsurrendered rebels, I tell you. Never signed a parole."

"But the general amnesty—"

"Bother general amnesty! Ballard represents the Federal government in this Territory, and Uncle Sam's army is here to protect the Federal government. If Ballard calls on the army it's our business to obey, and if there's any mistake in judgment it's Ballard's, not mine." Which was sound soldier common sense, and happened to be equally good law. This is not always the case.

"You haven't got any force to send," said Tuck.

This was true. General Crook had taken with him both Captain Sinclair's infantry and the troop (or company, as cavalry was also then called) of the First.

"A detail of five or six with a reliable noncommissioned officer will do to remind them it's the United States they're bucking against," said Paisley. "There's a deal in the moral of these things. Crook—" Paisley broke off and ran to the door. "Hold his horse!" he called out to the orderly; for he had heard the hoofs, and was out of the house before Corporal Jones had fairly arrived. So Jones sprang off and hurried up, saluting. He delivered his message.

"Um—umpra—what's that? Is it *imperative* you mean?" suggested Paisley.

"Yes, sir," said Jones, reforming his pronunciation of that unaccustomed word. "He said it twiced."

"What were they doing?"

"Blamed if I—beg the captain's pardon—they looked like they was waitin' fer me to git out."

"Go on—go on. How many were there?"

"Seven, sir. There was Governor Ballard and Mr. Hewley

and—well, them's all the names I know. But," Jones hastened on with eagerness, "I've saw them five other fellows before at a—at—" The corporal's voice failed, and he stood looking at the captain.

"Well? Where?"

"At a cockfight, sir," murmured Jones, casting his eyes down.

A slight sound came from the room where Tuck was seated, listening, and Paisley's round gray eyes rolled once, then steadied themselves fiercely upon Jones.

"Did you notice anything further unusual, Corporal?"

"No, sir, except they was excited in there. Looked like they might be goin' to hev considerable rough house—a fuss, I mean, sir. Two was in their socks. I counted four guns on a table."

"Take five men and go at once to the State-House. If the Governor needs assistance you will give it, but do nothing hasty. Stop trouble and make none. You've got twenty minutes."

"Captain—if anybody needs arrestin'—"

"You must be judge of that." Paisley went into the house. There was no time for particulars.

"Snakes!" remarked Jones. He jumped on his horse and dashed down the slope to the men's quarters.

"Crook may be here any day or any hour," said Paisley, returning to the doctor. "With two companies in the background, I think Price's Left Wing will subside this morning."

"Supposing they don't?"

"I'll go myself; and when it gets to Washington that the commanding officer at Boisé personally interfered with the Legislature of Idaho, it'll shock 'em to that extent that the government will have to pay for a special commission of investigation and two tons of red tape. I've got to trust to that corporal's good sense. I haven't another man at the post."

Corporal Jones had three-quarters of a mile to go, and it was ten minutes before noon, so he started his five men at a run. His plan was to walk and look quiet as soon as he reached the town and thus excite no curiosity. The citizens were accustomed to the sight of passing soldiers. Jones had thought out several things, and he was not going to order bayonets fixed until the final necessary moment. "Stop trouble and make none" was firm in his mind. He had not long been a corporal. It was still his first enlistment. His habits were by no means exemplary; and his frontier personality, strongly developed by six years of vagabonding before he enlisted, was scarcely yet disciplined into the military machine of the regulation pattern that it should and must become before he could be counted a model soldier. His captain had promoted him to steady him, if that could be, and to give his better qualities a chance. Since then he had never been drunk at the wrong time. Two years ago it would not have entered his free-lance heart to be reticent with any man, high or low, about any pleasure in which he saw fit to indulge; to-day he had been shy over confessing to the commanding officer his leaning to cockfights—a sign of his approach to the correct mental attitude of the enlisted man. Being corporal had wakened in him a new instinct, and this State-House affair was the first chance he had had to show himself. He gave the order to proceed at a walk in such a tone that one of the troopers whispered to another, "Specimen ain't going to forget he's wearing a chevron."

III

The brief silence that Jones and his invitation to supper had caused among the Councillors was first broken by F. Jackson Gilet.

"Gentlemen," he said, "as President of the Council I rejoice in an interruption that has given pause to our haste and saved us from ill-considered expressions of opinion. The Gove'nuh has, I confess, surprised me. Befo' examining the legal aspect of our case I will ask the Gove'nuh if he is familiar with the sundry statutes applicable."

"I think so," Ballard replied pleasantly.

"I had supposed," continued the President of the Council— "nay, I had congratulated myself that our weightiuh tasks of law-making and so fo'th were consummated yesterday, our thirty-ninth day, and that our friendly game of last night would be, as it were, the finis that crowned with pleashuh the work of a session memorable for its harmony."

This was not wholly accurate, but near enough. The Governor had vetoed several bills, but Price's Left Wing had had much more than the required two-thirds vote of both Houses to make these bills laws over the Governor's head. This may be called harmony in a manner. Gilet now went on to say that any doubts which the Governor entertained concerning the legality of his paying any salaries could easily be settled without entering upon discussion. Discussion at such a juncture could not but tend toward informality. The President of the Council could well remember most unfortunate discussions in Missouri between the years 1856 and 1860, in some of which he had had the honor to take part—*minima pars,* gentlemen! Here he digressed elegantly upon civil dissensions, and Ballard, listening to him and marking the slow, sure progress of the hour, told himself that never before had Gilet's oratory seemed more welcome or less lengthy. A plan had come to him, the orator next announced, a way out of the present dilemma, simple and regular in every aspect. Let some gentleman present now kindly draft a bill setting forth in its preamble the acts of Congress providing for the Legislature's compensation, and let this bill in conclusion provide that all members immediately receive the full amount due for their services. At noon both Houses would convene; they would push back the clock, and pass this bill before the term of their session should expire.

"Then, Gove'nuh," said Gilet, "you can amply vindicate yo'self by a veto, which, together with our votes on reconsideration of yoh objections, will be reco'ded in the journal of our proceedings, and copies transmitted to Washington within thirty days as required by law. Thus, suh, will you become absolved from all responsibility."

The orator's face, while he explained this simple and regular way out of the dilemma, beamed with acumen and statesmanship. Here they would make a law, and the Governor must obey the law!

Nothing could have been more to Ballard's mind as he calculated the fleeting minutes than this peaceful, pompous farce. "Draw your bill, gentlemen," he said, "I would not object if I could."

The Statutes of the United States were procured from among the pistols and opened at the proper page. Gascon Claiborne, upon another sheet of paper headed "Territory of Idaho, Council Chamber," set about formulating some phrases which began "Whereas," and Gratiot des Pères read aloud to him from the statutes. Ballard conversed apart with Hewley; in fact, there was much conversing aside.

" 'Third March, 1863, c. 117, s. 8, v. 12, p. 811,' " dictated Des Pères.

"Skip the chaptuhs and sections," said Claiborne. "We only require the date."

" 'Third March, 1863. The sessions of the Legislative Assemblies of the several Territories of the United States shall be limited to forty days' duration.' "

"Wise provision that," whispered Ballard. "No telling how long a poker game might last."

But Hewley could not take anything in this spirit. "Genuine business was not got through till yesterday," he said.

" 'The members of each branch of the Legislature,' " read Des Pères, " ' 'shall receive compensation of six dollars per day during the sessions herein provided for, and they shall receive such mileage as now provided by law: *Provided,* That the President of the Council and the Speaker of the House of Representatives shall each receive a compensation of ten dollars a day.' "

At this the President of the Council waved a deprecatory hand to signify that it was a principle, not profit, for which he battled. They had completed their *Whereases,* incorporating the language of the several sections as to how the appropriation should be made, who disbursed such money, mileage, and, in short, all things pertinent to their bill, when Pete Cawthon made a suggestion.

"Ain't there anything 'bout how much the Gove'nuh gits?" he asks.

"And the Secretary?" added Wingo.

"Oh, you can leave us out," said Ballard.

"Pardon me, Gove'nuh," said Gilet. "You stated that yoh difficulty was not confined to Mr. Wingo or any individual gentleman but was general. Does it not apply to yo'self, suh? Do you not need any bill?"

"Oh no," said Ballard, laughing. "I don't need any bill."

"And why not?" said Cawthon. "You've jist ez much earned yoh money ez us fellers."

"Quite as much," said Ballard. "But we're not alike—at present."

Gilet grew very stately. "Except certain differences in political opinions, suh, I am not awah of how we differ in merit as public servants of this Territory."

"The difference is of your own making, Mr. Gilet, and no bill you could frame would cure it or destroy my responsibility. You cannot make any law contrary to a law of the United States."

"Contrary to a law of the United States? And what, suh, has the United States to say about my pay I have earned in Idaho?"

"Mr. Gilet, there has been but one government in this country since April, 1865, and as friends you and I have often agreed to differ as to how many there were before then. That government has a law compelling people like you and me to go through a formality, which I have done and you and your friends have refused to do each time it has been suggested to you. I have raised no point until now, having my reasons, which were mainly that it would make less trouble now for the Territory of which I have been appointed Governor. I am held accountable to the Secretary of the Treasury semiannually for the manner in which the appropriation has been expended. If you will kindly hand me that book—"

Gilet, more and more stately, handed Ballard the Statutes, which he had taken from Des Pères. The others were watching

Ballard with gathering sullenness, as they had watched Hewley while he was winning Wingo's money, only now the sullenness was of a more decided complexion.

Ballard turned the pages. " 'Second July, 1862. Every person elected or appointed to any office of honor or profit, either in the civil, military, or naval service, . . . shall, before entering upon the duties of such office, and before being entitled to any salary or other emoluments thereof, take and subscribe the following oath: I—' "

"What does this mean, suh?" said Gilet.

"It means there is no difference in our positions as to what preliminaries the law requires of us, no matter how we may vary in convictions. I as Governor have taken the oath of allegiance to the United States, and you as Councillor must do the same before you can get your pay. Look at the book."

"I decline, suh. I repudiate yoh proposition. There is a wide difference in our positions."

"What do you understand it to be, Mr. Gilet?" Ballard's temper was rising.

"If you have chosen to take an oath that did not go against yoh convictions—"

"Oh, Mr. Gilet!" said Ballard, smiling. "Look at the book." He would not risk losing his temper through further discussion. He would stick to the law as it lay open before them.

But the Northern smile sent Missouri logic to the winds. "In what are you superior to me, suh, that I cannot choose? Who are you that I and these gentlemen must take oaths befo' you?"

"Not before me. Look at the book."

"I'll look at no book, suh. Do you mean to tell me you have seen me day aftuh day and meditated this treacherous attempt?"

"There is no attempt and no treachery, Mr. Gilet. You could have taken the oath long ago, like other officials. You can take it today—or take the consequences."

"What? You threaten me, suh? Do I understand you to threaten me? Gentlemen of the Council, it seems Idaho will be less free than Missouri unless we look to it." The President of the Council had risen in his indignant oratorical might, and his more and more restless friends glared admiration at him. "When was the time that Price's Left Wing surrendered?" asked the orator. "Nevuh! Others have, be it said to their shame. We have not toiled these thousand miles fo' that! Others have crooked the pliant hinges of the knee that thrift might follow fawning. As fo' myself, two grandfathers who fought fo' our libuhties rest in the soil of Virginia, and two uncles who fought in the Revolution sleep in the land of the Dark and Bloody Ground. With such blood in my veins I will nevuh, nevuh, nevuh submit to Northern rule and dictation. I will risk all to be with the Southern people, and if defeated I can, with a patriot of old, exclaim,

" 'More true joy an exile feels
    Than Caesuh with a Senate at his heels.'

"Aye, gentlemen! And we will not be defeated! Our rights are here and are ours." He stretched his arm toward the Treasurer's strongbox, and his enthusiastic audience rose at the rhetoric. "Contain yo'selves, gentlemen," said the orator. "Twelve o'clock and our bill!"

"I've said my say," said Ballard, remaining seated.

"An' what'll ye do?" inquired Pete Cawthon from the agitated group.

"I forbid you to touch that!" shouted Ballard. He saw Wingo moving toward the box.

"Gentlemen, do not resort—" began Gilet.

But small, iron-gray Hewley snatched his pistol from the box and sat down astraddle of it, guarding his charge. At this hostile movement the others precipitated themselves toward the table where lay their weapons, and Governor Ballard, whipping his own from his armhole, said as he covered the table: "Go easy, gentlemen! Don't hurt our Treasurer!"

"Don't nobody hurt anybody," said Specimen Jones, opening the door.

This prudent corporal had been looking in at a window and hearing plainly for the past two minutes, and he had his men posted. Each member of the Council stopped as he stood, his pistol not quite yet attained; Ballard restored his own to its armhole and sat in his chair; little Hewley sat on his box; and F. Jackson Gilet towered haughtily, gazing at the intruding blue uniform of the United States.

"I'll hev to take you to the commanding officer," said Jones briefly to Hewley. "You and yer box."

"Oh, my stars and stripes, but that's a keen move!" rejoiced Ballard to himself. "He's arresting *us*."

In Jones's judgment, after he had taken in the situation, this had seemed the only possible way to stop trouble without making any, and therefore, even now, bayonets were not fixed. Best not ruffle Price's Left Wing just now, if you could avoid it. For a new corporal it was well thought and done. But it was high noon, the clock not pushed back, and punctual Representatives strolling innocently toward their expected pay. There must be no time for a gathering and possible reaction. "I'll hev to clear this State-House out," Jones decided. "We're makin' an arrest," he said aloud, "and we want a little room." The outside bystanders stood back obediently, but the Councillors delayed. Their pistols were, with Ballard's and Hewley's, of course in custody. "Here," said Jones, restoring them. "Go home now. The commanding officer's waitin' fer the prisoner. Put yer boots on, sir, and leave," he added to Pete Cawthon, who still stood in his stockings. "I don't want to hev to disperse anybody more'n what I've done."

Disconcerted Price's Left Wing now saw file out between armed soldiers the Treasurer and his strongbox; and thus guarded they were brought to Boisé Barracks, whence they did not reappear. The Governor also went to the post.

After delivering Hewley and his treasure to the commanding officer, Jones with his five troopers went to the sutler's store and took a drink at Jones's expense. Then one of them asked the corporal to have another. But Jones refused. "If a man drinks much of that," said he (and the whiskey certainly was of a livid, unlikely flavor), "he's liable to go home and steal his own pants." He walked away to his quarters, and as he went they heard him thoughtfully humming his most inveterate song, "Ye shepherds tell me have you seen my Flora pass this way."

But poisonous whiskey was not the inner reason for his moderation. He felt very much like a responsible corporal to-day, and the troopers knew it. "Jones has done himself a good turn in this fuss," they said. "He'll be changing his chevron."

That afternoon the Legislature sat in the State-House and read to itself in the Statutes all about oaths. It is not believed that any of them sat up another night; sleeping on a problem is often much better. Next morning the commanding officer and Governor Ballard were called upon by F. Jackson Gilet and the Speaker of the House. Everyone was civil and hearty as possible. Gilet pronounced the captain's whiskey "equal to any at the Southern, Saint Louey," and conversed for some time about the cold season, General Crook's remarkable astuteness in dealing with Indians, and other topics of public interest. "And concerning' yoh difficulty yesterday, Gove'nuh," said he, "I've been consulting the laws, suh, and I perceive yoh construction is entahley correct."

And so the Legislature signed that form of oath prescribed for participants in the late Rebellion, and Hewley did not have to wait for his poker money. He and Wingo played many subsequent games; for, as they all said in referring to the matter, "A little thing like that should nevuh stand between friends."

Thus was accomplished by Ballard, Paisley—and Jones—the Second Missouri Compromise, at Boisé City, Idaho, 1867—an eccentric moment in the eccentric years of our development westward, and historic also. That it has gone unrecorded until now is because of Ballard's modesty, Paisley's preference for the sword, and Jones's hatred of the pen. He was never known to write except, later, in the pages of his company roster and such unavoidable official places; for the troopers were prophetic. In not many months there was no longer a Corporal Jones, but a person widely known as Sergeant Jones of Company A; called also the "Singing Sergeant"; but still familiar to his intimate friends as "Specimen."

Bill Gulick's second entry in these pages is wholly different from his first—an offbeat and moving tale of a Conestoga wagon train traveling west on the Oregon Trail and of the relationship between an indentured servant from Sweden and an "uncouth, ignorant, poorly dressed" frontier guide.

Where the Wind Blows Free

★★★★★★★★★★★★

Bill Gulick

WHEN the stranger rode into camp, Freda Eklunds was down on her knees before a pan of hot, soapy water, washing dishes. The dry June wind coming off the sage-covered desert beyond Fort Bridger had loosened a strand of her braided yellow hair, and, in exasperation, she had made a hasty backhand pass at it, succeeding only in getting suds in her right eye. With a cry of dismay, she lifted her apron, wiped the strong lye soap from the offended eye, and then looked up through a misty film as the stranger swung off his horse.

" 'Scuse me, ma'am. This the Wagner outfit?"

"Yes."

"Whar'll I find Lucius Wagner?"

"Over there," she answered, started to point, then, as a flood of tears came again, tried to stem them with her apron.

"Somethin' troublin' you?" the man said, concerned.

"Soap. Just soap."

As her vision cleared, she saw that he was tall, lean, and dark, wore ragged, greasy buckskins, and, despite his self-assured air, appeared to be only a few years older than she. His black eyes twinkled.

"Glad to hear that. Thought I'd busted in on a private cry."

Resuming her chore with an angry toss of her head, she covertly watched him lead his horse toward the wagon in whose shade the Wagner family was resting. Mr. Wagner, a hearty, red-faced man in his early fifties, was napping. Mrs. Wagner, a solid woman with a firm chin and disposition to match, was making sure that her six children—who ranged in age from nine to sixteen—were con-

159

centrating on their books to make up for the schoolwork they were missing. *I should have warned him that the Wagners dislike being disturbed at this hour,* Freda mused. *Well, he'll learn that soon enough.*

"Howdy, ma'am. I'm Jeff Clayton. Jim Bridger sent me over—"

"If you wish to see my husband," Mrs. Wagner cut in, "he cannot be disturbed. Come back later."

Mr. Wagner opened his eyes. "It is all right, Mama. I am awake. What do you want, Mr. Clayton?"

"Jim says you're lookin' for a guide to take you through to Oregon."

"We are."

"Wal, that's my business."

"You know the way?"

"Blindfolded."

Vigorously scrubbing a plate, Freda marveled that an uncouth, ignorant, poorly dressed man such as this one should approach the Wagners and ask for a job so casually. The Wagners were rich, socially important people of the best Pennsylvania Dutch stock. Back in Philadelphia, Mr. Wagner had owned a prosperous brewery, lived in a fine house, and circulated with gentlemen of means. Yet Jeff Clayton dared interrupt Mr. Wagner's nap and stand in Mrs. Wagner's presence without even doing her the courtesy of removing his hat. Mr. Wagner, who always conferred with his wife on important decisions, glanced at her questioningly.

"What do you think, Mama?"

Her sharp eyes surveyed the young man. "How much pay do you ask?"

"Four dollars a day."

"Two is plenty."

"Four, ma'am. Take it or leave it."

Freda stifled a gasp. Mrs. Wagner would send him packing, of course. Such insolence from a hired servant could not be tolerated! True, the guide that had brought the twelve wagons in the train this far had quit a week ago and headed for the California gold fields. Guides did seem to be a necessity in this country, and the enforced layover was making everyone restless. All the same, she was certain what Mrs. Wagner would say. She felt sorry for Jeff Clayton, despite his arrogance, for he looked like he badly needed the job.

Mrs. Wagner's eyes snapped. "Three. That is all we will pay."

Jeff Clayton turned to his horse. "Oregon lies due west. Good luck."

There was a murmur of discontent from the emigrant families

that had gathered around. Mr. Wagner scowled, conferred in whispers with his wife, then said, "Wait. We will pay you four dollars. But only on our terms."

The black eyes were amused. "And what might they be?"

"That you do not quit us whenever you feel like it, as the other guide did. That you take us safely through to Oregon City before you receive one dollar of your pay."

"Fair enough." Swinging into the saddle, he gave the Wagners an informal salute. "Now if you'll excuse me I got some business to do at the fort. See you in the mornin'."

Because she knew what it was like to be without money, a job, or friends, Freda was glad that Jeff Clayton had found work despite his lack of manners. She determined to teach him the Wagners' ways so that he would not offend them. Being far too timid to speak directly to a man she had barely met, she found an errand to do at the fort that afternoon and said her piece haltingly to Jim Bridger, whom she knew to be a kindly, understanding man. When she was done, he gave her a searching look.

"Kind of took to Jeff, didn't you?"

"Oh, no!" she said hastily, coloring. "It is just that I want to help him."

"He'll be obliged, ma'am."

Freda had cooked and served the Wagners their breakfast, next morning, when Jeff Clayton came nonchalantly riding into camp. One horrified look told Freda her well-meant advice had been completely ignored. He had not trimmed his hair, bathed, shaved, or changed his filthy buckskins, as she had told Bridger he must do. His eyes were bleary; he complained of an aching head and a stomach full of butterflies; he scorned the good breakfast she had kept warm for him; he drank three cups of coffee but said it was too weak; and then, when she indignantly refused his suggestion that she snitch a pint of "old man Wagner's whisky" and sneak it to him as an eye-opener, he stalked off muttering profanely that if he'd knowed this was going to be a dry drive damned if he'd have hired on.

Freda was so angry, she hoped the Wagners would fire him. But both Mr. and Mrs. Wagner were too preoccupied to notice his condition, and the wagons moved out in good order. Under his apparently casual guidance, they made good time across the high, sage-covered plains lying west of Fort Bridger, struck Bear River and followed its lush valley northwesterly, left it where the river swung south, and wound without incident through the rough, lava-strewn country beyond. Reaching the juncture of

the Portneuf with the Snake, two weeks later, Freda heard Jeff
tell Mr. Wagner that it would be wise to camp here for a few days,
readying the wagons and resting the oxen for the tough going of
the Snake River Desert ahead.

After breakfast, next morning, Mrs. Wagner said, "When you
have finished the dishes, Freda, the clothes you will wash. You
will need the big tub, wood for the fire, and lots of hot water."

"Yes, Mrs. Wagner."

Hurrying through the dishes, Freda put them away, went over
to one of the wagons, and struggled to lift down the big wooden
tub resting on the high tailgate. It proved stubborn to move. She
heard Jeff, who was lying on one elbow near the fire, say to Mr.
Wagner, "That's a heavy tub, Lucius."

"Yes," Mr. Wagner agreed. "It is a good, solid tub." He raised
his voice. "Your shoulder you should put under it, Freda."

Freda flushed. "Yes, Mr. Wagner."

She heard Jeff give a grunt of disgust. He rose, crossed to the
wagon, and lifted the tub to the ground for her. She thanked him
with her eyes, turned, and hastily picked up bucket and ax. To
her amazement he snatched them roughly out of her hands. "No
need for you to do that with all these husky kids standin' around.
Adolph, fetch some water. Ludwig, go chop some firewood. Hus-
tle, now!"

Freda whispered urgently, "Jeff, please!"

Mrs. Wagner's eyes shot fire. "You will give no orders to my
children, Mr. Clayton."

"Wal, they wa'n't doin' nothin', so I thought—"

"That is servant's work. Freda!"

"Yes, Mrs. Wagner! I go!"

"You wish she should have help, Mr. Clayton?" Mrs. Wagner
said with an icy smile. "Very well. You help her."

Freda saw Jeff's jaw drop. "Me? You're orderin' me to carry
water and wood like an Injun squaw?"

Panic-stricken, Freda took bucket and ax out of his hands and
ran toward the river. Catching up with her, he grabbed her arm,
stopped her, and said angrily, "Now, what'd you go and do that
for?"

"Please, Jeff, you must not argue with her! She will become very
angry!"

"That's no skin off my nose."

"You will lose your job! Four dollars a day is a great deal of
money!"

She saw his black eyes flicker, angry at first, then amused, then
thoughtful. "How much are they payin' you?"

"Oh, I am paid nothing. I am an indentured servant."

"You mean to tell me you work for free?"

"They give me my meals and bed."

Jeff gave a snort of derision. "They do that much for their oxen. How come you put up with it?"

As he cut wood and carried water for her, she told him. Back in Sweden, her homeland, her father had been a gunsmith, and the tales he had read about Oregon had fascinated him. A year ago he had brought his family to America, determined to make his future in that bright new land; but shortly after the family reached Philadelphia smallpox had taken everyone except Freda. She had been barely eighteen, homeless, and frightened. With no money, no relatives or friends in this country, and a hazy notion that Oregon was a place where all dreams came true, she had found the Wagners planning to emigrate there and indentured herself to them as a servant.

"For how long?" Jeff asked quietly.

"Five years."

"Then what'll you do?"

Shyly she lowered her eyes, her voice warm and full of hope. "If I am a good servant, perhaps when my time is up they will give me a little dowry. Then I can find a husband."

"What the devil's a dowry?"

She stared at him in amazement. "You do not know? Why, it is what every girl must have before she can get married!"

His eyes surveyed her from head to toe. " 'Pears to me you've already got all a gal needs—and then some."

"Oh, Jeff, do not joke! A dowry is a gift to her husband—a cow, a little house, a piece of land, a sum of money."

"You mean to tell me the fella gets *paid* to marry her?"

"It is not pay. It is a start for married life. How else can a young couple get a start for married life?"

He rubbed his chin, thinking that over. "Why, it's plumb easy. If a fella's got any gumption at all, he shakes the dust of his folks' farm off his boots, takes his gun, his horse, and his ax, and travels west till he finds a piece of land that suits his eye—"

"Who gives him this gun, this horse, this ax?"

"Nobody. He buys 'em."

"Where does he get the money?"

"Wal, his arms ain't broke, are they?"

Puzzled, she gazed at him. "What do you mean?"

"Jest that a little money ain't hard to come by if he ain't scared of work. He can take a job—"

"Why should he? His folks have land, yes? Why does he not stay home and work there?"

Her innocent questions appeared to irritate him. "You don't get the idea at all. Take me, for instance. My folks had a good farm back in Ohio, but we had a big family and my foot took to itchin'. So I said the hell with farmin', came west, and started trappin' beaver—"

"You were poaching?"

"Huh?"

"Who did the beaver belong to? Who gave you permission to trap them?"

Before he could answer, Katrina and Peter, the youngest of the Wagner children, came running up and told Freda Mama was wondering when she was going to start the washing. Jeff gave them a message to carry back to their mama that made Freda cover her ears with her hands; then, as he leaned over and picked up an armload of wood, he grunted, "You got a lot to learn about this country, young lady. Like it or not, I'm going to be your teacher."

"And you," she said primly, picking up the bucket of water, "have much to learn about manners. Perhaps it will be I who shall teach you!"

That settled, they went back to camp.

Jeff meant well, Freda knew, but the sad truth was he was short on patience. He was always preaching what a great thing it was to be free, but when she'd say: "Free from what?" he'd blow up and ask her what fool system of government had she been raised under, anyway? His bluntness hurt her; she would quit speaking to him; he'd come to her and apologize, saying he hadn't meant it personal, that it was he who was stupid not her, and why didn't she please learn him some manners?

She tried. For instance, she said, it was very rude of him to stare blankly off into space, pretending to be deaf and dumb, when Mrs. Wagner asked him to do some task. He disagreed. Just because he lent Freda a hand when her chores got too heavy for her seemed to give Mrs. Wagner the notion he'd jump when she said frog. But damned if he would. Only way of curing Mrs. Wagner of ordering him around was by giving her the deaf-and-dumb Injun treatment.

"But must you make her so angry?"

"I ain't her personal servant."

"Her husband pays your salary."

"As a guide, that's all."

"But if you displease her, she will make her husband discharge you. Then what will you do?"

"Wal, I won't starve, you can bet on that."

"How can you be sure? Who would take care of you?"

He threw back his head and laughed. "Hell, gal, long as a man's got his health, a gun, and a lick of sense, he can't possibly starve in this country. Beaver, buffalo, antelope, deer—why, they're all free for the takin'. So is the land."

"What land?"

"Most all of it." His dark eyes sobered. "Why, honey," he boasted, "if I had a mind to I could claim three hundred and twenty acres in Oregon. If I had me a wife, I could claim a whole square mile. After I'd lived on it long enough to prove I intended to stay, the government would give me title to it free and clear. I could cut down trees, build a house, farm, raise cattle, or do anything else I was man enough to do, without asking leave of nobody."

She thought that over. "How much land could Mr. Wagner claim?"

"The same as me, no more."

That, she guessed, was an outright lie. But she let him think she believed it, just to keep the peace.

One evening in early September the wagons made camp in a grassy valley on the western slope of a range of mountains Jeff said were the Blues. When Freda had finished her chores he took her for a walk. In the twilight they stopped and sat down on a rock. As Jeff filled his pipe, Freda gestured into the purpling distance.

"This is Oregon?"

"Eastern edge of it, yeah."

"Where is the free land?"

"All over."

"Here—right here?"

"Far as I can see, nobody's claimed this valley yet."

She sat quite still, her eyes taking in the wide, grass-covered meadow below and the sparkling stream wandering across it. The soil looked deep, rich, and free from stones, and, overlooking the valley, a tall, straight pine and hemlock trees, much like those of her own country, covered the higher slopes as far as her eyes could see. Her voice filled with awe.

"Jeff . . ."

"Yeah?"

"You could take a square mile of this valley for yourself?"

"Sure—if I had a wife."

"Why don't you?"

He puffed silently on his pipe for a time. "Wal, I guess I ain't ready to settle down yet. I mean, I'd have to find the right sort of gal. . . ."

"Don't you want a wife?"

"Someday . . ."

"Where will you look for her, Jeff?"

"Ain't give that much thought."

She averted her eyes. "I hope you fine one with a handsome dowry."

"Why would I want one with a dowry? My arms ain't broke."

She looked at him. "You have said that before. I do not understand what it meams."

"It means I've got some pride. I'm able to put clothes on her back, food in her mouth, and a roof over her head. Long as she had some git-up-and-go to her, I wouldn't care if she didn't have a dime."

Despite her efforts to master the English language, there were still occasional phrases Jeff used that Freda failed utterly to comprehend. This was one. Before she could ask him to explain it to her, Mrs. Wagner called from camp, "Freda! Freda, come here at once!"

Hastily Freda got up and went; but from the look Jeff gave her she gathered that this wasn't the kind of git-up-and-go he'd meant.

There was the damp chill of early autumn in the air when the wagon train made camp at the Dalles some days later. Westward, Freda could see tall mountains looming, slashed by a wide, rapids-filled river. She heard Jeff say to Mr. Wagner, "We got a choice to make here, Lucius. Oregon City lies a hundred miles west, beyond the Cascades yonder. But there's two routes we can take."

"Which is easiest?"

"They're both mean. We can take the wagons apart and raft 'em through the Gorge. Or we can cross the mountains on Barlow's Toll Road, which is jest one notch better'n no road at all. If we stick to the river, we'll get mighty wet. If we cross the mountains, we'll have some stiff climbin' to do."

"You are the guide, Mama says. It is for you to decide."

"Wal, I'd rather climb than swim."

Mr. Wagner smiled and clapped Jeff on the back. Freda was pleased to hear him say, "You have been a good guide, Jeff. Tonight we will have a little party to celebrate the nearing end of our journey."

It was a nice party, Freda mused as she watched the couples dancing and heard the men chatting jovially around the whiskey barrel

which Mr. Wagner had set out despite his wife's frown of protest.
Eyeing Jeff with concern, she hoped he would remember his place
and not drink too much, for with things going so well between
him and Mr. Wagner she had begun to entertain a secret dream.
Mr. Wagner would be an important man in Oregon, no doubt
about that. If Jeff chose to settle down, perhaps Mr. Wagner would
give him a job in his brewery. If Jeff worked hard, was sober, industrious, and thrifty, then by the time Freda's five years were
up . . .

She sighed in dismay. Urged on by the menfolk, Jeff had jumped
into the center of the firelit circle and was doing a wild Indian
war dance. That overcame whatever inhibitions he may have had
against sociable dancing, and he snatched her to her feet and gave
her a whirl that left her breathless. Well aware of what Mrs. Wagner's attitude would be toward having a servant girl join the party
uninvited, Freda tore loose from him, but Jeff, unperturbed,
grabbed first one, then another of the ladies and cavorted with
them. To Freda's horror, one of his partners was Mrs. Wagner,
which caused whoops of laughter from the onlookers. What Mrs.
Wagner thought of that, Freda had no chance to observe, for now
Mr. Wagner, carried away by the spirit—or spirits—of the evening, jubilantly seized Freda and danced with her.

That surely must have shocked Mrs. Wagner, Freda thought,
panic-stricken. But Mr. Wagner wasn't done yet. As the dance
ended he picked Freda up, whirled her around until her skirts
flew, and then gave her a juicy, alcoholic kiss square on the lips.

Mrs. Wagner broke loose from Jeff's grasp and crossed the circle. With a cry of outrage, she slapped Freda hard, jerked her husband around, planted an open-handed blow against his startled
face, then, her face like a thundercloud, read the riot act to all
present.

"Enough! Enough of this disgusting drinking, dancing, and
kissing! No more will I stand for!"

The party ended. Her face aflame, Freda stared down at her
shoe tips. "I am sorry, Mrs. Wagner. So sorry!"

In the sudden silence Jeff strode to her side, put his arm around
her quivering shoulders, and said hotly, "What's to be sorry for?
No harm was intended nor done. If you want my opinion, Mrs.
Wagner—"

"Your opinion you will keep to yourself, Mr. Clayton! You are
a paid servant, no more!"

"Wal, that's your notion," Jeff said, the anger in his voice so
deep it frightened Freda. "But mine happens to be a sight different. Any old time you start slappin' Freda around—"

"Jeff!" Freda begged, frantically squeezing his arm. "Be still! Please be still!"

He gave her a long, searching look. Then he turned abruptly on his heel and stalked off into the dark.

It took two weeks to make the mountain crossing. In all that wearying time Jeff walked not once with Freda of evenings. Nor did he associate with or speak to the Wagners except in the strict line of the business at hand. He was angry, she knew, and he was hurt. That he could be hurt touched her deeply; that she had hurt him while he was trying to protect her and she was trying to protect him made it all the worse.

The last hill which they must descend was so steep, the only way to get a wagon down was to tie a log behind its rear wheels as a drag, lock the wheels, and ease the vehicle downgrade by means of ropes belayed around the trunk of a thick fir on the height. Ordering the women and children to stand clear, Jeff supervised the men in the slow, hard, backbreaking work with a skill that made Freda marvel at his ingenuity. He got all but the last of the wagons to the bottom of the hill without incident. Then, as it inched along, halfway down, a frayed rope broke, and the wagon went tumbling end over end down the slope, landing on an immense rock that splintered it into kindling wood.

Jeff took it calmly. After making sure no one had been injured, he said to Mr. Wagner, "That's the first one we've lost. We're lucky, Lucius."

"Lucky?" Mr. Wagner stormed. "It was *my* wagon!"

"Wal, you started west with two, and you've still got one left. Outside of the wagon itself and a barrel of busted dishes, there's no damage done."

Down on her knees in the wreckage, Mrs. Wagner let out a frenzied howl. "Lucius! Those dishes were my Sunday-best china!"

The glint in Jeff's eyes warned Freda that he had been pushed almost as far as he would go. But Mrs. Wagner failed to see it. Lighting into him, she tongue-lashed him for five solid minutes before she paused for breath. He didn't interrupt, but his eyes got darker and darker. When Mrs. Wagner was done, he looked at her husband.

"Know what I'd do with that mouthy squaw of yours if she was mine?"

"Lucius!" Mrs. Wagner screamed. "Did you hear what he called me?"

"I'd cut me a length of sapling, like so," Jeff said, measuring off the proper length with his hands. "Then I'd lay it onto her good and proper. Makes 'em quit every time."

Freda saw Mr. Wagner's face turn red, then white. She saw him gaze vacantly off into the forest, as if looking for something. Then, recovering himself, he exploded: "You are discharged, Mr. Clayton!"

"You don't have to fire me. I quit." He pointed west. "The road's clear and easy the rest of the way. You can't miss it. Give me my pay and I'll be riding."

Trembling with anger, Mr. Wagner fished his purse out of his pocket. "I'll be happy to. How much do we owe you?"

"Ninety days I've put up with you. That's three hundred and sixty dollars, way I figger."

"Wait, Papa!" Mrs. Wagner said, a calculating gleam coming into her eyes. "Remember the bargain? No pay was he to get until safely we arrived in Oregon City. We have not arrived. Yet he quits. With his own mouth he said it. So no pay do we owe him."

"You are right, Mama." Mr. Wagner smiled at Jeff. "That was the bargain."

Freda gasped, for without a word Jeff had strode over to his horse, got his rifle, and turned around. As he started to speak, an involuntary movement on her part drew his eyes to her. He stared at her long and hard. She returned his gaze, silently imploring him to do nothing he might later regret. She saw his black eyes flicker with sudden decision.

"Lucius," he said quietly, "how much is Freda worth to you?"

Mr. Wagner stared at him blankly. "Freda? You ask how much she is worth?"

"Yeah. That indentured-servant guff don't shine out here. If she had the gumption, she could take her freedom. But she won't. She's scared to. So I'll buy it for her. I'm askin' you to make a choice, Lucius—give me my pay in cash or give me Freda. You got jest ten seconds to make up your mind."

Mr. Wagner looked uncertainly at his wife. "Mama—?"

"Servant girls we can get any day," Mrs. Wagner said scornfully. "Cash money is hard to come by. Give her to him."

"You heard that, Freda?" Jeff said.

"Yes."

"Go pack your things. I'll take you to Oregon City."

She did not move. "And after that?"

"Why, that's up to you, I reckon," he said irritably. "I got no use for a servant. But you'll have your freedom."

"What will I do with it?"

Jeff stared at her. "Do you mean to tell me you won't take it?"

"Not this way. Not by having you buy it."

"Wal, what difference does it make how you get it," he demanded, "jest so long as you're free?"

"A great difference—to me."

Anger flared in his face. She wanted desperately to cry out: *Please, Jeff—please understand!* but no words came. With a grunt of disgust, he turned and picked up his horse's trailing reins, jammed his left foot into the stirrup, and roared, "Wal, like it or not, you're free! Your debt to me is paid, Lucius. I'm headin' back to Fort Bridger to give old Jim a piece of my mind for ever tellin' me herdin' pilgrims beats trappin' beaver. But you let Freda alone, you hear me, 'cause if I ever get word you or your wife are pesterin' her—!"

"Jeff!" Freda cried, running toward him. "You must understand why I said what I did! You can't go this way!"

"Watch me! Jest watch me! I'm goin' back to the mountains, I am, and find me an Injun squaw—"

A horse always senses the mood its master is in, Jeff had once told Freda; thus, the wise man controls his temper when approaching his mount. But right now he was so mad, he threw wisdom to the winds. Just as he swung his right leg over the horse's back, that usually calm-natured beast snorted, stuck his head between his forelegs, and humped his body violently. Freda screamed as she saw Jeff sail through the air, do a slow half turn, then pile into the ground with a jarring thump.

She ran to him and helped him sit up. "Jeff! Are you hurt?"

He stared down at his limp right arm. "Busted a wing, seems like."

"Just what you deserve," Mrs. Wagner said unsympathetically. "Come, Lucius."

As the Wagners moved toward their wagon, Freda started to protest, but Jeff muttered, "Let 'em go. I'll make out. Now if you'll just fix up my arm—"

But Freda had a much more urgent matter on her mind. Getting to her feet, she called in a clear, firm voice—not at all a servant's voice, "Mr. Wagner!"

Surprised at her tone, he paused. "Yes?"

"Before you go, there are three things I want of you."

Amused, he gazed at her. "And what are they?"

"First, my clothes."

"You may have them."

"And my freedom."

"That you have already. Didn't you hear the agreement we made with Mr. Clayton?"

"I heard it, yes. But I am not a horse or cow to be sold in the marketplace. I am taking my freedom for myself. Do you understand?"

He shrugged impatiently. "Very well, Freda. You have it. Why argue how you are getting it?"

"Because," Freda said quietly, "if I am taking my freedom for myself, if no one is buying it for me, you still owe Jeff three hundred and sixty dollars. And before you leave, I insist you pay it."

Mr. Wagner laughed heartily. "Insist all you like, my dear. It will do you no good." His face darkened. "Now get your clothes and let us go."

Freda quite lost her temper. Stooping, she picked up Jeff's rifle, leveled it, and cocked it. "The money, Mr. Wagner—I want it right now."

Mr. Wagner reached for his purse. . . .

After the preacher in Oregon City had married them, Jeff said the sensible thing to do was wait till spring before they filed a homestead claim on that valley in eastern Oregon. By then, he said, his arm would be healed and he'd be up to doing heavy farm work.

Freda just smiled and said, "No, we need not wait. Let us go at once—tomorrow."

"But, Freda, all that work—"

"Who's afraid of work?" she murmured as she kissed him. "We're both free now, aren't we? And *my* arms aren't broke."

Wal, Jeff said, long as they had three good arms between 'em, he guessed they'd make out.

*Before settling in eastern Oregon, Ray Palmer Tracy (1886–1966)
lived in many different parts of the West and worked as an oil-well
drilling contractor, gold and copper miner, sheep rancher, and forest
est ranger in the Oregon Siskiyous—all of which provided him with
a wealth of background material for his fiction. He was a frequent
contributor to the Western and adventure pulp magazines of the
thirties, forties, and early fifties, notably* Street & Smith's Western
Story Magazine *and* Short Stories. *He also authored two full-
length Western novels,* Gunsmoke in the Hills *(1939) and* Fighting
Sheepman *(1951). "Critters of Habit," which takes place on the
Eastern Oregon Plateau, is an authentic portrait of early pioneer
days in that part of the Pacific Northwest and of some of the author's
thor's personal experiences with oxen.*

Critters of Habit

★★★★★★★★★★★★

Ray Palmer Tracy

I

THE early morning scent of full-blown summer was in the
bright air of the Eastern Oregon plateau. A kindly sun domi-
nated the sea-blue sky. It shed yellow rays over the deep green
of the pines which swept in stately pride up the mountain slopes
that held the valley of the Wineglass in protecting arms.

Scattered along the creek bank, in a strong, convenient pattern,
were the substantial buildings of the Wineglass cow outfit. A gay
hummingbird darted in and out among the honeysuckles that
climbed the south porch end of the rambling ranchhouse. And out
of the rear kitchen door streamed the Wineglass hands, finished
with breakfast and ready for the day's work.

Vic Ferris, the last man away from the table, could see no fun-
damental difference in this day than in any other that time poured
over the big ranch. A tall, loosely framed young man with a
slightly hooked nose, and the light of independence in the gray
of his eyes, he got out the makings, rolled and lighted a cigarette.

As he started on, from the shortcut trail over the shoulder of the west ridge, leading to Jack Belfont's Diamond-K spread, came a clatter of hoofs. Madge Belfont rode her sleek claybank along the south orchard fence and reined toward the back door of the house. Big Fred Lang, one of the Wineglass hands who had left the table just ahead of Vic, stopped her.

Although there had been no understanding between them, Vic and Madge had been going together, attending dances and the Lit'ry held in the white schoolhouse at the four corners. Since his arrival at the Wineglass the year before, Fred Lang had made determined efforts to cut Vic away from Madge.

The big cowboy did not fit into the Wineglass family like the other boys. This might have been due to his having ridden for one of the famous spreads of the Southwest. Perhaps it caused him to hold himself above the mill run hands as one of the saddle aristocracy. Big headed or not, at least he did his work well and was accepted by that standard of measure.

Vic saw Madge's strong white teeth flash in her generous mouth. "What is it, Fred?" she asked.

Fred, with an air of intimacy, mumbled something Vic couldn't catch. But he could see the dancing laughter in the deep blue eyes that made Madge's rather plain features so intensely alive.

"I haven't time to visit today," she said, and urged her horse.

Fred said something again.

"Afraid I'll be busy Sunday," Madge said over her shoulder, and rode on.

Madge was wearing scuffed boots, a tan denim divided skirt, an old flannel shirt Vic recognized as having belonged to her father, and a battered hat crushed on her short, brown curls. Her sleeves were rolled above her elbows, exposing round, firm arms sun-creamed to a velvety texture. They set an unmistakable pattern for the lithe, vibrant figure sitting so straight and easy in the saddle, and which the awkward clothing could not conceal. She pulled up beside Vic.

"What got you out of bed at this hour?" he greeted.

"The birds made such a racket in the tree outside my window I couldn't sleep," she smiled down at him.

"If the birds drove you over to see me, I'm coming over to the Diamond-K with a pocketful of wheat," he grinned back.

"I hate to hurt your feelings," said Madge, "but I didn't come over to see you. I'm here to borrow some jar rubbers from Mom Hazelton. Mother and I got a batch of canning started and found we were short on tools. I've got to hurry." She rode on.

*   *   *

Vic strolled toward the worn plot in front of the bunk house, where the wizened foreman, Jake Westing, made a morning rite of dealing out the day's jobs.

The lame, cantankerous old choreboy, Ajax Cully, Fred Lang, Swede Anderson, Chuck Baily, Penny Larch, and the other hands not up in line camps were already spread out on the "Auction Block" as they had named the site of the assignments. Trailing behind Vic, deep in an argument, were Jake and the owner, old Tom Hazelton.

Vic had long since ceased to pay any attention to the endless wrangling of the pair. It seemed to be Jake's policy never to agree with old Tom on anything. But just let any misguided hand try to curry favor with Jake by questioning the wisdom of the boss. He'd be lucky if Jake didn't chew him up and use his bones to pick the fifteen teeth he had left. Jake made it thoroughly understood that it was *his* privilege, and *his privilege* alone, to disagree with old Tom.

At the "Auction Block," with the others, Vic faced the approaching foreman and owner. Lean, rawhide-constructed little Jake bounced along, his wrinkled face upturned. A sweeping, frayed mustache hid the wreck a gun-barrel had made of his mouth in the wild days of his youth. And lumbering along beside him, like a tolerant Newfoundland dog overshadowing a yapping terrier, was old Tom.

It was hard to tell what old Tom was thinking by studying his round, smooth face which seemed almost untouched by the same years that had corrugated the features of his foreman. But once those small, blue eyes, which mingled shrewd justice with the chill of winter, looked into a man's soul, there was seldom any doubt in the man as to who was boss of the Wineglass or why it held the position it did and kept prosperous, even in these money panic days of the early nineties.

"I kinda cotton to a man with gumption enough to have and express an opinion of his own," old Tom rumbled down to Jake.

"Yus, you would," Jake snorted up at the tranquil heights above him. "It would never occur to you that it prob'ly warn't a mind of his own such a feller had, but a case of outgrowed britches. A feller—" He broke off as he glanced ahead and saw he and old Tom were getting within hearing distance of the hands. He did that often, giving the impression that he and the boss were settling the fate of the ranch, even though he had only been contradicting the old man's mild opinion that it looked like a dry spell.

Old Tom stopped at the fringe of the "Auction Block," while Jake went on and faced the semi-circle of waiting hands. His sharp, pale eyes singled out Swede. "Swede," he said, "hook Ben and Kate to the mower and cut the timothy on the lower medda. You can have Chuck and Penny again today for your crew."

"Ay gotta grind a mower sickle," stated Swede. "Somebuddy gotta turn the grindstun."

Turning the grindstone was a job no one wanted. Swede had learned the only way he could get a hand on the grindstone crank was to have Jake assist him the chore.

Ajax quietly limped to a spot behind the tall, wide frame of Fred Lang. Jake saw him. A little smile spread his mustache. "Ajax is so full of vigor this morning," he commented, "I reckon a spell at the grindstun will trim him down to around our size."

"I've gotta take the stock to water out of the dry pasture, and then irrigate the garden. I ain't got time," objected Ajax. A sort of pensioner, he was the only one who dared argue with the touchy foreman.

"You'll have time after the sickle is ground. Anyways, there's a moon tonight," Jake closed the debate.

Ajax's red-rimmed eyes were bitter. He had never become reconciled to the accident that had turned him from a rider into a choreboy. Making him turn a grindstone seemed pouring it on.

Jake's pale gaze skimmed over Vic to Fred Lang. "Fred," he directed, "saddle your horse and ride up to the line cabin in Fur Hollar. You he'p Ted Seevey move the dry she stuff over to Rubby Crick."

"On my way." Fred started for the corral.

Jake singled out Vic next. "You've been on the Wineglass four years," he said. "That's long enough so you prob'ly know more about running the ranch than I do. I'm going to let you figger how to get them new shakes for the calf shed roof down here from up the crick. You'd better take an axe and brushhook along in case you have to cut a wagon road through the rawsberry patch at the upper end of Rawsberry Medda."

Vic was tophand on the Wineglass and rated a riding job when there was one. To give him an axe and brushhook and send him out on a farm job and hand Fred what should have been his riding assignment was the rankest kind of an insult. His first impulse was to tell Jake to brush out the wagon road himself and then quit. Just in time he bit back the outburst. To quit would bring him a worse disaster.

He was proving up on a homestead. Leaning on his steady job, he had borrowed money at the bank in Crown Knob and bought the first whiteface cows ever offered for sale in that section. He just had to have a job to keep up his bank payments; and in these times of panic, competent riders were riding the grubline, vainly searching for work.

"What am I going to use for a team to haul down the shakes?" he asked as soon as he could trust his voice.

"That's right," nodded Jake. "All the teams is busy or turned out, ain't they? Well, you wun't need a team right away. It'll take you anyways two days to brush a trail through them rawsberries. We'll see about a team when the time comes."

Vic glanced at old Tom to note how this outrage registered with him. Old Tom's face, as usual, revealed nothing. Anyhow, old Tom never directly interfered with Jake's handling of the help.

"All right," Vic answered Jake, and went to the shop.

He got an axe and brushhook. Locating a file, he touched up the edges of the tools.

Fred rode away from the corral. A few minutes later, old Tom drove his buckboard team toward town. Jake mounted his hammer-headed roan, took the trail around the orchard fence, and disappeared toward the southwest. "Going to take a look at the grass on Sunflower Prairie," speculated Vic.

Swede Anderson and Ajax were coming toward the grindstone at the south side of the shop. Vic couldn't see them, but he could hear Ajax complaining in the whine he had developed since being relegated to a pensioner job in the ranks of the has-beens.

"I draw all the work nobuddy else can stomick around here," he croaked. "Feller'd think a choreboy was a dam' slave."

Vic had sympathy for Ajax but was in no mood to listen to his griping. He flung the file on the bench and started up the creek, wondering what in the world he had done to merit such shabby treatment. Something had got crossways of Jake's craw. But what?

It was as peculiar as it was unexpected. Without any warning he had been reduced to the status of a farmhand, and Fred had been promoted to his job. Thinking of Fred, he remembered that there had been a satisfied smirk on the big cowboy's face when Jake had given him the Fur Hollow assignment. Although he couldn't think of a thing Fred could have done to bring about this condition, a suspicion that he was at the bottom of it took root in Vic and began to flourish.

Sooner or later, if he kept his mouth shut and waited, the truth would come out and throw light on Jake's queer remarks and actions. Meanwhile, there was nothing to do but shrug off the insult and bide his time.

The faint wagon trail Vic was following clung to the bank of the creek. A quarter of a mile above the house it rounded the point of a spur sticking out from the west mountain ridge. The creek made a big bend around the point and then curved back toward the ridge only to swing sharply to the east again and enter the raspberry patch midway between the ridges.

The wild tangle of raspberry bushes and brambles laced together with creepers was an effectual barrier to the timber just above. Vic surveyed the jungle with extreme distaste. He climbed the steep west ridge to where he could look down on the patch and trace the route he was doomed to hack into a wagon trail.

The more he studied it, the more dismal the prospects of the next couple days seemed. He spent a futile hour looking for some way to get a wagon around the patch. But Jake had known what he was talking about in that respect. Reluctantly he went to the spot he had picked to begin and started swinging the brushhook.

There was no breeze down in the protected valley between the high ridges. The sun warmed as it began to arch over the blue vault above. Sweat poured out of Vic. The heat brought up tormenting pictures of Fred riding the cool, pine-scented trail to Fur Hollow.

In half an hour Vic's shirt was wet and sticking to his back. His muscles were hard, but he was bringing a new set into play and he saw he had to pace himself or he would tire badly. He laid down his brushhook and piled the brambles he had cut right and left. While it rested him, it also presented him with a couple bloody thorn scratches, which did not improve the temperature of his outlook.

The brush out of the way, he stepped back to judge what lay ahead of him against what he had already accomplished. "A fairly industrious hen with a brood of chickens could have distanced me," he concluded gloomily. "At this rate it'll take me a week."

Picking up his brushhook, he stepped up his tempo. Jake had mentioned two days. It was a two-day job or there would be more explanations. Then Vic thought of Wall-eye and Weak-will, the Wineglass's lumbering, bay oxen with the wide-spread polished horns tipped by gleaming brass knobs. He rested on his brushhook while he mulled over the idea that had come to him.

Vic couldn't recall ever having heard the exact status of Wall-eye and Weak-will on the Wineglass. There was an impression among the hands that the oxen were pets of old Tom. In the early days, old Tom had crossed the plains with an ox team, and it was rumored he had a sentimental streak about oxen and always kept a span.

Whether that was true or not, no one but old Tom ever yoked

Wall-eye and Weak-will. He always plowed the garden strip with them, and in winter skidded out the year's supply of wood.

Jake, who had no use for oxen, mostly, Vic suspected, because old Tom set store by them, made fun of the team. He claimed that old Tom had got so heavy and slow, the only things poky enough to exercise him were oxen.

Vic was thinking of the oxen and also of the high-wheeled dump cart old Tom yoked to the cattle when he wanted to haul things about the ranch. The tough-hided animals wouldn't mind the thorns on the raspberry bushes and would plod right through brambles and creepers, Vic thought. The dump cart with its high wheels and maneuverability rolling along behind would crush a trail.

The shakes could be loaded into the dump cart as well as into a wagon. A couple or three trips and the shakes would be down at the buildings ready for use. There would be no two days of whaling away in the heat with an axe and brushhook.

Of course no one had told Vic he could yoke up the oxen. On the other hand no one had forbidden him to use them. If he was successful, old Tom wouldn't say anything, and he didn't see how Jake could. And it would give him a chance to get back at Jake for giving Fred his job and handing him one that was cut to fit a farmhand.

There was no percentage in running unnecessary risks. He decided to handle the experiment without the benefit of witnesses. If it worked, it could make no difference. Should the project bog down, the oxen could be returned with no one the wiser. He would only have to work harder to make up for the time wasted.

At the present minute, Ajax would be a couple miles over the ridge taking the horses to water. It would be at least an hour before he returned to the house and then went down the valley to irrigate the garden. Old Tom was in town. Jake was on his way to Sunflower Prairie. Fred and the line riders were out of the way, and the other hands were busy below the turn down the valley. Only Mom Hazelton was at the house.

Mom and Vic were pretty good cronies and he was sure Mom wouldn't say anything even if she saw him, which was unlikely unless she came out of the kitchen at the wrong time. It was Ajax he had to look out for. Vic leaned his brushhook and axe against a tree and hiked back to the house.

Old Tom had turned the oxen on the stubble of the upper meadow. They were grazing across the creek straight east of the barn. Vic saddled his horse and drove them into the corral. He hurried as fast as he could to get through and out of sight before Ajax could show up.

Although he had watched old Tom handle the oxen, Vic had never driven an ox team in his life. Often he had heard old Tom say that oxen driving was an art. Maybe he said that to rile Jake. Anyway, it was a laugh. It looked to him as though anyone with the sense God gave geese in the north of Ireland could do the job. He had perfect confidence in his own ability.

It was an easy project to get under way. He simply followed the routine he had learned by watching old Tom. Wall-eye he yoked in the nigh bow, and Weak-will in the off bow.

The dump cart was outside the corral fence. Vic got the goad from the beam in the shed where old Tom kept it and then opened the corral gate. He rapped Wall-eye sharply across the nose as he had seen old Tom do. "Wah-hish!" he ordered with authority.

Being a good horse teamster, knowing the kind of hitch to make, and remembering the five commands, "Wah-hish! Haw! Gee! Back up! and Whoa!" he had no difficulty in putting the team in hitching position. Of course old Tom sometimes used the fancy command "Come here!" instead of "Haaw!" but Vic didn't need it.

He did forget the warning that Wall-eye was a dangerous kicker. The way he rolled his eyes and even the manner in which the light flashed on the brass knobs of his horns were warnings. Old Tom claimed Wall-eye could kick a chaw of tobacco out of a man's mouth at three yards.

On the other hand, Weak-will, the off ox, was gentle. He neither kicked nor hooked. The trouble with him was he always did just as Wall-eye dictated. That was why he was named Weak-will; no mind of his own.

Forgetting about Wall-eye's heels, Vic made his yoke hitch to the draw chain and then went back to remove the trigging from under the dump cart wheels, placed there to keep it from rolling down the grade into the creek. As he passed Wall-eye's bay rump, the ox let go a kick with a mighty cloven hoof that shot past Vic's face with such force, the wind stirred his eyebrows. He reproved Wall-eye by rapping him across the nose and commanding, "Whoa, there!" repeating the formula he had heard drop from old Tom's lips.

As customary with oxen drivers, Vic walked beside the nigh ox, Wall-eye, as he turned the team into the wagon tracks leading up the creek. Seemed like the dump cart made an unmerciful racket in the still day as the wheels bumped over rocks in the rough trail.

He looked toward the house but could see no signs of Mom's ample figure out at the south corner of the kitchen, her favorite spot when she was watching any ranch activity that interested her. He was glad when he reached the spur, made the turn, and was hidden from those down the valley.

Slowly the ox team poked around the bend, following the creek to the raspberry patch. Vic guided it into the beginnings of the road he had started to brush out. "Whoa!" he commanded.

Obviously, he couldn't walk through the brambles beside Wall-eye. He let down the dump cart tail gate, threw in his axe and brushhook, and climbed in himself. Now came the test as to whether this was going to work or not. "Wah-hish!" he shouted, and reached down and jabbed Wall-eye with his goad.

Wall-eye was not enthusiastic about pushing into the prickly wall. There was no place else to go, since he couldn't back up with Vic behind him. Reluctantly, he forged ahead. Weak-will went with him docilely.

Once launched, the steady oxen clambered through the bushes, brambles, and creepers, crushing them down, apparently insensible to any pricks or stings. The following wheels finished smashing a definite trail.

Vic grinned up at the hills. It gave him an uplift to be able to get back at Jake this way. It would be such a time saver, no one could object. Long before a man could cut a trail to the shakes piled between two trees at the upper end of the patch, the same man with the aid of the oxen could move the shakes to the calf shed.

It didn't take long, even at the slow ox pace, to weave through the raspberry patch to the timber at the upper edge. The shakes had been loosely corded between the two trees so the air could get at and cure them. "Whoa!" ordered Vic and studied the situation.

A small tree of axe size and a couple of brushhook size had to be cut out of the way before he could turn around and put the dump cart where he wanted it for loading. Picking up the axe and brushhook along with his goad, he jumped to the ground and went up ahead.

He had just trimmed the axe-sized tree for falling when the oxen started. They swung around and made for the road.

Vic dropped his axe, grabbed up his goad, and streaked to head the team. "Whoa! Wall-eye! Whoa!" he yelled.

Wall-eye paid no attention. He completed the turn, dragging

Weak-will with him. They beat Vic to the road by a full length of the team and dump cart.

Vic tried to get near enough to climb in the cart, but he tripped on a creeper just as he was reaching for the chain on the tail gate. He tried again and began to gain on the runaways now going lickety split through the raspberry patch. As the oxen got warmed up, they began to draw away from him in spite of his efforts.

The dump cart was a good six feet out of his reach when it burst into the clear meadow. On good footing, unhampered by creepers, Vic thought he could overhaul the outfit. But Wall-eye saw how it was. He let out another link in his lumbering gallop, and the dump cart still stayed out of reach.

Vic stopped. This was a peach of a how-de-do. If the team ran all the way home, it ought to get there about the time Ajax would be arriving from the horse pasture. And how Ajax would love to report that the demoted tophand had sneaked out the ox team and let it run away from him. Vic would be sure to lose his job, and he couldn't afford it.

The team slowed a little when Wall-eye saw the pursuit had stopped. It gave Vic new hope. The team was following the road around the big bend. By cutting straight across, Vic thought he might reach the spur point in time to get ahead of the runaways.

He had quit yelling whoa to conserve his breath. There was no use yelling at Weak-will, and Wall-eye was intentionally deaf. Bounding over the creek, he sprinted across the tangent of the bend. Wall-eye saw him and divined the threat to his liberty. He really got down to the running business. Weak-will, having no mind of his own, matched Wall-eye with all the genialness of his colorless nature.

Both the oxen and Vic were putting on a finishing sprint in the last yards of the race. Heads down, kinks in their tails and backs humped, the oxen were making the rocks fly. Vic, the goad gripped in his right hand, was running so hard, his feet seemed to be sprinting right out from under his body.

Vic had a slight edge. It appeared he was going to reach the point first. But Wall-eye didn't give up hope. He turned loose with a final spurt.

With a desperate leap Vic tried to clear the creek again. He would have succeeded only for a deceptive bunch of grass which he took to be springing from solid turf. Instead it was drooping over and concealing a vacant spot. Vic pitched full length.

He was up quick as he could pull his feet under him. But the slight delay was fatal. The oxen were almost on top of him.

Gamely he jumped into the road, flailed his goad, and gasped, "Whoa!" like steam escaping from a leaky flue in a nearly dead boiler.

Instead of slackening, Wall-eye showed his respect for the goad by leaving the road and turning west around the point which he had already succeeded in passing. The dump cart began to bound up the slope. Vic struggled after the runaways. If he could get them to circling on the bench above, he still might win out.

II

The bench for which Wall-eye was heading stretched along back of the Wineglass buildings. However, instead of remaining a level bench, a quarter mile to the north it pitched eastward in a gentle slope.

Directly back of the buildings, the slope was well watered by springs cropping from under the bluff of the ridge above. Old Tom had chosen the location for an orchard.

The down valley half of the orchard plot he had planted to trees he had brought with him across the plains. Some of them had lived. Others, chiefly the ones he wanted most, according to old Tom, had died. Three years ago, he had filled in this lack from a peddler who had driven through. Among the trees he bought were numbers bearing the great names of apples he had eaten in his native state when he was a boy.

There were Teatoskies, Ben Davises, MacIntoshes, Peach Apples, Yellow Transparents, and there were four thrifty specimens of sweet apple trees, which in the fullness of time would bear huge green, sweet fruit that nothing approached when it came to making cider.

Back on the old farm when old Tom was a boy, his father had raised this variety of sweet apple for the cider press. Only a little of the cider was used in its sweet state, mostly bottled by his mother after a careful process to be used strictly for church social purposes, where temperance was the watchword.

A little of the precious cider was set aside for vinegar. But the big barrels of it were brazenly set where nature could take its course and ferment it into something akin to royalty.

Along about the time the cold weather struck the cider would be getting ripe. When the mercury went plunging and froze the water in the cider, driving the unfreezable alcoholic content to the center, the elder Hazelton acted. He ran a redhot iron in the bung-hole of each barrel, burning through the water ice to the alcoholic core.

The core was drawn off and jugged. It became an applejack with authority and smooth as a dream of paradise, although Tom's mother said it was the broth of the devil and that his father was swilling himself into perdition with it.

The young trees in old Tom's orchard were thrifty. There had even been a few big sweet apples the year before. Next year old Tom thought he might have enough to make up a small batch of what he had decided to name "Pride of the Wineglass." It might be he would have to move his barrels up in the mountains to find proper freezing weather, as this country often had open winters.

But Wall-eye, Weak-will, and Vic were busily rearranging old Tom's plans. At the minute they were dodging about the bench above the creek. Wall-eye was trying to get back to the creek road and the corral. Vic, his goad flailing, was doing his best to corner the team against the bluff.

Winded and staggering, Vic jockeyed the runaways into a bluff pocket. Before he could rush in and close the trap, Wall-eye saw what was going on and charged out, almost running Vic down. The dump cart bounded past him, streaked along the bench, and cut down the slope toward the orchard.

Vic reeled along behind. The language he was using was so faint from lack of breath, it is doubtful if it rose high enough to be recorded against him; but it was plenty sincere. It was cut off like a spigot turning off water when he reached the break and could look down the orchard slope.

Instead of turning along the orchard's south fence and running back to the creek road, as they should have done, the oxen had kept above the west fence. But Wall-eye knew where his ultimate goal lay and about the wire gate just ahead.

The fact that the gate was closed made no difference to the runaway ox. The team, dump cart and all, barged through the gate as though it didn't exist. Then Wall-eye lined out for the gate in the east fence, the only barrier between him and the corral.

Not being concerned over how Weak-will was faring or even considering him at all, Wall-eye chose a course close to a line of apple trees and put his soul into his running. Unfortunately, the line of trees was on his off side.

The off ox, Weak-will, had to do something about it whether he had a mind of his own or not. Either he had to shove Wall-eye over or pull wide so the line of trees would pass between them. Not being an ox to foment trouble by crowding Wall-eye, he swung wide. Back of them bounced the heavy dump cart, poised like a grim reaper.

Vic moaned and shut his eyes. The fascination of the impending catastrophe wrenched them open again. The dump cart hit the Teatoskie tree. Came a loud snap and the whole top of the tree was mowed away.

A louder snap and the Ben Davis went home. Followed in rapid succession with no sign of slowing speed, the MacIntoshes, the Peach Apples, and the Yellow Transparents. And then horror really did sink the iron in Vic's soul. The next in line were old Tom's prized sweet apple trees.

Vic tried to turn his eyes away but could not move. There were four loud, separate reports, and nothing but splintered stumps were left of the trees which were to furnish old Tom with the wonderful drink to be known as "Pride of the Wineglass."

"Damn their bay hides to hell and back!" groaned Vic, his eyes on the ruin.

Wearily, Vic plodded after the team. He didn't hurry. The rush was over. It would have no effect on the inevitable whether the team now went quietly to the corral or tore down all the buildings on the place. In a sort of daze he watched the oxen crash through the lower gate, slow down, and swing to a stop at the corral.

Vic repaired the damage to the gate and closed it. Following the line of cruelly decapitated trees, he went down through the lower gate, which had not been much damaged. The blow had only broken the wooden latch.

Out of the corner of his eye, Vic saw Ajax standing near the shop. And at her favorite spot, Mom Hazelton, her capable hands under her apron, stood transfixed like a square, solid statue. If there had been anyone else within hearing, the racket would have drawn them out as well.

Vic pretended not to notice his audience. He went down to the corral where the runaways were standing in colossal innocence. Wall-eye looked as though butter wouldn't melt in his mouth, and Weak-will was sedately chewing his cud.

Now the damage was done, there was no sense in trying to brighten up their ideas with the goad or even giving them a cussing. In fact Vic took a narrow, selfish stand. He looked only from his own viewpoint. It concerned him not at all that he was letting the team get away with something they might remember. He was just too smacked down to think that far ahead.

Turning the team around, he put the dump cart in the spot where he had found it. He trigged the wheels and went up front to unhook the draw chain and drop the tongue. Wall-eye kicked at him again, just an expression of good spirits. It missed him by less than an inch. He was almost sorry Wall-eye hadn't connected. A good kick couldn't make him feel any worse than he did.

In the corral once more, he unyoked the team and returned it to the meadow stubble. Gloomily he contemplated his immediate future. He could have survived the audacity of yoking up the oxen and hauling down the shakes, had the operation been successful. But decapitating old Tom's sweet apple trees was certainly in the category of unforgivable sins.

The axe and brushhook were still by the pile of shakes. Vic returned up the creek. When he reached the road he had broken at such frightful expense to himself, he stood looking at it.

It wasn't a bad road. With a little work it could be made to do for a team of horses. Habit was strong. He hated to leave a job half done. Glancing at the sun, he was surprised to see that it still lacked several hours of dinner time. So much had happened, it seemed to him that time must have advanced well into day after tomorrow.

Working steadily, by dinner time he had brushed out the two wheel tracks and tossed the brush aside. The road was ready no matter what Jake decided to use to do the hauling. At least Vic had that satisfaction.

He dreaded to go to dinner and face the boys, but that trial was going to be as nothing compared to the ordeal of supper, when Jake and old Tom would be back. The only good thing he could think of was that Fred wouldn't be home that night to gloat.

Dinner in the ranchhouse kitchen was not as bad as he had anticipated. He looked so forbidding, no one ventured to question him on the story Ajax had so gleefully spread. Not even Mom mentioned it.

However, after the meal was over and the boys were in the open again, Swede, who was a great admirer of Vic's, said worriedly, "Ajax tells me you had a runaway with Vall-eye and Veak-vill. Did Yake know you was going to take them oxen?"

Vic shook his head. "No. It was my own bright idea."

"Wait till Jake gets home. He'll show you where God hid the plow," prophesied Ajax with sweet satisfaction. It gave him sadistic pleasure to see another in difficulties.

"Yeah, Yake is going to be putty mad, Ay bat you," worried Swede.

"He'll sure raise hell," was Vic's sincere agreement.

*   *   *

When the boys had gone back to work, Vic studied the destruction in the orchard. He got a huge chunk of beeswax he and Swede had taken from a bee tree the year before. He cut a chunk into a bucket and carried it along with a saw and axe to the decapitated trees.

The afternoon was nearly spent when he had finished. Bad as he was feeling, the oddness of the scene made him grin. Each apple-tree stump had been sawed off square, leaving as much stump as possible. Then the top had been split to receive one of its own branches which was then bound to hold it in place. He had followed this operation by pouring melted beeswax over the raw wounds, stopping the bleeding and shutting out the air.

"Not a bad job of grafting," he concluded, taking a mournful pride in his work.

Next, Vic cut up the balance of the apple-tree tops and neatly piled the brush. As he returned to the tool house, Mom came out of the kitchen and intercepted him. Her kindly eyes, still youthful in her aging face, were critical. "Vic," she demanded, "what possessed you to yoke Wall-eye and Weak-will to the dump cart? And how in glory did you manage to get 'em into the orchard?"

Vic told her about his attempt to save himself a lot of disagreeable work.

A faint smile wreathed Mom's lips as she listened. She said, "It's both funny and tragic, Vic. Jake won't like it. He's a good man, but he's one of them ghastly letter of the law fellers. He figgers a Wineglass hand is made especially to do exactly as he says and no other way. Besides, I'm afraid Tom will be riled."

Vic concluded he had never heard such understatements. Of course he was worried over how old Tom was going to look at it, but it was Jake who was going to take his hide off.

As Vic went down to the bunk house to pack his few belongings for the pending exit, his homestead was very much on his mind. So were his few whitefaces.

Vic had planned on getting into business for himself early as possible. The homestead he had taken up a couple miles down the valley from the Wineglass just suited him. It couldn't have been more conveniently located so he could prove up on it and at the same time hold his job at the big ranch.

Working Sundays and moonlight nights, he had done a lot to his homestead during the two years since he had filed on it. His log house and pole barn were exceptionally good. His tophand job at twenty-five dollars a month and found made his credit good in both the store and bank at Crown Knob.

When he had an opportunity to buy some whiteface cows, rare

in the country at that time, there seemed no good reason why he shouldn't borrow the money at the bank. That was what he did and bought six head of cows and a young bull.

How he was going to make his monthly payments at the bank with his job gone weighed heavily on him. It took a monthly toll of twenty dollars out of his wages to satisfy the bank. It kept him scraping to get along on the balance. When his wages stopped, he shuddered to contemplate what was going to happen.

Not many ranchers thought much of whitefaces yet, and he might have trouble selling them, even if he wasn't determined to do no such thing. They were his start on the sort of cowman's career he had planned.

There was little chance of getting another job in these hard times, at least not enough work to keep up his payments. If he could only hang on here. He didn't think there was much hope, but such as there was lay in the possibility of old Tom getting home before Jake. If he could make a clean breast of it to the boss himself, there might be a chance.

Vic watched the road to town, but the ranch buckboard did not come in sight. He saw Ajax ride up the orchard trail after the milch cows. Shortly afterward, on the same trail, Jake came riding his hammer-headed roan back from Sunflower Prairie. It just didn't seem to be Vic's day for luck.

Jake stopped at the corner of the orchard and surveyed the apple tree stumps, each with a branch sticking up like a plume. He rubbed his hand over his face as he always did under stress of emotion. Vic fancied he could almost hear the horny palm rasping over the wrinkles and feel the heat of a rising rage in the old foreman.

He watched Jake ride down to the corral and start to unsaddle. Hopefully he looked down the road. Old Tom was still not in sight. No use in putting it off. Besides, it was better to hunt Jake up than to have Jake hunt him up.

Vic was standing in the corral waiting by the time Jake had finished caring for his horse. Jake turned and gave him a penetrating glance. "Whut's on your mind?" he asked.

"Them trees up in the orchard," said Vic frankly.

"Yus?" rasped Jake. "If it ain't askin' too much, might I inquire whut the orchard has got to do with the road I told you to brush through the rawsberry patch? You takin' over the supervision of the Wineglass? Is that why, when I give you a job I come home to find you've bruk off the best apple trees on the place a good mile from where you was told to work? Well, why'n tarnation you standin' there gawpin'? Why don't you say somethin'?"

"I went up and started brushin' like you said," began Vic. "Then it struck me there was a quicker way."

"Yus. You yoked Wall-eye and Weak-will, hitched 'em to the dump cart, and figgered to smash down a road. Only the team run away from you."

"How'd you know?" Vic tried to look surprised.

"Ajax met me up the trail a piece and told me the good news," Jake confirmed Vic's opinion. "Anyways it made no difference. I ain't blind. I seen the dump cart tracks and the ox tracks all over the bench, and I sure couldn't miss them apple trees. Easy enough to figger whut happened."

"Yeah, that's right," agreed Vic.

"You prob'ly don't think so," Jake went on, "but when I told you to brush out that trail, I knew them oxen was out on the stubble just as well as you did. Only reason I didn't send someone with them and the dump cart to break a road was lack of a teamster. That lack didn't bother you none."

"I've got the road ready to use," said Vic.

"That ain't the p'int. Your britches are too small for you. You need a place with room to swing yourself. I'm going to give you a chance to go find one. Come up to the office and I'll make out your time."

Vic followed Jake to the house. This was just what he had expected, so he didn't make any useless pleas or excuses.

"You was paid up in full the first of the month," said Jake. "I make it that Wineglass owes you five dollars even. I ought to keep it and your horse and saddle to he'p pay the damage you've done. But all I'll ask is for you to go away. Here, I'll pay you the five out of my own pocket so you wun't have to wait for Tom."

Vic took the money but didn't leave. He said, "I've got supper coming, and I ain't got much to eat down at my homestead." He really wanted to wait for old Tom. There still might be a chance to hang on.

While he was down at the barn looking for an extra bridle he owned, old Tom returned from Crown Knob and put up his team. As Vic came out of the stable with the bridle in his hand, the old man was standing at the corner of the corral gazing with a bewildered expression at the strange row of apple trees extending up the slope back of the house. He turned an inquiring look on Vic.

"Some of my work," admitted Vic. He gave old Tom a complete account of the affair.

"So you grafted tops back on the apple tree stumps," was old Tom's unexpected and interested comment. "If they live, how long will it be before I can expect to be making cider from sweet apples?"

"Uncle of mine in California learnt me how to graft," said Vic. "With all them strong roots, you'll never know a thing happened in a couple years."

"Puts the Pride of the Wineglass back about a year," old Tom figured. He glanced at Jake's hammer-headed roan. "I see Jake's back from Sunflower Prairie," he said.

"Yes. I've already been fired."

Old Tom was silent a long time. Finally he asked, "You know why Jake give you that brushin' job this morning?"

"I ain't got the least idea."

"I wondered at the time," said old Tom. "Jake's funny about some things. Kind of bullheaded too. Didn't happen to say anything critical of him that could have got back to him, did you?"

"I never said anything he could get mad at no time. Anything I said could just as well be said right in front of him."

"You sure?"

Here was a broad hint that something had been said. Vic couldn't recall a thing.

"Plumb positive," he said.

"What you going to do with your homestead?" With that question, the faint hope that old Tom might interfere in his behalf vanished.

"I'm going to keep it," said Vic.

"What about that fancy stock of yours?"

"I'm hanging on to that, too."

"I'll buy it so you wun't lose anything," offered old Tom.

"Thanks, but it ain't for sale." You never could be sure about old Tom, but Vic thought the answer pleased him.

Silence settled over them as they walked away from the corral. Vic, all hope of reinstatement gone, turned off at the bunk house to wash for supper. Old Tom went on to the house.

All the boys were seated at the long kitchen table when old Tom and Jake came in from the office through the living room. As usual, they were deep in argument. Oxen was the subject. Knowing what inspired it, Vic kept his eyes on his plate, but his interest sharpened.

"So oxen is critters of habit?" inquired Jake, indulging in his custom of repeating old Tom's statements in the form of a question and then sniping at them.

Old Tom nodded and slipped into his place at the head of the table. "All a driver has got to do is learn the habits of his oxen and he knows what to expect and what to guard against."

"It's about time you capped that off by tellin' that old joke about driving oxen being an art," suggested Jake.

"Too bad you was never edicated to oxen," prodded old Tom.

"Yus, ain't it?" inquired Jake with extreme sarcasm. "All I know about oxen is that they're better'n horses in deep snow and rawsberry bushes. But we've got an expert with us. Give us the benefit of your experience, Vic."

"I never drove oxen in snow, and only once in raspberry bushes," answered Vic. "But if you want my opinion as to whether oxen driving is an art or not, I'd say it is."

Something like a chuckle rumbled in old Tom, but his face was straight.

Swede who was quietly coming to a boil over Vic being fired, broke in with, "Ay know a square head Svede ain't supposed to know much. But Ay think somebuddy shoot off his mouth behin' somebuddy's back."

"That's plenty," said old Tom, clamping the iron hand of authority on Swede. "The twenty and found I pay common labor is for work and not backbiting. The only man I've got less use for than a backbiter is the man who listens to him." He seemed unconscious of the suspicious look to which Jake was treating him.

After supper, Vic went down to the corral and saddled his horse. He stopped at the bunk house and loaded on his war-bag. As he rode past the house, old Tom and Mom came out. "You come back and see us," said old Tom.

"Come up for a hot meal any time you get hungry," invited Mom.

"Sure I will," said Vic. He knew they both meant it, and it made him feel better, even though wild horses couldn't drag him back to sponge a meal.

He rode on down the highway and turned around the point which hid the buildings of the ranch that had been home to him for four years. A great loneliness settled over him. It was still with him when he reached a sturdy gate in the right-of-way fence. On the squared beam forming the portal, he had burned VF, the brand he had registered, now worn by thirteen head of cattle and four horses.

Vic pulled up. Some of his blue mood departed as he looked at the solid little set of buildings on the knoll beyond the creek. The big log cabin was fashioned to become the main room of the house when he built the additions he had in mind. And across the front he planned a wide porch overlooking the bright pools of the creek and with a sweeping view down the valley and across the great plateau to the north.

Back of the house, and far enough from the creek so it would not contaminate it but still be handy for stock, was his barn, the nucleus of the great spread of buildings and corrals that one day would stretch around the knoll. And at roundup time, there would be a prime herd of sleek whitefaces winding down from the east ridge to winter range and the great auxiliary stacks of hay.

At times like this, he always pictured a smiling figure with vital life sparkling in her eyes, riding with him and taking pride in their possessions. Somehow he had to hang on and make this dream come true. Until now he had not realized how deeply rooted it had become.

With no job, five dollars in his pocket, no grub to speak of at his homestead, a mountain of debt ruining his credit at the store, and twenty dollars coming due every thirty days at the bank, the outlook was positively bilious. Yet he refused to consider folding up.

Starting on, he went through the gate, turned his horse in the corral, and entered the cabin. Worn out, he went to bed early. He was up at daybreak and made a dry meal out of hot cakes without butter or syrup.

In the pasture where he had summered his whiteface bull, Vic rounded up his old pack pony and cinched on the pack saddle with empty pack pockets. He then stepped up on his riding horse, pulled at the pack pony's lead rope, and started for town.

Crown Knob was located in a south gulchhead just below the brow of a hill. From the east, south, and west, the town could be seen for long distances. Fortunately, the gulch was fairly straight for the first quarter mile, for it became the main street of the town.

There was one of the country's rare springs in the gulchhead. It became a natural camping site. Then someone put up a store and a saloon, and Crown Knob came into being.

Crown Knob still boasted of only a small population. However, it was well located to become an important trading center. It now had one big general store, a couple blacksmith shops, a bank, and two hotels, besides the necessary dozen or so saloons to cater to the domestic as well as the traveling thirst.

Vic tied his horses to the hitchrack in front of the false fronted building housing the Crandle Mercantile Company. He went in the store and back where Abe Crandle was leaning his elbows on the counter and reading some advertising through steel-rimmed glasses set well down toward the end of his nose.

It would only be a question of hours before Abe would hear a couple versions of how the Wineglass tophand had been fired. Vic wanted him to have the true story. He told Abe at once.

Abe placed his bony hands on the counter and looked over his glasses at Vic. His mouth was compressed and his eyes thoughtful. "Nope," he said at last, "Jake didn't fire you for letting the ox team run away, not even for busting hell out of old Tom's apple trees. He had another reason."

"That's how I figger," agreed Vic, "but I dunno what it is."

Abe rubbed his hand over gray stubble on a jaw powerful all out of keeping with his bent, slight frame. Then he added, "Jake's as good an all-around cowman as old Tom, but he's onery and techy as all git out. Somehow you've rubbed his fur the wrong way. No use askin' him. Someday it'll all come out. What you going to do now?"

"Look for another job. Don't know where is one, do you?"

"I git that question asked me a dozen times a day. The answer is always the same. There ain't a loose job nowhere. If anyone can find one, you can. And don't worry about that bobbed wire you owe me for. I'll wait."

"Much obliged, Abe." Vic's face broke into a grin. The worried knot in his stomach relaxed a little with this gesture of confidence. "I only wish J. B. Ballard, over to the bank, would talk that way."

"J. B. ain't so bad," Abe defended him. "Only trouble with him is dyspepsia. Keeps him looking so much like he was walking around to save funeral expenses, it sort of jars on folks."

"J. B.," said Vic, "would skin a flea for his hide and tallow."

"J. B. is clus," admitted Abe. "But he's square, too."

"Yes," agreed Vic. "He wouldn't pick your eyes out unless you owed 'em to him." He left the store and crossed the street to the bank.

J. B., his thin hair carefully combed over the bald spot and his stringy neck thrust up through a sparkling batwing collar, leaned his arms heavily on the teller's ledge. The corners of his mouth drooped. His chisel nose was thrust close to the bars. He gave the impression that the motive power of his body had long gone and he was moving himself around by hand. But there was no lack of power or interest in the cold eyes with which he probed Vic as Vic told his story and felt the sweat start out on him.

"Maybe you better sell your stock and pay the bank," J. B. suggested at last. "Prices have gone down since you bought your whitefaces. It'll probably make a clean sweep to put you in the clear."

"I can't sell," balked Vic. "I never could replace them white-faces."

A wintry smile flitted across J. B.'s pinched features. "Old Tom has done very well with his scrubs," he said.

"Times are changing," replied Vic stubbornly.

"Maybe you can get a job; maybe not," said J. B. after a long silence in which Vic could almost see the banker's mind turning over every possibility. "I'll give you sixty days to find out. If you've got a job by that time, maybe I'll make arrangements not to crowd you. If you ain't got a job, you come in and settle up."

"Thanks," said Vic. "I knew I could depend on my bank to help me out in a pinch."

The sharp eyes bored into Vic. "Listen," came in dry, rustling tones. "Men run to the bank pleading for cash. They sign notes and make great promises. Then they hit a snag. The bank being a business institution either helps 'em out or shuts down on 'em according to the looks of their future. It has to protect its depositors. If the bank takes over, the man who borrowed, signed a note, and gave his word screams bloody murder that he has been bilked and robbed. Think that over, Vic, and someday let me know how it figgers out."

Vic was a little mixed-up as he pulled out of Crown Knob with his pack horse. He had a reluctant, vapory hunch that maybe J. B. might have something besides a penurious nature under his thin hair.

On the way home Vic made up his mind how he was going about hunting a job. It seemed to him that since the country closest to the Columbia River was where the bulk of the settlers were homesteading, and where they were roving around looking for work, his chances would be better across the mountains to the south.

First, he had to return home and finish his haying or he would have nothing to feed his whitefaces and horses during the coming winter. So he put in the next week cutting wild hay and stacking it in his stackyard, adding it to what he had had left from last winter.

That taken care of, he threw the pack on his old pack pony once more, saddled his horse, and cut over the mountains to the John Day Valley. He followed up the river, stopping at each ranch strung along the rich bottom lands, conserving his own meager supplies for times when he would be caught out in the open.

III

Like the plateau between the mountains and the Columbia on the other side of the range, there seemed to be no work, and every man with a job was clinging to it. Well up the Northfork Valley he stopped at the Turkey Track ranch. Jock Bixby, the lanky foreman, had come from the same section as Vic.

Jock said, "I don't figger you've got a chance in a thousand of landing a riding job, Vic. Seems like they's fifty men for every opening. I'll tell you what. About a day or so's ride up the valley and over the ridge in the timber, I hear the Worthings are grading a piece of road to connect the south highway with their mill on Box Creek. You might get a job doing something for them. Anyway it's a chance."

The next morning, Vic rode up the valley. He pulled into the pine timber and crossed a ridge that dropped over into Box Creek. That night he camped in the open, and the next day followed the creek up to the Worthing mill.

A white-haired old lady who must have been beautiful in her youth and still was erect and striking in her age was the only person about the premises. She was acting as watchman, she said.

"I'm Mrs. Pete Worthing," she introduced herself. "Pete and Dan—Dan's our son—are up at the head of the creek at Welch Gulch grading a bit of road. Looking for a job?"

"Yes," said Vic.

"Then you might's well turn around and go back. Pete and Dan are full up on hands."

"I've nothing to go back to," explained Vic.

"That's what they all say," sighed Mrs. Worthing. "But they all do come back. If you must go, just keep on the logging road up the creek above the mill pond."

"Thanks." Vic urged his horse and rode on. In prospect was just one more disappointment. Still, he might as well keep going.

The road led him through a small logged-off area and ended at Welch Gulch, which butted against a bluff of rocks. Across the gulch, the bluff softened to a steep, timbered slope. Opposite Vic and approximately on a level with him, a half dozen men with ox teams were shoveling out a dugway along the slope and hauling the earth to the head of the gulch and dumping it to form a fill.

On a wide, gravelly flat which was evidently flooded during early spring freshets was the camp. There was a mess tent, a cook tent, and a bunk tent. Beyond was a corral with feeding panels for the oxen. There was one ox team in the corral. Vic eyed it with interest and hope. Maybe the team needed a driver.

He certainly hadn't been looking for oxen, but any kind of a job at all suited him. Crossing the gulch, he left his pack horse on the flat and rode up the steep slope to the dugway where the work was going on.

A big, square-shouldered man about Vic's age, which was twenty-four, and wearing a bright logger's shirt seemed to be in charge. He had a shovel and was making a hand as well as bossing the job. Vic pulled up close to him. "You Dan Worthing?" he asked.

A pair of eyes keen and gray as Vic's own went over his visitor. There was neither friendliness nor hostility in the glance. "Yes," he acknowledged.

"I'm Vic Ferris, and I'm looking for a job," returned Vic.

Dan shook his head. "Sorry, Ferris," he said, "we ain't got a thing for you. We're just using our regular logging crew on this job along with our skidding teams."

"What Dan means is we ain't got no ridin' job," put in a sarcastic voice from above the dugway.

Vic's glance traveled up the slope. Seated on a rock, his chin resting on hands clasped over a cane, was a man even bigger than Dan. But the cut of the face and shoulders was the same. Only this man was far older. He could be no one but Pete Worthing, Dan's father.

"I ain't expecting a riding job. I'm looking for *any kind* of work," Vic said.

"I've never seen a cowboy worth a cuss for anything he couldn't do while camped in a saddle," said Pete.

"You never seen me work yet."

"Ain't likely to, either," countered Pete. "Cowboys is too good to do real work. All the job we've got open is skinning Bright and Brindle, them oxen down in the corral, I seen you sizing up."

"I'm an ox skinner," declared Vic.

"Sure! Sure!" jeered Pete. "A cowboy, the most wuthless cuss on the face of the earth, skinning oxen? That's good, that is! Dummed if I ain't got a notion to give you a chance." There was a sly, secret joke deep in his eyes.

"Look here, Dad," Dan spoke up. "We need that team to haul—"

"Shet up!" ordered Pete. "You was always wantin' to quit the mill to join the wuthless gang that rides the free, romantic range. I've got a yen to show you what you'd a-growed into."

"But the team—" started Dan again.

"Never mind the team!" roared Pete. "I'll tend to the team!" He paused and glanced at the sun. "Too late to do anything about it before dinner. Time to unhook, Dan."

Dan, who it now appeared was a straw boss working under the eyes of his father, called to the men to quit for noon. At the same time, the camp cook, a flour sack about his middle, came out of the cook tent and beat on a dishpan with a spoon.

"I can tell the time of day right on the nose," boasted Pete to Vic. He got up, and Vic saw the reason for the cane. Pete's right leg was badly bent, the result of a log, a break, and a bad set. He managed to get down from his observation post easily enough and hobble toward the camp. "Come eat with us," he invited Vic. "You get a chance to show what you can do afterward."

"How much does the job pay, if I make good?" inquired Vic.

"Dollar a day and found for you and your horses," Pete named generous terms.

Vic suspected Pete had added "horses" because he had no idea the cowboy would come through the test. But Vic had to make good. It was his one chance to land a job.

The food was plain but plenty. Vic studied the men and decided they were average. None of them seemed to have any idea what was going to happen at the driving test, judging by the puzzled expressions.

Pete made no explanations. He didn't even mention the test until dinner was over. Then he said, "Vic Ferris, here, is going to haul dirt with Brindle and Bright—if he can handle 'em. Them two have been eatin' all the morning. While the others are catchin' up, we'll go out and have Vic learn us how to skin oxen. That right, cowboy?"

"All I aim to do is drive 'em in my own way and let others figger out their own system," answered Vic.

"We'll go watch you yoke up. Brindle is the nigh ox. Bright works on the off side."

"Dad—" began Dan.

"Shet up!" said Pete. "As I was saying, Brindle is the nigh ox and Bright is the off. I'll show you which is which. The yoke is on the corral fence."

Vic glanced around. The puzzled expressions had given way to grins and the exchange of sly, amused glances. These old ox skinners knew something that Vic didn't. He wondered what it was. However, it did put him on his guard.

It was no more trouble yoking the oxen than he had encountered yoking Wall-eye and Weak-will. In fact Brindle and Bright reminded him of the pair that had wrecked his setup at the Wine-

glass. Bright was Wall-eye all over excepting in color. Brindle had
the same gentle manner as Weak-will and was under the complete
domination of the aggressive Bright.

There was one point of difference which struck Vic as odd. The
positions of the oxen were reversed. For some reason, Brindle was
the nigh ox, while Bright, the one that should have been closest
to control, was farthest away.

"You got to watch out or the team will bolt," warned Pete
frankly. "If they get away from you, your job goes with 'em."

This bit of helpfulness made Vic more suspicious than ever.
And there was grinning anticipation on the faces of everyone save
Dan, who seemed to be sore about something.

Lifting the wagon tongue, Vic slipped it into the yoke ring and
made the proper hitch with the draw chain. He picked up the
goad. As he did so, the others began to edge back out of the way.
It gave Vic the cue that whatever was going to happen was going
to take place right then and there.

Keyed up and tense, ready to jump for his life, Vic started for
his position at Brindle's head. As he passed the ox, he noted that
the hair had been worn off his side in a couple of places. The im-
port of it didn't register until one second late. But it did hit him
quick enough so he wasn't caught flat-footed. "Wah-hish!" he ordered, and smartly rapped Brindle across the nose in the approved
manner.

Brindle stepped out. So did Bright. Only the off ox surged into
his yoke, all twelve hundred pounds of him. He picked the front
wheels of the wagon right off the ground. And Brindle, who followed the leadership of Bright just as Weak-will followed that of
Wall-eye, was only a second behind in putting his share of the
power into the yoke. One jump and they were off at a gallop.

Even as his goad fell, Vic diagnosed what was being done to
him. So he started out to prove that a top cowboy was the only
kind of a hand who could drive these oxen with this particular
hitch.

Brindle had barely hit the yoke with his full power when Vic
left the ground in a flying mount to his slippery, loose-hided back.
The ox humped and tried to buck, but he was handicapped by the
yoke and Bright surging into the other bow of it at runaway speed.

Vic shifted ends with the goad. He leaned far over and brought
the heavy butt of the goad across the tender part of Bright's nose
with all his strength. "Whoa!" he yelled.

Bright paid no attention to the command, but the terrific whack
across his snout staggered and slowed him. Before he could shake

off the effects, Vic let out another ringing "Whoa!" and the goad butt whizzed down again.

This time Bright stumbled and went to his knees. It stopped Brindle's forward lunges so abruptly, he shucked Vic over his horns.

Flying low and hard, Vic was half dazed by the impact with the ground. Instinctively he staggered to his feet, danced in front of Bright, waved his goad, and yelled, "Whoa!"

The ox eyed the singing goad and shrank back. Then old Pete Worthing hobbled furiously around front and grabbed Vic by the arm. "What you tryin' to do? Kill my ox?" he bellowed. "Gather up your horses and get the hell out of here!"

"Look!" Vic's dander began to rise. "You hired me fair and square to drive them oxen! Well, ain't I a-drivin' 'em? First I've got to break 'em so they know the meaning of the word *whoa*!"

"Get off the place!" roared Pete, yanking at Vic's arm.

Dan came hurrying up. There was a scowl on his face but a twinkle in his eyes. If there had been any sense to it, Vic would have said Dan was pleased. Dan said, "Dad, you can make out my time and I'll leave along with Ferris. It's lucky for me that he come along. I might not have found out your word was no good until it was too late."

Old Pete let go of Vic's arm. He raised his cane as though he was going to slash at Dan. "My word no good! My word no good!" he repeated hoarsely. "You dare say that!"

"You promised Ferris a job if he could drive Bright and Brindle," reminded Dan. "The minute it looks like he could do it, you order him off the workings. You offered me a partnership in the business if I'd stay. I ain't going to waste my time hanging around if the way you're treating Ferris is what I'm heading into."

Old Pete carefully lowered his cane. There was a surprised look on his face. "That's so, ain't it?" he asked of nobody in particular. "I did promise Ferris a job. Who would have supposed a cowboy could drive oxen?" He was silent a moment, then he asked, "What we going to do for a team to haul hay for the stock if Ferris takes Bright and Brindle?"

"I tried to ask you that, but you wouldn't listen," said Dan. "I'll have to borrow Dave's mules."

Pete turned back to Vic. Before he could speak, Vic said, "If I'm going to work this team, suppose I put Bright back on the nigh side where he belongs."

Old Pete's face creased in a wry grin. "I reckon there's exceptions in cowboys," he admitted. "When I was a tyke, cowboys and cowmen run my family off from where they had squatted in Wyoming. It soured me on the hull kit and kaboodle. How'd you know them oxen were working on the wrong sides?"

Vic pointed to the hair worn off Brindle's hide. "Done by the draw chain," he explained. "He'd have to be on the other side to have it happen. Oxen, you know," he added sagely, repeating old Tom's words, "are critters of habit. They want things done in a certain, set manner or they object, like running away."

"You win," conceded old Pete. "Shift 'em over and get busy."

Vic had made a good impression on the road crew by the way he had handled the runaway oxen. No one suspected that he had never held a goad in his hands but once before. And when the oxen were shifted to the positions in which they belonged, they were steady and reliable.

Pacing his speed to suit the others, he took his place in the line. He filled his wagon, hauled it to the fill, and unloaded. Returning, he performed the operation all over again. Before night he was one of the gang.

Dan roved about with his shovel and gave first one and then another a hand at loading. A week later, while Dan was helping him, Vic tried to thank him for his timely intervention when old Pete had been about to chase him out of camp.

"Forget it," grinned Dan. "It's me who owes you thanks. You done me a big favor. Like any kid I wanted to be a cowboy, dash around on a pony roping cows and fighting Injuns."

"I run away from home to become a cowboy," nodded Vic understandingly. "And here I am, hauling dirt for a fill with oxen."

"Funny how things turn out," said Dan. "Trouble with Pop was he never noticed when I growed up and got where I could see the future of the lumber business. You couldn't chase me out of it. But Pop, hipped on the subject of cowboys, kept harping. You come along and shet him up. See why you don't owe me no thanks?"

"You're more'n welcome."

While Vic worked away at the fill, he had plenty of time to think over the events that had landed him here. Viewed with the advantage of time and distance, significant guideposts which had been obscure from close up now stood out boldly.

To him, Fred Lang had been just another rootless cowhand who had drifted into the country and would eventually ooze out the same way. Even the petty jealousy which had prompted the big cowboy to plot against a man who held a better job and drew higher pay than himself was understandable. There was plenty of that stripe roaming the country.

Now he really tried to analyze Fred, helpful details moved out of the shadows. The way Fred conducted himself in the bunk house penny-ante games was an indication of his character. Fred not only played to win, but his small winnings vanished in his poke. And there was a cold, calculating look in his yellowish eyes as he played; no joy of the game as with the others. Vic concluded it was greed and not jealousy that had top priority in Fred Lang.

As tophand Vic was receiving five dollars more per month than the others, and Fred evidently coveted it so much he was not above trickery to get rid of the obstacle standing in his way. Yet Vic was not quite satisfied with his deductions.

While Fred was not overlooking the pennies, he gave Vic the impression that he was a man who would have his eye on big game. When he thought of the answer to that it was so simple, he wondered how he could have overlooked it.

Fred Lang was planning to get his hands on the Diamond-K by marrying Madge Belfont. Vic was as sure of it as though Fred had told him. Others had tried to cut Vic out with Madge, but none had tried so persistently as Fred. It boiled down to the fact that Fred was not particularly interested in the tophand job. He wanted to rid himself of the man standing between him and Madge.

Nine times out of ten a tophand demoted as Vic had been would have quit. That had been what Fred had expected. Only Vic's homestead, his cows, and his determination to establish himself had kept him hanging on. Then, as though fate was pulling for the scheming cowboy, Vic had got fired, leaving what seemed to be a clear field for Fred.

One reason why this explanation had been so long in coming to Vic was that while he was interested in Madge, he had given the Diamond-K no thought. He was building his own spread and could stand on his own feet.

He wanted to go at once and warn Madge. Quickly he saw that was impossible, even if he wasn't anchored to this job as securely as though he were wearing an Oregon boot.

"Fred ain't going to get away with it, if I can help it," he murmured as he bowed his back and shoveled dirt for the fill.

The road was finally completed. Vic was paid off with sixty dollars in gold and a little silver. The money in his pocket gave him a feeling of strength. Riding the back trail toward Crown Knob, he had the satisfaction of knowing he had taken the first hurdle and was still in the running.

IV

Vic was anxious to get back to his homestead for a couple reasons besides Madge Belfont. The roundup must be about ready to start if it wasn't already under way, and he had to be on hand to look after his stock. Then there was his obligation to the bank in Crown Knob. He was already a couple weeks late in reporting to J. B. Ballard.

It was in the middle of the afternoon that Vic rode into the town. He went directly to the bank.

J. B., looking as though his end was near, was at the teller's window. "You been avoiding coming in, or did you get a job that lasted this long?" he greeted.

For answer, Vic emptied his poke on the ledge and shoved forty dollars through the wicket. "Gimme credit for that," he said.

J. B. got out Vic's note and made the notation. "I figgered you'd find a job," he admitted. "How about the next payments?"

"I thought maybe you'd let me have time on 'em," answered Vic. "Roundup is coming on and I'll have to ride after my cows. I can't earn money that way."

J. B. pursed his lips thoughtfully. "You'll have to make one more payment to put you over the hump," he decided. "After that the bank will wait till you sell your first beef. You might pay me now. You've got the money." He indicated the money still on the ledge.

Vic shoved the money in his poke. "No," he refused. "I owe Abe Crandle some money and he gets his share. Besides, I've got to live."

"Just so you have the other twenty dollars here in thirty days from now, giving you a little extra time," J. B. laid down generous terms. "Maybe you can get a job on the big roundup and get paid for rounding up your own cows."

"I'll be back in thirty days," promised Vic, and went over to Crandle's Mercantile.

Abe was unpacking a case of boots. "Well, well," he greeted, shoving his glasses to the extreme end of his nose so he could gaze over the rims better. "I've been looking for you the past week. Where you been?"

"Up at the Worthing Mill working on a road-grading job with a pair of oxen," grinned Vic.

"That ought to tickle Jake," chuckled Abe. "The roundup started a couple of days ago. The boys are going to miss you. Nobody seems to care much for that blowhard, Fred Lang, who took your place. The thing I don't like about him is to see Madge Belfont getting so thick with him. They've been going around together since you left."

It was just what Vic had expected, but it put a knot in his stomach to hear it from Abe. He thought that he must have been half expecting Madge to see through Fred and have little or nothing to do with the big cowboy.

He did his best to conceal his feelings. Pulling out his poke, he changed the subject with, "I've got some money to pay on my bill. Here's the twenty dollars I saved tender-hearted J. B. from getting his claws on after I'd paid him what I owed the bank to date. At the rate I paid J. B., your share will be about ten dollars."

"I'll take five on the bill and no more," said Abe.

"Then I'll spend the other five for grub. That," figured Vic, "leaves me ten of the twenty J. B. says I've got to pay on my note in thirty days."

"You keep all your money and pay him now," suggested Abe. "I'll carry you for what little grub you need."

Vic shook his head. "I'll treat you as good as I did old Uncle Ten Percent."

Abe took the money. "Maybe you're right," he acknowledged. He waited until he had wrapped up the things Vic had ordered and watched him depart. Then he went over to the bank.

J. B. looked up from a ledger without change of expression.

"You old bloodsucker!" accused Abe.

"Just because you figger a man is a good risk is no sign he's going to climb on the back of this bank and ride. He damn well ain't going to. He squawk about that twenty he's got to pay in thirty days?"

"Not him. I'm doing the squawking."

"Go ahead and squawk. I was afraid for a minute I'd made a mistake. If he's the kind of fella you claim, he'll be here in the bank in thirty days. If he ain't, I'll be out in the country shortly after looking for him. And I'll collect the works."

"You've got no heart," growled Abe. He decided it was no use to argue and went back to the store.

Riding home from Crown Knob, Vic was not even thinking of his shaky credit at the bank. What Abe had said about Fred and Madge getting thick was keeping him occupied. Maybe he had lost out completely by not being around to protect his interests.

He reached home in a low state of mind but was compelled to snap out of it. He unpacked his pony and then rode up in his pasture and drove a half broken cayuse down to the corral. This cayuse along with his top horse was to be his cavvy on the roundup. It was going to be tough on them, but they had to take it.

The roundup had used a lot of Vic's thought and planning during the summer. The Wineglass, the Rafter-M, the Diamond-K, and the Spade staged the roundup together with Jake Westing rodding the outfit. Jake being wagon boss complicated things. It was Jake that was forcing him toward the plan he expected to use.

Early in the morning, he loaded his pack pony with a meager supply of grub and his bed roll. Leading the pack pony and the other half of his cavvy, he took up the east ridge and swung around the head of Wineglass Valley to Fox Meadow, where the wagon would be camped.

He could hear the cook's axe going before he reached Fox Meadow. Reaching the edge of the timber where he could look down on the familiar scene, he pulled up.

At the far end of the meadow, the day jingler was keeping an eye on the cavvy. Off to the west was the great expanse of Empire Flats. Bunches of cattle were already drifting into the flats, forced down from the high range by the riders.

As always during the day, the wagon camp appeared to be practically deserted. The cowboys were riding the great circle. Soon they would be working the herd gathered on Empire Flats. Brands would be separated and reps would take the strays back into the territory of their own roundups.

Vic had to see Jake, the wagon boss, and didn't have any idea where to locate him at this hour. Looked as though he would have to camp and wait till night. Everyone would then be gathered at the wagon. He heard riders coming slowly through the timber to the east of him. He looked around to see Jake and old Tom riding side by side, as usual deep in an argument. They saw Vic and broke off the talk.

"So you got back to the country," greeted Jake. "I thought maybe you'd skipped out and left that funny beef of yours as a sort of a joke on us."

"I'm glad to see you home again," said old Tom.

"So you're glad he's back?" questioned Jake. "I dunno why."

"You ought to be glad to have me come and look after my funny beef," pointed out Vic.

"That's right, maybe I oughta on that count," nodded Jake. "You can join the wagon. Of course you ain't a cowman with that little dab of stock. You're just a homesteader with a few head, and will be treated as such."

Vic had been pretty sure Jake would take this dim view of his standing. The reps of the big outfits which conducted roundups of their own in widely scattered sections worked and lived on a reciprocity basis. Homesteaders had to pay board by the meal at the wagon.

There was no intention of Vic spending any of the ten dollars he had already saved toward what he must pay J. B. Ballard at the end of thirty days. "I'm going to conduct a roundup of my own," he said.

Old Tom coughed loudly. Jake turned and gave him a sour look and once more fixed his attention on Vic. "A one-man roundup?" he inquired.

"Why not?"

"I 'spose that's your wagon and cavvy?" He nodded toward the pack pony and the half-broken cayuse. He knew what Vic owned as well as Vic did.

"Such as it is, yes."

"Where you going to camp it?"

"Up at Willow Springs."

"That box canyon is plumb up near the top of the divide."

"Sure. I'm figgering to ride circle in the opposite direction from the big roundup."

Jake seethed. What Vic proposed to do was not so much different from any other rep; only he was removing himself from the control of the wagon boss and avoiding the tax on himself for meals.

"Speaking as one wagon boss to another," Jake said, "I'll have the boys of my roundup cut your stock back over the divide. I dunno why our roundup should pay hands to gather your funny beef."

"No you wun't," contradicted old Tom in the tone he used to warn all and sundry that there was going to be no argument. "It would cost more to cut the stuff back than to let it go as it is. Nobuddy around here is going to bite my nose off to spite somebuddy else's face."

"But Vic gets his cows rounded up free of charge," complained Jake. "All he has to do is pretend he's rounding up his cows and then cut his stuff out like any other rep."

"What of it?" inquired old Tom. "If roundin' up Vic's twelve head along with four-five thousand of four big outfits is going to put us in the red, we'd better quit the cow business and buy us some knitting needles."

Jake chewed the end of his mustache but offered no further objection.

"Thanks," said Vic to anyone who felt like accepting it. He turned his horse and rode toward Willow Springs. He had had at least one break, catching old Tom with Jake. Jake wouldn't lift a finger to help him, but neither would he allow any rider to do him an injury. Old Tom had said hands off, and Jake was literal-minded.

Willow Springs was ideally located for Vic's purpose. It was close up to the divide and it already lay above the narrowing circle of the roundup. The spring was sheltered in a little box canyon which widened into a bowl a short distance above the mouth and had a fair stand of grass, enough for Vic's purpose.

By use of a few poles the mouth of the canyon could be closed to form a little pasture. Since he had no day jingler or night hawk to look after his cavvy and no cook to tell him what direction the cavvy had taken if it pulled out, it was necessary to put his horses in an enclosure. Too, it was an ideal camp site.

When he reached the Springs, Vic unpacked his pack horse, got his axe, and fenced the mouth of the canyon. He made a set of pole bars to be used as a gate. Then he turned his horses loose to feed and spent the rest of the day fixing up his camp.

The next morning, he rode down to Empire Flats and took a look at the cows already there. He found one of his whitefaces and her calf. It required the rest of the morning to get them up to the box canyon.

In the afternoon, Vic swung down the mountain again and then worked his way up, intercepting bunches as the roundup riders urged them toward Empire Flats. He knew all the riders he met, and all had heard about this one-man roundup and were ready to give him any help they could.

Zack Webb of the Diamond-K said, "I'll tell you what's a fact, Vic. I ain't got any of your cows in my bunch, but I seen Bill Phelps of the Spade throw a couple head of yours in his bunch. He ought to be over in Wolf Run by now, about halfways down, I'd say."

"Sure they were mine, Zack?"

"I'd have to be blind not to know your stuff, Vic. Them white-faces make most of the stock on the range look kinda peaked. All the boys had mentioned it."

"Thanks, Zack," said Vic. He turned toward Wolf Run and jogged along at an easy trot. Open glades and patches of timber fell behind. Approximately where Zack had predicted, he found Bill.

Bill had Fred Lang with him. And Fred had just picked up another of Vic's cows with her calf.

It was the first time Vic had seen Fred since the big cowboy had ridden away as a replacement on Vic's job weeks ago. "Hello, Fred," he greeted.

"Howdy," returned Fred without enthusiasm.

"Probably thinks I ought to be folded up and out of the country by now," was Vic's thought.

When Vic wanted to hold the bunch up while he cut out his stock, Fred said, "We'll do that down to Empire Flats."

"What's the matter with doing it here and saving Vic the trouble?" demanded Bill.

Fred was clever enough not to press his suggestion, but he couldn't keep from giving Vic a jab. "You cut out cows about the way you drive oxen," he said.

"At least I never had to make up any yarns to get a man fired so I could get his job," retorted Vic.

"I never told Jake nawthin' but the truth," said Fred, taking the bait before he realized he was making an admission that he had told Jake something.

"Yeah?" Vic raised his brows. Then, because he couldn't afford open trouble with Fred right now, he turned his back and hazed his cows up the mountain.

His suspicions had proved to be well founded. Fred had got him fired from the Wineglass; but Vic still had no idea what Fred had told Jake.

Vic, however, had no time to spend on Fred for the next week. Two of his cows and their calves seemed to have vanished from the range. It would be a serious chunk out of his little herd, and he was badly worried. A loss of that magnitude could cause J. B. Ballard to revise his offer to extend the VF credit.

It would be easy to lose a couple of his cows and calves under the range conditions. There were plenty of men around the mountains who picked up what beef they needed for meat regardless of brands. What they looked for was something to furnish prime steaks.

After he had combed the country with no success, he joined the riders working the great herd at Empire Flats. His cows might be tucked away there somewhere. Until then he didn't know how much he had missed the companionship and the man talk around the wagon. This was where he belonged. Even his horse enjoyed the fast, rough work.

The flying dust, the smell of sweat and leather and burned hair and hide as some sleeper was dragged to the fire and branded, filled his nostrils. The yells of the riders, the bellowing of cattle, the rumble of multiplied breathing, and the thud of flying hoofs furnished a music he loved.

When he returned to his lonely camp near the divide and stretched out with only the distant stars for company, emptiness pressed against him. But there was no time to indulge in self-pity. He was too worried about his missing cows and calves.

Zack Webb insisted that he had seen both the missing cows and their calves on the bluffs across Three Pines Creek some days earlier. Vic combed that country for two days without locating a trace of his stock. To make sure, he started back for a third day of riding over there. On the way he ran into Zack again.

"You sure you seen them cows and calves of mine over Three Pines way?" Vic asked the Diamond-K cowboy.

"Positive. I got a good look. I could almost read your brand from where I was."

"Ain't hide nor hair of them over there now," said Vic.

Zack rubbed his short nose. "They might have wandered around the head of the crick and pulled over the divide up around Hammer Ridge," he suggested.

Vic gave him a sharp look. What Zack had just said didn't make sense, and they both knew it.

"Was anyone besides you riding Three Pines Crick country that day?" asked Vic.

"Fred Lang," answered Zack, still rubbing his nose and looking over Vic's head.

"Where's Fred now?"

"This morning, I heard him ask Jake if he couldn't go hunt a couple steers that broke back on him. He figgered they might have gone over Hammer Ridge. Prob'ly he's up on the divide looking for 'em now."

"Maybe I'd better look Fred up and ask him if he's seen them cows of mine anywhere," commented Vic.

Zack looked straight at him for the first time. "Yeah," he said, "it wouldn't hurt to inquire." His blocky figure motionless in the saddle, he watched Vic disappear in the direction of Hammer Ridge. Then he shrugged. "I didn't tell him nawthin'," he said. "He drawed his own conclusions."

As Vic approached Hammer Ridge, it occurred to him how easy it would be to scatter the stock he had gathered in the box canyon as a side enterprise to Fred's visit to the divide. It would do no harm to take a look.

When he reached the mouth of the canyon, the bars were in

place. Apparently his fears were groundless. Still, he had come this far, he might as well ride up to the bowl and make sure.

Dropping the bars, he rode up the canyon, his horse making little sound on the springy turf. One glance around the bowl reassured him. His stock was where he had left it. Then activity in his camp near the spring drew his attention.

Fred Lang's horse stood near Vic's bed roll, white in its tarp at the head of his bough mattress. Fred was over by his packs busy at something. Vic couldn't believe it when he realized what Fred was doing.

The big cowboy was busily scattering the meager supplies from Vic's stores. He wasn't doing it just any old way. There was a studied skill about it. At once Vic saw that he was tearing up things and hurling them in a messy pattern that would get the job blamed on a bear.

Fred was so occupied and felt so secure, sure that Vic was riding the Three Pines Creek country, he did not notice Vic's arrival. He kicked an empty pack aside, leaving it against a tree as though sent there by a bear's cuff. Obviously he was fixing the camp so the finger of suspicion would never point to him.

Vic touched his horse with a spur and rocketed up to the camp. Caught red-handed, Fred whirled around.

There was no shame on his face. Instead, a blaze of anger lighted his yellowish eyes, and his full mouth twisted. Deliberately he turned his back and finished emptying what was left of Vic's flour and then rubbed his feet in the little pile.

"What the hell you think you're doing!" yelled Vic.

"I'm just fixin' it so's a certain cheapskate can't go on deadbeating his way through the roundup." Fred faced about with a taunting air. He considered Vic helpless.

"You won't be able to lie your way out of this to Jake," said Vic.

Fred gave him a jeering grin. "It's my word ag'in yours," he said confidently. "And you notice how it come out last time. You got put to brushing a road through raspberry bushes. If you'd had any pride, you'd have quit. You had to wait and get fired. Anyway, I didn't lie. I only told the truth. That'll make what I say about this stick."

"You sure did lie that last time!" accused Vic.

"You know I didn't," insisted Fred. "All I done was to repeat what you said when me and you was cleaning out the last of the north haystack in the stackyard. You said you wished Jake had either put the stackyard near enough the feed lot so we wouldn't have to pack the hay to the stock, or far enough away so we could use a team. Showed pretty plain you didn't think much of the way Jake handled things."

There was no acting in Vic's amazement. "I didn't show anything of the kind, and you know it!" denied Vic.

"Then why didn't you explain to Jake just what you did mean and make him understand it when he set you to brushing out the road?" taunted Fred.

Vic saw Fred was laboring under the delusion that Jake had immediately accused him of what he had said at the stackyard. He wouldn't have made that mistake if he had known Jake better. But Jake had told old Tom. He had to do that, and it explained the puzzling things old Tom had said to him the day he had been fired.

"You know I was just making a crack that didn't mean a thing," accused Vic.

"Jake didn't think so," grinned Fred.

While he was astonished by the simplicity of it, Vic was also able to appreciate its diabolical cunning. It was one of those things that the way they are said the words mean nothing and the manner everything. Fred had repeated it as a sneer at an incompetent. It was a thing that would rile Jake more than a slap in the face. And Fred was the only witness. Such joking slips have ruined the career of many a politician and sent more than one innocent man to the pen.

"You worked it pretty slick," admired Vic. "But it's different this time. You ain't going to have no call to say anything to Jake because you're going to pay me the damage before you leave here."

Fred threw back his head and laughed with honest glee. "You're going to make me pay for that four bits' worth of flour, beans, and bacon!" he gasped. "Well, what'cher waiting for? Go ahead and collect!" He didn't even bother to brace himself, but stood grinning.

Vic walked quickly to Fred's horse. Before the big cowboy caught his intention, Vic stripped off the fancy saddle and flung it down close to his own mount. "I reckon I can sell that for enough to square the account," he explained.

"You put my saddle back on my horse before I break your neck!" bellowed Fred, and began to advance menacingly.

"I'll sell it back to you for what you owe me for the grub you've ruined, plus a dollar and a half to pay me for making a trip to town to get more. The whole bill will be two dollars and fifty cents."

"You'll sell me *my own saddle* for two-fifty!" Fred's astonishment nearly outdid his pleasure. "That's a good one!"

"You'll settle before you get your saddle!" Vic refused to back an inch.

Fred had awed most men because of his size and strength. He had taken it as a sure sign that he was all those who got out of the way of his swagger indicated. Vic really amused him. "Tell you what I'll do," he said. "I'll gamble with you. Double or nothing! You hold the saddle and you get five dollars. You don't hold it, you get nothing!" Without waiting for an answer, he rushed at Vic and swung a haymaker that would have settled things if it had landed.

Vic ducked the blow easily and shot in a right that stopped Fred in his tracks. It only angered the big cowboy and deepened his determination to use this opportunity to beat Vic out of his way once and for all. He struck again, club fashion. The blow caught Vic on the side of his head with force enough to stagger him.

"How you like it?" taunted Fred, and sprang in to finish the job.

Vic dodged but stumbled over the saddle. Before he could catch his balance, Fred flung his arms around him and lifted him from his feet.

Arching his back, Vic tried to withstand the pressure. In spite of his efforts, he caved in and was hurled to the ground.

Fred yipped his triumph and leaped forward, aiming a kick at the fallen man's ribs.

Vic rolled and grabbed Fred's foot, wrenching him off balance, and brought him to the ground heavily.

Both men scrambled to their feet. His rage fanned by what he considered Vic's lucky break, Fred charged in to smother and overpower the lighter man.

Vic, having felt the bull strength in Fred, backed away, rolling with the punches, letting the big man wear himself down.

As Vic ducked, covered, and backed away, never making a return, Fred grew contemptuous and careless. He rushed again and again, trying to get his hands on Vic. "Stand up and fight!" he panted.

Vic took him by surprise and accommodated him. Swiftly he slid inside Fred's careless defense and ripped a left to the solar plexus that whooshed the already damaged wind out of the big man and etched gray agony across his face. His hands half dropped from the shock, and Vic nailed him with a terrific right cross to the jaw.

Fred's knees buckled and he almost fell. Vic rushed him and knocked him off his wavering balance, dumped him on the ground.

It was the final shove and not the blow that put Fred down.
But even to be put on the ground by a man he had confidently
expected to slap into submission with little more than open-
handed cuffing, sent Fred berserk.

Still gasping for air, he bounded to his feet and rushed Vic to
wipe out the disgrace. Vic sidestepped and let him further wear
himself down with fury-driven rushes. Abruptly he slowed and
stepped back to recover his wind, suddenly realizing that he was
wearing himself helpless.

Vic didn't dare let him rest. His only hope was to keep Fred
going until he licked himself. So he went after the tiring cowboy,
pecking and slashing, keeping him on the move, never giving him
a second in which to recover.

Fear began to dawn in Fred's eyes, and his tortured breathing
could be heard all over the battleground. He had to do something
quick or he was going down to shameful defeat. Springing forward, he made a final effort to get his hands on Vic.

Vic was watching out for that. He saw the signal of the charge
spark in Fred's glazing eyes. Nimbly he slipped to one side so Fred
missed his frantic clutch. As the big cowboy stumbled past, Vic
swung from his boot tops, putting everything he had left into the
blow. He caught Fred under the ear. The big cowboy went down
and out.

Fred was out for so long, Vic began to get uneasy. He was just
going to examine him when Fred grunted and struggled to a sitting
position. Bewilderment was spread over his face. His eyes fell on
Vic, and the blaze of rage in their yellowish depths acclaimed that
all was now clear.

Fury and helpless humiliation struggled for mastery in Fred.
He had been whipped and knocked cold by a man forty pounds
lighter and with nowhere near his strength. Staggering to his feet,
he swayed on rubbery legs.

Everything in his nature called for him to hurl himself on Vic and
continue the fight. It was not lack of physical courage that kept
him from it. He was in the clutch of a terrible weakness from that
last paralyzing punch. To renew the fight was to get knocked out
again.

"If you've got five dollars on you, you can have your saddle,"
informed Vic, watching him warily.

"You didn't take up the bet I offered. All you get is the two-
fifty!" snarled Fred.

"You didn't give me a chance to either take you up or turn you down," pointed out Vic. "This is the first chance I've had to tell what I intend to do about it. I take you up!"

"I won't pay it!" refused Fred.

Vic shrugged. "Suit yourself. Swede Anderson has always wanted your saddle. He'll pay me five dollars for it."

Fred stood silent in the grip of a black rage. If he showed up with his face battered this way and without his saddle, he never could get away with a story of the fight he could otherwise frame up. "That little bit of grub ain't even worth the dollar you said it was," he protested.

"Double or nothing was your own idea," reminded Vic. "Double the grub and the trip to town is what you're going to pay!"

"All I got with me is two dollars."

"All right, I'll keep the saddle."

Fred got out his poke. He had no choice. Extracting a five-dollar gold piece, he turned it over in his hand, reluctant to let go of it.

"You called me a cheapskate," said Vic. "Now lookit you! After all the fun you've had you don't want to pay for it!"

Fred lurched forward and handed Vic the coin. "I'll square this with you," he threatened.

Vic watched him carefully as he took the money. He was running no risks of letting a recovered man of Fred's size and strength get at him again.

But the fight, for the present, was out of Fred. His revenge would have to wait. He went to his saddle, cinched it on his horse, and rode out of the canyon without looking back.

Vic stepped up on his mount and followed to put up the bars. Then he thought he had better keep his eye on Fred.

The big cowboy was heading for Hammer Ridge but swung straight for Empire Flats when he saw Vic watching him. That was queer since Fred was supposed to be after a couple of steers up on the divide. Knowing what he did through Zack Webb, Vic concluded the hint Zack had given him was close to the truth. He headed for the pass known as Blind Jump.

The pass led over the divide to a big bench on the other side of which was a long drop over a bluff. However, to the west, there was a rough game trail which led down to the river into broken country. It was a section more suitable for sheep than cattle and was mostly used by the woolies.

The first thing Vic saw after crossing the pass was his two white-face cows and their calves. There was no actual proof, but he was as well satisfied as though he had seen him that Fred Lang had run his stock over the divide. He suspected that Fred had a couple of steers stashed out so he could innocently ride into Empire Flats with them and account for his trip. And the whitefaces, once down in the breaks of the river, could be counted on to vanish completely and leave Vic in financial difficulties.

The idea of destroying Vic's food supply was probably an afterthought. Supposing the victim was far away over on Three Pines Creek, it was too good an opportunity for a man like Fred to pass up.

Instead of making it tough on Vic, it had turned out to give him five dollars of the needed ten he had to have to make the thirty-day payment to J. B. Ballard.

Vic returned his recovered cows to the box canyon bowl and then took stock of his wrecked supplies. He picked up most of his beans. What was left of his bacon he found up among the rocks above the spring where he never would have dreamed of looking for it had he thought a bear had wrecked his camp. Coffee and sugar could not be recovered.

Also his flour was beyond salvage. His potatoes had not been touched.

It was too late to start home that day, so Vic spent the night in the canyon, making the best of his restricted larder. Early the next morning he struck camp and shoved his whitefaces down the ridge. He had a straight, easy route to travel and arrived home just at dark. Tired and still sore from his fight with Fred, he was glad to get to his cabin, eat, and turn in.

He was up at daybreak and had breakfast. Once more he saddled his horse and stepped up. Leading his pack pony, he headed for Crown Knob. He arrived in the middle of the morning, tied his horses to the Crandle Mercantile hitchrack, and went in the store.

Abe's sharp eyes roved over the bruises on Vic's face. Before he could say anything, Vic asked, "How about trading a couple of five-gallon coal oil cans of venison ready for the table and a little jerky for a sack of flour, some bacon, and a few other knick-knacks?"

"Where's the meat?" inquired Abe.

"Running around the hills back of my homestead."

"It's a deal," nodded Abe. "Pick out what you need for grub," He glanced at Vic's face again. "Been fighting, I see," he stated.

"An argument with gestures."

"Girls cause a lot of trouble."

"This wasn't over a girl."

"The girl didn't weaken any of the gestures, I bet you."

Vic didn't answer, and Abe went on, "Zack Webb was down yesterday. He said Fred Lang came in with his face batted out of shape and putting out a big windy of how you sneaked up on him, knocked him out, and beat him up while he was helpless. It was on account of him getting your job and girl, he claimed. The story was so good, Zack said, nobody believed it."

"Got any empty coal oil cans?" inquired Vic.

"Talkative cuss, ain't you?" grinned Abe, and went rustling empty cans.

V

Within a week after his trip to town, Vic knocked over a couple of fat bucks and packed the meat down to his homestead. Part of the salvage he cooked in the cans and sealed out the air with melted tallow poured on top.

The balance of the meat he cut into strips and turned into jerky by spreading it on low racks with fires underneath to dry out the juices. He now had the meat ready to deliver to Abe. Besides, he had plenty left for himself.

Now he was home and could keep his eye on them, Vic turned his cows up on the east ridge of the valley. His weaner calves, he shoved into his homestead pasture.

While keeping his cows from wandering away, he hunted out down timber ready to be cut for his winter wood. This he sawed into logs of easy skidding lengths.

During this time he didn't see any of the Wineglass riders. He was well satisfied with that. It gave the marks of his battle with Fred time to fade.

The thing that was bothering him most at present was Madge. He hadn't been over to the Diamond-K to see her. Even if he hadn't been marked up, he doubted if he would have gone. It wasn't that he didn't want to see her. For once he was in the grip of uncertainty. It was possible that she might have changed toward him now she was thick with Fred Lang. Besides, if she hadn't changed toward him, she would expect him to invite her to go to dances; and how could he take her, broke as he was?

There were free dances. But if he couldn't take Madge where it wouldn't look like he was a pinch penny, he wouldn't take her at all.

When the date for the first fall meeting of the Lit'ry in the white schoolhouse at the four corners rolled around, Vic was of two minds. He wanted to go and he was afraid to go.

At the opening Lit'ry they always had a big feed. That had attractions for him after the plain fare he had been eating. The thing getting under his skin again was Madge.

First, there was risk of a turn-down if he asked her. If she did go with him, how was he to get around taking her to the pay dances? Finally he decided to go, but to go alone.

Another thing that annoyed him was the certainty that Fred Lang would take Madge if he didn't ask her, and maybe anyway. He hated to have that crook publicly beat his time. Still, he couldn't play dog in the manger. Maybe Madge had forgotten all about him by this time anyhow. The thought made him so blue, he decided not to attend the Lit'ry.

But when the time came, Vic greased his boots with deer tallow, put on his carefully preserved suit, and rode through the crisp fall air to the schoolhouse. As he approached through the early dark, light was streaming from the windows, and there were many rigs and horses lined along the schoolyard fence.

The Lit'ry, aside from being a movement to lift the cultural level of the rural community, was also a social event and a place to swap gossip. With no telephones and poor roads, it was hard to find out how the neighbors were getting along and to straighten out twisted rumors.

Purposely Vic had delayed his arrival until most of the others were on hand. The meeting hadn't taken up yet, and he circulated around visiting with folks he hadn't seen all summer.

Fred Lang and Madge were there as he had expected, but he managed to avoid them. In this he had the cooperation of Fred, who carefully kept his back turned. Uneasy and prepared to go on the defensive, Vic was surprised to find his exploits had made him something of a personage.

There were plenty of cracks about old Tom's oxen and the apple trees. And somehow a garbled version of his summer's experiences on the road grade had got around. But it was his one-man roundup which had really caught on.

Both Jake and old Tom were there and greeted him as though nothing peculiar had happened. Mom Hazelton, president of the Lit'ry, was bustling around supervising where the food should be placed and doing a last bit of gossiping before she called the meeting to order. She came up to Vic while he was talking to old Tom.

"I'm sure glad to see you, Vic," she said, throwing a glance at old Tom to make sure he was listening. "The place ain't been the same since Jake blamed you because the Lord used Wall-eye and Weak-will as instruments to punish Tom for his wicked purpose in raising them sweet apples. There ain't a soul on the ranch since you left that can drive a nail straight or I'd trust to saw a board."

"Fred Lang says he's a good carpenter," said a familiar voice.

Vic turned to see the slender figure of Madge Belfont. Her cheeks were pink, and her complexion seemed very clear above the dark color of her tightly fitting basque with the stylish leg o' mutton sleeves. The light reflected from under her long lashes matched the fire that came from the row of steel buttons up the front of her basque. Like Fred, she carefully avoided meeting Vic's eyes.

Right at her elbow, strutting with the air of a proprietor and ignoring the man he had displaced, was Fred Lang. He said, "If you want some carpenter work done, Mrs. Hazelton, I'll do it for you."

"No you wun't," refused Mom. "Vic promised to put up a shelf or two for me, and I'm holding him to it."

"Maybe Vic don't want to do it," said Madge.

"Fiddlesticks!" Mom disposed of that. "Besides, I saw a table in the bunkhouse that Fred made. If that's a sample of his work, it's plenty." Mom didn't like Fred and didn't care who knew it.

Fred was sore but tried to carry it off as of no consequence. "All right, let old One-man Roundup do the job," he said.

Vic looked straight at Madge. He said, "I'm beginning to think I've got a lot of unfinished business around the neighborhood."

Madge flushed and hurriedly began to talk to Mom about the late roundup.

Old Tom, who had been patiently waiting, addressed Vic again, "Mom is right about your carpentering. I never did see such a collection of butter fingers on one spread as I've got. When you get done for Mom, I've got a couple of jobs for you."

Jake heard that. "What's the matter with usin' the men we've got?" he demanded. "Swede is handy with tools."

"Swede?" questioned old Tom. "Yep, Swede is plenty good for rough stuff, like the cabinet work on a hogpen. I'm aiming to have a new window cut in my office, and I don't calculate to have to be ashamed and apologize every time company looks at it. Vic's going to do the job."

Jake knew by the way the old man spoke that it was settled. Any arguments to the contrary were already too late.

"For once, by glory, Paw," approved Mom, "you're talking sense!"

Vic glanced at Jake. He didn't seem to be annoyed. His face was just expressionless. Vic spoke for the benefit of all. "I'll be glad to go up and carpenter for a spell."

"Yeah, and while you're there, I want you to take a look at them apple trees you grafted and see how they're doing. They look all right to me. They seem to be snapping out of it fine, but I dunno much about such things and Jake is plumb useless."

"So I'm plumb useless about such things?" inquired Jake with vast astonishment. "How do you know when you never asked?"

"I don't have to ask you anything. I pumped you dry years ago. When I want to find out anything, I sort over what you know and then go somewhere else to ask questions."

"So you go somewhere else to ask questions? Sure does beat all how smart you are. You know all about earth dams and ice ponds." Old Tom had built a dam, against Jake's advice, of course, and the first freshet had washed it out.

The delighted crowd drew around. Everyone enjoyed these passes between Jake and old Tom, but all had learned not to agree with either one. This was a private vendetta and didn't mean a thing. At least it meant nothing to the public, and it was extremely dangerous to take a hand.

"I spose," said old Tom, "you're taking a roundabout crack about my telling you how to drive oxen. You see," he instructed the listeners, "Jake's paw drove an ox team to Californy way back in '49. He stuck it out but made such a poor job out of it he even filled pore, gullible Jake with so much prejudice he wun't even pick up a goad. Now me, I drove an ox team across the plains, only much later, not long before Custer had his set-to with Sitting Bull. I gotta lot of respect for oxen."

"Yeah, oxen are fine to exercise doddering old men," agreed Jake. "Ain't that so, Vic?"

"All I know is what I learned up in the raspberry patch," said Vic. "They gave all the exercise I could stand, and I ain't old nor crippled."

"All Jake knows about driving oxen in rawsberry bushes is from rumor and hear-say," criticized old Tom. "You know how 'tis. The more ig'runt a man is about a subject, the more full of information he is about it. It's like an old maid lecturing on fetching up children. I'd say off-hand, it would be a good idea for Jake to get him some experience driving oxen through rawsberry bushes before he takes cracks at them who has."

"Maybe you figger I can't drive oxen through rawsberry bushes?" Jake's voice began to rise.

"How would I know? I've never seen you operate. All I've got to go by is what I've heard; and it all might be bragging. Knowing the source, leads one to wonder."

"So now you're gone to wondering? Well, any time you need

convincing, I'll step right out with a yoke of oxen and make you take water," retorted Jake.

Mom called the Lit'ry meeting to order. It ended the argument, and the program began.

When the cultural part of the entertainment was over and the folks were arranging themselves for the refreshments, Madge shoved over on the bench she and Fred were sharing. "Come sit with us and tell us something about that grading job you had this summer," she invited.

Vic would have refused, only Fed scowled and looked so mad, he yielded to temptation and sat down.

"These benches ain't made for three," said Fred.

"No?" inquired Madge. "When the school was crowded one winter, May Carter, Mary Zigler, and I sat on this very bench and divided this very desk between the three of us."

"You was small then," argued Fred.

"You mean I'm overgrown now?" Madge's eyes were dancing.

Vic didn't want it to look as though it was his fault if Madge, the little devil, needled Fred into an outburst. He called out to Zack Webb, "Hey, Zack, hold that seat beside you while I go rustle us some cake and coffee!" He rose and left the bench to Fred and Madge.

When the meeting broke up and everyone was getting ready to go home, old Tom came over to Vic. "About that carpenter work," he said. "How about coming up and putting in the rest of the week?"

"Can't I put it off till the first of next week?" he inquired. "I ain't got my winter's wood down to the house yet, and I'm afraid it might storm up on the ridge."

"That'll be all right," agreed old Tom. "First of the week suits me."

Getting up his wood was not all the reason Vic had for postponing his going to the Wineglass to do carpenter work. He wanted time to think over the angles.

For instance, there were better carpenters than he among the homesteaders roaming around the country desperately looking for just such jobs as Mom and old Tom were offering. There was more to this than met the eye.

Vic got to thinking about that oxen argument at the schoolhouse. Old Tom had led the argument all the way. There was nothing new about his baiting Jake. But Vic had noticed long ago that when old Tom took the trouble to bring any certain topic into the talk and keep harping on it, it usually developed he had an object in view.

While he was skidding his wood down from the ridge and piling it on a rollway back of the house, Vic tried to fathom old Tom's object in stirring Jake up over oxen driving. He had badgered Jake into declaring his willingness to drive an ox team in a raspberry patch, only there didn't seem to be any sense to it. It wouldn't prove a thing as far as Vic could see.

Maybe old Tom was just hoorawing Jake and everything was as it appeared. Still, it was peculiar. If anything was going on, he was sure Mom was not involved. At that, he wouldn't have been surprised to find that old Tom was back of Mom's suggestion that he come up and put in the shelf so Jake wouldn't think he was going over his head in a delicate situation. Also it could be old Tom's way of giving him a chance to earn the money to pay off the bank. That would be like old Tom.

Saturday night, Vic sized up the pile of logs. He decided there were enough to see him through a hard winter. Soon as he got the Wineglass carpenter work done, he planned to saw his woodpile into stove lengths. When the snow was flying, he wouldn't have to get out and do his wood cutting in it.

Now he saw his way clear to fix up the bank so he could ride until he had some beef to sell; all he had to pay was his store bill. No matter what old Tom's reason for getting him up to the Wineglass, it would put him sitting pretty until spring.

Soon as it was time to put his cows out on the range, he would have to think up something. He couldn't stay with his cows and work for someone else. Neither could he afford to hire anyone to ride for him. He certainly couldn't expect to run his cows with the Wineglass stock with Wineglass riders to look out for them as he had done until now. It was going to be a tough nut to crack.

Monday morning, he saddled his horse and rode up to the Wineglass. He purposely did not arrive until after the jobs had been handed out. However, Jake and old Tom were still on the Auction Block waiting for him.

Jake scowled over his tardiness. "Vic is working for you, Tom," he said pointedly. "You can lay out his job."

Old Tom nodded. "Get some tools from the shop, Vic," he said. "Mom has decided to have three shelves put in. First, though, I want you to come up to the orchard and tell me how them grafts you made are doing."

"Huh!" grunted Jake, and went down to the corral.

"Jake is kinda set in his ways," chuckled old Tom as he walked up to the orchard with Vic.

The grafts on all the trees had grown solid. Vic was amazed at the way they had prospered. He got out his knife and began cutting off the suckers the strong roots had forced out.

"I figgered to attend to them suckers long before this," said old Tom, and got his knife and helped.

When they had finished the row, Vic looked over the lot with pride. "No," he said, as though carrying on the conversation he had had with old Tom the day of the catastrophe, "it won't set the trees back more'n a year. Year after next, with any luck, you'll be drawing off a core."

"Not bad after what happened to 'em," commented old Tom, and another chuckle rumbled in his chest.

Vic glanced around at him. Old Tom was looking down the slope to the calf shed, where Jake had Swede Anderson and Chuck Bailey tearing off the old roof. As Vic watched old Tom, he decided he was chuckling at some secret amusement. Something was going on behind the scenes.

While Vic went to the shop after tools, old Tom went to his office. He wasn't around when Vic went to work in the pantry.

The job was about half done when Madge Belfont rode over and joined Mom in the kitchen. It seemed that this was the day Mom had picked to can apples, and Madge had volunteered to come over and help; and incidentally get a few cans to carry home, as none of the Belfont orchard was in bearing yet.

Madge did not confine her activities to canning applies. When Vic went through the kitchen to get a board, she was making apple pies. He wondered if the fact that apple pie was his favorite had an influence, but concluded that he was getting ideas and that Madge was just helping Mom out.

It being natural to Vic to attend strictly to business when he worked, he didn't try to talk to Madge. He kept right on with his measuring, sawing, and hammering until Mom called him away. She raised her voice to an unnecessarily loud pitch. "Let up for a while, Vic," she said. "I reckon the job will keep if you take five minutes for a slab of hot apple pie."

Beyond the living room, the office door opened and old Tom came tramping into the kitchen. "Did I hear somebuddy mention hot apple pie?" he inquired.

"I was talking to Vic," said Mom.

"If Vic can have a piece of hot apple pie, so can I," grumbled old Tom, and dropped into a kitchen chair where he could look out the window.

Vic saw the twinkle in the old man's eyes and followed the direction of his gaze. Once again he was looking at Jake and his crew working at the calf shed roof.

The shelves were completed by dinner time. Vic had just cleaned up his shavings and sawdust when the boys came in to eat.

Fred Lang was surprised to see Madge. He didn't like that sort of surprise. "You didn't say anything to me yesterday about coming over today, Madge," he complained.

"Should I have?" inquired Madge.

Chuck winked at Vic across the table. He said, "Seems natural to see you here putting it away. Going to try them oxen again?"

"Not till somebody tops my record," replied Vic.

"There ain't no reason for letting a team of oxen run away," Jake seized the opportunity. "It wouldn't happen to a real teamster. Of course there's them who hold a different opinion."

"The thing to remember is that oxen are critters of habit," said old Tom.

"So oxen are critters of habit?" questioned Jake. "You ever hear the expression *Dumb as an ox*? Oxen ain't got brains enough to be critters of habit."

"Experience would cure you of them idears," said old Tom with exasperating complacency.

"See whut I mean?" Jake appealed to the table at large and pushed his mustache aside with his fingers while he fitted the saucer of his coffee cup to his mouth.

"Oxen ain't like horses," old Tom went on in a tone that sounded suspiciously like he was instructing a child. "You can reason with a horse, but not with an ox. Just like I said, he does his doings from habit. Once he gets a habit formed, it's tough to break him of it. In that, he's like you, Jake."

"You got me mixed up with somethin' else," said Jake. "I can't be druv a-tall."

"I've been taking that into account for thutty years. What I was talking about was the grade of intelligence."

"How would you know anything about that?" inquired Jake in vast amazement. "It's easy enough to get your number right. Just lookit whut you associate with! Oxen!"

"In order to drive an ox you've got to know more'n the ox," said old Tom. "It ain't never been proved how much more. I only know I've had good luck driving oxen most of the time. All I've got to do is watch a man drive an ox team and I can tell what kind he is."

"Hear that, boys? That's the way Vic got found out," put in

Fred slyly, pretending he thought old Tom was taking a swing at his onetime tophand.

Jake ignored him. It was meant for him, and he started right in to deal with it. "So you can tell whut kind he is?" he inquired. "I spose that up to now I've been on probation. Sounds like you'll have to see me poking up a team of thick-headed cattle before you can make up your mind whether to hire me or not."

"Anyway, I'd find out if you can handle oxen," said old Tom, "or put that noise down to a loose board banging in the hot air that's been lashing this place for years."

"Want me to give you some lessons in oxen driving?" inquired Jake, getting sore.

"Now you mention it, I dunno why you ain't tried to give me lessons before this," said old Tom. "Never be a better time than now. We've got them shakes to haul down from the pile up the crick. Now Vic's here to put the roof on the calf shed you can't put it off no longer."

"Me put it off!" Jake's mustache bristled. "Every time I mentioned it you had something that needed doing worse."

"That's right," agreed old Tom. "But that's the job we're right up against now. And it's an oxen job. It'll give you a chance to put up or shet up."

Jake's mustache billowed in and out with the puffing of his lips. "Lookit here," he croaked, his eyes full of suspicion, "have you been putting this off, laying for me with that rawsberry patch and them cussed oxen?"

Old Tom gaped at him with convincing, wide-eyed astonishment. "I'm trying," he said, "to run the Wineglass with such help as a man can pick up. Help is getting so uppity I don't scursely dare make a suggestion."

Jake considered the answer. Vic wondered if the foreman could make anything of it. He could see Jake weighing it, suspicious that there was a pitfall hidden in it somewhere, his experience with old Tom being what it was. "All right," he said at last, "trot out your stone-age team and I'll learn you how to haul shakes with it." He shoved back his chair and looked toward Chuck.

"Vic will go along as helper," put in old Tom before Jake could pick anyone else. "I'll trail along to see if you really know which end of an ox to yoke, or is it all talk that's been beatin' on my ears till I'm near deef."

The hands wanted to stick around and see the demonstration, but they all had to go back to the jobs they had been working at during the morning with the exception of Fred. Old Tom suggested that Fred work on the calf shed roof with Chuck and Penny to speed things up.

Jake sent Vic up in the pasture to haze Wall-eye and Weak-will down to the barn.

As he rounded up the big, bay brutes that had caused his downfall, he was wondering about this sudden interest in oxen. He had been on the Wineglass four years, and what had been said at the Lit'ry and at the dinner table today constituted the longest conversations about oxen he had heard in all that time. To hear old Tom, one would suppose oxen was all they talked about.

One thing Vic had learned about the boss. He handled Jake pretty slick. More than half the time, he was sure, Jake actually thought the ideas he was carrying out were his own. And he was a good foreman. If he hadn't been, he would have been long gone from the Wineglass. As to what this oxen business meant, Vic didn't have the slightest idea. But old Tom had something in mind. He always did.

Vic ran the oxen into the corral, and Jake yoked them. He got the goad from where Vic had left it, opened the corral gate, and closed to the proper distance from Wall-eye's head. He rapped the ox sharply across the nose. "Wah-hish!" he commanded.

The oxen moved out in their deliberate way. "Haw!" ordered Jake, rapping Wall-eye on the shoulder. Wall-eye swung slowly and headed for the waiting dump cart.

Vic watched Jake expertly put the oxen in position on either side of the dump cart tongue. Showing his knowledge of Wall-eye, he made a wide detour to remove the trigging from under the dump cart wheels. In fact, Jake seemed so perfectly at home handling the oxen, there was no doubt in Vic's mind but that Jake knew his business. He glanced at old Tom.

Old Tom was watching Jake critically but with no sign of disapproval. Vic thought that if old Tom had been expecting Jake to make a fizzle of driving a team of oxen, he was doomed to taking a fall for once.

"Wah-hish!" Jake swung the oxen into the trail up the creek. The oxen moved along at their snail's pace, the heavy dump cart rumbling and banging over the rocks behind them.

Vic fell in behind the dump cart. Old Tom walked behind him. Jake glanced back. He said, "Keep your eyes open back there and you'll pick up some pointers about handling oxen." But he was uneasy. Vic saw him glancing back often.

It was a fine fall morning. The leaves of the shedding trees were still mostly clinging to their branches. They were waiting for the wind to dry them out before cascading them down in a rustling shower. Their colors made vivid streaks in the almost solid green of the upsweeping pines.

The dump cart poked around the bend and followed the road through stretches of dried grass where the Wineglass herd would pick winter feed.

Jake slipped in ahead of the team and let it follow him up the trail until they reached the end of the raspberries. The foreman stopped the team beside the pile of shakes in the same spot where Vic had stopped it weeks before.

"Vic," suggested old Tom, "le's me and you walk around to the other side of these shakes and see how they've cured on the sheltered side." He led the way around the pile.

Jake, confronted with the same problem that Vic had faced, went on ahead just as Vic had done to pick out a route in which to turn and place the dump cart for easy loading.

Suddenly there was a shuffling of hoofs. The draw chain rattled.

"Whoa! Whoa, there! Whoa, Wall-eye!" roared Jake. He made a frantic dash.

There was the beat of hoofs and the rumble of wheels as the team and dump cart swung around. Wall-eye galloped into the open roadway well in the lead of Jake. Weak-will, still having no mind of his own, went with him.

Jake was tough and nimble, but he lacked the incentive to run his heart out in pursuit of the runaways that Vic had had. He stood still in the opening and watched the dump cart bound along in the wake of the oxen. He turned to old Tom and Vic as they came around the shake pile. "What in tarnation started them oxen?" he demanded accusingly.

"How should I know?" inquired old Tom. "I ain't teamstering today. Besides, me and Vic was on the other side of the shakes."

"I went up ahead to see where I could turn around with the outfit," explained Jake. "I hadn't gone twenty yards when the team started. Before I could head it, they were hightailing it for home."

"Well, if you figger to show us how you can drive oxen, we'd better shank along back and pick up the demonstrating team," suggested old Tom.

No one had much to say as they trailed the runaways. Vic wanted to laugh. Ostensibly, Jake had fired him because the team had run away from him and torn down a row of apple trees. And here was Jake with the oxen running away from him in the very same spot. Only this time there was no one at the point to turn the team up to the bench so it could reap a destructive swath through the orchard on the way back to the barn.

They followed around the long bend in the creek to where they could see the buildings. Wall-eye and Weak-will were patiently standing by the corral gate, waiting to be turned out to pasture. They had got away with it once, and there seemed to be no reason why they shouldn't do it again.

As they approached, Vic saw that the ox team hadn't gone directly to the corral gate. They had run around the barn and come up from the lower side. The ranch hack had been in the way. The front part of it looked as though it had been hit by a train. One front wheel had three spokes on it. The other had one.

Jake glanced at old Tom. There was nothing contrite about the look. There was smoldering anger as he surveyed old Tom's bland face.

Old Tom appeared not to notice. He stooped over and began gathering up the scattered wheel spokes. "We better save these," he said. "Lots of times a piece of good seasoned hickory comes in handy to make a wedge or a hammer handle or somethin'. Kinda looks like we'd have to get a new hack. Well, Mom's been after me for quite a spell. She'll probably thank you for the kind of ox driving you do, Jake."

"My drivin' is all right!" bellowed Jake. "It's them consarned idjuts of oxen! How'd I know you never half broke 'em to work? Nobuddy could be blamed for havin' a runaway with them half-wild, dumb-witted, mishandled cattle! They wouldn't have acted that way if I'd had a hand in learning 'em whut was whut!" He stopped suddenly, and a queer expression come over his face.

"Now what's biting you?" asked old Tom.

"Say," demanded Jake, "did you know them oxen was going to run away?"

"It didn't surprise me," said old Tom. "But I warned you so you could be watching."

"So you warned me? That was nice of you. I'd like to know when."

"I pointed out one time after another that oxen are critters of habit. If you'd listened when Vic told about his runaway, you'd have known right where them oxen started from. Shows how much you know about oxen or you'd have asked Vic."

"That's it, try and lay your low tricks on Vic," said Jake. "You can't get away with it." He walked over to Vic. He said, "Vic, I didn't know Tom had ruined them oxen breaking 'em before you borrowed 'em to make a road. It warn't fair to fire you for his blundering. You're back on the payroll at your old job and pay, if you want it, with one proviso."

"What's the proviso?" inquired Vic warily.

"You gotta give Wineglass first choice of them whiteface bull calves of yours." Jake gave old Tom a defiant look.

"The only thing you can do under the circumstances is give Vic his job back," agreed old Tom. "As for your proviso, where'd you get the idear I can't see good beef as fur as you can? But Vic don't have to give us first choice unless he wants. Of course we'd like to have it."

"You can have first choice," said Vic. And right there he cleared up his range troubles for next summer and for the summers following. "One thing I'd like to ask," he said. "How could you be sure them oxen would light out and run away from Jake?"

"I wasn't sure. But the conditions were all there. As I keep saying, oxen are critters of habit. They do a thing a time or so. If they benefit by it, they've formed a habit. When they run away from you, they got turned out. Why not again?"

"I see," nodded Vic. "Well, long's they're all hitched up, suppose I take the ox team and haul them shakes down to the calf shed? Now I know what to look out for, I figger I can make out."

Old Tom shook his head. "I've got more carpenter work waiting at the house. Jake can figger out a way to get them shakes down. They's more men than can work right good on the shed roof," he hinted, and exchanged a long look with his foreman.

Jake faced the calf shed. "Come down here, Fred!" he yelled.

Fred approached the corral warily. He acted as though he suspected something might explode under his feet.

"Take Wall-eye and Weak-will up to the shake pile and haul them shakes down to the calf shed," ordered Jake. "If there's any time left, you can start cleaning out the corral, using the oxen and dump cart. That job will take you the rest of the week."

Fred's cold, calculating eyes went to Vic. "Driving oxen is more in Vic's line. I'm a rider," he said bluntly.

"You ain't a rider here anymore," replied Jake. "Vic is back as tophand. You're just an extra laborer around the ranch."

"I ain't never been set down this way!" Fred's voice rose.

"You have now," said Jake.

Fred didn't ask the reason. He said, "I'll quit first."

"It's up to you," Jake gave him his choice.

Fred turned to old Tom.

"If you want my opinion," said old Tom, "there ain't no place on the Wineglass for a feller who'll pull the trick you did to get

Vic fired so you could get his job. And then there's that licking
Vic gave you at Willow Springs that seems to kind of got tangled
up in your memory till in the confusion you figgered you won it.
Anyway, that's the way you told it."

"Vic lied to you about that fight just like he lied to you about
me trying to get his job," accused Fred.

"Now I call that right interesting." Old Tom's tone matched
the cold glint in his eyes. "You see Vic never so much as mentioned you to either me or Jake."

"Then how did you find out?" Divided between anger and surprise, Fred practically confessed that old Tom had the right of it.

"It's my business to know what goes on around the Wineglass,"
said old Tom in a tone that cooled Fred to silence. He turned from
Fred to Jake. "Make out Fred's time, Jake. He's resigned and
we've accepted his resignation."

Jake said to Vic, "Looks like you'll have to haul down them
shakes after all. You can work for Tom tomorrow." He followed
and overtook old Tom, who was already on his way to the house.
Before the pair were out of hearing, their voices were raised in
argument. Vic grinned. Oxen were not the only animals that were
critters of habit.

Vic picked up the goad and went to the head of the team. He
turned the disgusted oxen back into the road and up the creek.
"Wah-hish!" he commanded.

As he went back over the events, Vic found he was not surprised
at what had happened. Fred was not clever enough to pit himself
against men who knew their way around like old Tom and Jake.
He had never fooled old Tom for a minute, and Vic doubted if
Jake had been deceived for long. But Jake was too stubborn to
admit he had been wrong. So old Tom had gone to work with his
devious but effective methods.

Happiness for Vic would have been complete only for one thing.
He wasn't sure how he stood with Madge. The fact remained that
he had been going with Fred. Maybe she had really fallen for him.

He was worrying about it when he came down from the timber
with the first load of shakes. Madge was at the corral getting her
horse to ride home. Vic headed the oxen against the corral fence
so they wouldn't run away again and went around to the corral
gate. Madge was already mounted. When she saw Vic coming, she
waited.

"I didn't have a thing to do with getting Fred fired," Vic explained as he came up, although he had had no idea that was what
he was going to say.

A little smile tugged at the corners of Madge's mouth. "The only one Fred ever kidded was himself," she said.

Vic thought that over. "If you ain't going to be busy, I'll drop around Sunday," he ventured cautiously, feeling for the old footing.

"Come early and have dinner with us," Madge picked up her cue. "Pa and Ma were asking when you were coming to dinner only this morning."

The old words and manner were there, but Vic was conscious that a new element had entered their relationship. Its potency made him light-headed. Confused by it, he grimly stuck to the old safe formula. "I'll be there," he promised.

Whatever had come over him was also affecting Madge. The blood was flooding to her cheeks. To hide her turmoil, instinctively she whirled her horse and rode away. As she went around the corner of the house she twisted in the saddle and waved her hand. There was something intimate and knowing about the gesture. It was an acknowledgment that Madge understood and accepted that new something that had just entered their lives.

He watched Madge ride from sight and then backed the oxen away from the fence. He threw off the load of shakes at the end of the calf shed. When he had finished, his eyes turned down the valley to the east ridge above where his homestead lay.

Once again he pictured himself shoving a sleek herd of whitefaces down the slope to the VF with its barns and corrals and the big house with the wide porch and the wonderful view. And riding with him was a girl who could express volumes with the wave of her hand.

"Wah-hish!" he started the oxen. Slowly they plodded up the creek. Vic didn't notice the rocks in the trail. To him it was a smooth highway he was following into a full future.

About the Editors

Bill Pronzini has written numerous Western short stories and such novels of the Old West as *Starvation Camp* and *The Gallows Land.* He lives in Sonoma, California.

Martin H. Greenberg has compiled over 200 anthologies, including Westerns, science fiction, and mysteries. He lives in Green Bay, Wisconsin.

$\overset{2}{5}9$

$\times \ 3$

$\overline{177}$

179

$\overline{3\,56}$

$\overset{2}{5}9$

$\times \ 3$

$\overline{177}$

179

$\overline{3\,56}$